MW00892159

# The Storyteller

Michael Frickstad

Copyright © 2012 Michael Frickstad

All rights reserved.

ISBN-10: 1479369586
ISBN-13: 978-1479369584

# DEDICATION

To Diane for finding me, supporting me, and loving me. You are proof of the words "All things work together for good for those who love God."

# CONTENTS

# ACKNOWLEDGMENTS

Thank you to Diane, Ian Graham Leask and his writing classes, Amy Rea, Mary Ann Straley, and everybody else who contributed to the evolution of this project from "a sappy little love story" into something far more interesting to write.

Just so you know, references to sacred texts are no indication of any expertise of my own, but rather the result of the contributions of translations, commentaries, and/or the writings of others. Quotations from the Word are modifications or paraphrases of many ancient writings, such as the Bible, the Koran, Tao Te Ching, or the sayings of Buddha. I must also credit the more modern chroniclers of Greco-Roman (Edith Hamilton) and Ojibwe (Basil Johnston) mythology. The writings here are not meant to faithfully adhere to any one religion, but rather reflect a unity that exists at least in my mind based on the limited exposure I have had to the various texts. The cosmology of the Word, Flame, and Earth Man is totally imaginative sprung from that exposure.

Sources used include, but are not limited to the following:

*The Bhagavad-Gita: Krishna's Counsel in Time of War*. Trans. Barbara Stoler Miller. 1986. New York: Bantam, 2004. Print.

*Essential Sufism*. Ed. James Fadiman and Robert Frager. 1997. New York: HarperSanFranciso, 1999. Print.

Hamilton, Edith. *Mythology: Timeless Tales of Gods and Heroes*. New York: Mentor, 1969. Print.

*Hua Hu Ching: The Unknown Teachings of Lao Tzu*. Trans. Brian Walker. 1992. New York: HarperSanFrancisco, 1995. Print.

Jacobs, Alan. *The Principal Upanishads: The Essential Philosophical Foundation of Hinduism*. London: Watkins Publishing, 2007. Print.

Johnston, Basil. *The Manitous: The Spiritual World of the Ojibway*. St. Paul: Minnesota Historical Society, 2001. Print.

*Teachings of the Buddha*. Ed. Jack Kornfield. 1993. New York: Barnes & Noble, 1996. Print.

Tzu, Lao. *Tao Te Ching*. Trans. Charles Muller. New York: Barnes & Noble Classics, 2005. Print.

# PROLOGUE

## 1

Once, the Word reverberated in every ear, shaped every mouth, moved every tongue.

All heard.

All knew.

All proclaimed.

But then all turned to themselves. The deaf became blind. The blind became mute. Silence reigned.

The Word went unspoken. It longed for and searched for a speaker, a writer, a preacher, a singer, a storyteller to break through the darkness of the world and pronounce the message which says:

*I am old,*
*Older than the story.*
*I am new,*
*Newer than your next breath.*
*I am every life.*

*I am the innocent and the guilty,*
*The virtuous and the profane.*
*I am Brutus and Caesar.*
*I am Judas and Jesus.*
*I am Lucifer and Michael.*
*I am the Giant Cannibals and Mother Earth.*
*I live in every man and every woman,*
*In every people,*
*In every generation,*
*In every country.*
*I live in every rock and every tree,*
*Every lake and every stream,*
*Every deer and every bear.*
*All –*
*All live in me,*
*Unknown, unknowing,*
*And I live in all.*
*I am the Word…*
*The shimmering Word that excites the eye,*
*The honeyed Word that lies sweet and savory on the tongue,*
*The healing Word that nurtures and caresses,*
*The ambrosial Word whose perfume intoxicates the gods,*
*The melodious Word waiting to be sung.*
*The Word that Man ignores.*
*I am old, but never tired...*
*Young, but never blind.*
*The Story lives in me.*
*It must be told.*
*I am here.*

In times of greatest need, the Word leapt forth from the unknown, the unexpected. Throughout the millennia of human existence, in obscure country villages and opulent throne rooms across the earth, humble carpenters and enlightened princes spoke the truth of the universe until their very names – Jesus, Lao Tzu, Muhammed, and Buddha – radiated the beauty of the eternal Way .

During the unusually warm spring of 1989, on the edge of the western plains of Minnesota, a new name joined them: Beecher Jones – husband, father, high school principal, unwilling messiah.

## 2

No matter what time of day or how busy the restaurant was, each time the front door to the Plains Cafe opened, conversation halted. Heads turned en masse and the regular customers — farmers, bankers, shop owners, along with the waitresses and the owner/ cook peering through the kitchen window — inspected each newcomer, his clothes, his hair, his demeanor. If the person passed this initial scrutiny, the rest returned to their food, their conversations, or their dice cups.

Their examination, they argued, came not from judgement nor fear, but instead from tradition. Like other businesses in Jefferson, Minnesota, the Plains was not a private club, but its owner and faithful customers expected certain conventions to be followed. Over the decades of its existence, the Plains had developed a certain clientele, and outsiders, though not overtly shunned, underwent this period of "indoctrination" in order to achieve acceptance.

For most of the intruders, this meant the furtive glances and whispered commentary that faded throughout their first visit and transformed to heartfelt welcome by their third time.

Certain people, however, could not and would never pass the primary evaluation.

On an unusually warm Friday in March, the loyal customers turned to see a young Ojibwe couple with their little girl enter, search for an empty table, and then take a seat at a window booth.

In the kitchen Hattie Berg, the cafe's rotund owner and chief cook, looked over the counter into the dining room. Three of her chins flopped and jiggled as she squinted and assessed the three newcomers. Disgust twisted her face.

She shook her head and muttered, "Indians. I hate Indians."

Chief waitress Clarice Olson came to the window to pick up an order. She saw Hattie's angry face, and asked, "Something wrong, boss?"

Hattie nodded at the front of the dining room. Clarice saw the family and immediately understood the problem.

Jefferson sat equidistant between three Indian reservations — Red Lake, Leech Lake, and White Earth.

Although Bemidji, Crookston, and Grand Forks had more to offer in shopping and services, natives still showed up in this town, unappreciated and uninvited. Hattie, in particular, left no doubt these "damn foreigners should just go back where they came from." Because most of the town shared her sentiments, nobody corrected her with the historical fact that the Norwegians, Germans, and Swedes that inhabited Jefferson were the real foreigners.

Clarice turned back to Hattie and mouthed the words, "I'll take care of it."

First, she filled three glasses of water and slipped two menus under her arm. She placed the glasses on a small tray, pasted on her best Jeffersonian smile, and approached the booth.

She set the water in front of each person, saying a little too loudly, "Mornin', folks. How ya doin'? Can I get ya anyt'ing ta drink?"

"Coffee for me," the husband said in the clipped diction that identified him as a probable resident of Mahnomen or Waubun.

"Yeah. Me too," said his wife.

"Sounds good. Sounds good. And you, little lady?" Clarice asked the girl.

The girl looked at her mother. "Can I have pop, Mommy?"

Her mother said, "Autumn, it's still breakfast time. Have some orange juice instead."

The girl's shoulders slumped and, hiding behind her mother's arm, she mumbled at Clarice, "Orange juice, please."

"'kay. I'll be right back," Clarice said.

When Clarice entered the kitchen, Hattie whispered, "What are you doing? I thought you were going to handle this."

Clarice kept her head down as she filled two cups with hot water. "Just hang on," she told her boss. She dropped a tea bag in each cup, then filled a small glass with apple juice and took them to the booth.

As she laid out the drinks, the three outsiders looked at Clarice, confused. Clarice, oblivious to their reaction, chirped, "Here you go. Did you decide whatchew wanted to eat yet?"

Autumn, the little girl, looked at her glass, Clarice, and then her mother. "I wanted orange juice," she whispered to her mother.

Her mother looked at Clarice and said, "She wanted orange juice, and my husband and I ordered coffee."

Clarice asked, "Are you sure? I could have sworn you said tea and apple juice. Okay. I'll be right back." She gathered up the drinks and went back to the kitchen. In a moment she came back with two half cups of coffee.

"Here you go," she said to the couple. "I'm sorry, though," she told Autumn. "We're out of orange juice. I can get you some prune juice."

The mother began to protest, but her husband stopped her. "No, that's okay. She can just have water. That's okay, isn't it, honey?"

The little girl nodded sullenly.

"Okay," Clarice said. "And to eat?"

Before the husband could begin to order, Clarice interrupted, "Oh! By the way, we had a big run on breakfast this morning, so we're out of a lot."

The mother looked at the clock. 8:30. Usually the heart of breakfast service. "Seriously? It's only…" she asked.

"Oh, God. I know. I was supposed to go to the store last night after my shift and get supplies. But then the alternator on my car died, and I was stuck tryin' to get that fixed. I'm really sorry. I promise we'll have a full menu tomorrow."

The husband and wife looked around at the other diners with full plates of pancakes, bacon, omelets, and hash browns.

"What do you have left?" the husband asked.

"Well, I can probably get a couple bowls of oatmeal and a slice of toast or something."

The woman looked around the dining room again. She bit her lower lip and began to breathe heavily. Angrily, she bent over the table and began, "Are you kidding—?"

Under the table, her husband grabbed her knee. "No, that's all right. We'll try later after our doctor's appointment," he said.

"But, Daddy," I'm hungry now," Autumn protested.

"We'll stop at the gas station and get you a candy bar or something," he said sliding out of the booth. "Come on, honey."

His daughter pulled on her jacket, while his wife glared alternately between him and Clarice. The man zipped up his brown leather jacket and urged his wife, "Let's go, Heather."

Angrily, the woman rose, slipped into her coat, grabbed Autumn's hand and stomped out the front door. The man paused a second, debating what to say. Then, he followed the others sheepishly until he stopped at the front door and turned back to Clarice who watched him steadily. The man saw her resolve and averted his eyes. He mumbled, "I'm sorry for wasting your time."

The eavesdropping customers jerked their eyes back to their tables and sipped their drinks. No one acknowledged that anything had just happened. They were simply happy to have their cafe to themselves again.

Hattie came out of the kitchen and joined Clarice at the window, watching the family get into their rusty pickup and drive away.

Hattie smiled and said approvingly, "That was subtle."

"Thanks," Clarice responded. "I don't think they'll be back."

"Good job," Hattie said, patting Clarice's back and waddled back to the kitchen.

Then Clarice saw it. Building and looming above the buildings across the street. A wall of fog bearing down on the town.

"Hattie! Wait! Come back. You gotta come see this!"

Hattie glanced toward the window, saw the imposing cloud, and squeezed her bulk between the tables, tipping plates and glasses onto the floor. Clarice pushed the gathered customers aside to give Hattie a clear view out the window. The cloud built higher and more threatening until steadily, the fog enveloped the lawyers' offices and the newspaper building across the street, the parked cars in front of the Plains, and finally the cafe itself.

Outside, the streetlights popped on. Barely anything moved, just a few confused and disoriented pedestrians caught on the sidewalks as the fog tumbled over the roofs and obliterated the streets.

Water droplets grew and clung to the window glass, blocking any light from entering or escaping the cafe. The gathered crowd of stunned patrons stared as the moisture gathered into ever larger drops that slid down the glass in small rivulets like rain.

"What the hell is that?" Hattie asked breathlessly, leaning against the booth table in front of her.

"Never seen nothin' like it," Clarice replied, her mouth agape.

Nobody else could say anything. Only the tinny rattle of the kitchen radio broke the quiet.

"There can't be anything good in this," Clarice whispered, astonished.

Hattie stared, then simply nodded and tottered back to her kitchen.

## 3

Long icicles dripped from the metal awning above the front door of Thorstad's Perfect Plumbing on the western edge of downtown. Although the morning air temperature gently rose above freezing, the frigid concrete sidewalk quickly glazed over from the dripping water, turning the entrance into a mini-skating rink. The bell above the door rang and the muttering, hard-faced Frank Thorstad emerged, muttering curses and scattering salt to melt the ice.

Knees bent to keep his balance, he reached into his bucket and flung handfuls of the sparkling crystals left and right, listening for the tell-tale crackling and popping to indicate the salt was doing its job. The sidewalk's icy surface soon became pock marked and Frank stood up, satisfied that customers could get into the building without falling and suing him for a few billion bucks. Just to be sure, he lifted the bucket and dumped the little remaining powder in front of the door for good measure.

There was one more thing he had to do. He cracked open the door, set the bucket inside, and then walked gingerly to the end of the building for his daily mid-morning smoke.

For all five years the store had been open, Frank's wife Sammi had nagged him that the smell of tobacco turned away customers the same way it repulsed her.

"Shit, the whole place smells like smoke. Always has," Frank replied.

Still Sammi begged.

She reasoned.

She threatened.

Finally, she had had enough and in a torrent of obscenities from her normally innocent mouth, her final ultimatum convinced Frank to smoke only outside, both at home and at the store.

As he once explained to his assistant Art Benson, "Smokin' outside in the winter is a bitch, but if the weather is warm like this all the time, I could get used to it. Besides, if Sammi keeps feedin' me and givin' me a little pussy now and then, it's no big deal."

Frank leaned against the corner of the patched red brick facade of the building, lit his cigarette, took a deep breath of smoke, and blew it straight up into the air as he carelessly tossed the match to the curb.

He rested his head against the wall and closed his eyes. The moist air grazed the scar that ran from the left corner of his mouth to his ear, the scar that Jeffersonians said defined his personality, the one he received so many years ago while hunting, the one which led him to break his phy. ed. teacher's jaw.

Even before that event, Frank's attitude frightened townspeople more than the scar itself, so when the hospital pieced him together after the hunting incident and released him, the local citizens knew to ignore the scar's existence and to ask no questions, make no comments. Mr. Darwin, the brash football coach and teacher, ignored the rule and told Frank the scar made him look perpetually pissed off.

Frank smiled as he remembered the loud crack as his fist splintered Darwin's face.

"Almost made the year in Fergus worthwhile," he thought, as he smirked and took another drag on his cigarette.

Frank had had countless run-ins with the juvenile justice system throughout high school, almost all of them related to anger and violence issues, particularly after whatever happened in the woods. Breaking a teacher's jaw was the last straw for the authorities, however. The juvenile court judge washed the county's hands of attempting to control Frank's outbursts and turned him over to the state mental hospital in Fergus Falls to determine and treat the source of his constant rage.

"Lotta good that did 'em." He turned his head with his hands until his neck cracked. "S'pose I should get back at it," he thought. Taking another drag on his cigarette, he blew the smoke high into the air again, watching the light breeze blow it away from him.

He coughed and spit. A loose strand of tobacco irritated the gum between his upper lip and teeth and would not move. His mouth contorted and pushed at the leaf until he gave up and finally dislodged it with the fingernail on his right pinkie. He flicked the leaf away and spit again to rid his teeth of any remnants that might be left.

"Shit!" he muttered, tossing the butt to the sidewalk and smashing it under the heel of his boot. With his toe, he jammed what was left of the cigarette into a crack between the sidewalk and the building. Then he turned toward the door.

He took a step toward the door and slipped. "Fuck!" he spat, reaching his hand to the wall to steady himself.

Then he saw the sky. His mouth fell open.

"*Holy* fuck!" he mouthed.

He kept his feet flat on the ground, slid to the door and threw it open, yelling inside.

"Art! Art! Come out here. Ya gotta see this!"

Art, Frank's bent and deformed hired man, shuffled out of the storeroom and grunted, "Wha'?"

"Come 'ere." Frank ordered, beckoning him outside.

Art steadied his broken body against the sales counter and then scuttled against the wall until he reached the door.

"Come out here and look at this," Frank said.

As Art's bent body emerged from the door, Frank turned him toward the east.

Behind the low buildings of the downtown stores and the dominant hulk of the town's grain elevator, a towering wall of fog loomed and lurched toward the town.

Frank leaned his head over Art's hunched shoulder, close to his ear.

"You ever see anything like that?" he whispered.

Art raised a finger to silence his boss. Then the two watched as the cloud devoured the town in front of them, crawling steadily toward them.

Finally, the cloud paused briefly in front of the store, investigating Frank and Art's significance.

Art shuffled forward, measuring the height of the cloud with his eyes. He leaned toward and sniffed.

Frank furled his eyebrows and demanded, "What are ya doin'?"

Art reached out as if the wall were solid. The thick moisture nibbled at his fingers, then swallowed the two men and the store.

Frank straightened a bit and placed his hand on Art's back.

"What the hell just happened?" he asked.

Art said nothing. He simply shambled forward into the darkened streets.

"Art! Where the hell are you goin'?" Frank yelled after him.

The sound of Art's limping feet vanished into the fog.

"What the…?" Frank muttered. He stared into nothingness for a moment. Silent drops of water clung to his face. "I thought I was nuts," he said, taking one last look into the darkness before reaching inside the front door to turn on the lights.

# I ART BENSON

## 1

Earlier that unusually warm Friday morning in March 1989, the muskeg surface of Grave Swamp rested on a murky brown lake that swelled and shifted as an errant breeze blew through the branches of the scrub brush that clung to the rolling ground. As the finely knit fabric of mud, roots, and moss rose and fell with the wind or the weight of lost wildlife, the bushes struggled for survival by sucking nutrients out of the muck below.

A small island of stable, solid ground rose near the center of the bog, and on the island a tall, decades-old swamp cedar grew unmolested by humans or animals. The Ontario Ojibwe, who did not know the swamp's history, would have called the tree holy. The animals and Art Benson who watched it that morning knew better. Birds that would normally have looked to the tree's dense branches for shelter from the weather instead opted for the barren twigs of the scrub brush below. The numerous insects that could have fed on the cedar boughs and bark shunned the island entirely. As if defying the world to invade the sanctity of the island, the cedar stood proud and tall, a well-armed sentinel looming over the bog, guarding what lay below.

That morning, the Word had spoken and Art had returned. Just before sunrise, he stood on the ridge above the western bank of the swamp. A full moon set behind him, and the first streaks of dawn peeked over Angler Hill across the bog. Art's bones and muscles turned against themselves so his right ear rested on his right shoulder. His back and neck ached in remembrance and premonition as his body questioned the sky.

The sky was not long in answering. Blotting out the rising sun, billowing thunderheads rolled over the hill like giant snowballs, building on each other, piling higher and ever higher into the air. A gust of wind from the prairie to the West blew over the ridge through the trees, shaking their limbs and pushing Art to his knees. The wind gathered round the swamp below him in a great circle, and spiraled inward at increasing speed. Like the brush that grasped the muskeg on the surface of the swamp, Art clung to the grass beneath him and watched. With strangling hands intent on twisting the life out of the tree, the circle of wind tightened its own grip around the tiny island and the base of the cedar, shaking and pulling at the tormented island.

Finally, the current blasted a hand straight up into the sky and pulled down a single lightning bolt that tore the sky and opened a great gash in the trunk of the tree, splitting the ground below the cedar's roots. The earth shook and the trees swayed violently. Art hung on tightly and watched while the muskeg around the island heaved and writhed, as if the sky were an eagle ripping into the swamp's belly and feeding on its entrails. The bog convulsed and twisted as the island rose in a paroxysm of pain. Just as the island was about to fly into the morning air, the fissure beneath the cedar let out a groan that shook the forest around the swamp and echoed off the face of Angler Hill. Then, with a resounding thud and splash, the island fell back.

The tree quivered once, twice.

And all was silent.

The air was still.

Art sat back and leaned against a birch tree that still shivered from the lightning and earthquake. He waited while the clouds dissipated. The swamp shone red in the morning light. Even from where he sat hundreds of feet away, Art saw the pale flesh of the cedar exposed by the lightning. It glowed a burnt yellow, a yellow that slowly grew in intensity, then stopped and turned a dull grey. From the point where the fissure in the ground met the wound of the tree, a wisp of fog danced upward, at first formless, then weaving itself into a great drunken man who stumbled and fell to the ground. Behind him came attendants, tiny wraiths that lay around their fallen leader, kissing his smiling, inebriated face. Other fantastical creatures, some half reptilian-half mammal, others part human-part dog, sprang out of the ground and tree, dancing, frolicking, and cavorting until the whole island was a raucous, hedonistic congregation worshiping before a prostrate god.

Art's jaw, broken and fused years ago, ached in recognition. "The Earth Man," he thought. The others were the Earth Man's evil spirits, the matchi-auwishuk. Art could not speak; he could only watch.

As the sun rose higher, the assembled throng melted into fog, a fog that spread across the island floor and oozed out over the swamp, heading toward Jefferson. Art's eyes watered and his nose ran in the morning air. The fog rose and darkened the sky. Art wiped his nose on his glove, rose, and limped through the woods away from the swamp. At the bottom of the ridge, he heard a loud commotion above him and turned back to see a mass of sparrows hurry across the darkening sky, squeaking and squawking their warnings to the world.

Art did not need the birds. He heard. He saw everything. The Word filled him. It spoke with a voice even louder than the thunder and the broken earth. The Evil Ones, the matchi-auwishuk, had returned to the place of their birth. But these spirits were not just Anishinabe. Tales of their cousins have been told by the Norse, the Greeks, the Christians, the Sumerians. Art saw them all and understood.

This day the spirits rose from the earth as fog to provide the Great Mask, the fog that hides the world from heaven. Under the cover of mist, the Evil Ones would search for sacrifice and disciples. Those inclined to excess would be the first rewarded and first destroyed. The spirits' aim was to blot out the Word, to bring darkness, and destroy the seekers of the light. As the Maskers' strength increased, only the Storyteller who saw both the spiritual and the temporal worlds, the one who could expose one to the other, could keep the Word alive. As with Jesus, Buddha, and Muhammad, the Storyteller would become the Story, and only the Story, in concert with the Herald and the Flame, could eradicate the Evil Ones.

As Art stood rapt in the scene before him of the fog spreading through the forest toward Jefferson, the Word spoke the Storyteller's Name from the still frozen earth.

The Name startled Art. He looked up into the barren branches of the birch against his back and saw faces, pained and hungry, lost and hiding, frightened and frightening. He recognized the Storyteller. Art also knew, like John the Baptist, this story was not and would not be his own.

## 2

Art forced himself to leave the marsh. There was no more to see than he had already seen many times. The legend of the place terrified the countryside, but instead of paralyzing him, Art's experience and first-hand knowledge spurred him to action. While the spirits he had just seen menaced Jefferson and its residents, he relived the truth and assessed his options.

Grave Swamp was an infamous, floating bog hidden deep in the woods just east of Jefferson at the foot of Angler Hill, a mile or so north of Highway 2. All of Jefferson knew of it. Few spoke its name. Even fewer allowed themselves to see it.

Native legends say the ghosts of long-forgotten Dakota and Anishinabe hunters, French fur trappers and misguided Norwegian settlers haunt the swamp. To the Children of the Flame and to those who replaced them, the spot was sacred. According to these native people, the Snow God, the White Deer, and, most importantly, the Great Flame emerged from this earthly womb.

But, as the stories say, those gods, called manitous by today's Anishinabe or Ojibwe, disappeared. They fled from the Evil Man of the Swamp, also known as the Earth Man. Chased by this master of the underworld and his spiritual minions, the manitous abandoned the Children of the Flame to the Great Flood, a vast glacier-formed body of water known to modern geologists and historians as Lake Agassiz.

When the floodwaters receded, new manitous and peoples arrived, yet the earliest legends prevailed. As if vapors from the ground permeated them with knowledge, the tribes of hundreds of lost generations of Anishinabe, Dakota, and Europeans realized the swamp, once sacred, was now cursed, possessed by the Earth Man, his followers and an ever-increasing, ever-more dangerous horde of carnivorous demons that ate human flesh – the Giant Cannibals, or Weendigoes.

Age after age, the lies and temptations of untold riches from seemingly human charlatans prompted war and torment across the valley left by the vanished lake. Beguiled people clamored and brawled to enrich themselves, only to fall victim to the devouring jaws of the weendigo.

Yet, even when they knew the beast's name, each generation of humans failed to learn the true nature of the demon that afflicted them, that they and their human nature were responsible for a spiritual being's physical survival. Children and adults alike feared the violent death and knew to run from the name "weendigo," but did not recognize what was most fearsome about the evil manitou, that these weendigoes hungered not only for the meat of their victims; they yearned for the lust and greed in each person. After consuming their quarry and all its innate desires, these weendigoes grew in proportion to the control that lust previously had on their victim.

However, this nourishment proved both sustenance and plague.

True, the creature needed the victim's meat to survive, to sustain life, but the lust contained in it also caused a weendigo's skeleton to grow rapidly, faster even than its skin. As the creature grew, its skull and ribs stretched tighter and tighter against its hide, nearly tearing its flesh to shreds. And then, the desire in the weendigo's belly turned to hunger, a hunger that outgrew the monster's physical size.

This then is the irony of the weendigo's existence: He needs to eat human flesh and lust to survive, but eating causes hunger that can never be satisfied. Each meal devoured threatens to destroy him with starvation.

When the current incarnation of Art was a young man, his vision quest, the Ojibwe rite of passage, took him to Grave Swamp. There he met and battled the weendigoes himself. Years later, his back still ached in recognition of their name. But on this day, the day of the all-consuming fog, on the day the Name of the Storyteller came to Art, he knew that the weendigoes were not the only spirits which appeared with the mist, nor was mere survival their only aim.

## 3

On his way back to Jefferson, the Word spoke to Art and revealed the necessary truths.

*The Number is three.*
*It is not holy.*
*It is not magical.*
*It simply is.*
*What you see,*
*The Earth Man,*
*The Matchi-auwishuk,*
*Evil itself,*
*Is incomplete.*
*It seeks the Number.*

Art remembered. The righteousness of the Word is found in the Number: The Herald, the Storyteller (The

Reluctant Messiah), and the Flame. Together, it is whole, complete.

What he saw at Grave Swamp aspired to be completely evil. It was not. The total degeneracy of wickedness had yet to complete itself. It was the mission of the Earth Man and his Great Masking, the fog, to do so.

Art also knew two of the Word's Number. He knew the Word had brought him to the swamp as Herald, and he had heard the name of the Reluctant Messiah. Beecher Jones, the town's high school principal. The third name, the embodiment of the Flame, was still to come. As Herald, Art's role was to convince Beecher of his responsibility, find the Flame, and to join the three together to defeat the Earth Man.

## 4

Art Benson himself is difficult to describe.

On the surface, *Art Benson* is just a name given by human parents to an unsuspecting infant. The child did not know who or what he was, had been, or would be. In time, he would learn he was far more than man, yet far less than god.

Even more difficult to explain is what he was at the time of the previous Great Masking, the one before Beecher Jones, the one that left Art's body deformed and his soul in transition so he would not talk of occurrences repeated for centuries, of occasions of legend and redemption, and of the circumstances of other Great Maskings.

In Beecher's time, Jeffersonians knew Art as the "Blue-eyed Indian," the curiosity, the oddity causing people to stop, to stare. His spine bent his body into a perpetual question mark. His legs carried him forward in limps and lurches. His jaw muscles clenched his teeth and stifled his voice. His course through this life meandered and spun into the wall of humanity, blocking and reversing, unsettling and halting.

Children grabbed at his clothes and taunted him. "You a hunchback? Huh? You a monster? You the Boogie Man? Huh? C'mon, freak. What are you?"

When Art shuffled to work at Thorstad's through the early morning light, dogs strained their leashes, growling and barking. Faces gathered at windows and the blinds closed.

They did not understand that the world in which Art lived, a world of man and spirit, the world that was in fact theirs as well, was and is inhabited by ancients and moderns.

According to Art, at the time of Beecher's Great Masking, the world was struggling to regain an identity lost thousands of years before. It was a world invisible to those who did not want to be bothered by truth and reality. It was a world that "does not exist" except to those who exist in it. And so it is today.

As a child of the earth, Art learned to speak and think in the languages of his time and in languages long forgotten; however, then as today, words cannot account for the wonders Art saw. As he would say, "The languages of man are not meant to describe the universe as it is. Only the Word can do that and the Word needs no sound, no symbol, simply an open spirit."

Who Art Benson was and is became the foundation of who Beecher Jones became, the foundation of Jefferson, Minnesota, the foundation of the world known and unknown today.

## 5

Art was born into Beecher's time in a small cabin near Naytahwaush, Minnesota, on the White Earth Indian Reservation. His mother was Anishinabe – Ojibwe – Chippewa (The labels have become interchangeable to the white man); his father was Norwegian. But Art was of the whole earth and whole sky, of all man and all manitou. His mother knew this and his father denied it. Still, from the moment he could stand alone, gaze into the night and marvel at the stars, from the moment he could hear the voices of the birds and the wolf and understand their words, from the moment he could think and speak truth, the reality of his transcendence of earthly definition and labels was obvious... and daunting to his parents and himself.

Time did not then nor does it now hold any limits for him.

While other children daydreamed, Art had spells, periods when the world suspended its journey and he stood apart, watching, listening. During these spells, he saw what no human sees. He heard what no human hears. He knew things no one else knows – the past, the future, the minds of others, the ways of the unseen forces ruling the universe. Because of the spells, the conventions of time confused Art. They meant nothing. In terms of grammar, he said, tense is irrelevant. To him life is an endless continuum extending across time upwards, downwards, partially, wholly. Many bodies, many ages, but one life. In the brief moments of these spells, he comprehended all. That is how he knew what happened, what is happening now and what is still to be. In those moments, he knew Beecher Jones when Beecher was born. He knew Beecher before the land formed out of the Great Water. He knew him at the Great Revelation to come.

Art saw the spells as a gift. Through them he sat at the feet of Jesus and Buddha, Lao-Tzu and Muhammad. From those man-spirit lips he heard the Word spoken without the distortion of history, the anger of culture, the perversion of religion. Early in the age of Beecher Jones, the priest and nuns at the Catholic Church's reservation school taught him what had been printed:

> *In the beginning was the Word, and the Word was with God, and the Word was God. He was with God in the beginning. Through Him all things were made; without Him nothing was made. In Him was life, and that life was the light of men.*

But for all the times the nuns read the words, *they* did not see. For all the times, the priest spoke them aloud, *he* did not hear. Though the Word exists, they did not know it. Because of Art's spells, he did.

Art's parents did not understand the spells. His mother said he was oblivious to her cries, her shaking, her pleading with him to wake and speak to her. She said words came from his mouth, yet he spoke in languages she had never heard. His father said at other times Art stood motionless for a half hour, a wooden statue with empty eyes turned to the sky, yet both his mother and father felt Art's soul wandering, lost in a mental labyrinth with no escape. They could not bear to watch him.

As Art grew older, these interludes of unconsciousness grew longer, more catatonic in their outward appearance, yet more intense in their revelations. By then, his father called them "hysterical trances" and prescribed beatings until he "outgrew" them. The nuns and the priest called him demon possessed and prescribed the rite of exorcism. The neurologist at the University of Minnesota called the spells "extended petit mal seizures," a form of epilepsy, and prescribed drugs. When Art told his mother what he saw and heard and felt in those "lost moments," she called him the reincarnation of Cheeby-aub-oozoo, a man-spirit who conversed with the manitous, the spirits of the Anishinabe people. She urged him on his vision quest.

In the teachings of the ancient mystics of civilizations known and unknown to the modern world, Art Benson learned the Word's truth and grew in the nurture of the Flame, the fire that burns and cleanses. For millennia, in whatever incarnation, he dwelled in their presence as their servant, warrior, disciple. At his dawn of realization, he sought their love. In the innocence of his youth, he found joy in their radiance. Throughout his age of responsibility, he served them in battle and in devotion.

His father said on the day before Art left on his vision quest, Art stood in the center of the room of their Naytahwaush cabin with a vacant stare turned to the sky, oblivious to his father's anger. His mother pleaded with him to awake and speak to them, but he would not. When Art finally gained consciousness an hour later, the words and sounds he spoke confused them and his eyes would not focus in the room.

Art later said he had seen Beecher Jones. He didn't know his name, but he knew his soul. It was also the first time Art saw the Evil Ones, the Great Maskers.

Like a saying of Lao-Tzu or Buddha, Art said, the Great Mask is a paradox, one he didn't understand at first, nor can it be fully explained now. Art knew that people teach that masks conceal, hide. But on his vision quest, he learned the Earth Man used the Great Mask to reveal, to disclose those who would leave what they had and follow Him. According to human nature, when a person is exposed, he will cover himself, hiding who he really is. The true self is suppressed. However, when a man already considers himself hidden, anonymous, he will act true to his nature, revealing the unseen, the unknown, the uncomfortable. So when the maskers bring their fog – the Great Mask – people in its path become hidden. They become who they are, no longer simply people, but prey to the Earth Man and his matchi-auwishuk, evil spirits.

Art had seen them in his visions, but on his quest, he found the Evil Ones at Grave Swamp, preparing their first attempt at Jefferson, Minnesota's Great Masking. He had only seen one other masking generations before, so he was unprepared for what was to come. He did not know his role that time. It was because of his lack of knowledge in that first battle of Grave Swamp that he lost two fingers and part of a leg, broke three vertebrae, and nearly died of exposure. In that confrontation a weendigo, a Great Cannibal, cracked Art's jaw. The bone healed badly, becoming nearly immoveable, thus confining Art's speech to barely audible, monosyllabic grunts. His spine also became deformed, curving into a question mark, constantly asking questions no one could or would answer.

When the battle ended, Art felt he had failed the Word. The Earth Man and his matchi-auwishuk had escaped but would come again, stronger and more determined. Art could not stop them, nor could he leave Jefferson. Only the Storyteller, a human touched and infused by both the Word and Flame, could reveal, confront and defeat them. Art knew he was not the Storyteller. In shame of his inadequacy, he set himself apart. As time went on, he became waebinigun, in the language of his mother – unwanted, cast aside, ignored. No one understood. No one listened.

In the week of his quest, which consisted of fasting, prayer, and struggle for survival, he learned the truth of the nuns' verses. He also learned the verse they didn't teach, the next verse:

*The light shines in darkness, but the darkness has not understood it.*

That week, through battle and revelation, he saw the light and the darkness. He learned that all the religions of his father's people, all the traditions of his mother's, all the moral codes ever devised and imposed upon the planet, all exist in darkness, ignoring the light of the Word and its Flame.

Those man-spirits who sought and found the Word in the past discovered it in ways wholly unforeseen. Jesus went to the desert and the garden to hear, and He touched the hand of God. Buddha went to the river to see the Word's truth and heard its laughter. Muhammad, groping along the cave walls for direction, tasted the sight of an angel. Lao-Tzu, sickened by the corruption and violence of humanity, rode off to die in the torrid heat of the desert, only to drown in the cool, life-giving fragrance of the Tao.

At one time everyday people listened and watched for direction. Some even heard. Art's father's people heard the Word in the teachings of Jesus, Moses, and Abraham. His mother's people read the Word in the sway of the cedars, in the flight of the eagle, and the rush of the wind. But his father's people became blind, his mother's people deaf. Jesus, Moses, and Abraham gave way to nothingness. All the manitous of the Anishinabe –

Kitchi-Manitou, Muzzu-Kummik-Quae, Maudjee-kawiss, and more – are no longer welcome in their native home, turned away in favor of indifference. No one misses them. None calls them back. The darkness of humanity, as well as the power of the matchi-auwishuk, has blocked the light.

In the time of Beecher, the Earth Man returned, but with Art's broken jaw and his outcast life, he could not speak the Word to break the Earth Man's power. Besides, Art's mouth was full of too many voices. He was, in the words of the nuns, a modern-day John the Baptist, "the voice of one crying in the wilderness."

An unlikely herald, Art was to convince Beecher Jones of the truth of who he was. Neither he nor any others knew. To himself and the town of Jefferson, Beecher was a husband, a father, and high-school principal. In reality he was the Word's ultimate warrior. Art needed to reveal to him what the Word taught, to lead Beecher out of the world into reality, to turn him into the Storyteller who would deliver the only truth, the truth of the Word. The Flame would burn away the confusion of the world and inspire him with truth.

# II BEECHER JONES

## 1

Early on Monday morning, three days after the Earth Man's return to Grave Swamp, Art stood on the fog-enshrouded street near Beecher Jones's house. Within Art lived Beecher's world – his home, Freedom High where he was principal, the future which would engulf him, the ever-thickening fog that had already engulfed the whole town for three days. His daughter Jeannie's laughter bubbled in Art's belly. His wife Sarah's mystery vibrated and burned in Art's teeth.

Art knew that to Beecher, as with the other citizens of Jefferson, he was simply the broken-down, "blue-eyed Indian," the unfortunate deformity who worked for the town's psychotic plumber, Frank Thorstad. An educated person like Beecher would not listen to Art about the Word or the Flame or the Earth Man or anything. But Art knew he must tell him.

Especially since the Great Masking had begun. Friday, the fog from Grave Swamp inundated Jefferson and paralyzed business and movement. That included the operation of the school.

As high school principal, second in command to Superintendent of Schools Sam Haake, Beecher needed to determine if the weather were safe enough to hold school. When the fog rolled in Friday afternoon and hid all but the glow of street lights, he canceled afternoon classes. And while the students loved his decision which gave them a just-short-of-three-day weekend, Beecher's judgement was not popular with the townspeople, particularly the unofficial ruling council, the Norske Junta. Besides fielding angry calls from upset mothers who had to leave work to care for their children and from irate storeowners who lost those workers, Beecher also had to meet with the mayor, two city councilmen and the chairman of the school board – half the Junta.

That Friday afternoon, sitting in a court-like semicircle in the back room of the Plains Cafe, the Junta grumbled and grunted in their usual state of agitation. Tough-set scowls predominated the room which prevented tidy food consumption and coherent expression of thought by the scowlers. Wiping a dollop of ketchup and angry spittle from his chin, Mayor Einar Nordhaus spoke forcefully for the group. "We'll accept snow days, but fog days? That's ridiculous. This ain't gonna happen again, is it?" Beecher recognized the words more as a directive than a question. The other members of the Junta glared in agreement with Einar's command.

Beecher shrugged and replied, "I don't control the weather."

Einar and company harrumphed, stood, and left. They muttered to each other, implying that weather mastery, while not specifically spelled out in Beecher's contract, was most certainly within the realm of his duties. They left him alone to pay the check and tip the waitress. Beecher sighed. Not only was he expected to follow their direction, he was expected to pay for listening to it as well.

In frustration, he left through the back door, walked sulkily down the alley through the fog back to his office, and called the superintendent who was in St. Paul, lobbying the legislature for more special education funding. Sam told Beecher, "When it comes to the children's safety, it doesn't matter what the boys down at the Plains think. Err on the side of caution."

"What do I do if the fog's like this on Monday?"

"Like I said, err on the side of caution."

Over the next three days, the murky haze only worsened, stranding Sam in St. Paul. By Monday morning mist was so dense in Jefferson, only the very foolish dared enter it. Without Sam around, the decision again fell to Beecher.

As he looked out his own front window, Beecher knew what his decision would be. However, he needed to assure himself of the necessity of losing another day of class.

The manitou in Art watched Beecher and listened to his mind as he emerged from the house into the morning gloom and crept gingerly to the end of the block. In Beecher's section of town, there were very few streetlights. Besides, the fog was so thick, their illumination was worthless, with each light simply a shining globe, hanging in the air. The first street corner he came to didn't even have a lamppost. Beecher stood hesitantly, fearfully, before stepping into the street, turning, and blindly feeling his way along the gutter, one foot against the curb, the other searching for obstacles ahead.

Three blocks later, things were no better. Barely able to find the curb with his outstretched foot, Beecher made his decision. This fog wasn't going to lift; it was becoming thicker. "Sam's right. To hell with the Norske Junta," he thought. "Better to be safe and leave the buses in the garage."

As Beecher moved through the darkness from one tiny, glowing pool to another, the fog infected his imagination until Jefferson became one surrealistic vision after another. Bushes became wolves crouching, waiting in ambush. Branches hanging like snakes from treetops turned trees into gorgons. At times the mist around him even took on human form – a laughing woman with yellow glowing eyes, or a hooded figure beckoning him toward some unknown ceremony, or a hunchbacked half-breed staring at a malevolent sky.

Beecher tried to shake the thoughts from his head. He wished he had had more sleep.

As he continued toward school, Beecher wondered why his fantasies distorted the innocuous into the bizarre. A psychiatrist would probably tell him they were arising from some hidden fear. His Christian fundamentalist college roommate would tell him they were warning him of his "impending doom." Beecher came to a simpler conclusion: Three days of incessant fog had finally driven him crazy.

He did not see the whole truth – that the fog which covered also revealed.

He simply desired that things get back to normal – students back in school, learning; teachers back in school, teaching; parents back at their jobs, working. But they couldn't. The fog made it unsafe to move, unsafe to breathe. Nothing would or could be normal until the fog disappeared.

Standing in the foggy shadows, Art nodded. This was truth.

Beecher inched his way along the gutter toward school until he came to an unlit intersection where he stopped abruptly. Ahead he saw nothing but darkness and mist. There was nothing to guide his feet. "Now what?" he wondered. He needed to cross the street, but how would he find the other side? He wasn't even sure where he stood. Near downtown, he knew, and closer to school than home. If he could find the curb on the other side, he could find his way to his office. He had to move forward, but he could not see his way.

After several minutes of indecision, Beecher forced himself into the street. His feet slid forward, slowly, one tentative step at a time. Hundreds of tiny steps later, there was still no curb. He stopped and looked about frantically. There was nothing to see, no sound to guide him. Alone and trembling in the mist, he soon realized he had veered into the middle of the intersection and was now walking down one of the intersecting streets. But which one? Was he on that weird diagonal street that led downtown and away from the school? He couldn't tell. His breath shortened and he pulled nervously on the back of his neck. He didn't know what to do. Even if he found another gutter, where was it going to lead him? The darkness paralyzed him, and he stood in the street, lost and terrified.

From a distance, screams pierced his thoughts. First, he thought he was imagining again, but then the shrieks grew louder, more insistent. He couldn't hear what the voices cried, nor could he tell if they were human.

"He can only hear with his ears," Art thought. "He must be taught who he is."

Art could no longer stay hidden. He stepped out of the fog and grabbed Beecher's arm. "Come!" Art grunted through his tight lips.

"What the...?"

"You ... stop them." Art winced from the pain in his jaw, but kept tugging on Beecher's arm.

"Art, what the hell are you doing here?"

Art leaned close and looked up at Beecher's eyes. He knew that all Beecher saw was Art Benson, a short, hunched, probably drunken half-breed who worked at the plumbing shop.

"He does not know himself," Art thought. "How can he know me?"

Art clutched Beecher's wrist and hurriedly dragged him down the street through the thickening mist toward the terrifying wails, giving him no time to question where they were going. Reluctantly, Beecher let Art lead him through the gloom until he saw a faint glow in the distance. He stopped short and pulled back on Art's arm. "Benny's?" he asked. "Is that Benny's Amoco sign?"

Art said nothing. His jaw hurt too much. He kept tugging Beecher toward the cacophony that became more horrifying as they moved toward the light. Then Beecher's eyes could see. Hundreds, perhaps thousands, of sparrows, birds of the manitous sent by the matchi-auwishuk, the birds Art had seen at Grave Swamp on Friday. They screeched and flapped their wings wildly, swirling and crashing into the mural on Benny's brick wall, the picture last year's art classes had painted of the forest and prairie surrounding Jefferson. Hundreds already lay twitching and dying on the sidewalk. Hundreds more swarmed out of the darkness like squadrons of kamikazes, diving into the unforgiving wall of concrete trees, then falling helplessly to the equally unforgiving sidewalk below.

At first, Beecher stood in stunned amazement. Then, as if he could actually stop their suicidal onslaught, he rushed forward, shouting and waving his arms to scare them away. Yet, no matter what he tried, the whole flock seemed bent on death. One after another, the sparrows slammed into the brick and dropped to the concrete around them. The swarm never ended.

In the midst of the mayhem, Art stopped. What triggered his spell, he never knew. He later remembered standing on the corner watching the birds fly out of the sky above the streetlight and Beecher scurrying up and down the sidewalk, flailing his arms. Beecher and the birds disappeared, and Art saw the spirits, there in the dark, flowing about the faces he had seen in the branches of the birch at Grave Swamp. A woman. No, two women. A child. A red-eyed, snarling man growing out of his skin. Fire, sex, blood, death... Art saw the Name. Beecher's real name. He heard the Word compelling him to reveal Beecher to himself.

"Art, aren't you going to do anything?" Beecher yelled.

The matchi-auwishuk overcame the faces, grabbing them by the hair and circling the streetlight. They smiled evilly, lust and power dripping from their lips like blood, and flew off in the direction of Grave Swamp. Art blinked and awoke.

Ahead of him he saw Beecher, waving and howling, until the last befuddled bird slammed itself into Benny's wall. Then the air was quiet.

Beecher stopped in his place, flopped his arms and roared in despair. His body shook and twisted as he swallowed a sob. He leaned down and put his fist to his mouth to prevent vomiting. He paused. Then he turned his head and glared at Art. He straightened his back and strode viciously toward the distracted hunchback.

"Damn it, Art! What the hell's wrong with you? Why didn't you help me? They didn't all have to die."

Art stood motionless, looking up at the empty sky. The faces were gone. Art lowered his gaze to Beecher and told the truth. "Not…my story. You. You…stop them."

"I tried! They're all dead! Look around you." He paused as his anger turned to confusion. "What do you mean it's not your story?"

Art looked at the sidewalk littered with dead birds, then said, "Word…h's spoken. You… stop them." Art nodded to Beecher and slid away into the fog.

Beecher watched Art disappear and murmured, "Stupid drunk."

In the darkness, Art grinned to himself. He had heard the insult, but it was all right. Beecher had begun to learn.

Through the mist, Art watched as Beecher saw one of the few live sparrows at his feet. It lay on its back, quivering. He bent and picked it up, holding it gently in his hand as it trembled in pain and fear. He knew nothing about caring for injured birds. He didn't even know what type of bird this was. All he could do was hold it until the spasms slowed,… slowed,… then stopped, and the bird was dead.

Beecher stroked the bird in his hand. The impact with the wall had twisted its head back against its wing. Beecher stared at it a moment, looked down the street where Art stood invisible, hidden in the fog, his own head resting on his shoulder.

Then Beecher gazed at the carnage at his feet. It was too late to stop them now. In the light of Benny's Amoco sign, he stood alone in the vacant parking lot, a mere shadow in the fog, surrounded by the bodies of twitching sparrows. He knew this was no hallucination, no fear-induced vision. This was real. The Word spoke quietly to him. He heard partially.

"It's the fog," he said. "It has to be the fog." He tilted his head and peered up through the mist to the light and the darkness beyond, wondering what Art had seen there.

"He is still young to the Word," Art thought. "If the fog is now an extra-natural force to him, that is a beginning. He will soon learn all."

However, it would not be now. To Beecher the night was still silent. He could not hear the laughter of the spirits in the air.

At the base of Benny's sign, he set his bird apart from the others, sniffed, and wiped his nose with the back of his glove. He had begun to feel. The learning had begun. As Art stood hidden by the fog and rubbing the pain in his back, Beecher turned away from the bird and walked to school.

## 2

At his empty desk, Beecher leaned back in his chair and closed his eyes, trying to erase the events of the morning. He could almost forget the birds, their frantic screams, even his own terror of being lost in the fog.

However, for some reason, he could not shake Art's words: "Not…my story. You. You…stop them." What did he mean by *story*? What did that have to do with what they had just seen?

Beecher knew stories. For most of his life, he had searched for a story to tell. What he did not know was that the Story he had long searched for was now his.

From the time he could remember, Beecher wanted to be a writer. Wisely, his father warned him daily that the road to success for an author is exceptionally difficult. Still Beecher persisted. As a teenager, when he had finished his math, history, and science in the evenings, he sat with a notebook, experimenting with characters and settings, words and phrases, plots and subplots. In college, he filled notebook after notebook as he developed twists into rising action. Even now, after his wife and daughter went to bed, he sat at the keyboard of his new computer, pushing words together, crafting paragraphs, agonizing over descriptions, searching for a climactic theme, ultimately saying nothing.

It wasn't for lack of ideas. Beecher had stories. He had imagination and creativity which alternately endeared him to and annoyed his teachers and peers.

And his personal life provided enough inspiration for dozens of pieces. Adopted at birth by two college professors from Bemidji State, his life was a persistent cultural conflict. At home he grew up around books, classical music, and discussions of history. The town, however, was more appreciative of action movies, country/rock, and the merits of wood-fueled stoves. So while Beecher collected books and built shelves in shop class for his personal library, his school friends collected hunting trophies and built gun cabinets and trophy mounts. While Beecher read F. Scott Fitzgerald and William Shakespeare, his friends read Louis L'Amour and *Field and Stream.*

Even though Bemidji State provided a mini-oasis of art and literature for the escapees/students from the Twin Cities who still desired a modicum of culture, the school's effect upon the inclinations of the local inhabitants was minimal. The high school and the business community insulated themselves from the influence of the college's outsiders.

Therefore, determined that Beecher would know as much of the "real world" as possible, his parents resolved to show him the earth, at least the American part of it. Each summer vacation, no matter how short or long, they took the family to different parts of the country, so by the time Beecher was 17, he had seen 45 of the fifty states.

Strangely, on all those trips, he had seen very few tourists. His parents always sought the offbeat, avoiding places found in the tourist guides. Instead, each ethnic community, each outlandish hotel, each quirky restaurant in every region of the country gave him a view of society few of his classmates had.

Not that many of those classmates cared much. Beecher was just a weird kid. He read books. He watched old movies and classic television videos. He listened to classical music. He took interest in the legends of the Ojibwe, despite the anger it evoked from the townspeople and the suspicion of the natives that came to town from the Red Lake and Leech Lake reservations to shop.

Some adults argued he never had a chance to be normal. His ostracism began with his name.

The week after his parents brought him home, his father sat with a group of colleagues around the faculty table in a far corner of the student union. After all the obligatory "How big is he?" and "Where did you find him?" inquiries, Dennis Milliken, a curmudgeonly, gray-bearded history professor asked what the whole table wanted to know: "Jones, what the hell kind of name is Beecher for a kid?"

"It's a great name," Beecher's father responded. "We named him after Henry Ward Beecher."

"Who's that?" asked biology professor Reese Gannon.

"Just one of the greatest antislavery preachers in American history. Harriet Beecher Stowe's brother? She wrote *Uncle Tom's Cabin*?"

"I know Harriet Beecher Stowe," Gannon replied. "I'm not a total biology goon."

"I'm no goon either, but evidently Jones is," Milliken grumbled.

"What is that supposed to mean?" Beecher's father asked defensively.

"Henry Ward Beecher? You don't know?"

"What's to know? His preaching brought an end to slavery. He turned 19th Century Christianity away from the orthodoxy of Puritanism. I think that was a pretty remarkable feat for that time."

"And...?" Milliken's puffy, bloodshot eyes scowled over his glasses.

Beecher's father shook his head questioningly. "And what?"

Milliken sat back, set his coffee on the table, and crossed his arms on his more than ample midsection. "Jones, you need to get away from the encyclopedia and do some real research. Not only was Beecher a bombastic, self-serving minister, he was boinking a parishioner."

"What?" the table exploded.

Milliken smirked and nodded his head.

"That... that was never proven," Beecher's father stammered. "As far as anybody knows, they were just friends. Besides, that doesn't erase the accomplishments and the influence he had on history and religion."

"Yeah, yeah, yeah. The truth is he was boinking a parishioner. Can't imagine her husband was too happy about it, let alone the rest of his congregation," Milliken said.

"Millken, how would you know? It was 1870, for crying out loud," Beecher's father said.

Milliken smiled and picked up his coffee. "1870 or now, it doesn't make any difference. Boinking is boinking," he sneered and gulped his coffee.

Of course, in a few short days Milliken's claim of "Boinking Beecher" became common knowledge throughout the town, and as the baby Beecher grew into a boy, his classmates used the information to harass him. One of two nicknames followed him throughout elementary and high schools. Many seized upon the preacher's relationship to Stowe, saddling young Beecher with the nickname *Harriet*. However, as he and his classmates approached adolescence, their focus shifted to the minister's alleged dalliances, re-crafting *Beecher* into *Boinker.* Although Beecher's peers used both names to humiliate and shame, their usage rather instilled in Beecher a strength not found in any *Jason* or *Bob* in Bemidji.

Instead of vainly retaliating against their taunting, Beecher turned into himself and to literature. He relished what his books taught him. Besides literature, he enjoyed the piano, despite the overwhelming popularity of the guitar. In his developing life view, he contemplated issues of science and God. He searched for definitions of the Ojibwe town names that dotted the countryside. He haunted the college library's philosophy section for meaning. He ignored the conventions of high school wisdom concerning drugs, alcohol, and sex. Contentment consisted of being himself.

Therefore, it surprised no one when he chose to attend Middlebury College in Vermont, rather than Bemidji State. As expected, he focused on literature, convinced his future lay there. Aware that Beecher was Beecher and admiring his ability and determination, his father urged a more practical, more salable profession than writing, one in which Beecher could earn a steady income and still have time to pursue his passion. Eventually, Beecher relented and took up the family business of education, determined to seek teaching jobs in the East where he would have access to every opportunity he felt valuable.

But then, just weeks after Beecher's graduation, his father drowned on a trip to the Boundary Waters near Ely. With his father's death, Beecher's plans for a life in the East ended. His mother's loneliness plus the safety and security of the Midwest drew him home to Minnesota. For five years he lived with his mother and commuted daily to an English teaching job on the Red Lake Indian Reservation, but the demands of commuting and of the job proved too wearing and forced him to reevaluate his commitment to teaching.

The appeal of writing still intrigued him. However, his father's words rang true: the choice of writing as a career proved riskier than he was willing to pursue, at least now when his mother needed him. So he decided to return to college for his principal's license. If nothing else, he would spend less time in the classroom, have less contact with students, and could spend more time helping his mom. For now, writing could wait.

That was his plan.

Even as he began his administrative program, he knew he was deluding himself. He had seen. He knew how hard principals worked. He saw the students these people had to work with on a regular basis. But he would have to settle. And he was persistent. His mother needed him.

After two years at St. Cloud State coming home every weekend, he received his certification and scrambled to find an administrative job. In 1982 the town of Jefferson, an hour or so west of Bemidji, needed an interim principal to replace a man who had developed "emotional issues," administrative-speak for an inappropriate relationship with a student's older sister.

Shortly after Beecher signed his contract, just as he felt his future was settled, his mother died. The doctors called it a heart attack, but her friends said she died of depression, that she never really recovered from her husband's drowning.

Beecher was alone.

Early one August morning, he stood on his parent's porch, looking across the street at the brick and spruce-shaded campus entrance arch. He bit his lower lip, shook his head, and sighed. Unlike when he left for college, this time his departure was forever. Even though he had lived in this house most of his life, it was no longer home. Always a loner, this was the first time he knew loneliness. The time to leave for good, if good even existed, had come. He sold his parents' house, car, and furniture; packed his own meager belongings; and left. He would not look back.

Beecher's new life began quickly, and a new job was only the beginning.

His first week in Jefferson, he attended the weekly Lions Club meeting. Sam Haake, the school superintendent, told him the town expected all school administration to be members of the club. Beecher did not know whether Sam was teasing him or not, but he decided to attend anyway.

The club met at 6:30 a.m. Tuesday mornings in the downstairs dining room at Inga's Truck Stop on the eastern edge of town. Sam drove them.

Even at such an early hour, the lot was full. Sam parked his car in the last available spot at the far end of a long line of vehicles. Beecher hesitated before getting out. He looked over the parking lot and asked, "Is it always this busy?"

"Nah. People are just curious and anxious to meet the new high school principal."

Beecher let out a long sigh. "Great."

"Ya nervous?" Sam asked him.

Beecher brushed a stray thread from the leg of his new dress pants. He took a deep breath. "I guess a little."

"You'll be fine," Sam told him. "Just forget that you're the new guy and the youngest principal we ever hired. They'll love ya. No sweat."

"No sweat," Beecher muttered to himself. "It's just my whole life."

The meeting was mostly a blur of introductions, awkwardly stifled and mumbled songs, and incomprehensible business motions. Then, even though he wasn't looking, Beecher saw. A woman. Young, yet confident and assured. Smiling. Alive.

He didn't mean to stare, but he couldn't help himself. When she glanced at him and smiled, Beecher caught his breath.

He nudged Sam. "Who's that woman?" he asked.

"Which one?" Sam asked.

"With the short hair."

Sam scanned the room, confused. All the women had short hair. In Jefferson, it was still the style after 25 years. Sam shook his head and looked questioningly at Beecher.

Beecher pointed toward the exit. "The one in black. Sitting at the table by the door. Next to the guy with white hair."

Sam craned his neck, then said, "Ah. Sarah."

"Sarah?"

"Sarah Bjornson. Owns a woman's dress shop in town… actually *the* woman's dress shop, the only one in a twenty-mile radius. Nice girl. Graduated here… I don't know. Eight years ago?"

"From Freedom High?"

"Yep. Right here in town. Graduated with honors, I think. You should meet her. You'd like her." Sam nudged Beecher with his elbow and smiled.

When the meeting ended, Beecher did not wait to be introduced. He brushed past Sam and other members and sought her out.

Sarah stood talking to a waitress next to the till, until she noticed Beecher wending his way toward her. She smiled at him, patted the waitress on the arm, and cut short their conversation. The waitress, at first confused, turned and saw Beecher looking at Sarah as he shifted his weight from foot to foot. The waitress glanced at Sarah, smiled, nodded, and walked away.

Sarah turned to Beecher and offered her hand. "Sarah Bjornson," she said.

Beecher smiled nervously and took her hand. "Beecher Jones. New principal," he said.

Sarah laughed and nodded. "Yeah. I caught that. Nice to meet you."

Even though she was far shorter than he, Beecher thought Sarah was an intimidating woman. Almost devastating. Black hair cut just below her ears. Silver eyes so bright they glowed. Transparent, yet mysterious. Everything she was seemed out of place in what he knew of Jefferson so far. Yet everything she was, was what he wanted. Although she was obviously younger than he was, within moments there was a familiarity, a commonality they shared.

"Um… Not to use an old cliché, but do I know you?" Beecher asked.

"Maybe," Sarah suggested, turning her head slightly and grinning seductively. "Where did you come from?"

"Bemidji."

"I graduated from Bemidji State four years ago."

As the two talked, they discovered that although Beecher had worked out of town, they knew many of the same people. "I suppose we could have met somewhere," Beecher said.

Sarah nodded. "At the very least, you could have seen me somewhere around town."

"But I just can't think where it would be," Beecher said.

"Whatever," she said. "It doesn't matter. You know me now."

"You're right," Beecher said. "That's all that's important."

"So," she said, "do you need a ride back to school?"

"Yeah… sure..." Beecher stammered. "Let me tell Sam."

As he shouldered his way through the lingering members to find his superintendent, Beecher thought to himself, "She's the one."

For two weeks, Sarah and Beecher found ways to be in the same place at the same time – the grocery store, a football game, Benny's Amoco and Convenience Store. Beecher's colleagues and employees saw the relationship's ultimate destination before the two of them did. And though the townspeople delighted in the happiness of "young love," they were not totally supportive of Beecher and Sarah's romance. Sarah's family had died in a car-train accident when she was in high school, and she still carried scars from their deaths. Despite people's repeated warnings, Beecher did not heed their advice nor hesitate to pursue her. He could not turn from her arresting eyes. He could not ignore her dark voice which pierced his thoughts through his work, his daydreams, and his sleep.

Beecher's time with Sarah was the most secure, most intimate he had ever spent with a woman. Although none had ever outrightly rejected him, the women closest to him had always instilled a feeling of alienation. He had never known his birth mother, and his foster mother was always what Beecher called "too Norwegian and too Lutheran" to ever show warmth toward him or his father. Yes, Beecher knew she loved him and he loved her, but they never felt a part of each other. Maybe that was the price of adoption.

He never had any female siblings. In high school, no musings about a Bemidji girl had ever kept him awake nights. In college, he was too Midwestern to attract any Middlebury coeds save the occasional curiosity seeker. He had led an unintentionally celibate lifestyle, waiting for the right person and the right opportunity. From the time he first left home, he felt alone, empty.

And then he met Sarah. One month after they first met, they slept together. The next morning, even though he felt ecstatic, Beecher thought he should feel some twinge of guilt, but he didn't. True, the echoes of his high school classmates taunting initially rang in his ears: "Boinker! Boinker!" but he easily shut out the voices. He was not a "boinker." He loved Sarah. And now she was a part of him and he was part of her, which was the relationship he always craved. So, the night had not been simply a sexual encounter, a natural outgrowth of their time together; it was a marriage proposal.

She said yes. Beecher felt complete.

He did not know.

In January, a year and a half after their summer wedding, their daughter Jeannie was born. They realized they had become parents more quickly than they had planned, but her birth united them even more. The first thing they decided to do was remodel the old two-story house they bought in the Larson Parcel, which was Jefferson's original residential section on the north side of town.

The project began simply. They painted. They wallpapered. They laughed as Jeannie waved her arms and gurgled from her infant seat, directing her parents' next move.

At home they shared everything from household duties to parental obligations, from mowing the lawn to changing diapers, from washing clothes to washing bottles.

Even outside the home, they worked together. Often, Beecher worked Saturdays in Sarah's store. Many weeknights, after a full day in the shop, Sarah picked up Jeannie from day care, grabbed a carryout meal from the Plains, and met Beecher at the school. Beecher fed Jeannie while Sarah cleaned Beecher's office and helped fill out his state report forms. Because she knew Beecher's true ambition was writing, she bought him a new typewriter and every night kept Jeannie, an ever-growing toddler, out of his office so he could create in peace. The Joneses' was the perfect Jefferson marriage.

Except it wasn't.

As years went by, Sarah's business success accentuated Beecher's writing failures. While women from as far away as Fargo drove to Jefferson to shop in Sarah's store, Beecher's rejection letters from publishers could have wallpapered their living room. Rather than causing arguments, the situation became the topic of non-conversation. Beecher and Sarah both avoided speaking about each other's situation, and their silence drove them into themselves and away from each other.

Beecher's job at school was secure. He did it well and conscientiously, but it wasn't writing. It never would be, and it hurt to accept the reality. Beecher acknowledged the problem to himself, but didn't know how to fix either his marriage or his literary failures. For all his education and life experience, he could not understand why the words would not come. He had nowhere to turn.

Or so he thought.

Had he asked Art Benson, Art could have told him. Beecher's problem was the same as the rest of Jefferson. Despite what he thought when he married Sarah, he was not complete. He did not know who he was. Because his personal mask hid him from himself, he did not even know his name, the Story. He could only see with his eyes and hear with his ears. His spirit remained hidden.

Instead he struggled aimlessly in front of a blank piece of paper, desirous of the perfect plot and the perfect words that would attract a publisher, that would make Sarah proud. He neglected the words of the Tao:

*Ever desireless, one can see mystery.*
*This appears as darkness, darkness within darkness.*
*The gate to all mystery.*

Instead of being desireless, his desire to write consumed him, blinded him to what he needed to see, blinded him to what he and his family were.

That is why his name surprised Art that day at Grave Swamp, but the Word had been clear. The Word may confuse Man, appearing to be darkness, but the Word is always light. So, Art knew, the Story was now Beecher Jones. Not a story for him to tell, but the Story which would tell him.

3

Back at the plumbing store, Art sat on a stool behind the sales counter and contemplated Beecher's memories. What struck him most was that Beecher should feel guilt. This equipped him for the coming battle because it indicated that he believed in good and evil, virtue and sin.

Art lifted his shirt and rubbed his throbbing lower back.

*Sin* is a curious word, he thought, completely devoid of the ability to describe what it stands for. Few know its depth and substance.

Living in antonyms, some use their concept of sin to define God, but their concepts of both God and sin are too small. They see God and the Word as a super-good-man, sin as a super-bad-man. They do not see the spirit world, nor do they want to. If they could, they would see the beauty of order in chaos; they could glimpse infinity upon infinity. They could see the width and breadth of evil hiding within this earth and on every planet, the shackled force straining against the bonds of time, thought, and the terrestrial crust to escape and run unfettered throughout the multitude of universes seen and unseen.

Sadly, Art knew, what escaped from the muck of Grave Swamp that Friday morning was beyond the comprehension of those who use the word *sin* most often – priests, ministers, evangelists. This clergy usually sees *sin* solely in "impure thought," sex, drunkenness, thievery, and murder. For millennia they taught right and wrong, to follow the rules, the virtuous reward of heaven for the moral and righteous, and the devastating condemnation of hell for the wicked. The knowledgeable and scholarly had no sense of the magnitude of either good or evil. Especially evil.

They claimed to know sin, yet none had seen anything but a foretaste of the Earth Man and the Matchi-auwishuk, the Evil Beings. Friday's earthquake, bolt of lightning, and emergence of fog carried a wickedness the cloistered intellectuals could never recognize, a malevolence that slowly, almost imperceptibly, transforms people.

Consequently, on that late winter morning, the Matchi-auwishuk and their leader, the Earth Man, knew the world would never notice their existence in a small, out-of-the-way village; Jefferson, Minnesota, was the perfect place to begin their assault. They thought the Word had forsaken Grave Swamp and Jefferson. They did not know the bog and town were like Christ's stable in Bethlehem, Mohammed's cave on Mount Hira, and Gautama's village of Gaya – a central arena in which the Earth Man and his allies would do battle against the Word. And they did not know about the sleeping blind man Beecher Jones.

Art's drowsing head jerked up at the words skating through his brain. "*Sleeping blind man*. A horrible phrase," he thought.

He heard the jealousy in the words, the jealousy that clouded his vision, obstructed the Word's voice in his ears. It had originally hidden the truth about Beecher from him. However, the still small voice of the Word became thunder and revealed all. Art's early recognition of his emotion was enough to prevent it from gaining control.

When the Word spoke to him in the darkening, gray Monday afternoon, three days after he watched the Earth Man arise from Grave Swamp, Art put aside his pride and listened. Then he knew. Beecher's spirit had been born. The shrieks of the birds had hailed the arrival of Beecher's soul, the nativity of his senses. His pangs of regret unstopped his ears so he could hear.

Art laid his head on the counter and closed his eyes. His vision shifted to the nearly deserted high school.

In the office, Beecher stood at his office window staring out at the fog. He was aware that his cosmos had altered, that the fog had brought a presence he could not describe.

Art raised his head again. He must help Beecher see and understand. He recalled the ancient story:

*Once a man asked the Buddha, "Are you a god? A magician? A man?"*

*When the Enlightened One answered, "No," the confused man asked, "What are you then?"*

*"I am awake," the Buddha replied.*

Newly born, Beecher was awake, Art knew, but he was groggy, just learning to use his eyes and ears. There was much he did not comprehend.

Most importantly, he must learn not to fear. What he had yet to realize was that with the fog, the Word had also arrived, quietly, unknown to the Earth Man and the Evil Ones, to reveal to Beecher a universe of truth.

Beecher had seen only a blurred vision and was oblivious to who he was, where he was, and why he was. Like most of humanity, he preferred to live in a dream called reality, unaware that in truth, reality existed beyond the walls of his office, the confines of his mind, and the boundaries of his life, birth and death.

Throughout the day in his cold, empty office, Beecher continually relived his morning – his hallucinations of evil, his disorientation panic, the flurry of wings flying out of the darkness and smashing into the concrete wall, and finally, the quivering, dying sparrows scattered on the ground at his feet. Even though the Word spoke to him, showing him that the fog was more than mist, he did not understand. He was like a baby looking at the mobile above his crib, fascinated, but uncomprehending. His immaturity and human limitations told him to dismiss evidence of the Word as the result of an overactive imagination.

Occasionally, he laid his glasses on his desk, pushed his brown hair back, and rubbed his bony face. He then raised his arms over his head, stretched his long legs, rose from his desk, and searched the thickening haze outside the window for a hint of illumination, direction, and meaning. He found nothing. He did not know that like Buddha, to see the light, he must first close his eyes and see the darkness.

Most stores down the street, including Thorstad's Perfect Plumbing where Art worked, closed for the afternoon due to lack of business. Far down the highway, beyond where Beecher could see, Art shuffled and lurched across the street through the fog, his head twisting to hear what nobody else could hear – the sounds of fear, anger, and regret; his eyes peering through the dark and fog to see what nobody else saw – already maimed lives twist, mutate, and evolve; and his nose sniffing the breeze to smell what nobody else smelled – the stench of death blowing through the trees.

Across the highway from the high school, Art lowered himself onto the step and huddled in the empty doorway of Eaton's Ace Hardware under the cover of the Great Mask. He watched Beecher's silhouette in the light of the office window, and knew much of the man Beecher did not know himself.

Beecher had always lived in ignorance of himself and his history. Yes, he knew he had been adopted, but he was unaware that his birth mother, a girl from northern Wisconsin, abandoned him on the streets of Duluth shortly after his birth. He never knew her. Still, even with his broken beginning, evil did not touch him. His adoptive parents raised him to be a good Lutheran, to shun the dark, to deny its existence by only facing the light. If he couldn't see the darkness, they told him, it couldn't exist.

But it did exist. It had just not found Beecher yet. That is why the Word had chosen him.

Art knew. He had seen evil. He had fought the Matchi-auwishuk. He had lost his battle. He no longer needed to fight himself.

He now knew Beecher was the innocent, the pure and untested infant warrior the Word needed. In his nascent spiritual state, nodding between dreamland and reality, he had to be roused slowly, carefully, to prevent the dark's crushing weight from collapsing upon him. That was why the Word had told Art to approach Beecher with care. That is why Art now sat in the hardware store doorway, concealed in fog. He stared into the sky and felt the earth slip away into the world of vision.

For hours Beecher aimlessly rearranged piles of mail on his desk and listened to weather reports on the radio. He realized schoolwork was impossible. He could not concentrate. Instead, from his lower desk drawer, he pulled a three-ring binder labeled "Writing Journal" and sat down to search for ways to incorporate the fog and the sparrows into the screenplay he had been writing for nearly twenty years. In private times like this, alone with his aspirations, Beecher seldom visualized himself as a high school principal. Instead he saw himself as "a writer in search of a story," not realizing he was a story in search of a writer.

Beecher pulled off his glasses and rubbed the bridge of his nose. Absently, he ran a finger over the small lump he had inherited from his unknown Scandinavian ancestors, an annoying "character-defining" knob that conveniently held his glasses in place. Leaning his head back against his chair, he yawned and again stretched his arms toward the ceiling. He was tired, but he could not bring himself to go home. Uncertainty had crept into his house and he did not know how to deal with it.

As Beecher rolled his head around his neck, the Word directed his thoughts again to the fog outside his window.

Fog itself was not an unusual occurrence in Jefferson, he knew, especially in the low-lying areas and swamps. However, that type of fog was short-lived, burning off by 10 o'clock or being whisked away by the constant wind blowing in from North Dakota.

This was different. On Friday, as the mist engulfed the town, the Word first whispered to Beecher. He did not know what he had heard, so he spoke the truth jokingly, "There is evil in this." Now, three days later, Beecher knew the joke was no longer funny. The fog was still there, silent and immovable. The people he knew – the townspeople, the students, his staff, his wife – everybody was acting strangely, even the birds.

And Beecher could not stop all the peculiar images arising in his mind. He did not recognize the source. He slowly swiveled in his chair and again looked outside. Jefferson looked as if it had been submerged in the cloudy waters of Mud Lake. Perhaps, Beecher envisioned, the ghost of Lake Agassiz had materialized, intent on reclaiming its birthright from the careless and sacrilegious humans. He heard the words of his script's disembodied narrator: "A pestilent vapor as thick as the murky waters of the Red River spilled from an unknown spring on the ancient lake's eastern shore, down into the valley, rising, thickening and spreading across the primordial lake bed, bent on destroying every human trace along the path of the long-extinct glaciers."

"Oh, yeah!" Beecher rebuked himself, shaking his head. "That will keep people in their seats. Charlotte Brontë meets Edgar Alan Poe."

"Killer fog," he thought, laughing to himself. "That's what happens when you spend all night watching too much Alfred Hitchcock and *The Twilight Zone* as a boy. I couldn't just watch what everybody else was watching. *I Love Lucy. Bonanza. My Mother the Car*."

Whatever the source of his thoughts, Beecher was certain that what he saw outside his window was more than fog. Somehow the mist had worked its way into his brain, unleashing a phantasmagoric image of Jefferson as a miniature Atlantis, a world of dancing naiads, swimming, swirling, cavorting, and swimming with the shimmering white globes released from their lampposts. Bjerkland's Grocery faded into a formless gray mass to which people glided like prehistoric fish or giant trilobites, slipping in and out of the darkness, about to be destroyed by the world that once sustained them. Beecher snorted. "Either that or they just need to buy some milk," he thought. He had begun to see, but still could not comprehend the meaning.

"What's da good word, Mr. Jones?"

Beecher started, whirled around in his chair, and saw the school's head custodian Karl Jurgens leaning against the door frame.

"Sorry I scaredja." Karl wiped the shine from his head, shifted his weight and shoved his hands deep into his pockets. "So, we gonna have school tomorrow, den?" he asked, shuffling into the room and slumping into the chair opposite his boss.

Beecher shrugged.

"Say, ya hear about all dem birds down at Benny's dere?" Karl asked.

"I was there when it happened."

"Really? Oof dah. Dat musta been spooky. Benny said dere vass like a t'ousand or so chust piled up on the sidewalk dere."

Beecher nodded. Karl looked down at his shoes and shook his head. "Yep, pretty spooky."

Beecher stared out the window a moment. "Spooks. Ghosts. Something is out there," he thought. He wondered if he were the only person in town who knew it.

"Karl, don't you ever go home?" he asked. "Every time I come up here, you're working."

"Got stuff to do. Gotta be ready in case we're here in da mornin'." Karl opened one of his shirt buttons, scratched his protruding belly, and then opened his mouth into a wide yawn. "I vas doin' a little service work on da boiler dere, just makin' sure everyt'ing vas okay"

A typical Jeffersonian, Karl was unassuming and unaware. Immersed in his vision on the hardware store steps, Art would not have been surprised if the Word had selected Karl to be the Story instead of Beecher.

For 25 years, while vacuuming rooms and waxing hallways, Karl reached out to people in ways that were both endearing and annoying. He was omnipresent, always working, always whistling, always listening. True, his appearance was at odds with his actions. His heavy round Buddha belly and shuffling gait made him appear lazy; still he never missed a day of work. The school was always clean. The furnace always ran flawlessly. He never hurried, but he was always on time, greeting everybody he met with a two-fingered salute and a raspy "What's da good word?"

Beecher once said, "The students love Karl, the teachers rely on him, and the school board underpays him." Karl didn't know, nor would he have cared if he did. He simply kept working, whistling his undecipherable tune, and asking for the "good word."

Underneath the image Art saw in his mind of Becher and Karl, he heard birds screaming. He smelled the Swamp.

"Oh, yah. I vanted to tell ya, too," Karl said. "I yust about got your Chevy fixed. Yust vaitin' on a couple parts to come in down dere at NAPA. Then y'll be all fixed up."

"Good. Sarah needs her Buick, and I'm tired of walking."

"How is da missus? I ain't seen 'er fer awhile."

Beecher hesitated. "Sarah? She's… she's fine."

Karl looked at Beecher, unsure of his response. After a moment, he leaned forward and asked, "Everyt'ing okay, Mr. J?"

Beecher nodded slowly. "Yeah, I think so. It's just..."

He looked at Karl. There was a unmistakable aura about this unattractive man that, despite his appearance, invited people closer. To Beecher, not only was Karl omnipresent; he was omniscient. No matter how many masks you wore, no matter how high and thick the façade you erected, Karl could look past them into your soul and see the truth. His presence nearly forced your confession from your lips and lying to him as useless as lying to God. That was his most endearing and annoying quality.

Across the street, Art sat straighter. He knew Beecher saw the Word in Karl. Art heard something else.

"You should have been a principal," Beecher said, leaning back in his chair and clasping his hands behind his head. He sighed, pursed his lips, and began. "I don't know. We've had our ups and downs. I guess we're just having one of the downs right now. It'll be all right."

"Ya don't sound like yer real sure."

Beecher examined Karl's round face. "I can trust you, can't I, Karl?"

"Heck, I don't tell nobody nuttin' that ain't deir business."

Beecher knew that. Karl had the reputation of being the only person in Jefferson who believed in everybody's right to privacy. Consequently, everybody forfeited that right and told him everything. Karl consumed details of Jefferson life like an unordained father confessor, storing up stories and never disclosing a word entrusted to him.

Beecher leaned forward, picked up a paper clip, and turned his chair to the side. He thought for a moment, remembering some long forgotten story of salvation. "Forgive me, Father, for I have sinned," he thought, then smiled, and began straightening the wire. Then he began. "I tell you, Karl. Something's wrong, and I don't know what it is."

Karl turned his chair sideways and gazed at the floor. "Like what?"

Straightening the clip into an impromptu nail file, Beecher sat back and began cleaning his fingernails. "Well, for three days, Sarah has been so quiet, almost as if she doesn't want me around. I don't have a clue what I've done or haven't done or should want to do."

Karl scratched his belly again, pinched his nostrils and thought for moment, trying to appear philosophical while meditating upon a snag in the carpet. He asked, "Well… you know what vomen want?"

Beecher looked up from his hands. "What?"

Karl looked at Beecher. "I vas chust askin' if you knew."

Beecher laughed. Karl smiled and continued, "Heck, me tell you? How should I know? You're da vun who's married, not me. If anybody should know vhat a voman wants, it should be you."

They both chuckled a moment before returning to their respective tasks, Beecher cleaning his thumbnail, Karl pushing at the snag with his toe. "I don't know, Mr. J." He leaned forward, trying to push and pull the fabric back into place. "You're good people. It'll be fine."

Karl leaned back, took a paper clip of his own from Beecher's desk, and began unfolding it. "Yup. If dere's vun t'ing this here job's taught me, it's how to tell the good people from the bad people."

Beecher looked up at Karl. "It has, huh? Like who?"

Karl thought for a minute. "Okay. For example, home ec. teachers? Good people. Phy. ed. teachers? Bad people. I mean, look at Coach Forseth dere. Every day dat feller whines and complains about his gym, how it's too small, how it's too dirty, how it's da 'showplace of da school,' how it should get the most attention and all dat crap. Big jerk. Ever'thin's all about him. All the stuff I done for him, you think he ever thanked me? Not once! But then you got Miss Grapnic. She just kinda goes along, doin' her job, no complainin', not givin' nobody no grief. Always slippin' ya a cinnamon roll or piece of cake or somethin'. A good person."

Beecher's memory flashed on Friday morning, the day the fog rolled into town. He realized the town's transformation had begun even then. He hadn't recognized it at the time, but the altercation between his phy. ed. teacher/track coach Wally Forseth and his home ec. teacher/drama director Laura Grapnic had been the beginning. A disagreement over the use of the combination gym-auditorium had nearly turned bloody.

Beecher twisted in his seat and his face became serious. "You notice anything strange about those two lately, Karl?"

"Whataya mean? Ya t'ink dey got sump'n goin' on?"

"No, not that. I don't know. Something happened on Friday. It was like... like somebody snatched the real Wally and Laura."

Karl looked up from his paper clip and stared at the wall, his face blank. His hands lay paralyzed in his lap.

Beecher hesitated. "Karl?"

The chubby man did not move.

Beecher leaned forward and asked, "You okay, Karl?"

"Huh? Oh, yeah. Ga 'head."

Slowly, Beecher sat back in his chair, watching Karl's eyes. "Promise you won't say anything?"

"'kay," Karl said quietly.

"Before school, both Wally and Laura were in here because they both wanted to use the gym that afternoon..."

Karl's face became animated as he interrupted, "Miss Grapnic had rehearsal. Wha'd Coach need it for?"

"Track team conditioning. He said the weather was too wet and cold to go outside."

"Yah, but her show's dis week."

Beecher picked up the silver letter opener from his desk and turned it in his hand. He ran his index finger along the edge. "Right. And you know how Laura is – quiet, timid, the most easily manipulated person on staff. Normally, she'd have given in without a word. But Friday she dug in her heels and threatened if she couldn't have the gym and stage, she'd cancel the show and resign."

"Good for her. Wha'd Coach say?"

Beecher twisted his paper clip and shook his head. "He said, 'Go ahead. Ain't nothing but losers in your stupid play anyhow'."

"Oooh," Karl grimaced.

"I know!" Beecher said. "And then this little woman – What? Maybe five foot, maybe 100 pounds – gets up, picks up this letter opener, circles behind Wally, yanks his head back by the hair, and threatens to lose the letter opener up his nose if he doesn't apologize for calling her kids losers."

Karl clapped his hands and leaned forward, giggling gleefully.

"No, it was scary," Beecher protested. "Wally was all stretched out with his back rigid and his arms and legs out to the sides, trembling. And his eyes… his eyes were the size of cantaloupes, staring past this silver point right into the eyes of a crazy woman. When I told him maybe his runners could come in after rehearsal, he just squeaked 'Okay' and left without saying or doing anything."

Karl slapped his leg. "Good for her. Teeny little Miss Grapnic beatin' up big old Coach Forseth. That's great."

"But that's what I mean by weird. I've never seen either of them like that. Laura, a vengeful Amazon; Wally, a squashed bug."

Karl sat quietly for a moment. "Wait. Dat vas Friday?"

"Yes."

Karl slapped his knee again. "Dat's what vas goin' on. Sure. Dat makes sense now. Uff."

"What do you mean?"

"Well, on Friday yust before ya canceled school, I vas in the gym dere, and Miss Grapnic vas up on stage, checkin' her scenery wit' some of her kids, and one of the... Whataya call 'em? Flat braces? ... come loose, ya know? So I'm givin' her a hand, screwin' it back on, an' Coach comes up to me, holdin' my broom and giffin' me shit 'bout how I vasn't sweepin' his floor. Miss Grapnic looks at 'im real stoney-like and says real slow and quiet, 'Karl's helping me right now.' An' I go, 'Yeah, I'm helpin' Miss Grapnic right now.' I mean, he looks at her and he looks at me, puts down the broom, and says sump'n like 'Well, soon's ya got time,' and he starts walkin' away. Well, now I'm feelin' kinda cocky, ya know? I mean I feel like I yust won da big battle. So I start gettin' bucky with 'im. I yell, 'Yeah, ya darn right 'when I have time.' Ya know what, Coach? I ain't one o' yer kids ya can bully around, ya know?'"

Beecher gazed at Karl. "Karl, that's not like you either."

"I know, but Miss Grapnic's kinda smilin', and I start tryin' to suck in the gut, tryin' to be da lean, mean lovin' machine. An' I yell at 'im again, 'Hey, Coach, you know where ya can shove dat dere broom.' Well, now Miss Grapnic's laughin', and I start t'inkin' like the kids, 'Okay, Karl. Babe magnet!' Anyhow, Coach jus' walks out. He's gone, and Miss Grapnic comes up an' pats me on the back and says 'Good job.' So now I'm thinkin' this could be my chance. Maybe I should ask her out or somethin'. I'm kinda like her white knight, ya know? But geez. Now! Now, I know Coach vasn't scared a me. He vas scared a her!"

Beecher smiled, despite the thoughts gnawing at him. "So, are you going to ask her out or what?"

"Oh, yah, sure. I just gotta cut my hair and keep her away from letter openers, I'll be fine."

"Karl, you don't have any hair.

"O, yah. I'm all right den."

Both men laughed. Then Beecher placed the straightened paper clip on his desk and said, "The point is Laura's never been violent in her life. Wally would usually have beaten the crap out of you for smarting off to him. And you! When have you been mouthy with anyone? What happened to 'the good word'? And dating Miss Grapnic? Where did that come from?"

Karl shrugged. "I dunno. Maybe I'm in love." Beecher raised an eyebrow, then looked back at the paper clip in his hand.

"Maybe somebody spiked the water fountains." Karl continued. "Maybe it's the fog."

Beecher glanced up abruptly. "You think so?"

Even through the brick wall and across the street, Art felt the Word in Beecher's office. Art's vision became more than just sight.

Karl hesitated and stared at Beecher, who leaned forward, threw his paper clip on the desk and laughed.

"You're right," he said. "I'm going nuts. I need to go home, take a nap, listen to the weather, watch the Academy Awards..."

"Now, see. Dat's wrong. If yer havin' trouble vit' your wife, ya gotta find out what she wants to do. I mean if she vants to watch the Oscars, fine. But if she doesn't..." Karl shrugged his shoulder. "You don't need to watch 'em anyway. Heard on *Entertainment Tonight* that *Above and Beyond*'s gonna win everyt'ing anyvays."

Beecher shook his head. "*Bright and Shining Star*. Great movie. Great writing."

"Ain't heard much about dat vun. Y'see it in town?"

"Jefferson?" Beecher shook his head. "No, I'm afraid there's not much of an audience for it here. Sarah and I saw it in the Cities."

"What's it about? Like *Star Wars* or somethin'?"

"No, it's not like that... it's more... more of a spiritual odyssey, the search for true happiness."

Beecher thought for a moment. The Word was speaking. Neither Beecher nor Karl knew. Beecher looked up and saw Karl eyeing him skeptically.

"Seriously. It begins with a woman just out of college looking for some kind of sign to give her direction, a reason for living, kind of like the Star of Bethlehem. She looks all over the country and finally ends up as a waitress in a little truck stop in some dinky little town. There she has this epiphany..."

Karl shook his head. "This what?"

"Epiphany. A moment of enlightenment. You know, like when all of a sudden everything in life makes sense?"

"Hell, I'm still trying to make sense of my mop."

Beecher smiled. "Anyway, she believes her purpose on earth is to help people wherever she finds them, even in the restaurant. So she does and becomes a messiah figure to everyone she meets. Instead of *looking* for the 'bright and shining star,' she *becomes* the 'bright and shining star'."

"Any dirty parts?" Karl interrupted.

Beecher smiled and shook his head. "A little at the beginning."

"I dunno, Mr. J. Sounds like a chicken flicken to me..."

"A what?"

"A chicken flicken."

"You mean a chick flick?"

Karl thought for a second. "Yeah, okay, whatever. Anyhow, I'm more inta war movies and action stuff myself. Didjer wife like it?"

"Yeah, she did."

"See dere? You guys got somethin' you can do tonight. Watch t.v. Cheer for *Bright Chevy Star*.

*"Bright and Shining Star."*

"Whatever. At least it's a beginning."

Beecher nodded. "Well, we'll see. I better get going. Let me know when the car's ready."

Karl got up and walked to the door. "Sure t'ing. If the fog lifts, we'll get the parts tomorrow, and then it'll just be a day or two puttin' 'em in. Now, go home and talk to your wife."

"That's your good word?"

Karl smiled. "Yep. My good word. Well, just gotta couple things to check on in the locker rooms. Then I'm goin' home."

"Keep safe," Beecher said.

"Always do. 'member the good word," Karl said on his way out to find his way home in the fog.

"We'll see how good it is," Beecher thought.

Just as he was reaching for his coat, the phone rang. It was Sarah.

"Hi," he said. "I was just thinking about you."

"Hm. You coming home soon?"

The Word had vanished. Beecher looked at his watch. 5:00. "Geez, yeah. Sorry. Time just got away from me, I guess. Anything wrong?"

"No, it's just that some of us are meeting down at the Plains for supper to talk about our class reunion this summer."

"Have you looked outside?"

"Beecher, we're all in town. It's not as if we have to drive to Fosston or anything."

"But how do you expect to drive in this stuff?"

"If we have to, we'll walk. It's no big deal. It's not as if you and I had anything planned."

He wasn't sure that was meant to hurt or not. Sarah had become too close. He had stopped listening, stopped seeing. He closed his eyes and decided to leave it alone. "What time are you supposed to meet everybody?" he asked.

"Around 6:30. Is that a problem? Or should I try to get a sitter because there are 'more important' things to do at school?"

The sarcasm was unmistakable now, but he pushed it farther away. "No. I'll be home in a few minutes." Before Beecher could say good-bye, the click on the other end told him there was nothing more to say. "So much for good words," he thought.

He hung up the phone and again looked out the window. This time there were no shadows, no naiads, no fishlike humans swimming past. Just a vast, gray blankness of fog.

"There's something out there," he thought. Then he shook the idea from his head, switched off the light and headed back into slumber. The sound of the Word was but a murmur.

## 4

The earth returned for Art. He felt the concrete step beneath him and breathed the moist air floating past the hardware store. He leaned forward, looking left, then right. The highway in front of him was deserted. The trucks and cars hurrying between North Dakota and Duluth had disappeared until tomorrow's sun could burn off the fog. Art struggled to his feet and leaned against the glass door behind him. Across the street, the light was out in Beecher's office. Art listened for instructions, but none came. The fog was thick, blocking the Word.

Art felt this once before when the matchi-auwishuk danced with the manitous, beating out the Rhythm of Despair, blinding the sun. Now the Earth Man and his followers sang and danced to a new song that enticed and deafened the earth. The new song would surely claim the weak. Art could not allow Beecher to dance to it. He struggled across the highway and limped off toward Beecher's house.

The Word did not speak, but led Art through the alleys to a leafless bush across the street from Beecher's two-story home. He arrived just as Beecher climbed the steps into the four-season porch, before entering the front hall.

Beecher heard Sarah upstairs, walking back and forth between their bedroom and the bathroom, trying on different outfits, putting the finishing touches on her makeup, making sure everything about her appearance was perfect. Even after years of marriage, Beecher gasped at the sight of her, whether she wore makeup or not, whether dressed in a formal gown or in jeans and a T-shirt, but especially when she wore black. Black was her special weapon, worn not just to impress, but to annihilate anyone who saw her. The combination of her ebony hair framing her face and the darkness of her clothes accentuated the radiance of her hypnotizing eyes. As Sarah came to the head of the stairs, the scent of her perfume drifted down to the entryway.

"Oh, good. You're home," she said, hanging a thin gold chain around her neck. "Jeannie's in the kitchen eating. I'll be right down." She smoothed the front of her black sweater and went back to the bedroom.

Beecher hung up his jacket in the closet beneath the stairs and walked to the kitchen, afraid of what awaited him at the table. "Sarah is a great mom," he often told his friends, "but everything she cooks comes from a box, a can, or has the word *hotdish* in its name." Her limited cuisine and paltry cooking skills led to numerous confrontations over the years, confrontations that usually descended into wild swings of volume from wall-rattling clamor to deafening silence. Beecher realized in the most recent incidents, food and cooking covered the actual issues between Sarah and him, but he had no real idea what those issues really were.

When Beecher walked into the kitchen, his daughter Jeannie knelt on her chair, poking at her food with her fork. Beecher kissed her on top of her head. "Hi, Baby. What's for supper?"

She looked up and scowled. "Speesaroni."

"Speesaroni?"

"Mm-hm. Spam, cheese, macaroni – mash them all together you get *speesaroni*."

"Does the name make it taste any better?"

Jeannie giggled. "No."

"Tell you what," Beecher said. He looked around to make sure Sarah was out of earshot, then whispered, "If you eat a little bit, when Mommy's gone, we'll throw away the speesaroni and have ice cream. Okay?"

Jeannie's face brightened. "Like last time?"

"Uh-huh. But don't say anything, all right?"

"I won't," she whispered. She speared a chunk of unnaturally pink meat, shoved it into her mouth, and grimaced. She strained to smile as her mother walked into the room. Beecher grinned as Jeannie fought to keep the mashed variation of pork from sliding between her teeth and down her throat.

Sarah finished putting on her earrings as she came into the kitchen. "Bed by 8:30, Jeannie. You have kindergarten tomorrow."

Jeannie tried to pound her fork in protest, but broke into a cough, accidentally swallowing her Spam. Beecher patted her back and handed her a glass of milk.

"If there's school," Beecher replied.

Sarah set her jaw and glared at Beecher. Emphasizing each and every word, she asserted, "Even if there's not, she still needs her rest."

Beecher and Jeannie glanced at each other. Jeannie quickly returned to her speesaroni. Beecher rubbed his finger along the edge of the table and muttered, "You're right. 8:30."

"Be good for Daddy," Sarah said, giving Jeannie a cursory hug and peck on the forehead.

Beecher followed her to the front door. As she turned the doorknob, he asked, "Sure you don't want to stay home and watch the Oscars?"

"Movies are your thing. I really have to go to this meeting. Tell me what happened in the morning."

She turned to leave, but Beecher interrupted her exit. "How late are you going to be?"

"I don't know. I'll try to be home by ten, but if I'm not, don't wait up." Before Sarah could pull the door open, Beecher pushed his hand against it, looked behind him to make sure Jeannie hadn't followed them to the front hall.

"Sarah, what's going on?" he whispered insistently.

"What do you mean?"

"Are you mad at me or what? Did I do something wrong? Say something wrong? What? This meeting can't be that important."

Sarah sighed, as she pulled on the hooded black cloak Beecher had given her for her birthday. Her silver eyes flared. "I don't have time for this right now. I have to get downtown. We'll talk about this later."

"When? This has been going on for —"

She cut him off. "I don't know," she hissed. "Later."

"Why not now?"

"Because I have to go!" she bellowed.

Beecher hushed her, nodding toward the kitchen.

"I have to go," she whispered harshly. The fierceness in her eyes told Beecher there would be no answer to his questions. He knew that look all too well. He had seen it far too often.

Beecher lowered his eyes from hers, bit his lower lip, and shook his head.

She pursed her lips, then quietly repeated, "I have to go." She kissed his cheek almost mockingly. "You can keep the car. I'll walk. Don't wait up," she said.

She opened the door and hurried off into the night fog.

Beecher stood on the porch, watched her dissolve into the dark, then returned to the kitchen.

Jeannie slowly stirred her speesaroni. He sat down at his place and stared at the concoction on Jeannie's plate.

"Daddy?" she said quietly, her voice quivering.

"Yes?"

"You 'member when we went to Disney World?"

"Sure, I remember," he said. "Why?"

"I liked that time."

"Why's that, Baby?"

"'Cause you and Mommy didn't fight then."

He looked up at her. She had already separated the pasta and the meat into two piles, and was now experimenting to find which pile would hold her fork in a vertical position, stabbing it first into the macaroni, then into the Spam. Her mind, completely detached from the action of her hands, was lost in that happier time of smiling parents, Winnie the Pooh, and Tigger. In her face the darkness disappeared; even in sadness, there was light. He reached out and touched her shoulder.

"Know what?"

"What?" she mumbled.

He took the fork from her hand and laid it on the plate. "We're gonna have ice cream!"

Jeannie cheered as Beecher scooped up the pot from the stove and scraped the prescribed meal into the garbage can. She hopped down, grabbed her plate, pirouetted to her father's side, and with the flair of a tiny ice dancer, swept her food into the trash. Beecher laughed, hugged her, and went to the cupboard for bowls, chanting, "We're gonna have ice cream. We're gonna have ice cream." Jeannie marched around the table like a drum major, using the ice cream scoop as a baton, joining Beecher's refrain. "We're gonna have ice cream. We're gonna have ice cream."

As they had done whenever Sarah left them alone with a particularly revolting supper, the two of them bagged up all the garbage in the house and took it to the garage to hide their deception. On the way back into the house, Beecher lifted her high above him, tickled her tummy with his head, and marched around the table again. Jeannie's screams and giggles became a new song that filled the air, drowning out the song of the Earth Man. For now the house was safe. Still the fog gathered itself and hung like a shroud about the windows, nearly obscuring the glimmer from the light pole across the street.

Omniscience is a puzzling burden. While it is true only the Word is truly omniscient, there is nothing else to call what occured during Art's spells. The voices of a hundred mouths, the desires of a hundred hearts, and the breath of a thousand sighs enveloped him, concealing his own experience from his eyes. Through the lengths of space and time, all human longing, misery, and suffering reached forward and shouldered aside his world until he no longer recognized the difference between himself and the universe. The stronger the Word lived in him, the more he became the whole of reality and the border between his life and that of others ceased to exist.

Art waited behind his bush across the street and listened to Beecher and Jeannie's song. It was powerful and sweet, glorious and real, human yet holy. The Word was present. It existed within the house, within the singers. It would be spoken. The time was near and Beecher must understand.

Art knew Beecher's world was still of his own experience – his adopted childhood, his Middlebury education, his books. True, the birds' shrieks had awakened his senses, but he did not hear the truth the birds spoke. He listened to Karl Jurgens' good word, but did not see Karl's soul. He melted under his wife's eyes, shivered under the touch of her skin, but could not feel the deformity growing inside her. To live beyond himself, Beecher still had much to learn – as did Art.

As he hunched in the mist, Art knew that the Word had chosen Beecher Jones as the Storyteller and the Story of this generation. The Flame would arrive to inspire him with truth. What confused Art was that along with the consideration of the Flame, he detected another presence, a person, someone he had never seen, a Jefferson outsider, somebody, like Beecher, chosen for the Word's service. A woman. In his visions, he saw her quiet face and smelled her hair. He heard the voices of her past, sensed the forces drawing her near, and felt her breath on his neck. Again he heard the name revealed to him in Grave Swamp along with Beecher's, the name he had ignored. The voice that revealed her name spoke with the authority of the ancients.

Art knew the voice was truth. He realized his role in the Story. He was the third. He wanted to be more.

Beecher and this woman were the lead players; Art was but the blind oracle of Greek tragedy, the Tiresias, the soothsayer who merely forewarns the world, but in himself accomplishes nothing. He saw himself in theatrical terms as nothing more than a Shakespearean spear carrier.

As he thought the words, Art tasted bitterness on his tongue. Anger rumbled in his belly.

The Word spoke softly in the breeze to his jealousy:

*Your feebleness is envy*
*Your cowardice strength*
*You are afraid to do nothing*
*Stay silent and know there is honor in stillness*
*I am in you*

*You are in me*

*You are more than nothing*

"What?... Tell me... If I ...am more... than no-... thing, what... am I?" Art mumbled.

*You are my voice*

"Don't want... to be... voice! Want... to be... heart!" he exclaimed into the silent night. He sobbed his disappointment. "Want... to be... heart," he whispered.

There was a moment of quiet, then:

*Blinded by pride you are*

*Grieving where no grief should be*

*You would act, but to act is nothing*

*Far greater is to think rightly*

*To look to what has been taught*

*Seek refuge in your soul*

*Have there your heaven*

*Remove the mask*

Art pulled himself to his feet. He hung on to a branch to keep from wobbling. "The Word is true," he thought. "In this struggle with the Evil Ones, pride has blinded me. I want to defeat their power and claim the glorious victory for myself, not for the purposes of the Word."

*Remove the mask.*

A new truth struck Art, one that, as oracle, he should have known, the truth of the fog, the Great Mask: Nobody, nothing was immune from its influence. Not even him.

The Word had to be followed. The Evil Ones and the Earth Man must be purged even from his spirit.

Jealousy is a poison for which the Word is the only antidote. Krishna's ancient advice spoke again: He must *shake off the tangled oracles* of worldliness and become the Word's true oracle. He must simply speak and act as instructed.

*This is Yog – and Peace!*

As Art closed his eyes and sat quietly on the moist ground, he felt the earth rotating toward its destiny. The spell was upon him.

He was once more in the life of Beecher Jones. He saw Beecher inside his house playing Candyland with Jeannie and he felt their joy and laughter. In a voice of wonder and trust in Beecher's infallibility, she asked him questions about the stars, the fog, and love. In his replies, there was strength and faith that his simple answers could satisfy her. After he put Jeannie safely to bed and sat down to watch the Oscars, the Word spoke to Beecher and he knew the answers would never be simple again.

The voice was small at first, an annoying whisper during "the most horrible Oscar Awards show in history." In the decades-long history of the show honoring film's artistic performances, no ceremony had been as ill-fated as this year's. The worldwide satellite television broadcast began with a few minor glitches, such as gremlin-infected teleprompters that sped the words past the readers at superhuman rates or microphones that refused to work, but then the night quickly disintegrated into chaos – falling scenery, injured dancers, and politically minded actors who championed every cause from ending hunger in the Sudan to preserving the birthplace of Millard Fillmore. Like millions of viewers around the world, Beecher watched in shock as halfway through the awards, emcee Dudley Rimes, host of the television game show *Here Comes the Bride*, collapsed on stage of a heart attack. The program, already a disaster, now descended into tragi-comedy as actors-turned-amateur-theologians offered prayers of supplication to every deity from Jesus to Allah, Mother Earth, Father Time, and, in a distasteful bit of whimsy, Spot the Wonder Chicken, all the while invoking the ancient cliché "The show must go on." And it did, although there was now a sense of sacrilege about the whole proceedings.

To make matters worse for Beecher, in the two hours of the show, his favorite movie *Bright and Shining Star* had yet to win a single Oscar, and neither had the media's favorite *Above and Beyond*.

Beecher winced at his own insensitivity. A man was at the edge of death while Beecher and a calloused show-business world concerned themselves only with next year's trivia. "Life is more precious than a stylized chunk of metal," Beecher thought.

Disgusted with himself, he rose and climbed the stairs to check on Jeannie. He stood at the door and watched her tiny body breathing quietly, peacefully. Like a protective mother, she hugged her Tigger.

Beecher glanced at his watch. Sarah should be home soon.

Softly, he walked over to Jeannie, pulled the covers over her shoulder, and kissed her forehead. Beecher smiled. Amid the disruptions of the world outside, he thought, this room felt safe, calm, protected.

When he returned to the living room, the show was still on, but Beecher had lost interest. He resigned himself to the fact that *Papa John,* a dimwitted, speculative story about William Shakespeare's father, was going to be the big winner, even though in most Americans' minds the title evoked more images of pizza than of Elizabethan England. It had already won four statuettes, including one for best supporting actor and best costume design. Beecher couldn't remember what the other two were for, nor did he particularly care. *Bright and Shining Star,* the touchstone of his own attempt at screenwriting, had been shut out thus far, and, given the way the night was progressing, this wasn't likely to change. Beecher sat down in the recliner and stared blankly at the television, thinking about the lifeless, unfinished script he had just recently resurrected from a box in the garage.

He had hoped the old play would jar something loose in his writing. It had not. His efforts to complete the script remained unfocused, uninspired. His story said nothing. The words lay dormant on the page, meaningless, even to Beecher. *Bright and Shining Star,* with its blend of spiritual and temporal themes, had stimulated him to create a new world which did not follow the usual rules of physics and convention, but

Beecher's new world was still unformed, uninhabited, and overshadowed by the presence of the real world.

Beecher turned off the lamps and sat quietly in the flickering light of the television screen. Tonight, he thought, the real world was more fantastic and surreal than he could imagine. An infectious fog had encompassed Jefferson, and he seemed to be the only one in town to know its power. Alone in the television's blue glow, Beecher remembered the sparrows, their screams, their self-destructive flight, his futile attempt to save them, their dead bodies lying at his feet, the mocking silence of the mist.

And what was Art talking about? "You stop them." Stop who? The birds were already dead. Maybe the fog had even taken hold of the "blue-eyed Indian."

Across the yard, the street, and into the alley, Art heard Beecher's thoughts and smiled. Beecher was learning, beginning to understand.

The skeptic in Beecher told him the fog's power was only a trick of the mind, but the fact that Sarah in her black cloak walked alone out there somewhere... The birds' screams still terrified him.

The sight of Casey Sturgis on the television screen interrupted Beecher's thoughts. Sturgis had already won the best supporting actor award for playing William Shakespeare in *Papa John*. One of the lesser tragedies of the evening, Beecher thought, but still, Beecher hated him instinctively. The actor spoke in his faux British accent and read haltingly from the teleprompter, afraid of another gremlin attack: "As we watch a movie, it is… it is easy to believe the story just happens, that the actors create their own words, that the director points the camera in a peculiar… particular direction and the scene naturally unfolds before the lens. This is not the cease… uh… case. Somewhere, sometime, somebody sat. Before a blank piece of paper… sat before a blank piece of paper and developed the characters, the story, the dialogue, the entire movie. That somebody is the screenwriter. The nominees for this year's best original screenplay are Randall Holmes for *Papa John*. Yea, Randall."

The audience giggled nervously.

Beecher grimaced as Sturgis over-smiled.

"Sorry," Sturgis said. "Randall Holmes for *Papa John*, Ansel Stone and Wesley Barnes for *Beyond Truth*, Amanda Wilson for *Bright and Shining Star...*"

Beecher sat up on the couch. To him, a win for *Bright and Shining Star* would confirm the presence of a deity in the universe. "Come on, *Bright and Shining Star*," he prayed.

"And the winner is..."

"*Bright and Shining Star.* God, let it be *Bright and Shining Star,*" Beecher mumbled to himself, leaning forward, his hands folded in front of his closed eyes.

"Amanda Wilson for *Bright and Shining Star*."

Beecher sat back and stared at the screen, amazed. "They got it right. I don't believe it."

The whisper of the Word in Beecher's ear became a shout, but the picture on the television screen distracted him. Simultaneous listening and seeing was a skill he had yet to develop.

An unassuming, quietly dressed woman in her early thirties rose from her seat. "More the Midwestern normal than the movie glamour queen," Beecher thought, "but then again she is a writer, not an actress."

She looked quite ordinary as she strode down the aisle in a simple floor-length forest green sleeveless dress with a high collar, her blonde hair drawn back in a simple ponytail, but the aura about her displayed far more grace, modesty, and elegance than anyone Beecher had seen on screen all night. The quiet smile under downcast brown eyes made Beecher sit up. As she stood behind the microphone where that night so much arrogance, fear, and bedlam had reigned, her lightly freckled face conveyed humility, inner satisfaction, dignity and a trace of loneliness. In the midst of the show's plastic display of excess and sensuality that had crumbled into disorder, Amanda Wilson was a beacon of tranquility, innocence and virginity.

"Okay, maybe virginity's a stretch," Beecher thought. Still he found this quiet writer far more alluring than the actresses who had preceded her to the stage or were likely to follow. "I think I'm in love. Damned fog!" he joked to himself.

Amanda cleared her throat, looked directly into the camera, and spoke in a dusky voice that resonated deep in Beecher's stomach, "There are literally hundreds of people I should thank for making this possible, but there's not time. When you see *Bright and Shining Star* and the credits roll at the end of the film, those are the people. Please take the time to read all their names. It's not as if being the first one to your car is going to get you out of the parking lot any faster anyway. Somebody not on that list, however, is my mother Lois who read my first story when I was seven, a little classic I called 'Scruffy and Tiger Eat Wally the Worm.' She told me, 'Keep working, honey. Someday your writing will make you famous.' Mama, I guess you were right. Thanks."

And then she was gone. Beecher knew he had seen and heard something, but he wasn't sure what. He sat back and shook his head to clear his mind, but as the television played a raucous beer commercial, the quiet image of Amanda Wilson remained before him. He stood and turned the sound off. Instead of deciphering the Word's message, however, he reflected on the gift of beauty.

Art knew the face on the screen the moment Beecher saw her.

Physically, Beecher knew, Sarah was far more beautiful than any woman he had ever met, but this Amanda Wilson, a simple image on a television screen, intrigued him. Whereas Sarah's beauty attacked you, slapped you senseless, then stepped back haughtily and dared you to react, Amanda Wilson's hovered above you, delicate, almost ethereal, sinking upon you unannounced. While men, especially those raised on the painted stars of television and movies, satiated themselves on the traditional and obvious sensuality of the Sarahs of the world, it was the Amanda Wilsons whose quiet, open elegance mysteriously wended its way into men's thinking, overwhelming them with subtlety, enticing them to break from convention and establish new lifetime priorities for one more glance at her tranquil face.

While the Word would have him listen to the name, remember the innocence, seek out the virtue, Beecher misinterpreted what he felt as the origins of lust, his physical side. He did not recognize the Word. Instead he concentrated on living up to practical reality as dictated by long-established mores. Beecher loved his wife; in a world limited by the city limits of Jefferson, Sarah was perfect. The sublime Amanda Wilsons waited for somebody else on an economic and social plane far above Beecher's. He could not waste his time dreaming of impossibilities, and so he dismissed what he had seen.

"Besides, what kind of speech was that?" Beecher thought, returning to reality momentarily. "Scruffy and Tiger Eat Wally the Worm?" He closed his eyes and for a moment imagined himself in Amanda's place, holding the Oscar, looking out upon thousands of Hollywood's elite, feeling the eyes of millions of people worldwide, reveling in his own sense of accomplishment. He stood up, held his can of Coke, faced the armchair, and spoke aloud, "I'd like to thank my wife Sarah and my daughter Jeannie for their love, my mom and dad for taking me to my first movie, Alfred Hitchcock and Rod Serling for their inspiration, President William Howard Taft for not letting appearance stand in his way of achieving great things, Rocket J. Squirrel and Bullwinkle J. Moose for making me laugh..." at which Beecher set his can on the coffee table, chuckled and shook his head. "Oh, yeah. That's much better. Thanking the family, a bunch of dead people, and a couple of cartoon characters. You're dreaming again, Beecher. Shut up and be real. Time for bed."

The Word would not let him go. He glanced down at his watch and saw it was just after ten o'clock. He flipped the station for the local news from Fargo to see if he could get any word about the weather.

Channel 5's ancient forecaster, Don Olquist, rated each day's forecast on a scale of one to five "Smiling Sols," yellow smiley faces with orange rays to represent suns. One represented overcast with little chance of blue skies; five was bright and sunny. Since Friday, one was the most generous Olquist could be, but tonight he was giving tomorrow's weather two Sols.

"Good. Maybe we'll be able to have school," Beecher thought.

Beecher flipped back to the awards show, which was in the middle of the last presentation of the five best song nominees. He looked at his watch again. It would be at least another half-hour before Best Picture, he thought.

He stood and stretched, but instead of heading upstairs to bed, he walked to the kitchen and made himself some hot cocoa. Sarah hadn't called. The meeting had already taken an hour longer than Beecher thought it would, but that's what happens when people start talking about old times. He took his warm cup and shuffled back to the living room. The show no longer seemed important. He looked at the television a moment, took a sip of his cocoa, then decided to sit on the screened-in porch to watch the fog.

The air was full of spirits Beecher could neither see nor hear. The temperature on the porch was barely cooler than that in the house. To help with the fuel oil bills, Beecher had put on storm windows in November and they had done a good job absorbing the heat from the daytime sun and keeping out the cold wind at night. Raising his mug, Beecher toasted himself on his foresight, then sat down on the old couch and propped his feet up on his bicycle that had been stored on the porch for the winter. He took a sip of his cocoa and looked across the street toward the streetlight. The six leafless oak trees that shaded the house in summer were now simply gray silhouettes against the light.

The spirits began to move.

Beecher thought of Sarah and wondered what he had done to cause her bitterness. Maybe he spent too much time at school. Maybe he ignored her. Or maybe they just needed to get away from Jefferson for a few days, weeks, months, decades. He had no idea what she thought or felt. At one time he had, but whatever spiritual connection they once had no longer existed.

Stealthily and steadily, the fog grew thicker.

Beecher did not notice. He finished his hot chocolate and put the cup on the floor. It had been a long day, and his limbs had begun to stiffen. Beecher stretched his arms and legs straight out in front of him a couple seconds, then relaxed, leaned his head back and closed his eyes. He tried to let go of the birds, the weather, school, Sarah, all the troubles of the day. He breathed long, deep breaths until his body felt light, weightless, and he let himself drift into the world of dreams.

## 5

It is in the world of dreams the Word speaks most clearly. The message enters with each breath and flows in the blood from heart to brain and back again. It spreads into each part of the body, rising from the sleeping toes upward and outward into the fingertips until the person becomes the message.

As Beecher's breath slowed, the dream began, slowly, quietly. The fog invaded his senses until all sense of proportion and clarity distorted. He watched as the earth, incited by the fog, rebelled against the laws of nature and man. He entered the reality that Art saw in his spells.

In his front yard a great cloud of mist billowed up from the ground, growling and hissing like dragon's breath, and rolled toward the streetlight to extinguish its glow and plunge the street into total blackness. The trees, however, marshaled themselves to preserve the light and save the home. Silently, they summoned the wind, and their limbs became human arms, swinging madly at the cloud with knifelike fingers that cut through the mist and scattered the moisture into harmless vapor. The fog fell dumb and subservient at the feet of the trees, and the wind hushed.

The illumination now safe, the trees looked forgivingly on the mist, blessed it, and then turned their attention back to the light. With loving arms they reached up and pulled the glowing electric ball from the pole and brought it to earth. Reverently, they set it upon a great altar that rose as a concrete table from the sidewalk between them. Resting sanctified on its bed of devotion, the light turned from a steady bluish-green fluorescent glow into red, flickering flame, as the sacred hearth spread its warmth in an ever-widening circle. The heat dispelled the cold and gray while the trees sang their hymns of praise.

As Beecher watched the fire and marveled at the music of the trees, something or someone moved behind the big twin oak. He craned his head left, then right, but could make out nothing. Beecher shivered and tried to shake off the chills. He stood and rolled his head around his shoulders to get the kinks out of his neck. "It's nothing," he thought. "Just the late night and the fog, or a dream within this dream."

He tried to awaken, but the Word grabbed him and held him conscious only within his vision. It forced him to stand at the door motionless, watching the yard, waiting. There was no movement, only the song of the trees, but Beecher felt someone there. Finally, he opened the door and stepped out.

"Sarah?"

There was no answer.

"Sarah, is that you?"

Again no answer.

The trees transformed their hymn to a march and raised the mist like a gauze curtain around the divine circle, tantalizing Beecher with little more than flickering shadow. The trees raised their limbs over the yard in great Gothic arches surrounding the fire and lifted their music to the sky. Beecher was about to step down, but halted when he saw the shadow of a dark, hooded figure approach the altar from behind the twin oak, carrying a package wrapped in a gray blanket. Three times the shadow circled the flame. Then it knelt and raised its offering to the light in humble supplication. The music became a whisper.

"Sarah?" Beecher called again.

Silently, the figure rose, placed its offering on the altar, stepped back and watched as the flames sprang upward, engulfing the bundle. Beecher recoiled in horror, yet he could not stop watching. After the fire consumed the bundle, the billowing flame calmed, and the form moved to the other side of the altar and stood facing the house. With its head hidden beneath its hood, the figure folded its hands across its midsection and waited.

Beecher gathered the courage he could only find in dreams. "Who are you?" he demanded.

The figure slowly raised its head, but the shadow under the hood still hid its face. Deliberately, the figure reached out its arms and invited Beecher to enter the temple.

"I'm not coming out there. I don't have any shoes. Just tell me who you are so I can wake up and go to bed, okay?"

At once a stinging fanfare rent the air, the fire flashed high into the night, and the trees dropped their misty sheet. There stood the figure, clean, now brilliantly white, and a flaming altar against the black background of the empty street. Once more, the music whispered around them. Again holding out both hands to him, the figure whose face was still concealed urged Beecher to join the ritual.

"Okay. This is just weird, mystical bull shit," he thought. "Probably something the *Papa John* producers would love…and get the Oscar for."

The figure did not move. It just stood there waiting his response. He shivered, then called, "What do you want?"

A shadowy finger pointed at him.

Again Beecher tried to wake himself, but the Word was insistent that he hear. He swallowed and asked, "Me? What for?"

The figure stood still. Beecher's breathing became rapid and irregular. He pursed his lips, sucked the lower one under his front teeth and bit down. "This is nuts," he thought. He could feel the blood race through his brain, his heart pound erratically against his ribs and against the whispered rhythm of the march. He had to get back to the couch and lie down, but the invisible constraints of the Word held him motionless. Then, without any prompting from his brain, Beecher's right foot stepped down. His left foot followed, and soon he was on the sidewalk, inching slowly, one stockinged-foot at a time, toward the apparition.

The music crescendoed as he moved down the sidewalk past the twin oak and entered the temple, stopping just short of the altar. As he stood before the flame, the march again became a hymn, now rising out of the earth beneath him. It was as if the whole planet sang. Mystified, Beecher looked down into the fire and saw the sacramental flame had completely consumed the figure's sacrifice. Beecher looked across the table and attempted to see beneath the figure's hood. "Do I know you?" Beecher asked.

There was no answer, no movement, no acknowledgment whatsoever. "May I see your face?" and again there was no answer.

He slowly reached across the altar with both hands to push back the hood, but, indignant at his blasphemy, the music crashed and the flame billowed, propelling him backward onto the ground. Beecher sat confused and rubbed his forehead. Evidently he was only allowed to see, not touch. Cautiously, he stood again and faced the figure across the altar. With its head still lowered, the figure reached up and pulled back its hood revealing the long blonde hair of a woman. Slowly, she lifted her head, then her dark brown eyes. Her lightly freckled face smiled at him.

Beecher knew her at once, but he was confused. "Amanda Wilson? Why are you...?" She raised a single finger to her lips to silence him. She smiled, then reached into the fire with both hands and lifted it high above her head.

The night burst into light and sound. The ground trembled at the music, and radiance poured down upon her, first, from the fire in her hands, and then from the sky. Liquid light flowed over her face, a face already glowing with its own illumination. The light streaming down upon her and emanating from her, the sheer volume and glorious harmonies of the music forced Beecher to his knees before the altar and he hid his face in his hands. Just as he was about to rise and flee back to the house, the light and music softened. Still afraid, he glanced up and saw the woman lower her hands and step around the altar toward him. He could not stand. He could not rise. All he could do was again hide his face in his hands and pray for invisibility. The woman touched his shoulder. Her hand was gentle, reassuring.

Beecher raised his head. She held out her hand, offering him the fire. Beecher looked down at flame. The fire burned, but her hands did not. Rather than scorching her skin, the heat and light had seeped into her pores so she was now the fire. He raised his eyes to her beatific face. She stood above him like a goddess, offering to share and bless him with her most cherished gift, the gift of spirit, the Flame. Beecher sensed that if he took the fire he would not be burned, yet he could not bring himself to touch it, let alone take it. Its intensity, her generosity terrified him. He rose and stepped back from the altar, shook his head, and ran back to the house.

The music became a chant again. With a look that was neither disappointment nor judgment, the woman placed the flame back on the altar, raised the hood back over her head, circled the flame three times, and bowed to the light. The trees again lifted their curtain of mist, and the woman walked off into the blackness. The night became silent.

## 6

The Flame had come in the hands and person of Amanda Wilson and Beecher did not comprehend. He had rejected it. To him it was just a dream. He did not know that to dream is to hear the Word. He also did not know that to reject the Flame was to reject the Word.

Art rose and looked across the street. He heard the Word speaking in the night.

"He must understand the fog, the music, the ceremony," It said. "Beecher has lived his whole life unaware of who he is. The parents he knew were not his. He thinks he is complete in himself, but he can not be what he is. He is man without spirit.

"Sarah is his worldly wife; Jeannie is his worldly daughter. They are gifts of that part of Me, the Word, that grants the physical, the earthly, the temporal. But Beecher does not know the Flame, which only comes from the spiritual, and is necessary to complete the soul. With the Great Masking and the Earth Man to face, he needs to be whole."

Art squinted across the street, but could not see to the house. He did hear Beecher slam his fist against the doorjamb and curse. He heard Beecher's thought. "This woman offered me the power and energy of fire and light, and I refused the gift. As usual, I am a coward. I am afraid of the fire, of her, of myself," he fumed.

Art smiled and whispered to the Word, "He does understand."

" At least in part," It replied.

Beecher lay back on the porch couch. He closed his eyes in frustration, trying to push away this dream and find another, but before he could, a voice above him said, "I thought I told you not to wait up."

Beecher started. The voice shattered Amanda Wilson, divine guardian of the Flame. The porch was suddenly frigid. Confused, Beecher opened his eyes and saw the street again bathed in fog. The altar, the temple, and the choir of trees vanished. He was back on the couch on his porch, wrapped in a blanket, shivering and looking up into Sarah's cold, stern face.

"I told you I might be late. What are you doing out here?" she asked him.

"I... uh... I was just watching the fog and I fell asleep, I guess. What time is it?"

"A little after one. Aren't you cold?"

"Yeah, kinda. How come you're so late?"

"After the meeting, some of us stopped at Ralph and Bonnie's. Time just got away from me, I guess."

Beecher felt a twinge of guilt, hearing the same words he had spoken to Sarah that afternoon. He leaned forward, rested his elbows on his knees, rubbed his eyes, and groaned. "Man, I'm tired."

Sarah stood quietly, then forced herself to ask, "Jeannie okay?"

"Perfect."

Beecher sniffed. The air smelled different. Sarah had probably had a drink or two at Bonnie's.

"Who won best picture?" Sarah asked.

"I don't know. I came out here for a second and fell asleep. Probably *Papa John*. It was winning everything else. *Bright and Shining Star* won for best original screenplay, though."

"Good."

"Yeah."

There was a long silence as they both looked at the floor. There was another smell. Beecher sniffed again. He knew it from somewhere, but like the air, his brain was foggy.

Sarah shifted uncomfortably and said, "Well, I better get to bed."

She put her hand on the doorknob, paused, and glanced at Beecher. She looked at the floor and said, "I'm… uh… I'm going to sleep in the spare room tonight. Okay? You've been awfully restless the last couple nights and I really need to get some sleep."

"Why didn't you wake me and ask me to move?"

"I don't know." She paused, then turned toward the door. "I'll see you in the morning."

Beecher looked up from his seat on the couch. "Sarah?"

"Hm?"

He waited until she looked at him. "Are we okay?"

She crossed her arms and turned her gaze to the floor. She paused. "We'll talk tomorrow, all right?"

After a long pause, it was obvious to Beecher she was not going to look at him or offer anything more. "Yeah. Fine."

She stood motionless for a second, eyes firmly entranced by the toes of her black leather boots. She twisted to her left, then back, and mumbled, "Good night."

As she moved to the door, Beecher stopped her. "Sarah?"

"Hm?"

"I love you."

She looked down at him, saw the earnestness in his eyes, looked away and nodded. "Hmph," she said as she walked into the house without him and closed the door.

Beecher leaned his head back against the couch and bit his lip. His thoughts echoed in the night and drowned out the message of the Word. "What am I supposed to do for her?" he wondered. "What does she want? What does she need? I don't know her any more. She's not the same woman I met at the Lion's Club years ago."

He looked out at the silhouette of the tree and remembered his vision of Amanda Wilson, the heat from the fire as he reached for her, the glow of her face under her uplifted hands, the liquid light pouring over her. He could have had it, had her. But he ran away.

The memory was vivid, alive, hardly dreamlike. He sat forward. "Of course, it was a dream," he thought. "Another hallucination of the fog." He rose and shuffled toward the inside door.

As Beecher reached for the doorknob, the light shifted behind him and a shadow raced across the porch. Beecher spun toward the street. A billow of fog burst from the sidewalk next to the tree, took the shape of a laughing woman, who pointed an accusing finger at him and instantly tumbled away into formless mist.

Astonished, Beecher stared at the empty sidewalk and the darkening shadows beneath the streetlight. He did not understand the assault that had just begun. He picked up his cup, turned his back on the cruelty of the fog and escaped into the emptiness of his home.

# III ART BENSON

## 1

Mohammed wrote: *Thus God leads astray whom He pleases, and guides him He pleases; and none knows the hosts of thy Lord save Himself.*

Somewhere, Art thought, the Word had led him astray. Labels no longer meant anything. Savior. Soldier. Servant. Simply sounds with no impact. The Word had spoken and Art could not understand. How could Beecher? His vision was his, not Art's. The Word spoke differently to both of them.

When Art first heard Beecher's name, he knew there was more – more to him, more to fighting the Earth Man. When he had heard the Word's proclamation, he had heard Amanda's name, not Sarah's, and he did not know Amanda Wilson. And what of the laughing woman Beecher had seen? Obviously, Art thought, he barely knew Beecher.

Before he could speak and explain to Beecher, he must listen and find sense in the messages he had received.

Art's temples throbbed and he fell to his knees, holding his head. The night became oppressive with too many dreams, too many lives, too many spirits. However, it was in the whispers of the spirits the answer lay. Art knew he must seek them out. He stumbled to his feet and staggered to the eastern edge of town.

At the city limits, he left the road and crossed the bare field, stumbling into the darkness over clods of earth. He soon found the grove of elms surrounding the Lutheran cemetery and crawled under the chain link fence. His back ached as he grabbed the fence, pulled himself to his feet, and inched his way up the hill amidst the tall headstones. At the crest he found a backhoe parked next to the brick mausoleum that stored winter dead awaiting spring burial. He clambered up onto the seat, struggled up onto the backhoe's cage, and over to the mausoleum roof. Pain shot up his spine and down his left leg as lights flashed behind his eyelids, driving him down to the asphalt roof. He lay motionless, throbbing in agony.

When he could finally move, Art gently raised his body and sat cross-legged, awaiting the voices of the spirits. His body again broken, his ears opened. Below him the unburied dead lay fitfully, forsaken and alone, speaking the secrets of the past. Out in the mist, the living inhabited their nightmares, eating the truth and tasting their own fear. Art closed his eyes and waited for revelation.

The first person he saw was the laughing woman. He knew partially. She had been here before. In another life, she had been of the Sky, a glorious servant of the Word and Flame. Now she was of the Earth, an underling of the Earth Man and his followers. Her return now saddened Art. Her appearance so soon after the Ceremony of the Flame threatened the clarity of Beecher's spirit and mocked the ceremony's sanctity.

That was how the Matchi-auwhishuk, the Evil Ones, worked. They cared little for the sacred, nor did they care about humanity. Their mission was to rummage through the depths of the human soul and revel in the darkness, to disclose the repressed truth and give it life. By masking with fog, they unmasked the soul. Most of them avoided Beecher's house, recognizing the power of the Word protecting Beecher and his family, but there was plenty of time for them to recruit from the others who walked the streets of Jefferson, those whose defenses were weak and, like the laughing woman, could be enlisted into their ranks. Art could do nothing to help those people. All he could do was watch and listen in the night and strive to protect Beecher.

## 2

Joe Engstrom, Jefferson's police chief, hid his squad car behind the bushes at the entry to the Mud Lake campgrounds, then walked up the dirt road fifty yards in each direction to make sure the car would be invisible to oncoming traffic. He shined his flashlight toward the bushes and saw nothing but brush. He shut off the light, then checked the parking area. Again, nothing but brush. The cold, damp fog seeped under his collar and made him shiver. As he pushed his way back through the bushes to his hiding spot, dead branches clutched at his jacket like a spirited skeleton desperate to pull him near.

Inside the car, he picked a dead leaf from his precisely pressed pants and dropped it into the empty ash tray. He twisted the rearview mirror and checked his hair, then worked on his fingernails with the file he kept in the glove compartment.

Joe hated stakeouts, but the Norske Junta had heard stories that kids were holding "bonfires," drunken orgies that, according to the town's chief electrician Pete Carlson, "not only threaten the moral fiber of our youth, but reflect poorly on the values of the community."

"Values. Yeah, like screwin' your neighbor's wife while you're supposed to be rewiring their house. Great values there, Pete," Joe muttered as he peered through the fog first to his left and then to his right.

Even though he detested this part of the job, duty was duty. So in spite of the night's visibility and the fact the lake was beyond his jurisdiction, Joe would spend the next six hours watching the fog drift over the deserted road and parking lot.

Not only was the campground beyond the city limits, it was outside Jefferson County. It was all politics, Joe thought, and politics was as big a part of his job as catching bad guys. He had explained to Einar Nordhaus, the town's ancient mayor, all he would be able to do was "scare the shit out of the little buggers by waiting until they were all pant-pissin' drunk, then flip on the cherry top and watch 'em all scatter." If he was lucky, he might beat a couple of them back to town and arrest them for drunken driving. Einar agreed it was a stupid plan, but it gave the Junta the illusion that Joe was actually doing something to "eradicate the immorality of underage drinking."

Joe snorted. "Wonder what the assholes'll do when they find out it's their own kids havin' the parties." It didn't matter. Conforming to the Junta's whims was the key to his job's survival.

Joe picked up his thermos, wiped the top clean with a tissue, and then poured a cup of coffee. After smoothing down his hair with his free hand and checking his appearance in the rear-view mirror, he leaned his head back against the headrest, and watched, fascinated by the fog that grew thick around his car before dissipating into a light mist. Someday, he thought, he would shake himself free of the Junta's authority and be his own man.

Two hours and a full thermos of coffee later, he was ready to give up and drive back to town. Nobody was going to let their kids out in this weather.

He leaned against the door to relieve the pressure on his full bladder. He really had to pee. He could use the campground outhouse, but the thought of the cobwebs clutching at his face and the stale, putrid stench of years-old human waste solidified his decision to wait until he got back to town. Sure, he could piss in the bushes, but that always made him feel dirty, weak, exposed. Besides it was only a few minutes back to town.

As he reached for the ignition, Joe saw a pair of headlights approaching from the North. A dark gray Chevy Blazer pickup with a topper, probably the most popular vehicle model in Jefferson County, emerged from the mist and pulled into the campground parking area and turned around to face the entrance. The engine cut off and the lights went out.

Joe shifted uncomfortably in his seat. He could nearly taste the pressure below his waist. He had to go, but he couldn't remember how to turn off the dome light so he could open the door without giving away his position. Did he move the light switch to the middle? All the way forward? Backward?

Sweat broke out on his forehead as he gritted his teeth and tried to concentrate on the car and driver. Just as he was about to say, "To hell with it," step outside, and give release to his bodily functions, he saw another car slowly approaching from the South. The car seemed unsure of where it was and approached at a crawl. "Shit, if you're comin', get here, will ya?" Joe gritted, squeezing his urethra shut with every muscle in his groin.

The car, a classic 1960 black Mercedes 300 SL Roadster, stopped across the entrance. Joe had only seen pictures of this car in magazines down at the barber shop. Obviously, this was not a local vehicle. For years, the Junta had Jefferson on a "Buy American" kick, and nobody in town dared to be so unpatriotic as to buy a foreign car. Even if somebody had the temerity to try, there was nobody in the area who would service one.

The Mercedes backed up, waited, then slowly turned into the campgrounds.

Joe squeezed his thighs together, wiped the sweat from his eyes, and searched for a pen to write down the car's license number. He looked up and watched as the Mercedes inched toward the parked Blazer. Joe's groin and jaw quivered uncontrollably, and the steering wheel shook in his hands. There was no way he could hold back the flood long enough to watch whatever business transpired between the two drivers. But then again, neither could he give away his presence. This could be the bust that finally got him out of Jefferson.

He frantically scrambled for options. He couldn't open the door, but he couldn't piss his pants either. Then he looked down at his empty thermos.

The thought disgusted him. If he ever had to drink from that bottle again…

He looked out at the two cars sitting side by side, sensing something bigger than the beginning of a teenage beer bash or a romantic encounter. The Mercedes passed the other car and followed the border of the parking lot, stopping at the back, fifteen yards behind the Blazer.

Joe glanced again at his thermos. He had no other choice. He unzipped his pants, unscrewed the thermos top, shoved his penis into the opening, and let the caffeinated urine flow back to its source. The relief was immediate, and Joe felt his whole body relax. As his bladder drained, he tried to keep watch over the drivers' business with one eye and with the other make sure the thermos didn't overflow.

The Mercedes turned and moved forward, pulling alongside the Blazer so both vehicles faced the entrance. Joe watched as both drivers examined their surrounding, searching for intruders. Finally satisfied they were alone, the Mercedes driver lowered his window.

Joe took a quick look down. His thermos was already two-thirds full and the flow was still steady.

The Blazer driver opened his door slowly and stood up. He was a chubby, bald man and held a large envelope. Again, he looked warily at the surrounding trees, then eased around the Mercedes to the driver's side. He leaned against the door and talked to the man inside.

Joe couldn't afford to look away, but he could feel the warmth of the steaming urine against his exposed skin.

The man in the Mercedes asked the Blazer driver something and he nodded. Inside the Blazer, the man leaned over, picked up a package off the seat and handed it to the Mercedes driver, who in turn handed over his envelope.

Just then, Joe felt the thermos overflow into his hand and onto the seat. "Shit!" he hissed, pulling his penis out of the thermos. While trying to hold the bottle steady between his legs, he hastily stuffed his member back into his pants and tried to zip them up. The thermos began to tilt and he jerked forward to catch it, bumping the horn. The sound blared in the quiet night air.

The other two drivers, startled at the sound, sprang immediately into motion. The Mercedes roared and sped past Joe's hiding place, spraying dirt and ice into the brush as it turned onto the road. The panicked Blazer driver threw his package onto the seat and struggled to start his engine, his lights dimming as the starter drained power from the battery.

Joe still held the now-straightened-but-urine-filled thermos between his legs as the Blazer whirred helplessly. Maybe there was a chance, Joe thought, as he cranked the key on his own ignition. The squad car's engine growled and thundered to life, but before Joe could shift into gear, the pickup engine finally turned over, burst to full power, and lurched forward past Joe's hiding place, nearly overshooting the approach. The Blazer swerved wildly, tipped onto two wheels, and hung over the ditch across the road. Somehow, the driver managed to stay on the dirt surface and race off in the opposite direction of the Mercedes.

Joe switched on his lights and siren and punched the gas pedal. That was enough to tip the thermos. Before Joe could grab it, the contents spilled over the seat, down his leg, and onto the floor. "Damn it!" he bellowed as he grasped for the bottle, forgetting his speed and the need to turn. His car flew over the ditch, broke off a fence post, landed in Milo Ostlund's empty cornfield and slowly sank into the soft, wet earth.

Joe watched helplessly as the Blazer's taillights disappeared into the mist. Urine dripped from his nose, the steering wheel, and the dashboard. He wiped his nose with his sleeve, then switched off the ignition. He rubbed his hands on his already soaked pants, then slowly opened the door and dumped the few remaining drops from his thermos onto the ground. Carefully, he swung his legs over and stepped from the car to inspect the damage. As he lit the sides of the car with his flashlight, everything seemed to be intact, but the wheels had buried themselves to the floorboards. He needed a tow truck, but how would he explain this mess to the driver? What would he say to the Junta? He reached into the car, picked up his radio and called dispatch. The fog had caused a number of accidents that had backlogged all the wreckers within twenty miles. Dispatch estimated at least three hours before they could get to Joe. He would have to wait.

"There has to be a better way to make a living," Joe thought. The mist danced like a fairy ballerina in front of his headlights as his wet pants clung to his legs. He could just sit and wait, or he could start walking. He exhaled, then trudged through the mud back to the broken fence post and onto the road. The air was quiet as he began his way toward town.

Joe hadn't gone far when in the distance he saw approaching headlights. As the car neared, he turned on his flashlight and waved for the car to slow down. The engine had a familiar whirring sound as the driver shifted into a lower gear and slowly advanced toward him. It was the Mercedes.

The driver stopped and idled the motor, waiting for Joe to approach. Cautiously, Joe walked toward Mercedes until he could see the face behind the headlight glare. He stopped, letting the flashlight hang at his side. With his head, the driver motioned for Joe to get in. Except for the Mercedes's engine, the night was quiet. Joe kept the driver in sight as he tentatively moved to the passenger side and felt for the door handle. He took a deep breath and hesitated before opening the door. The air felt like laughter.

## 3

The phone rang, interrupting Betty Nordhaus's first erotic dream in decades. As mayor for the last twenty years, her husband Einar often got late-night calls from cranks and disgruntled constituents, but for some illogical and selfish reason he insisted the phone remain on her side of the bed.

After the third ring and Einar still hadn't answered, Betty elbowed him in the back until he woke up. Finally, he stirred and reached across her for the receiver. "Watch out for my teeth," she told him. Phone in hand, he raised himself on his knees and elbows, forming a bridge over Betty in a vain attempt not to disturb her further.

Forty-five years of marriage to a smalltime, self-centered politician plus raising three ungrateful children had burned away most of the sexual desire Betty had once had. However, the sensuality of her dream had stirred the ashes so now the smell of Einar's wrinkled, hairy, and flabby skin hanging so close to her face ignited the need for passion. As he talked above her in curt sentences, Betty breathed deeply until all the sights, sounds, and sensations from her sleep came alive. While Einar grunted "Yeah… uh huh… course not," Betty reached up under his pajamas and caressed his round belly. Einar tried to brush aside her hand, but she was insistent. She pushed the shirt aside, leaned up and kissed the bare flesh jiggling in her hands. Again he tried to push her away, but she was sucking his skin between her lips and nibbling on him with her toothless gums. Her bites distracted his thoughts, and she smiled when he had to ask the caller to repeat himself.

Betty compounded Einar's distraction when she pulled the pajama bottoms over his hips and took his gray-haired penis into her mouth, reliving what they once called "saving ourselves for marriage." Einar abruptly cut the phone conversation short. "I can't t'ink right now. I'll have to call ya in da mornin'," he murmured. Shaken by Betty's insistence, he bounced the phone off its cradle just missing the glass with Betty's soaking teeth. The receiver crashed to the floor, and Einar fumbled with the cord until the phone was back in place. When Betty released him, Einar collapsed on her side of the bed, breathless and exhausted. Betty smiled, pulled the covers over them both and snuggled into Einar's back.

"Who was on the phone?" she asked.

Einar thought a moment, then laughed. "For the life of me, I can't remember."

Betty smiled and reached down for him again. "Good."

Confused, Einar turned to the wife he had never seen and asked, "Why are you doin' dis, woman?"

Betty pushed him back down on the bed, straddled him, and reached for her teeth from the bedside table. She leaned over and nipped at his hairy earlobe. "I want to," she whispered.

In the glow of the clock radio, the wrinkles, the bulging stomachs, the silvered hair disappeared, and the two gazed at each other. Einar reached up and pulled her to him. "Me too," he mumbled.

Outside, the fog pressed itself against the glass, delighting in each creak of the long-worn springs and ancient bones.

## 4

The sky was black as the mist hung thick in the trees above the small, one-story house on the west side of town where Laura Grapnic lived. The house was slightly farther than walking distance from school, yet not so far away that Laura would bother starting her Chevy Malibu on warm spring days. In the light, everything about the house and yard was neat, tidy, precisely placed. Even the way Laura parked her car in the driveway seemed designed to be aesthetically pleasing.

On this night Laura had neglected to close the living room drapes, and the eyes of darkness watched as she sat cross-legged at her desk, writing a letter to her brother back in New Ulm. Unlike the neatly composed woman she appeared before her home ec. class in school, tonight she looked harried and frustrated over the loss of another day of play rehearsal. Dressed in jeans and an overly large sweatshirt that diminished the large breasts beneath it, she chewed absent-mindedly on a tendril of her brunette hair that hung over her face.

She wrapped her arms around her legs, leaned her chin on her knees, and stared at the piece of paper on the desk. Her brother had wanted to know why she never used the FACS acronym for her classes at Freedom High. "Are they that far behind the times up there?" he wrote.

"Yes, we're behind the times," she wrote, "and I like it. Besides I hate the acronym. Family and Consumer Science? Hah! Are you kidding? We can't talk about FAMILY planning because we'd have to mention birth control, which would mean sex education, which would mean we would have to acknowledge that humans have sex. (Nobody in Jefferson has sex, especially me. Sad, I know) CONSUMER here means somebody who eats, not somebody who buys. And SCIENCE? How can science explain how to look good or make baked potatoes?"

Her words stopped her. Was she being too harsh? She really liked her job, but sometimes it just got to her. Maybe, she thought, she was just depressed because of the weather. She scowled at the page and scratched her chest with her pen. She crumpled up the paper into a tight ball and tossed it into the wastebasket across the room.

"Two points," she said, pulling a new piece of stationery from the box.

Outside, Karl Jurgens stood on the street, watching the glowing window. For four nights, he had left his gray Blazer parked in his driveway and walked to Laura's house. Usually, the windows glowed green as the living room curtains filtered the light from Laura's desk.

Tonight was different as he stood and watched. Tonight the light shone bright yellow. He could see Laura at her desk writing, but she could not see him. Stuffing his hands into his pockets, he looked down and scraped the ground with his toe. Maybe tonight, he could summon the nerve to do more than just watch. As he gazed at Laura's window, the air became heavier and slid down from the trees.

## 5

Across town in his apartment above the lumberyard, Wally Forseth stood next to his entertainment center and picked up the MIAC (Minnesota Intercollegiate Athletic Conference) All-Conference Award he won as a running back at Concordia-Moorhead. The living room was a shrine to Wally's high school and college athletic past, as well as his accomplishments as a high school coach. The trophies, the certificates, the photographs had once made him proud, but tonight they made him feel small, insignificant, worthless. He placed the certificate back on the shelf, turned off the light, and felt his way back to his bedroom.

He flopped down on the bed, stared up into the darkness, and felt nothing. No anger, no desperation, just nothing, a great hollowness, as if his body housed a vacuum and all he had ever wanted to be had been sucked out of him.

Jefferson saw him as strong, proud, arrogant. His stocky six-foot frame, his shoulder-length curly blond hair, his confident swagger portrayed a controlled and controlling personality that intimidated students and parents alike. His record of accomplishments as an athlete and as a coach garnered respect from townspeople and from his opponents. However, since his walk home through the fog after Friday's confrontation with Laura Grapnic, he realized all he had ever worked for was no longer meaningful; all he had ever achieved was irrelevant.

What people did not know was that his life was not his own. That is, nobody knew but Laura. They had dated off and on for a year, slept together once, and then broken up. At work they kept up the appearance of friendly colleagues. They concealed their relationship so well that few people in Jefferson even suspected anything had been going on in the first place, even themselves.

But in the short amount of time they had been together, each had learned more about the other than either had intended. Laura certainly knew far more about Wally than he wanted her to. What frightened him most was she knew that the Wally Jeffersonians perceived was merely a charade. As she said that fateful last night together, his arrogance, his self-assuredness, his swagger were all a put-on by a "weak, frightened, little shit head."

Wally could not disagree. And on this night, he hated himself for its truth. Since high school, everything he said and did had been an effort to impress. Those fooled by his facade ultimately meant nothing to him, leaving his endeavors futile, his successes pointless. Had he taken his own path through life, had he followed the voice within him, he may have become something worthwhile. He had once had a chance with Laura, but that was long gone. And now, after Friday's incident in Beecher Jones's office, there was even less. She would always see him as shallow, crude, and self-absorbed.

"She's right," he thought. "Especially tonight." Tonight, he was just an empty bottle floating on an empty ocean. No message. No destination. Tonight, the feeling of uselessness gnawed at him stronger than at anytime since he began teaching.

Wally lay on his bed, reached over and turned on the bedside lamp. He harshly brushed a tear from his cheek and reached under his bed for his Bible. He usually hid his religious leanings even from himself, but before sleep he often searched for guidance from the words he had learned from his pastor-father's confirmation classes back in eighth grade.

He wiped a dust bunny off the cover and ruffled the pages over the side of the bed. "Hmph! Most people probably don't even think I know how to read," he thought.

As he often did, he closed his eyes and simply allowed the book to fall open. He then pointed his finger at a verse, trusting God to speak through the whims of chance. When he opened his eyes, he saw the verse. Job 7:16: *I despise my life; I would not live forever. Let me alone; my days have no meaning.*

Wally shut the Bible, put it back under his bed, and turned off the light. Again surrounded by darkness, he laughed sarcastically. "Thanks for the encouragement, God," he said.

The Word had spoken to a non-listener.

## 6

The darkness had entered Beecher's house and lay at Sarah's side as she stared at the wall, her blankets wrapped tightly around her shoulders.

For three days she had done nothing but think of The Man, and she didn't understand why. He was vulgar and grotesque, a crazy drunk who beat his wife and son. Sarah couldn't even call him by name. He was simply The Man. Even in high school when the judge sent him to the mental institution in Fergus Falls for attacking a teacher and the town's "true Christians" expressed their sympathy for his tormented soul, Sarah felt nothing but contempt.

Friday when he walked into Sarah's store looking for a gift for his wife, Sarah's stomach felt light, her brain airy. She followed him about the store, telling herself she was protecting her merchandise, but honestly wanting to be near him, desiring his stare, relishing the accidental touch of his hand on her hip.

The emotion was not logical, she knew. Nor did it make sense that she purposely passed his house while driving home from work that afternoon. It didn't make sense that her lust for him distracted her every thought, her every action. Most of all, it didn't make sense that after what happened outside his house tonight, she still wanted to see him again more than ever.

While Sarah was in high school, her family died. With the help of friends and through her determination, she fought through the grief and loneliness. After graduation, she had gone to Bemidji State where she sought comfort wherever she could find it. Sex was the most satisfying for her and by the end of her freshman year she classified herself as "mildly sluttish," although nothing she would classify as promiscuous. After a while, though, every back-seat wrestling match, every late-night naked foray in the dormitory stairwell became tired and boring, and she turned inward, throwing her efforts into her studies and earning her degree in business.

After receiving her degree, she came home to Jefferson to open a successful clothing store, successful at least by Jefferson standards. However, she was unable to establish a social life and her loneliness returned. The women, even old friends, shied away from her (except for fashion advice) and the men left her alone entirely. One of her clerks attributed the problem to Sarah's looks:

They crazed the women with jealousy and intimidated the men with the dominance of her silver eyes and black hair. Whatever the reason, Sarah felt abandoned and, for some reason, guilty about her early college years.

Beecher changed that. The mutual attraction shocked and consumed them instantaneously. They met in September, and in June they married and moved into a classic two-story house on the north side of town near the Baptist church. They spent every moment possible together, and Jeannie's birth cemented the "perfect" marriage that others only wished for. Nobody wished for it more than Sarah. She liked being married, but her emptiness persisted.

The reunion meeting at the Plains broke up about nine, and she and her clerk Cathy stopped at Ralph and Bonnie Bjerkland's for a drink. An hour and three Southern Comforts later, Sarah stood up to leave.

"Sarah, you okay? I haven't had anything but Seven-Up. You want me to drive you home?

"That's okay. I'll be fine. I can still walk," Sarah said.

Minutes later, she walked the familiar street past The Man's house. Above her, the bare branches of ancient elms hung silently as the fog swam among them. She slowed as she reached the end of his sidewalk. She stopped, glanced at his house, and pulled her hood over her head, partially to protect her hair from the dampness in the air and partially to hide her face should anybody pass by.

Her glance transformed into a stare.

As she peered through the fog at the man's window, she could barely distinguish his form sitting in front of the television. He stretched and rose from the couch. Standing at the window, he scratched his crotch, then leaned over and turned off the television. He picked up a pack of cigarettes and began walking toward the door.

Swiftly, Sarah ducked behind a tree just as he came onto the step. Her heart raced and her breath quickened from fear that he might see her. She peeked her head out just as his face glowed in the match light and the smoke mixed with the fog around his head. She hesitated briefly, then pulled her head back behind the tree. Had he seen her, she wondered? If so, did he recognize her? She leaned out again. He sat on the top step, calmly drawing the smoke into his lungs, looking out at the sidewalk, as if he were waiting for her to appear. She stepped out and faced him.

Although Sarah could barely see his face through the fog, she felt his sneer. He flicked the butt into the yard and breathed smoke high into the air. Then he stood up and ambled toward her. There was insolence in his step, an assuredness that frightened her. She wanted to run, but unseen forces rooted her to the spot. He bent down and gazed upward, smirking, seeking to discover her face. She remained motionless as he stood in front of her. He reached out and pushed the hood back. She jerked her head and turned her face. His hand caught her cheek and turned her to him. He smirked, nodded, and drew her head toward his. She felt his rough, hard, angry mouth on hers.

The time accelerated. Kiss became gasp became fumbling hands. Her black cloak fell to the frosted grass. The rest of her clothes tumbled from her body, and she pulled him to the ground with her. Grasping, pulling, groaning, she ripped at his shirt as he scrambled out of his pants. Their steamy, naked bodies rolled naked across the icy grass until he was on her. Desperately, Sarah wrapped herself around him clutching the heat of his body on her, in her. His hungry breathing roared in her ear, obliterating the sound of her heartbeat. The cigarette smoke in his hair filled her nose and mouth, choking and gagging her as she strained against him, pulling him further inside. She bit his neck and gouged her fingernails into his back, feeling the warmth of his blood under her hands.

Above her the branches and the fog danced crazily – jumping, whirling, laughing voyeurs sharing in her lust. Giving in to her passion, Sarah pushed her hips upward and heard herself scream. A dry, calloused hand clamped across her mouth and stifled her into silence. Then she heard a voice – a different voice, not hers, not his. Younger. Frightened. Angry. A face – misty, cloudy, barely human.

She closed her eyes so she couldn't see. When she finally opened them, the face and The Man were gone.

Again, she was alone, abandoned. She lay naked on the cold grass, staring up at the fog, her hand in her mouth stifling her sobs. The faces of her dead parents and brother hung above her momentarily, then disappeared.

Sarah gathered her clothes, dressed hurriedly, and ran crying to the dress shop to clean off the filth she felt all over her body. In the rest room she stood naked, frantically scrubbing her arms, her legs, her breasts, her genitals, her neck, her face, but no matter how hard she tried to scour herself clean, she could still feel the foulness everywhere, blocking her pores, contaminating her skin, sinking into her soul. Then she realized it wasn't just on her; it was in her. She could smell it. She could smell him, and no soap, no scrubbing, no perfume could ever remove the stench. She finally gave up, dressed, struggled to gain her composure, and walked home. When she found Beecher sleeping on the porch, she wanted him to take her upstairs, to hold her, to tell her everything would be all right. But she couldn't ask him. She couldn't even sleep in the same bed for fear she would infect him with what she had done.

So here she lay alone in the guest room, praying for sleep to take away her old and new guilt. She rose to sit on the window seat and meditate upon the fog, but the sight of her own sidewalk, her own trees, reinforced the depths of her betrayal. The sounds, the smells, the man's face, the dancing fog, all overcame her, and she curled up again on the bed, clutching her pillow to her stomach. She struggled to reclaim her innocence, the sad times when her mother had stroked her hair and told her how beautiful she was, the happy times when her father had hugged her and told her she was his good little girl. If only she could go to sleep, dreaming of her family.

Sarah pulled the pillow over her face and turned to the wall, smothering her cry. She couldn't let Beecher know she was crying. When her sobbing stopped, she turned onto her back again and struggled to turn off her memory.

## 7

Art heard all in his vision atop the mausoleum – Joe Engstrom's curses, the Nordhauses' love-making, Laura Grapnic, Karl Jurgens, Wally Forseth, Sarah Jones. There was more, but he could no longer listen. He sat up, rose and climbed down from the roof, knowing the Great Masking had grown stronger.

He walked back to Jefferson, wandered the streets of town, and saw the faces. He heard the voices. He felt the cries. And he knew. The Evil Ones had found their home.

The force of three had lost its equilibrium. The three energies of the universe had been thrown off-balance. Earth, heaven, and hell strove against each other for supremacy in the souls of Jefferson. The three centers – the belly, the mind, and the heart – no longer sought to integrate; they sought to dominate. Art felt the need to re-establish the world's stability.

Back in town, he huddled in the doorway of the hardware shop and tried to plan. Through Sarah, the Earth Man had found his way into Beecher's home. There must be a way to protect Beecher, to protect Sarah, but before Art could seek the Word's counsel, Jefferson disappeared. A different vision appeared.

Art sat at the feet of Lao Tzu and heard the words he did not understand. The master who knew the Tao, who knew the Word, spoke in riddles, in paradox. Art struggled for clarity each time Lao Tzu spoke.

*Who can save the world?* He asked.

*Perhaps one who devotedly follows these teachings,*
*Who calms her mind,*
*Who ignores all divergences,*
*Who develops a high awareness of the subtle truths,*
*Who merges her virtue with the universal virtue and extends it to the world without expectation of reward.*

*She will indeed be the savior of the world.*

The explanation would come, Lao Tzu said. Know the savior and the savior's savior.

A semi rumbled past on the highway.

Art awoke.

*She.*

The master had said *She*. If Beecher were the savior, *She* would be the savior's savior.

Art need not ask who, for he already knew the answer. As he walked, a lighted sign shone above him. *Sarah*'s, it said.

Art knew the sign mocked him. Its message was from the Matchi-auwishuk. He turned his eyes to the sky above the drug store across the street. For a brief moment, the mist reshaped itself to reveal the innocent face of a freckled woman, brown eyes, her long, blond hair pulled back into a pony tail.

# IV AMANDA WILSON

## 1

The Word had spoken. Art now knew. Beecher was not alone. And his wife was not his savior, his companion. She was only his earthly wife. He would not confront the Earth Man with her. He would confront the Earth Man *and* her.

Art rose and walked to the decaying building where he worked. He carefully approached the tired concrete block building, hoping Frank had not had another fight with Sammi and was holed up in his office.

In another lifetime the building had housed a bowling alley, a pool hall, and the local American Legion Club. Frank had taken few efforts to remodel the place. The bowling alley became the shop's showroom, with toilets, bathtubs, and showers straddling the gutters and pink-topped ball returns. The pool hall became Frank's office with the biggest table in the center of the room.

Frank gutted the Legion Club and turned it into his warehouse. The exterior remained basically the same save a black awning with hand-drawn letters that attempted to say "Thorstad's Perfect Plumbing," but ran out of room, reading "Thorstad's Perfect Plumbi-." Tonight the awning seemed to warn Art away, but he jiggled the front doors anyway.

Locked.

He slid along the north wall to the rear of the building where he found the spare key Frank hid above the back door that led into the warehouse, which still smelled like cigarette smoke from its years as the Legion Club. Art furtively checked the area around him to make sure he was alone, then slipped inside.

Some people, when they are confused or tense, hide under the blankets of their bed. Art could not think in his two-room shack that sat mere feet from the railroad track. Each time a coal train rumbled through town on its way from North Dakota to Duluth, the floors and walls shook so hard that dust and paint chips filled the air and choked Art in his sleep. When he needed quiet, a place to think, to reflect, to hear the Word clearly, he instead hid amidst the toilets and tubs at Thorstad's Perfect Plumbing.

The ghosts of bowlers, pool players, and drinkers had long ago left the building to porcelain and metal. It was peaceful, and even when the store was open, people left Art alone in the warehouse.

That night he needed to think. He had heard more than he could process. He recognized the face in the fog as the one Beecher saw on television. Amanda Wilson. But what did a movie screenwriter have to do with him?

Keeping the lights off, Art fumbled his way to a porcelain pedestal bathtub Betty Nordhaus, the mayor's wife, had special ordered for her bathroom remodeling. He crawled in and leaned his head on the back of the tub.

Closing his eyes, he saw Amanda Wilson's face again. His breathing slowed. His muscles relaxed. He waited for the Word to tell him more. The answers came with the questions.

"Who is Amanda Wilson?" he asked.

*Amanda Wilson is alone.*

"Alone?"

*Alone. The parents she knows adopted her; the parents who conceived her are lost to all but Me. From ten earth years until now, she has felt disconnected from the universe, isolated, unknown even to herself.*

*On the sand dunes overlooking the southern shore of Lake Superior in Sand Creek, Michigan, she often joined spirits with the iron ore ships far out on the water on their way to and from Duluth. On the rolling waves, the giant boats looked small, fragile, and alone, about to be swallowed by the water and sky, but still they pushed on until they vanished over the horizon.*

"Her parents?" Art whispered.

*Her terrestrial adoptive mother Lois still lives in Sand Creek, but since she revealed Amanda's adoption, she and Amanda are no longer close. That day of Lois's revelation*

*Amanda had thousands of questions her mother couldn't or wouldn't answer. She never would. Even today, she still will not reveal details of Amanda's birth parents, exactly where she was born, or the circumstances of her birth. All Lois will say is, "You were not born in Sand Creek, but somewhere in Minnesota." The questions have persisted, and the more Lois stubbornly refuses to supply answers, the more defiantly determined Amanda is to find her true identity.*

"And her father?"

*Dead… to your world.*

"How? What happened?"

*It was time.*

"What has Amanda Wilson to do with Beecher Jones? With Jefferson? I do not understand."

*Shhh. Breathe. Listen. Watch. Know.*

Amanda's story unfolded as Art stared up at the ceiling. The Word's voice softened. It was warmer, quieter, more feminine than he remembered.

Then he knew. It was Amanda's story. This was her voice.

*By the time I reached eighteen, I had determinedly scoured every room in my parents' home, seeking hiding places for missing documents, old pictures…whatever I could find that would reveal something of my origin.*

*One day in the summer after high school graduation, I went to my father's workbench in the garage to find a can of Three-in-One oil for my bike's brakes. I loved that bike and hated when it became dirty or the brakes squeaked.*

*I like doing things for myself. Always have. So when I spied a metal box high in the rafters, among the cardboard cartons of discarded clothes, I did not wait for help. I was curious then. I mean right then. There was no later. There would be no waiting. I set up a stepladder, pushed the clothes aside, and pulled down the box. The latch had rusted shut, but with a quick pry of a screwdriver, the latch gave way. I began paging through my elementary school report cards, pictures I had drawn, and stories I had written, including the original, hand-scrawled copy of "Scruffy and Tiger Eat Wally the Worm."*

*At the bottom of the box, I found a pocket file with a stack of official-looking documents inside. An oversize elastic cord bound the bulging folder. Slowly, carefully, I removed the brittle cord and slid the documents onto the workbench. There were five stapled documents each covered with a blue legal cover. One was a loan agreement for a car I had never seen in our garage. Probably before my time. Another was a deed to a house in Wisconsin my grandma Wilson once owned. The legal copy of my parents' marriage certificate from Sand Creek County also had a decorative Lutheran church version stuffed between its covers. A copy of my mother's graduation certificate from secretarial school covered the last set of papers.*

*When I picked it up, the first thing I saw was an official looking arched* Minnesota *over the state seal on the cover. I slowly opened the cover and found them, my adoption papers.*

*Hurriedly, I read, anticipating answers my mother would never give me. The legalese, however, did little to clear up my long list of questions. No mother, no father, their identities protected by the state. However, the papers did reveal my birthplace – Jefferson, Minnesota.*

*A car slowed on the street out front of the house, and I scurried to replace the papers and box in case it was Mom or Dad coming home. I peeked out the side door and saw the driveway was still empty.*

*I knew part of the answer, but it wasn't enough. I went inside the house, found my dad's travel atlas inside the kitchen cupboard and took it up to my room.*

*The first thing I did was to find Jefferson on a map. It was in northwestern Minnesota right on Highway 2. I traced the road with my finger through Minnesota, northern Wisconsin and into Michigan's Upper Peninsula. At Ironwood, Highway 2 meets Highway 28, the road that follows the southern shore of Lake Superior through Marquette and into Sand Creek.*

*I paged to the back of the atlas to find out the population. 1500. Far less than Sand Creek's 12,000, but not miniscule. Very similar to the towns of Michigan's Upper Peninsula. Someone would have answers, I thought.*

*Without knowing why, I called the bus station to find if Greyhound had service to Jefferson. The agent told me Greyhound only went as far as Duluth, but I could transfer to Dakota Lines there, which would take me where I wanted to go.*

*I hung up the phone and rummaged through my desk drawer to find my savings account passbook. Having paid fall tuition at Northern Michigan the week before, there was only $300 left, but I believed that would be enough to get me to Jefferson, spend a few days, and get back home in time before school started. I had to go.*

*I ripped a piece of paper from one of my old tablets and began to write a note explaining where I had gone, but the words of explanation, of guilt, of insolence, of remorse collided in my brain. Finally, I simply wrote,"Have gone to Jefferson, Minnesota. I'm sorry. I'll be back. Amanda." My father might be insulted, but my mother, even if she did not approve, would understand why. She could try to explain it to him until I got back.*

*As long as my aunt Kathleen, my father's sister, never found out, everything would work out in the end. Kathleen's tongue twisted and reshaped stories until what had been a Ladies Aid meeting at the Congregational church turned into a drunken orgy. Kathleen loved her brother Doug, but she was a bitter woman who resented my mom and my relationship with him. Her bitterness reveled in every opportunity to tear our family apart. If Kathleen learned that I had gone to Jefferson, Sand Creek would instantly hear and know that I was "an ungrateful little bitch who left the parents who raised her to find her drug addicted slut of a birth mother."*

*Still, I was resolute. I was going. I packed my bag, tiptoed downstairs, left my note on the kitchen table and crept out the door. Sneaking through the alleys, I walked downtown and hid behind the bus station/flower shop until the westbound bus arrived.*

*After nine hours of bouncing across northern Michigan and Wisconsin, changing buses in Duluth, and sleeping through most of northern Minnesota, I awoke as the bus pulled into a truck stop on top of a hill at the east end of Jefferson. I was the only person to leave the bus. I stood in the nearly empty parking lot and looked toward town. The sky glowed an angry red above the prairie, burning the grain elevator and the water tower into black silhouettes. As the bus pulled out of the parking lot and back onto the highway, I realized it would soon be nighttime and I had no place to stay.*

*I picked up my battered suitcase and entered the café. There was a line of booths against three walls, a counter opposite the front door, and about five tables in the middle of the room. I found a booth and shoved my bag across the bench against the scarred paneling.*

*At the counter, two truckers slopped up their pot roast gravy with a dinner roll. In the window booth in front of me, an older couple argued about what the other liked to eat. In the back corner six teenagers scrunched into a booth, balancing towers of cups, saucers, and silverware as high as gravity, faulty design, and a half dozen toothpicks would allow. I thought it was odd that nobody sat at any of the tables, as if we all avoided the center, and thus, each other. In fact, the whole room seemed empty, as if those of us who were there looked on from the outside.*

*I turned around, looking for a waitress. I saw a brunette serving coffee to the truckers. Her name tag said Geri. When she spied me, she waved and said, "Hey, Hon. I'll be right with you."*

*I looked down at the scuffed and dirty floor, kicked absently at a loose tile, and folded my empty hands. I realized that before loneliness and guilt overcame me, I should call home and tell everybody I was all right.*

*The pay phone with its thin, ragged, yellowing phone book was near the check-out counter. I got up and edged around the tables and saw there was also a panel of local ads next to the phone. My finger trailed down the list and found two motels, neither of which advertised their prices. I took a deep breath. Judging from how light had faded the panel, any prices would be out of date now anyway. For all I knew, both places were out of business. It was then I realized I had no idea how much a motel room cost nor how long I was going to stay or how much food cost or… I should have asked my mom. Then I remembered why I had originally come to the phone.*

*I'd have to call collect. Without any idea how far my money would go, I would have to conserve. I realized how rude it was, calling home to say, "Hey, I'm in Jefferson, Minnesota, trying to find who my real parents are. By the way, will you pay for the phone call?" If my mother answered, I'd get an hour's lecture both on the phone and when I got home. If it were my dad, the silence would be excruciating, almost as much as the disappointment on his face would be.*

*"Yes, operator, I'll accept the charges."*

*Instead of either my mother or father's voice, it was Kathleen's, filled with accusation as she barked into the receiver.*

*"Kathleen?" I asked.*

*"Amanda! Where are you? Your mother is frantic."*

*"I'm fine. Can I talk to her please?"*

*"She's not here. She's at the hospital with your father."*

*I shivered. "Hospital? Why? What's the matter?"*

*"I don't know. I'm still waiting to hear. They wouldn't let me see him. I'm only his sister. He collapsed at the dinner table and they had to call the ambulance. Wherever you are, you better get your skinny little butt straight home. Do you understand me? Straight home."*

*"I… I'll try to get there as quick as I can."*

*"Good!" The line went dead.*

*"Whatever is wrong is your fault!" the click said.*

*I was sure it was.*

*I hung up the phone, shakily, and leaned against the wall, trying to figure out what to do next. I had to go back, but there wouldn't be a bus east until the next day. Hitchhiking in daylight was dangerous; at night, unthinkable. Uneasily, I walked back to my booth and sat down, trembling.*

*Geri the waitress delivered an order to the couple at the window and stood joking with them. Something she said struck the man particularly funny, and he laughed loudly as he leaned far across the table for the sugar for his coffee.*

*I sniffed and wiped a tear from my cheek. As the man sat up, he saw me. Quickly, I averted my eyes and turned away. The wife started her own story when the husband interrupted her. I glanced back. The wife's scowl indicated interrupting her thoughts was something that seldom occurred and she didn't like it. Unaware of his wife's glower, the husband pointed to me and whispered a question to Geri. She looked at me and shook her head. I wanted to sink under the table, but could not move. I didn't want to cry, but my mouth quivered, my breath halted, and tears overflowed my swelling eyes. Geri excused herself and walked toward me.*

*I looked around for a method of escape, but before I could move, Geri sat down next me, cutting off my flight. She patted my hand and asked, "Honey, you all right?"*

*Through tears and quivers, I tried to say yes, but Geri's open face and the lace handkerchief she offered me inspired honesty. Between sobs, I explained my situation, how I needed to get back to Sand Creek as soon as possible. I didn't want to say anything, but there was no hiding from this woman. Her look, her voice, her touch drew everything out of me.*

*Tenderly, Geri coaxed an explanation as to exactly where Sand Creek was, then patted my hand and told me to wait a moment. She rose, walked to the couple near the window and talked to them briefly. First, the husband, then the wife nodded. Geri smiled, hugged each person's shoulder and then returned to me.*

*"Honey, I have it all figgered out. You wanna come with me?"*

*I nodded, and Geri took me by the hand to meet the couple. "Honey," Geri said, "this is Martha and... Albert, is it?" The man nodded. "Albert. Folks, this is... I'm sorry, sweetheart. I didn't catch your name."*

*"Amanda."*

*"This is Amanda. Now, honey, Martha and Albert are on their way from Rugby, North Dakota, all the way to Montreal, Quebec, Canada. Doesn't that sound like a nice trip?"*

*I nodded, returned Geri's handkerchief, and then reached for a paper napkin to use as a tissue. I didn't feel right using her clean hanky. She smiled and patted my shoulder.*

*"Well, the really nice thing is they were planning to drive right through Sand Creek on their way, and they tell me they'd be awful grateful for some company. I told 'em you could pro'bly help them, at least as far as Sand Creek. You know. Talkin'. Keeping each other awake. Maybe even sharin' the drivin'. What do you think?"*

*"That would be great," I sniffed. "Thank you."*

*Albert said, "Sure. If ya wanna just wait a second dere, Amanda, while we pay our bill..."*

*Geri interrupted. "No, that's okay, baby. I'll take care of it. My way of saying thanks for helping our friend Amanda here."*

*I took Geri's hand and thanked her. Instead, Geri enfolded me in her arms and said, "Honey, that's why God put us here, to help each other when we need it. Now, I'll be praying for you and your family. Okay? You take care, now." I nodded my head against her shoulder. Geri stepped back and kissed me on the forehead.*

*I picked up my suitcase and followed Martha and Albert to their car. After squeezing my bag into the trunk, I took one last look back at the café. Geri stood at the door waving. I smiled and waved back. As Albert turned onto the highway and headed east, I turned to the back window and watched the Jefferson elevator and water tower fade into the blackness of night.*

Art struggled to relate the past he observed to the life he lived. He barely knew Inga's Truck Stop, but he easily recognized the emptiness Amanda first saw in the room. He had been there once after his last battle at Grave Swamp and felt the stares, the disdain of being Indian, of being different. That would have been long before Amanda had been there, probably long before Geri.

Art thought for a moment. There was something out of place with this waitress. He recognized her, but not from then. From now. Somewhere. He didn't know how. And what did this have to do with Beecher? He dared not ask the Word. More story pulled him back to the car headed east years ago.

*It soon became obvious that the need for company was Geri's idea, not Martha and Albert's. They didn't need it. Martha was somebody who loved to talk whether anybody listened or not. I thought she would be just as happy conversing with a potato as with another person. Martha babbled nonstop from Jefferson to Duluth. It was also clear that Albert enjoyed the sound of his wife's voice. He would occasionally mumble "Uh-huh" as he looked back at me in the rearview mirror and smiled. We stopped for the night in Duluth and the couple insisted on paying for my room.*

*In my bed, I marveled how there was never any real malice in Martha or Albert's voice. Arguing was just their way of communicating.*

*The waitress... Geri? Was that really her name? I can't remember... The waitress understood that and saw the true Martha and Albert. She knew what I needed. Martha and Albert were it. And not just for the return ride to Sand Creek. On the ride to Duluth, I saw what they were to each other in the patience, love, and happiness that filled their car, their marriage, their lives. Geri had seen the same and brought them to me when I needed them.*

*The qualities I saw in Martha and Albert were qualities I saw in my parents, yet never knew myself. I couldn't remember being happy. Sometimes content, but never happy. Leaving Jefferson without finding my birth mother promised to drive out even contentment.*

*By the time Albert and Martha dropped me off at home the next day, it was noon. Cars lined the street, and people filled the house. I slipped around the back of the house and entered through the kitchen. Food filled the counter and stovetops. At the kitchen table Kathleen harangued Pastor Gleason. When she saw me, she stopped short. One look at Kathleen's grimace and Pastor Gleason's over-practiced, sympathetic eyes and I knew the truth. I put down my suitcase and attempted to steel myself. "Where's my mother?" I asked.*

*Kathleen approached her accusingly. "She's in her room, resting. Where have you been? Just what the hell did you think you were doing?"*

*Pastor Gleason reached out and touched her shoulder. "Now, Kathleen…"*

*I ignored Kathleen's interrogation and pushed past her into the living room. "Mom?" I called*

*The crowd in the living room parted as I scrambled past them upstairs to my parents' room.*

*"You can't go up there! I told you she's resting!" Kathleen screeched from the kitchen.*

*I slipped quietly into the room and closed the door behind me. I stood in the darkened room, waiting for my eyes to adjust. I heard my mom's breathing. I hesitated, then finally whispered, "Mama?"*

*"Amanda?" Mom turned over and sat up. "You're home?" she asked turning on the bedside lamp.*

*My chin quivered. "Mm-hm."*

*"Come here, baby."*

*I sat next to my mom and the two of us hugged in silence for several minutes. I patted my mom's back, then reached over to the bedside table for a tissue.*

*"Do you want one?" I asked.*

*Mom smiled and nodded. "With the size of this nose, I better have two," she said.*

*"Mama, I keep telling you. It's not that big. There's just a little hump on it," I smiled.*

*"Uh-huh, and there's just a little sand in the Sahara."*

*We both laughed, blew our noses and fell back into a hug, rubbing each other's back and crying even more.*

*Finally, Mom leaned back and said, "He's gone, Amanda."*

*I nodded. "Mama, did… did I..."*

*My mom looked at me quizzically until the question was clear in her mind. She hugged me again. "No, Amanda. This wasn't your fault," she said stroking my face. "The doctor said it was bound to happen. His heart was weak for some time. He hid it from everybody. From you. From me. From Kathleen."*

*"But my note..."*

*She kissed my forehead, and I flinched. The kiss was familiar. I felt the same love I had felt from Geri's lips back in Jefferson.*

*Mom held my face in her hands and looked straight into my eyes. "Amanda, he never saw it. I didn't want him to worry. It wasn't your fault."*

*"Kathleen thinks it is. How did she know I was gone?"*

*"I had to tell her. I'm sorry. After the ambulance took your dad away, I was scared. I didn't know how to find you."*

*I took my mom's hand. "Mama, I just wanted to find..."*

*She stopped me. "I know, Amanda. I'm not angry. I'm just glad you're home."*

*During the funeral, whispers pounded against my brain, crushing my spirit into dust. At the gravesite, I panicked. Hundreds of imaginary hands closed around my throat, choking the air out of me until I collapsed in tears, gasping for breath next to my father's coffin.*

*Two pallbearers supported me and walked me back to my mother's car where great sobs convulsed my body as I laid my head in Mom's lap. She stroked my shoulders and hair until the caresses soothed and tranquilized me enough so I could again form words. "They think this is all an act. They think I'm… I'm wicked, that I killed him," I said as I wiped my nose with the back of my hand.*

*"I know, Amanda, but they're wrong."*

*"Mama, when this is all over, can we… can we go somewhere and never come back?"*

*"Run away?"*

*I nodded.*

*"Amanda, We can't do that. This is our home. We've lived here since..."*

*"So what? They hate me."*

*She took my hand. "Amanda, in just a couple months you'll be going to college. You'll be away from town. They'll be away from you. They'll forget. It will all work out fine. You'll see."*

The scene faded from Art's eyes. Still he wanted to know more. He asked the Word, "And did it all work out fine?"

*It did not. Sand Creek is, after all, human.*

"What happened?"

*In her absence, the stories about Amanda's role in her father's death increased in number and magnitude. By the time she graduated from college, Amanda could no longer embarrass her mother by coming home. The vindictive spirit of the town, so palpable that gray day, now stood like Cerberus at the gates of hell preventing her return. Listen.*

Again Art heard Amanda's voice. This time older, more resigned.

*I never told my mom this, but years after I graduated from college, I returned unnoticed one last time to visit my father's grave. As I stood by his gravestone, I looked across the field of headstones to the trees and stone fence that surrounded the cemetery. Behind those trees and that fence, I saw Highway 28, the town's main street. Along that avenue were the church where my parents had been married, the meat market Dad owned for twenty years, Talman Ford where Mom worked since she and Dad began dating, and finally the house in which they raised me.*

*A block away, a vigorous breeze off Lake Superior shook the treetops outside the high school. Through the cemetery gate, I saw the flag above the post office ruffling in the wind. Next door a pickup pulled up in front of the hardware store. The driver stepped out, waved a greeting to a passing Chevy, and spoke to a little boy and his puppy standing by the door.*

*I now knew why my mom couldn't leave. Lois Wilson was… .and still is… an admired name in that town. Sand Creek was where she worked, married, and lived with her husband for over three decades. Me? I was lost forever. For the actions of one day, I knew I would always be an outsider, a pariah.*

2

Art's leg jerked and he awoke in the porcelain tub in the plumbing warehouse. He caught his breath and raised his head. The room was dark and quiet, yet there was light and sound. He saw Lois Wilson's face, heard her voice. The Word spoke to him. He understood more, but not all. Amanda's past, Beecher's present, Art's future, Lois Wilson were all linked. Where this knowledge would take them, how it involved the Earth Man and Evil Ones was still unclear. And Art still saw no Sarah. There were even more questions than before. The answers would be in the world of dreams, yet he realized he would know soon. So would Beecher.

Art let himself out of the building and locked the door. His legs and back cramped him into a ball in the front entryway. In his pain, he knew more visions were upon him.

Beyond the plains to the West, over the mountains, and among the twinkling lights and steady buzz of the Los Angeles night, Amanda Wilson had had enough of Oscar celebrations. She was going home.

She pushed herself through the paparazzi waiting for a glimpse of singer Chynna Dahl with her tongue stuck in director Martin Fiorinni's ear or producer Steven Harper playing celebrity grab-ass. With cameras loaded and ready to flash, the photographers paid little attention to Amanda escaping Casey Sturgis who had groped her three times before he puked into the punch bowl.

Amanda stood apart from the throng and smiled as they jostled for position to catch each new arrival. When her limousine pulled up, one reporter noticed her clutching her Oscar and shouted, "Hey! Hey, you! Who are you? You have an Oscar. You gotta be somebody. Who are you? "

The street full of photographers began to rush toward her, and she ducked into her car as the night sparkled with the flash of thirty cameras praying for "The Shot." Amanda slammed the door, and urged the driver, "Go! Go!" The car lurched forward and the crowd around them separated and turned to the next limo in line.

Once on the freeway, Amanda leaned back in her seat and watched the traffic speeding past her. She tried to be happy, but her smile was as artificial as the party and the people where she had just been. The night should have been a celebration shared with the people she loved, but her mother was home in Michigan, her best friend Sherman Lubovich was in New York, and her agent Herb Strickland and his wife Maggie were on vacation in London. The only place she had to go was the empty beach house she had shared with Herb and Maggie since beginning the *Bright and Shining Star* script.

The city became a neon blur until the car pulled off the highway onto a seaside street leading to the beach. She looked down at the Oscar she held in her lap. The biggest night of her life and she was alone.

The chauffeur parked and got out to open her door. He was shorter than he looked while he was driving. Still, she thought about asking him to share a bottle of wine with her to celebrate. "Sorry, it was such a short night," she told him, taking his extended hand and rising from her seat.

"That's okay," he told her. "I don't usually get home before my wife's asleep, so this is great."

A wife. So much for that. Amanda forced another smile. "Newlywed?" she asked.

The chauffeur nodded and grinned. "Three months tomorrow."

Of course. "So you have some celebrating to do yourself," Amanda said.

The man's grin widened. "Yeah, celebrating. I guess you can call it that. Something like that, anyway."

Amanda smiled, stepped away from him, and moved toward the house. "Go home and have a good time," she told him, turning to the door to hide her disappointment.

As she inserted her key into the lock, the chauffeur waved out his window, called out his congratulations again, and watched her close the door behind her to make sure she was safely in the house before he drove away.

After the tail lights disappeared up the driveway, Amanda sighed, set her Oscar on the dining room table, and went upstairs to change out of her dress into something warm.

Within minutes, she was on the beach, a blanket draped across her shoulders and a wine glass in one hand and a bottle of Chardonnay in the other. Above the shoreline, she spread her blanket on top of a sand dune. She sat down on the blanket and pulled the hood of her Northern Michigan sweatshirt over her head to warm her against the cool ocean air. After pouring herself a glass of wine, she lifted it to the moon, and whispered sadly, "To Amanda and to Oscar, the man in her life." She took a sip and wrapped her arms around her shins. With her knees tucked under her jaw, she watched the moon sink lower in the western sky. The moon grew larger, stretching its silver arms across the waves, inviting her closer. She shook her head and took another sip.

Twelve years ago she had left home to find who she was; twelve years later she was no closer to knowing. Geri the waitress had become the heroine of *Bright and Shining Star*. The kindness, happiness, and love Amanda envied in North Dakota's Martha and Albert had become its theme. Her father was dead; her mother still lived in Sand Creek. Amanda existed in the relationship vacuum of Los Angeles. Even though she and her mother never mentioned the place, maybe it was time to return to Jefferson.

When she finished her wine, she lay back in the sand and felt the moonlight gently caress her cheeks. She closed her eyes, let the sound of the traffic on the Pacific Coast Highway fade off into the distance, and invited whatever dreams could erase the loneliness she felt on this night she when should be ecstatic.

In her dream Amanda saw a tall, thin man below her in the moonlight writing something in the damp sand. As he was about to finish, the gentle waves reached forward and erased the words. After the water receded, he simply looked down, sighed, and began his task again… and again… and again. Amanda smiled. That was her favorite poem in college:

*One day I wrote her name upon the strand;*
*But came the waves, and washed it away:*
*Again, I wrote it with a second hand;*
*But came the tide, and made my pains his prey...*

The image of the man's love in Edmund Spenser's poem and that before her, a love so strong one would fight the very forces of nature to declare it, was her ideal. A love that the waters of loneliness could not wash away was her dream and her desire.

The dream man stood up and held up his right hand to keep back the water. The waves responded by stopping and pulling back to see what the man would do next. He bowed to the sea in gratitude, and raised his hands in supplication to the moon swollen and sinking into the horizon. He kicked off his shoes, rolled up his pants legs, and stepped into the water and foam. When he had waded out to where the waves reached his knees, he knelt, reached his arms out in front of him, eased his body face down into the water, and floated motionless. He then turned onto his back and floated, smiling up at the night sky.

Amanda felt her heart drawn to this man and smiled, too. If only for a moment, she could share joy with another person, even if he didn't know she was there. It was several minutes before he rose and waded back to the shore. As he emerged from the water, Amanda laughed at the pant legs that had been rolled so carefully and which were now drenched.

As he approached his message on the sand, the man pushed the wet hair back from his face with both hands and exulted in the feeling of the air on his face. Amanda noticed the man's unique nose, long with a bump on top of it. The man stopped before his words and looked down. He nodded, peeled off his soaked shirt and pants, and stood naked, silhouetted by the moon. He raised his hands to the sky again in silent entreaty to the forces of the universe. Facing the ocean again, he inhaled deeply, and ran headlong toward the water, releasing his breath in one long howl.

Amanda laughed aloud. How many times had she wanted to do this same thing, run naked into the ocean, squealing and laughing like a schoolchild? His hands slapped the water. He jumped high and fell backward into the sea. He threw his hands into the air repeatedly, sending water heavenward, to have it fall back into his face like rain. All the while, his exuberance rang through the air, overflowing into Amanda, making her dizzy with delight. She closed her eyes, feeling close to another person for the first time in years.

Then the splashing stopped. Amanda looked out to the ocean to see what was the matter. The surface of the sea was empty. "Is the dream over?" she wondered. Suddenly, the man's head broke the surface, gasping for air. The splashing was now frantic, not joyous. He managed to keep afloat a few seconds, but then vanished beneath the water.

Amanda dashed to the shore. Intent only on saving the man, she flung off her sweatshirt, pulled off her pants, and raced headlong into the water, swimming frantically toward the place she had last seen him. Behind her, unnoticed in the excitement, fog boiled up out of the mountains to the East and rolled madly toward the shore, free of the laws of nature.

A hand reached up in front of her, followed by the man's head. Amanda swam behind him to prevent him from grabbing her and dragging them both under. She grasped a handful of hair and began pulling the struggling body to shore.

But the shore was gone.

The fog had raced across beach, swallowing the lights of the city behind it, and had engulfed Amanda and the drowning man. She couldn't see. She had no idea where she was, where she should go, and how she could save this person and herself. By reflex she prayed desperately, crying over and over for deliverance, for the safety and security of the beach.

Her own screams woke her. She was back on her dune, clothed, alone, haze all around her. The fear from her dream still gripped her. Breathlessly, she turned her back to the sound of the waves and searched for Herb and Maggie's house, until through the vapor she detected the faint glow from the porch. Hurriedly, she pulled her hood over her head, grabbed the glass and bottle, and ran towards the light.

# V BEECHER JONES

## 1

Beecher jolted awake.

A shriek of terror.

Was it his? Had he been dreaming? He didn't remember.

Was it Jeannie? It didn't sound like her.

He sat up listening in the darkness. At first, he heard nothing, then there was a rocking, a whimpering. He rose and stepped silently to the door. The sound was somewhere down the hall.

He eased his way down the corridor and stood outside Jeannie's door. He cracked the door open and peeked in. She lay on her bed quietly hugging her stuffed Tigger he and Sarah had bought her at DisneyWorld.

Beecher pulled the door shut again and listed more intently. The rocking whimper came from down the hall.

The guest room.

"Sarah!" he gasped.

He pushed the door open and burst inside. He could hear her whispers in the dark. Clicking on the desk lamp, he asked, "Sarah, are you all right?"

Sarah sat on the edge of the bed, shivering violently. She hugged herself, her head tilting to the side, muttering, "Oh, my God. Oh, my God." Beecher knelt in front of her and clasped her hand.

"Sarah, what's wrong?"

Sarah looked at him, her face twisted by terror. "I saw them, Beecher. I saw them."

"Who?"

"My mother, my father, my brother. I saw them."

"Why is that bad?" Beecher whispered as he pushed the hair from her face.

"I saw them die!"

She slid to the floor into Beecher's arms and sobbed into his shoulder. "But, Sarah, you weren't there. You couldn't have seen them die," he whispered, holding her head close to him.

"I did! It was like, like I was the car looking in at them. Dad was driving. Jeff was next to him in front. Mom was leaning forward in the back. Jeff told one of his stupid jokes and they were laughing. They were laughing! They were happy. Then I wasn't the car anymore. I was outside on the tracks. They were coming toward me, and… something was wrong. The train was coming and the crossing arms wouldn't go down."

Her voice rose and Beecher pulled her face to his chest to muffle the sound so they wouldn't wake Jeannie. When Sarah paused to catch her breath, Beecher leaned back and found the door with his outstretched arm and pushed it shut. He kissed her sweating forehead.

"The crossing arms wouldn't go down?"

Sarah gulped and continued. "The arms wouldn't go down. I waved my own at the car to make them stop, but Dad couldn't see me. The train horn blared and blared. And none of them in the car could hear.

"Then I could see everything inside the car again. I watched the train hit them. I watched the car doors push together, crushing Jeff and my dad between them. The blood exploded from their bodies. My mother slammed against one door while the glass from the other side sliced through her throat. Her blood splashed all over the car, mixing with Jeff's, with Dad's.

"I wanted to stop the bleeding. I had to stop the bleeding. I stretched out my hands, but I couldn't move. I couldn't reach her. Someone, something pulled me away."

Sobs again wracked her body. Beecher held her closer and said, "It was a dream, Sarah. Just a nightmare."

He rocked her in his arms, kissing the top of her head, rubbing her back, until her breathing became more even and her body relaxed. When her crying finally stopped, she leaned back, sniffed, patted his chest and told him, "You need to get some rest. Go back to bed. I'll be okay."

"You want me to give you a back rub until you go to sleep?" he asked as he wiped her face.

Her jaw trembled and her breath quavered. She shook her head.

"You sure?" he asked.

She nodded. "I'll be okay. Thanks," she whispered. She reached up and touched his cheek. "Get some sleep."

He kissed her forehead again and tasted the fear in her sweat.. "I love you, Sarah," he said.

She nodded, patted his chest again, and got into bed. Turning to the wall, she curled her body around her pillow and closed her eyes to erase the image of a lover's smirk as he pulled her away from her bleeding mother. She struggled to forget him dragging her from the car into the fog. She prayed not to dream.

Beecher stopped at the door and looked back. There was a smell in the room – a rank, musty odor, the same he had smelled on the porch when Sarah came home. He sniffed his hands. The smell of Amanda Wilson's fire hung mockingly in his nostrils, like a broken promise, but there was something else in the room, something more raw, more fierce, more animal. Confusion held him at the door, watching, breathing, wondering. When Sarah began to turn toward him, he quickly slipped into the hallway.

He stood a long time listening to her toss sleeplessly in her bed. That was more than a nightmare she had. He had never seen her so horrified, so sick with fear.

He checked on Jeannie one more time, walked toward Sarah and his room, then stopped. He thought, then huffed and fumed. He hurried down the stairs, out the door, and into the fog. His face contorted with rage as he gazed at the mist about him.

"What?" he demanded. "What are you trying to do? Huh? The birds, Wally and Laura, those little hallucinations, that dream, Sarah's dream… Come on. What? What the hell do you want?"

There was no answer as the fog slowly drifted past the streetlight. Beecher shook his head.

"Come on, you chicken shit!" he shouted. "What?"

Everywhere was silence.

"Screw you," he muttered, walking back to the house. As he closed the door behind him, he felt the fog peeking through the window, smiling.

Art sat in the shadows across the street and nodded.

Beecher had chosen sides. It was time. He was the Voice and the Voice must speak the Word, tell the Story about the Earth Man, the Evil Ones, the Great Mask, and Truth.

Art struggled to his feet and shuffled off to his shack.

## 2

After a fitful night of angry tossing and broken dreams, Beecher finally surrendered, dressed and made himself a hearty breakfast of an English muffin and coffee. His aggravation increased as he buttered his muffin and reflected on the night's events. The Word fed his righteous indignation with glimpses of the Earth Man and the Matchi-auwishuk. He did not recognize them for what they really were, but he knew they threatened life as he knew it.

After draining his coffee in three gulps, Beecher set his cup on the kitchen counter and vowed defiance. He didn't know what a small-town school administrator could do to halt the cosmic forces moving about him, but he couldn't stand idle.

This fog was more than water. This fog had an aim. Beecher's dream of Amanda Wilson, Sarah's dream of her parents' death, the suicidal birds, the school employees' irrational behavior – all this signified something, a power beyond the terrestrial.

He pulled a chair away from the table and straddled it backward, laying his chin on the backrest. He stared at the linoleum on the floor and sighed deeply

He didn't consider himself a particularly heroic person. Especially since he couldn't save any of the sparrows down at Benny's. Still, like the knights of old, he knew he had to destroy the mysterious forces before they destroyed him, his family, and the whole town of Jefferson.

"It's all about the fog," he whispered. To accomplish his goal, he needed to discover the fog's origin, its mission, its weakness.

The first step was to engage it and challenge its power, to call it out and learn its strengths, to ascertain its characteristics and probe its weaknesses, and finally to destroy its dominance over Jefferson.

He decided his first move would be to reopen school.

Sitting on his bed, his back against the crumbling plaster wall, Art heard Beecher's thoughts and slumped in disappointment. Beecher's ambition bore no knowledge of the truth of the Earth Man and the Evil Ones. The fog, the Great Mask, was nothing, simply a weapon, a tool. The enemy lay deeper, hidden within the Jefferson psyche, within the souls of the very people Beecher chose to defend. Without that knowledge, Beecher's efforts would be pointless. There was much to teach, Art knew, before Beecher became the Story. He rose from his bed and entered the threatening mist.

Beecher's phone rang. He hopped up and knocked his chair to the floor. Stumbling over it, he fell against the wall and quickly grabbed the receiver before the ringing could wake Sarah and Jeannie upstairs. He fumbled the receiver and it dropped onto the floor.

The tinny sound of the caller vibrated from the floor.

"Hello? Mr. Jones? Hello? Is anybody there?"

He immediately recognized the raspy cigarette voice of the school's transportation supervisor Rowena Schmidt. Beecher pulled the cord until he could grab the receiver and put it to his ear.

"Yeah. Yeah, I'm here. Just dropped the phone. Sorry. What's up?" he said breathlessly.

"I hate to say it, Mr. Jones, but I t'ink we're gonna haveta cancel school again. I got at least eight drivers who say dey ain't goin' out until dey can at least see a block ahead of 'em. Can't say as I blame 'em."

"Rowena, we can't keep putting off classes. We have to go back sometime. Can't we just see how many kids we can get in...?"

"Seriously, Mr. Jones, dey're safer at home. I chust drove from my house to the bus garage – What? A half mile? – Oof dah! –nearly hit a parked car, hopped da curb a couple times. I don't know how I'm gonna get home."

"The forecast says..."

"Uncle Don ain't been right once dis week."

Beecher seethed a moment. Finally, he and Rowena agreed to delay opening for two-hours, then reassess the situation.

It was no use. By eight o'clock the fog was thicker than ever. It eclipsed the light of the rising sun and the town stood still, quietly cloaked in darkness. At 8:30 Rowena called again and Beecher finally relented. Fighting the battle did not mean risking the lives of students and staff to satisfy his own ego and quest for sainthood. Beecher hung up, poured himself another cup of coffee, and called the radio station.

With the cancellation official, Beecher stood at the sink, sipping his breakfast, furious at his inability to defy the force behind the fog. From the bottom of the window, the laughing woman burst up, twirled twice, and pressed her face against the glass. Beecher's cup crashed into the sink, shattering and splashing coffee onto the curtains, the wall and the floor. Outside, the woman danced out to the yard, took a deep breath, and blew across her up-turned, open palms. Instantly, the fog lightened, letting enough sun through to reveal buildings, trees, and the street. The woman pointed at him, laughed, twirled again, and vanished.

As coffee streamed down Beecher's face, Sarah came into the room, putting on her earrings. "Who was on the phone?" She stared at Beecher's dripping and the soaked curtains. "Beecher, what's going...What happened?"

Beecher grabbed a dish towel and looked at the remains of his cup, the spattered wall, and the now light fog outside the window. "There won't be any school," he said through his teeth. He wiped his face with the dish towel. As he clenched his jaw, his lips disappeared. He did not know the laughing woman's face, nor could he tell whether she was mist, spirit, or hallucination, but he knew it was the same face he had seen the night before outside his house, not Amanda Wilson, but the mocking woman who dared him to make the next move, challenging him to enter her world.

Sarah stood silently, hesitant to move or speak, fearful of Beecher and what he might know. As she watched, Beecher plucked the larger shards from the sink and tossed them angrily into the garbage. "Excuse me," he muttered, pushing past her into the hall where he grabbed his jacket and stormed out of the house.

Coffee still dripped from the wet curtains. Sarah crossed to the window and gazed out at the gray morning. She looked back at the door Beecher had stormed through. Her chin quivered as she went upstairs to find Jeannie.

3

As Beecher burst out his front door, Art rose from the bushes and crossed the street to meet him. His eyes fixed on the frosty ground in front of him, Beecher didn't see the hunched creature headed toward him. Rage consumed him and he cut diagonally across the yard, kicking at the glazed grass and muttering curses under his breath. Shifting course, Art hurried to catch Beecher, but pain sliced into his hip and back, slowing him. He could not raise his voice without screaming in agony. But even his screams were lost as his heavy breath turned them to wheezing. The gasping moans slowed Beecher, and he spun on Art, his face grimacing in anger.

"What the hell do you...? Damn! Art." His face softened when he recognized the hunched back. He had thought the sound was the laughing woman. "Why do you keep sneaking up on me like that? You scared the shit out of me again."

Art could only huff short bursts of air. Intelligible words twisted into garbled coughs and phlegm. He struggled for air, fell to the ground, his hands flailing helplessly clutching for sound.

"Word," Art gasped.

Beecher's face furled in confusion. "Yeah?"

"Word… fog... Matchi-auwish..."

"Majee-what? What are you trying to say?"

The air fought against Art, grappling with the sounds of his throat. The words were incomprehensible. Still he forced them forward. He clutched at Beecher's legs and panted, "The Story… you… must… Flame..."

"Story? Flame?" he asked, pushing Art's hands away. "What the hell are you talking about?"

Still Art reached for him. "You… know. You… saw."

As Beecher pulled away from him, Art collapsed to the sidewalk, resting his wrinkled cheek on the cold concrete. Beecher looked down at him with an expression of pity and disgust. "Damn it, Art. You have to do something about your drinking. This is getting ridiculous. You're going to hurt yourself or somebody else."

Art felt Beecher's eyes examining him, waiting for a sign of life. Beecher knelt next to him and placed his hand on Art's shoulder. "You hear me, Art? You okay? You want me to call Joe to take you home?"

Art managed to raise his head and whisper a strained "No."

"You sure?"

Art nodded and watched as Beecher turned and walked away toward the school. For a moment Art found his voice and croaked, "Word... Flame..."

Beecher stopped, turned quizzically, then with a shake of his head dismissed "the drunken, blue-eyed

Indian," crossed the street, and disappeared around the corner.

Art laid his head down and felt the air lift. He knew he could stay no longer on the field of battle. He must bring Beecher to neutral ground, somewhere out of the fog, to explain the Great Mask.

Before he could move, the world shifted. Lights disappeared. The laughing woman, Amanda Wilson, Beecher, Sarah, Jeannie – their faces swirled before him, and the sidewalk rose and fell in great waves beneath him. He rolled to the gutter and curled into a ball, vainly trying to wrap his arms about the curb. His mouth fell open and a trail of drool slid from his lips, down the gutter and into his pants. He did not care. He had failed to bring Beecher the Truth. Right now, Beecher only saw "through a glass darkly"; Art knew he must be taught to see "face to face."

Art lay on his side and waited for the Word. And he heard. With the Evil Ones, the Great Cannibals, came death, and with death, victory. Whose victory had not been determined. The battle swarmed around Beecher, Amanda, Sarah, and Art, and Art realized that he was the only one to know there were sides to be chosen.

4

In his present state, Beecher could only deal with the earthly effects of the fog – adjusting schedules, calling the weather bureau, waiting. The mist had lightened, but the air still hung heavily over the town. He didn't know what to call it, but he felt the spirit of the

Evil One coursing through the streets, the stores, and the houses. Beecher stood at his office window, convincing himself travel was still unsafe though the mist had faded, persuading himself his decision to close school was correct, despite the traffic moving easily past his window.

Rather than confront what his spirit spoke, his mind returned to the mundane. "People are amazing," he thought. "They're so intent on regaining a sense of normalcy." He laughed at himself. "Then again, here I am, working on a day off."

Beecher wasn't alone. All morning, teachers filtered into the building to take advantage of the quiet in their rooms. Beecher's secretary, Peggy Nordahl, sat at her desk, working on attendance reports. Even students hung in the halls, presumably to retrieve books and unfinished homework. The only one Beecher hadn't seen was Karl, but Beecher knew he was somewhere in the building, whistling his formless tune, cleaning some vacant room, repairing everything from pencil sharpeners to boiler plates, asking somebody, "What's the good word?"

The activity, while soothing, lacked the comforting busyness of everyday school life. For some reason, the atmosphere was slow and sluggish. An aura of fatigue, of grogginess, surrounded the building, as if the weather had become a mental and physical burden weighing it down and sapping its energy.

The day hung leaden over the town, burdened by unwept sorrow, a sorrow even beyond Art's sight, a sorrow that awaited its birth.

## 5

At the Plains, the Norske Junta met under the rusty Coke sign. They had barely arrived when a black Mercedes pulled up beside them and let out Einar Nordhaus. Inside the car, the tall, black-leather-clad driver leaned forward, saluted the group, and drove away. The Jefferson intelligentsia looked questioningly at Einar. He managed a weak grin and said, "C'mon. We got work ta do."

The men looked at each other quizzically. Pete Carlson stared after the Mercedes as it turned onto the highway and headed east.

Einar bellowed at him. "Pete! C'mon! Let's go!"

Pete turned to Einar and pointed after the car. "But who…wha'..?"

"I'll explain inside. Let's go."

Pete looked at Einar who held the door open. "Yeah. Okay," he mumbled and went inside.

The two proceeded through the dining room, past the kitchen, and into the back room. The Junta had nicknamed the room "Hattie's" after the Plains' owner Hattie Long, but it was really their room, the unofficial government center that controlled the city, the school, and the county.

Even though Beecher's position as principal made him a de facto member of the group, they pointedly excluded him from this meeting.They had too much to say, too much to arrange, too much business to conduct.

6

As the morning progressed, a steady pressure behind Beecher's eyes echoed the townspeople's fuming over another school day lost.

Beecher understood. The school was the lifeblood of the town. When it was open, the town was vibrant and alive. When weather or calamity closed it down, the town shut down as parents stayed home to care for their children.

But the fog was dangerous, more dangerous than they knew. It had put Beecher in a no-win situation, and he didn't feel like defending his decision.

Still, the phone call from Einar Nordhaus was not unexpected and Beecher knew he had to answer.

"Damn it, Beecher. How many days off are ya gonna give dem kids?"

"Morning, Einar."

"Why the hell'd ya close school? There ain't hardly no fog out there."

"Not now, but there sure was earlier. Weren't you awake?"

Einar hesitated. "Well… yeah, I was up, but..."

"Einar, I can't take chances. I have kids, drivers, teachers..."

"Well, the boys are pretty pissed off..."

"Who? The Junta?"

Einar grunted. Beecher felt Einar's exasperation through the phone. "I really resent you using that name," Einar said.

Despite his frustration, guilt gnawed at Beecher, chastising him for his disrespect. "I'm sorry," he said, "but I resent everybody second-guessing every decision I make. I don't enjoy this. I can't take the time to consult you and the rest of 'the boys' every time I need to blow my nose."

Einar took a breath to measure his words. "Beecher, you need to… you need to think a little more about who you are responsible to."

"I'm responsible to the students and parents..."

"There are other people to consider." The words hung ominously in the silence.

"Einar, are you threatening my job?"

"No. I'm not. But there are forces..."

Beecher stared at his desk coldly and gripped the receiver tighter. "Forces. What does that mean?"

"Just be prepared for changes. And soon."

It was not like Einar to be cryptic. Every day he and the Junta celebrated with frankness their latest intimidation of employees, contractors, and suppliers. Detecting traces of subtlety at Hattie's was preposterous. Yet Beecher would not let himself be bullied. "If you're finished, Einar, I have some work to catch up on."

"Just remember what I said."

Beecher hung up the phone, stifling his rage.

## 7

The school was the neutral space Art needed to enter, to teach. Its relation to the mistakes of history and science intimidated him, but the Word told him this is where he could reach Beecher.

Art shuffled through the darkened hallways until he stood quietly waiting at the door to Beecher's outer office. When Peggy looked up from her computer, she started, then forced a smile and asked, "Can I help you, Art?"

Art pointed at Beecher's closed door. "See Mis... Mister... Jones." He kneaded his painful jaw.

She looked protectively at the office. "He's busy right now. If you could come back later..."

"'ll...wait."

Peggy hesitated, then picked up the phone and punched the intercom. "Mr. Jones, Art Benson is here. He wants to see you."

She listened, glanced at Art, then said, "I can't tell. All right. Thanks." She hung up the phone. "He'll be right out," she said.

Art nodded. Beecher opened his door, anger still clinging to his face. "You wanted to see me, Art?"

Art moved toward his office, but Beecher stepped forward to stop him.

"What's this about?" Beecher asked.

Art looked inside Beecher and saw his apprehension, his doubt, his unnerved spirit. To him Art was the cry in the night, the infectious fog, the essence of what haunted the town.

"…Know," Art told him, pointing at his own chest.

Beecher looked at him quizzically. "You know...?"

"Fog."

Beecher glanced at Peggy, who smiled and hid her face behind a hand.

"Hmmm. Well, that's good."

Art pointed to himself and said, "Must talk." He then turned his finger to Beecher. "Must hear."

Beecher looked up at the clock. "Yeah. Okay. Come on in. I guess I have a few minutes."

Art passed him into the office. "Peggy," Beecher said, "if you need me for anything..." The unspoken words said, "Get me out of this quickly."

"Okay," she answered, and Beecher shut the door behind him.

"All right," Beecher said, taking the seat behind his desk. "Sit down."

"…'ll stand."

Beecher leaned forward and narrowed his eyes. "Art, don't take this the wrong way, but have you been drinking?"

"Don' drink."

Beecher's skepticism permeated the air. "You mean 'any more'? Are you in recovery or...?"

"Never…" Art swallowed… "have."

"Ever?"

"Ever." Art raised his eyes to meet Beecher's.

Beecher had never seen their color before. He had only heard the rumor of a "blue-eyed Indian." The cobalt irises opened the other world to him and shook his feigned calm. He sat back and thought for a second. "All right," he said. "What must I hear about the fog?"

Pointing at Beecher again, Art nodded and said, "Know the… answer. Heard…the Word, seen…Matchi-auwish..."

"Matchi-auwish. You said that out on the street. What is this Matchi-auwish? What is this Word you keep talking about?"

"The Word…" Language failed him, so Art touched his own lips, then Beecher's chest. "…inside you." Art touched Beecher again. "Heard it… Heard in birds." Art nodded at him "…Know."

Beecher examined Art's face. Art heard Beecher's eyes blink, and he watched as Beecher weighed the image of the self-destructive birds and the day that had passed.

"What is it I know?"

"Matchi-auwish. Earth Man. Evil One." Art stretched his hands in front of Beecher. "Lives apart… from Word." Pointing to the window, he added, "Uses fog…for own…purposes."

" Matchi-whatever. Earth Man. Evil One. All of them?"

"All one."

Beecher nodded sympathetically and twirled a pen on his desktop. He paused. "Is this something your people believe? I read a lot of Ojibwe history, but never heard anything about it, even when I was teaching up at Red Lake."

Art shook his head. "Not what believe. What is. Universe has… lost balance. Word forgotten, rejected, … denied. Flame ignored. Good must… come back. Matchi-auwish walks…in fog…seeking own." Beecher's face contorted in confusion. Art laid his palm on Beecher's chest. "Must stop him."

Beecher pushed Art's hand aside and laughed. "I must stop him? And how do you propose a Norwegian Lutheran stop an Ojibwe devil?"

Art tugged on his right ear, then tapped Beecher's forehead. "Listen what know. Trust what believe. Word lives in you."

Beecher scowled and said, "Please don't do that, Art." He then shook his head at Art and added, "Well, if he's talking, I'm not hearing."

Art moved to touch Beecher's ears, but Beecher stepped away. Art shook his head and told Beecher, "Hearing. Not listening."

Peggy's phone rang outside, then stopped. A moment later, the intercom buzzed. "Excuse me a moment," Beecher said, pushing the bar on the phone. "Yes?"

"Mr. Jones," Peggy said. "It's Joe Engstrom on line one. Says it's important."

"Okay." He looked up at Art. Both felt the world shift. "I need to take this," Beecher said. "Can I talk to you later?"

Art looked beyond Beecher to the street. The fog had returned. It hung in sheets from the trees and window awnings. The Earth Man walked.

"Art?"

Art could not find the words that would stop Beecher's pain and confusion. "Listen," Art said. "Word speaks. Listen."

Beecher nodded. "I will."

Beecher only wanted Art to leave; however, the Word would be spoken and Beecher would have no choice but to hear. Art walked out of the school and headed for work, all the while listening as Beecher picked up the phone to speak to Joe Engstrom.

"Hey, Joe. What's up?"

"Um… Mr. Jones, can you come over to city hall? I think we've got a problem."

"What's wrong?"

"I'll tell you when you get here. Bye."

Beecher looked at the dead phone in his hand. "Now what?" he wondered. He put down the receiver, put on his jacket and walked into his outer office.

"Peggy, Joe wants me to come to his office. You know what's going on?"

She shook her head. "What did Art want?" she asked.

"To give me a lesson in Indian theology. Did you know he has blue eyes?"

"I heard that, but never paid much attention. He always kind of hides his eyes when I look at him. It's an old Indian trait around here."

"Then he wants to talk to me and I don't understand anything he says. Talking about some word and the evil one and..."

"Has he been drinking again?"

Beecher smiled. "He says he doesn't drink. Never has."

"Yeah, right."

Beecher shrugged. "That's what he said."

"No one could work for Frank Thorstad as long as Art has and not drink."

"True," Beecher agreed. "You sure you don't know anything about what Joe wants?"

"Probably another pot-smoking basketball player or something."

"Damn kids," Beecher joked. "Back in a bit. If Sarah calls, tell her where I am."

## 8

Beecher walked the three blocks through the thickening fog to the police station, while eyes peered out of store windows and followed him. The news pulsed across the town gossip line, and Beecher sensed secrets hiding behind walls, peeking out of windows, ducking behind buildings. He was not prepared for what he was about to find out.

Outside Joe's office, an unfamiliar black Mercedes stood in front of Joe's white squad car. Joe's car was normally spotless, but now it rested against the curb with mud and grass clinging to the wheel wells. Dirt streaked the windshield and a dent caved in the driver's door. "Must have chased one of the Junta's kids through some field," Beecher thought. "Probably wants me to talk to the dad. Like hell I will."

The office door opened and a tall, dark-haired man in a black leather jacket pushed by Beecher. Not even acknowledging Beecher's existence, the man cooly slid into the Mercedes, revved the engine, squealed the tires, and sped away. Beecher shrugged, shook his head, and walked into the reception area.

The room had an antiseptic odor powerful enough to strip wallpaper and kill cockroaches, almost as if the cleaning crew had bathed the room in a bizarre concoction of Lysol, Raid, and Listerine. Joe sat behind the counter, rubbing his forehead. "Who was that?" Beecher asked.

"Hm? Oh. Another unsatisfied customer," Joe said. "Beecher, thanks for comin'. Ya wanna come with me?" Joe led Beecher into his private office in back. When the door opened, Beecher saw Laura Grapnic sitting in the corner, biting her wrist and crying silently.

"Laura?" Beecher asked.

The waif-like teacher looked up at her principal. "Mr. Jones, I didn't know who else to call. I just... I..." Her voice broke, but her lips kept trying to form coherent words. Finally, she gave up and broke down, hugging herself and sobbing.

Beecher knelt in front of her, gently touching her face. "Laura, what's wrong?" She couldn't answer. She simply pulled away and held herself tighter. Joe closed the door, and Beecher turned to him. "What's going on?"

Joe walked behind his desk. "Have a seat."

Beecher pulled up a chair and sat next to Laura, taking her hand as she stared at the ceiling, as if praying for deliverance. Joe took a deep breath and exhaled. He looked down at his desk, then up at Beecher. "Beecher, I was going to call you later," he said. "but... I thought Miss Grapnic would feel more comfortable with somebody she knew and trusted. She suggested you."

"Fine… I guess. Joe, what's...?"

"Well, sir, there's been a… uh..."

Joe's reticence frustrated Beecher. "What? What's happened? Has this anything to do with your car?"

Joe's face flushed. "No. That… that was something else. This is... Well, this is worse. There's been… a tragedy. I don't know what else to call it. We found Karl Jurgens dead this morning."

A chill formed at the top of Beecher's skull, traveled down the back of his neck and spread out across his back. His jaw slackened. "Karl? He... No, because... How?"

"He… uh... As far as we can tell right now, he broke his neck."

Beecher stared at Joe, then turned his gaze to the floor. Beside him, he felt Laura's shoulder tremble and heard her breath quiver. He looked back up at Joe. He tilted his head toward Laura. "What does Laura have..."

"We found him outside her house."

Laura's face contorted, and she buried her head in her hands, sobbing again.

"Do you think she...?" Beecher asked.

Joe shrugged. “I don’t know what to think. It doesn’t make sense that she could, but...”

Beecher recalled the image of Laura standing over Wally Forseth with the shiny letter opener poised under his nostrils when he had called her actors “losers.”

“Is she under arrest?” he asked.

“No.”

“Can I talk to her a minute alone?”

“I don’t think so. I need to hear what she has to say. It’s not as if you’re her priest or lawyer.”

Beecher turned to Laura and asked, “Laura, do you want me to get you a lawyer?”

She shook her head.

“Are you sure?”

She nodded.

“Miss Grapnic,” Joe said, “you know you’re entitled to have an attorney, right? I can call Darin Wolstad and get him over here in just a couple a minutes.”

Laura shook her head.

“Okay. You wanna tell Mr. Jones and me what happened?”

Laura sat up, wiped her face with the back of her hand, and began.

“I... I don’t... I came out this morning... I didn’t see him at first. He was lying in the snowbank under my window... I had decided to come to school today and talk to Mr. Jones about what to do with the play...”

“Whaddaya mean?” Joe asked.

“Well, we haven’t had a rehearsal since last week and now school’s been canceled every day this week, so I didn't know what we were going to do. Anyway... I walked out of my house and began backing my car out of the driveway and I saw... I saw him. I saw Karl. He..."

Joe leaned forward and asked gently, "Do you know how he got there?"

Laura shook her head. "No, I... Not really... I just..."

"You just what?"

She looked up at the policeman. "I... I had this dream."

Beecher saw the hooded face of Amanda Wilson, heard Sarah's screams in the night. He glanced at Joe.

"A dream," Joe repeated. "Yes, go on."

"I dreamt he was stalking me."

"Karl Jurgens stalking you?" Joe asked.

"Maybe not stalking," she said, "but he was always trying to be near me, always watching me. At school he was always hanging around my room; at the grocery store he was behind me at the checkout; at the Amoco he was at the pump next to me; at the theater in Bemidji, he sat two rows behind me. It didn't matter where I went, who I was with, Karl was there."

"This was your dream, though. This wasn't actually happening, right?"

"Right. I mean Karl has always been very nice to me. He never did anything like that."

Beecher remembered Karl saying how he wanted to impress Laura, how he had shrugged and said, "I dunno. Maybe I'm in love."

Laura continued, "Anyway, he was doing all this weird stuff and then he tried to kill me." Her hands began to tremble again. Beecher held them tighter, trying to calm her.

"Kill you how?" Joe continued. "What did he do?"

"I was working at my desk at home, typing this test. And then – I don't know how – I could feel someone watching me. I turned around and looked at the window, and there was Karl, just standing there in the fog, smiling.

"But it wasn't just Karl. He had this huge snake draped around his neck that kept tapping its head against the glass, like it was trying to get into the house. I walked to the window to tell Karl to leave, but when I got there, the snake looked at me with these red eyes. Its head started swaying back and forth, slowly and rhythmically, like it was trying to hypnotize me. I wanted to tell Karl to take it away, but I couldn't speak. I opened my mouth, and no words came out, no sound, nothing."

"And?"

"Karl lifted the snake from his neck and held it in his hands, handing it up to me like an offering. I just stood there and shook my head. It was as if I had hurt his feelings. He nearly cried. He lowered the snake, looked at it sadly, and placed it on the ground. It looked up at him disgustedly, slithered up into the tree, and rested on a branch, glaring back at my house with its tongue flicking toward me. Karl stood at the window, his eyes pleading with me to come out into the fog with him and the snake. When I shook my head again, he walked up next to the tree and lifted something up to the snake. It was as if they were talking."

"What did they say?"

"I couldn't hear. I was still inside. Then Karl turned back toward the house. His face was a twisted mess of – I can't even describe it. Now *his* eyes were red. His body was hunched over almost like Art Benson, and there was this… venom dripping from his teeth. His awful smile said he was going to swallow me and my whole house. He crouched, took two steps, and then flew headfirst at the window. His arms were stretched at me, and as he flew nearer, I could see farther and farther down his throat. I threw the curtain shut, and there was this sickening crunch. Then I woke up in my bed screaming."

Beecher brought a fist to his mouth and chewed on his finger. Joe looked at Laura impassively. "That's a scary dream," Joe said.

"But why Karl?" she asked. "That's doesn't make sense. He's not horrid like that. And then I came outside this morning and there he was, lying dead below my window."

Joe looked at Laura intently for a moment. "Okay, Miss Grapnic. You wait here. I'm going to talk with Mr. Jones for a second. Then I think I'll let you go. All right?"

Laura nodded. Joe rose and opened the door, letting Beecher out before him. As he closed the door behind him, Joe turned to Beecher, shaking his head.

"What?" Beecher asked.

"Her dream fits the evidence."

"What?"

Joe nodded. “It looks like Karl ran as fast as he could head first into her wall.”

“You’re kidding.”

Joe shrugged.

“And the snake?” Beecher asked.

“No, there’s no snake, and of course, Karl couldn’t fly, but… she dreamt he crashed into the wall, and it looks like he did.”

“On purpose?”

Again, Joe shrugged. “Looks that way. Was Karl all right? I mean, was he depressed or anything? Did he seem… stable?”

Beecher thought for a moment. “Well, he mouthed off to Wally Forseth the other day, but...”

“That qualifies him as stupid, not insane. How ‘bout him and Miss Grapnic? He been stalkin’ her, ya think?”

“Well,... I think he kind of liked her, but I just can’t see him...”

“Yeah, I know. Hell, I thought he was kinda… well, you know… a little fruity.”

“You mean gay?”

“Yeah.”

“No. At least I don’t think so. I don’t think he was psycho either.”

“He take drugs?”

“Not that I know of.”

“Hm.” Joe shook his head.

“What are you going to do with Laura?”

"I don't know. Sending her back to her house might be kind of hard on her. She got any friends she can stay with?"

"I can ask the choir teacher."

"Good. She'll have to stick around, though. She can't leave town. I may need to talk to her again."

Joe drove Laura home to get a few things. Beecher rode with her in the back seat of the patrol car. The same antiseptic odor he had smelled in the police station permeated the car. Beecher cracked the window until they reached Laura's house.

Laura avoided the front steps, taking the men into the house through the kitchen door. While Laura quickly packed a bag, Beecher and Joe walked into the living room to look out the window to where the body had lain. Neither spoke.

When Laura finished her packing, Joe drove her and Beecher across town to Sandy Daniels' apartment. Beecher offered to help in any way he could, but Laura thanked him and assured him she would be all right.

Back in the car, Beecher asked Joe, "You think she did it?"

Joe shook his head. "No. Funny how dreams work, though, ain't it?"

Beecher nodded his head. He lowered the window again. "What did you do in here?" he asked. "It really stinks."

Joe's face flushed. "Had a little accident last night. Spilled some… some coffee and had to try to keep the stuff from staining the seat."

"What did you use?" Beecher asked. "Smells like somebody pissed on a pine cone or something."

Joe looked straight ahead and said nothing. He dropped Beecher back at the school and drove off.

The weight of all that had happened finally settled on Beecher, and he slouched into the school. Peggy was still waiting at her desk.

"You hear?" he asked.

Peggy nodded, rose from her chair and hugged Beecher, as much for her own comfort as his. She wiped away a tear and asked him, "You going to be all right?"

"Yeah. I don't know about you, but I'm done for the day."

"Me, too," Peggy agreed. "You want a ride home?"

"No, I think I need to walk."

"You want me to come in tomorrow?"

Beecher shrugged. "We'll see."

The two walked quietly to the door, hugged again, and parted, Peggy walking to the parking lot, Beecher heading home.

He intended to go home, but found himself nearing Laura's house. He stopped out front and stared at the darkened window. Slowly, he walked up the sidewalk to the front step, and examined the scene.

The fog thickened, but Beecher ignored the gathering gloom. He found the dent in the siding where Karl's head had struck, and the remnants of a snow bank hidden from the winter sun by the house still bore the imprint of his body. A few drops of blood still dotted the snow. Beecher climbed the steps to get a better look at the wall. At the point of impact, he saw what appeared to be a crack in the siding. Leaning over the railing, he reached out and touched it. It moved. Beecher took off his glove and picked out one of Karl's few remaining hairs embedded in the wall. Beecher looked down at it, twirled it between his fingers, and whispered, "What's the good word?"

A snap in the tree above him startled him. He glanced up and saw the branches crawling with snakes, some huge, some small, all with red eyes, all swaying in a hypnotic fashion, all flicking their tongues at him.

Beecher fell back against the door and slid down to the top step. The largest snake leaned forward out of the tree, opened its mouth as if to swallow Beecher whole.

Then it vanished.

Cautiously, Beecher lowered his arms. The snakes no longer existed. Instead, the fog swirled and danced like Karl's hair between Beecher's fingers. He remained motionless, anticipating the arrival of the laughing woman. She never came.

To Beecher, the laughing woman was the face of the force he could not name, the force that must be stopped. Gathering his strength, Beecher stood up, and bellowed, "You want me, too? Here I am, bitch. Come and get me!"

The fog gathered under the tree and twisted itself into the form of Karl Jurgens. The specter advanced on the house, leering at the living room window, waiting for Laura to appear.

"No!" Beecher screamed, the sound reverberating through the afternoon air. The apparition evaporated as

Beecher fell to his knees, grabbed the back of his head with his hands, and pulled his head to the cold concrete beneath him.

When the tension in his limbs passed from his body into the steps below, he looked into the mist and asked, "What is this? What do you want?"

From the gloom Beecher heard Art's voice saying, "The Word. Matchi-auwish. Listen."

"The Word. Matchi-auwish. Listen," Beecher repeated. He sat quietly and opened himself to the sounds of the earth. "I hear evil," he said. "I hear danger. I hear..."

"Do not say. Only hear," the voice in the gloom said.

Beecher looked around him, seeking the voice's body. He stood but found nothing. The voice speaking inside him frightened and confused him. "I need to find Art," he murmured, hurrying back downtown to the plumbing shop to find him, but Art was gone.

Art watched the celebration from the ridge above Grave Swamp. The Evil Ones danced around the Earth Man who stood in front of the scarred tree from which they had all emerged. Out of the brush of the floating bog, a human-shaped figure with a snake wrapped around its shoulders divided the revelers and progressed toward the Earth Man. The figure lifted the snake to the Earth Man, who took it, kissed its tongue, and placed it on the ground. As the beating of the dancers' feet and hoofs shook the swamp, the snake wrapped round the human figure's legs and up its body to its face. The snake's forked tongue slid into the figure's mouth and the two bodies merged into one, creating a snake-man, a slithering, reptilian body with the head of a human, the face of Karl Jurgens. The force of the Matchi-auwishuk had increased by one.

Art closed his eyes and felt them turn back into his head. Perception shifted, and the throbbing swamp transformed into a rolling sea.

# VI AMANDA WILSON

## 1

The Word speaks to all, in dreams and visions, in hopes and desires, in disappointment and despair. It allows the mind to see the near and the far, the true and the false. It erases distance and time, allows us to discern the actual from the supposition, the truth from the lie.

As the Word spoke to Art, his body yearned for sleep, but there was more to see, more to know about Beecher, his wife Sarah, the Matchi-auwishuk, the Earth Man… and Amanda Wilson.

The nightmare of the drowning man plagued Amanda all night. With each recurrence, her confusion and terror intensified. When she awoke on the bedroom floor embroiled in a death struggle with her bedsheets, she decided to stay awake. Shaken and battered, she rose, made herself a pot of coffee, and took her cup to the deck to watch as the rising sun behind her burned off the morning fog lying over the ocean.

As the light slowly revealed the waves sprinkled with purple, orange and red sparkles, Amanda's anxiety eased. The rhythm of the lapping water, the warmth of the cup in her hand, calmed her nerves. Still, the night of fearful dreams and lost sleep gnawed at her. Dreams were just dreams, she knew, yet the drowning man and her inability to bring him to safety made her feel weak and helpless, a sensation she despised.

The phone rang. When Amanda answered it, her mother was already crying.

"Amanda, I'm so sorry I wasn't there last night. I'm just... I don't know... It's so hard to get away from work and everything. I watched it on t.v., though. I am so happy for you."

Work was only an excuse, Amanda knew. And her mother could have called her anytime last night, but that was not the way her mother operated. Amanda just accepted it. Even though she and her mother loved each other, the practice of avoidance had become habit and they had worked it into an art.

"Did you like the speech?" Amanda asked.

"It was very sweet. Thank you. I didn't know you still remembered Wiggles the Worm." Her mother's voice halted. "We're all… we're all so proud of you."

Amanda spoke quietly, soothingly, as her mother sniffed, slurped, and sobbed into the receiver. This was one reason Amanda didn't phone home more often or look forward to her mother's calls. Her mother's sentimental outpourings always elicited a combination of guilt, happiness, loneliness, joy, grief, and love.

As usual, the issue of Amanda's birth went unspoken. For years it was never far from Amanda's thoughts, but now was a time for celebration, not for recalling the issue that had separated them long ago. Since Amanda left home, the two approached the matter like moths circling a streetlight on a hot, sticky August night, flitting dangerously close, but never near enough to cause themselves any real harm.

However, the underlying tension tore at them until after an hour, their emotions a scrambled mess, it was time to hang up. Amanda said good-bye and placed the wireless phone on the deck railing. The air grew chilly. A cold sun from behind the house shone on the sand and waves. The temperature reflected the bitter emptiness in Amanda's heart, a void that could only be filled and warmed when she finally knew who she was. Last night she had reached the pinnacle of professional success, success that verified her worth to society. Now it was time to verify it to herself.

The tautness from the nightmares kneaded itself into her shoulders. The morning air, a drowning man, an absent mother, and an urge to move, to travel, to seek the past, to find the truth – all linked by the frigid hollowness inside her – alternately spurred and paralyzed her.

The phone rang again. The sound rattled inside her belly. Amanda's mood lightened when she heard Sherman Lubovich's voice. Sherman was her best friend from college who now lived in New York and worked as a book editor for McKinley-Hurst. Besides her mother, Sherman Lubovich was the one person Amanda had wanted with her at the awards ceremony, but like her mother, Sherman's work had kept him away.

"It was a shit meeting," he told her. "My boss thinks this asshole is the second coming of Fitzgerald or Updike. So on the biggest night of your life, your best friend is stuck listening to this cretin explaining the subtle nuances of his protagonist's obsession with creative masturbation. Not even someone as brilliant as you could make a film out of this pile of crap."

"Oh, yeah. I'm a genius."

"You are. And beautiful. If I weren't involved..."

"Yeah, your boyfriend would probably object."

"Probably. Intolerant little bugger. Always causing trouble."

Amanda loved Sherman's laugh. He always knew how to lift her mood.

"Speaking of trouble," he said.

"Yes?"

"You're the one who's in for trouble now."

"What do you mean?"

"The machine is out to destroy you."

"What machine?"

"The great movie machine. They're never going to be happy until you write a sequel. First, they'll offer you money, then they'll appeal to your artistic nature, and before you know it you'll be sucked into writing *Bright and Shining Star II: The Wonder Continues.*"

"Yuck!"

"Get out of town now. Leave before they call. Run far away to where nobody lives."

"Actually, I was just thinking of that."

"Don't think. GO! If you let them get to you, it will be blasphemy. I'll have to hunt you down and torture you with white-hot safety pins until you see the error of your ways."

After they had teased each other unmercifully, they laughed their goodbyes and hung up. Amanda barely had time to put the phone down before Sherman's prediction came true. Three minutes after she said goodbye and firmly vowed to resist the temptations of demon Hollywood, Amanda's agent Herb Strickland called with his typical morning greeting, "Hey, Mandy! You up?"

Herb was the only person Amanda ever allowed to call her "Mandy." The familiarity and the condescension inherent in the name usually irked her, and she would imagine herself slowly decapitating the person with a fingernail clipper. However, with Herb she had come to accept the nickname as a term of fondness. There was something fatherly and endearing about Herb. She just could not tell him how much she detested that name.

"Yes, Herb. I've been up since 6:30."

"6:30? Are you crazy?"

"Probably, but that's another long story. I'll tell you about it sometime. How's London?"

"Wet. So, Gorgeous, are you feeling righteously pompous and arrogant today?"

"No, not really."

"Why the hell not? Not many people in the world have an Oscar to prove how great they are. You should be strutting around the house, reading your press clippings, sipping champagne..."

"It's a little difficult to feel anything when you haven't slept most of the night."

"Really? That sounds interesting. Who is he?"

"Not that. Just some weird dreams."

"Speaking of dreams, how'd you like to make some serious money?"

Here it comes, she thought. "I thought I had been."

"Mandy, Mandy, Mandy," he clucked. "We've only been on the beginning track until now. Do you know how much we can demand with that little man on your mantle?"

"Lots?"

"Gobs and gobs. After *Bright and Shining Star*, we're talking nearly the total annual budget of the state of Rhode Island, and after *Bright and Shining Star II*..."

"*Bright and Shining Star II*? Wait. Herb, I love you, but there will be no *Bright and Shining Star II*. Remember what you always say: 'Sequels suck!'"

"Yours won't."

"How do you know?"

"I have faith in you."

"Herb, I can't do a sequel. The story is over. All the main characters are dead. There's nothing more to say. My head feels like mush. There's not enough in there to come up with a story that would even interest a brain-damaged aardvark."

"Mandy, the studio wants a sequel and they want you to do it. I mean, they hold the rights anyway, so they're going to do one with you or without you. Wouldn't you rather have control over what happens to your story? They're talking guaranteed six figures. All you have to do is come up with something I can sell and..."

"Herb, no. I really need to shift gears for a while, fly to Alaska, maybe write a novel..."

"A book? I don't sell books. I sell scripts. I need a script, not a novel. How do you expect me to get rich if you write a book?"

"Herb, you can't tell me this house belongs to some destitute hillbilly. You're doing okay."

"*Okay* is not the goal, sweetheart. Rich… rich is the goal. We want to be rich. Maggie has her heart set on buying Scotland."

"Herb, I can't. I'm going nuts. Last night I had the same nightmare over and over. I was trying to save this drowning man, and by the end the person who really needed saving was me. That's what I'm going to do, save myself from drowning in all your Hollywood bull shit."

"Mandy..."

"Come on, Herb. Make up some kind of excuse. Tell them I'm researching. Tell them I'm waiting for my muse to instill me with a plot that will make the gods jealous. Hell, tell them I sprained both hands playing badminton. I don't care. I really need to get away."

There was silence on the other end of the line.

"You still there?" she asked. "Hello?"

"Yeah, I'm here. I'm just trying to figure out a way to tell Maggie she can't have Scotland."

Amanda laughed. Herb was back on her side.

"How long are you going to be away?" he asked.

"I don't know. A month or two... or eight. When I'm ready, I'll come back, and I'll have something bigger than *Bright and Shining Star*," she assured him.

"Promise?"

"I promise. Hug Maggie for me."

"All right. We'll talk when I get home."

After she hung up, Amanda felt both liberated and lost. She walked back inside and replaced the phone. Standing at the door, her eyes closed, she listened to the waves, hoping the water would speak to her. When it didn't, she walked back to the living room table, picked up her Oscar, and sat on the sofa, looking out over the ocean.

A bronzed man walked his golden retriever along the beach, occasionally tossing a piece of driftwood for the dog to fetch. Every time the dog returned with the stick, the man reached down, ruffled its fur, and spoke words of praise and encouragement.

Amanda looked down into the statue's featureless face and felt the metallic coldness of its skin against hers. There was no expression of happiness or despair, of love or hate, of wishes achieved or lost, simply a stoic blankness that portrayed as much emotion as she had ever allowed herself to feel.

Outside, the man and his dog sat down in the sand and watched the waves. The ocean swelled into large billows that broke long before reaching the shore and then slid slowly up and down over the beach, pulling pieces of the land back with it into the deep.

Amanda remembered the man in her dream, his writing in the sand which the waves always washed away, his reverence toward the moon and sea, his running naked into the water and his joyous splashing, his disappearance beneath the waves, his wet hair in her clutching hand. She wondered. What happened to him when she woke up?

The phone rang.

"Miss Wilson, this is Tommy Molten over at Serenity Studios. I'd like to talk to you about doing a film for us."

In rapid succession she heard from Eagle's Claw, Winding River, and New Jerusalem studios, all with the same proposal – a follow-up to *Bright and Shining Star*. She pulled the phone plug from the wall and hid the phone in the refrigerator.

She grabbed a swig of orange juice from the bottle, then went into the living room and plopped down on the sofa.

Leaning her head back against the sofa, Amanda closed her eyes. At first, all she heard was silence. Then the swell and surge of the surf outside the open doors turned to voices – her aunt Kathleen accusing her, her mother forgiving her, a gentle waitress telling her, "Honey, I've got it all figgered out." The words resonated. Amanda opened her eyes. Clouds now obscured the sun, and the cold wind had chased the man and his dog off the beach.

Amanda stood and placed the statue on the mantle. Quickly, she walked to her room to pack. The Oscar's face mirrored the blankness of the horizon, darkening with thickening clouds.

## 2

Amanda woke briefly when a bell above her sounded and the "Fasten seat belt" light came on. The plane shuddered and bounced as the sky outside disappeared into a grayish purple hue. High above the northern Great Plains, Amanda glanced out the window at the patterns of winter on the land far below her. The snow had seeped into the farmland like white paint onto a black canvas, revealing a monochromatic impression of civilizations past, of native hunters, of deified animals, of lost wanderers.

She forced herself to sleep again as the plane shivered.

Her dreams were like Art's, revelatory fantasies within a vision. In one dream, she was running *from*; in another, she was running *to*. In both dreams the destination was the same, and at the end of her flight awaited the feared answer, the desired unknown.

Far across the country, Art saw and heard her dreams. What was most important now was that she did not yet know him. But to become who she really was, she needed to, for he knew Beecher, the Matchi-auwishuk, the laughing woman, and Sarah. Amanda did not.

As the plane flew over the North Dakota plains, clouds increased. The air became riddled with invisible potholes that jostled and shook the fragile jet. Amanda woke when the flight attendant gently touched her shoulder. "Ma'am, would you please straighten your seat? We'll be landing soon."

"Thank God," Amanda thought. She brought her seat back forward, then stretched her legs. She held her chin in her hand and looked out at the light flashing on the end of the wing.

She had won the Academy Award for Best Original Screenplay. She had gained the respect of a world far larger than she could have ever imagined while she was in Sand Creek, Michigan. She knew that her mother, Sherman, Herb and Maggie loved her.

None of that was enough.

Somewhere there was something, someone to complete. In a philosophical flash of insight, she thought, "The world of humans consists of threes. Triangles. Trios. I am only one. There must be another person. Two other people.

Maybe her "trio" was an internal trait, not a person, she considered.

"Traits like what?" a voice inside her asked.

"There is inspiration." This she knew she had.

"There is creativity." This she also had.

"And?" the voice asked.

Amanda paused. There must be one more.

She nodded. She had to seek the "Bright and Shining Star," the light, the flame, the passion for herself, not for the fictional characters of her writing.

The plane jolted and bounced twice before it settled smoothly onto the runway at Fargo's Hector Airport. Amanda hadn't seen the ground until they were on it. The fog was thicker than she had seen in her dream at Herb and Maggie's house.

"Ladies and gentlemen, this is your captain. Welcome to Fargo, North Dakota. As you can see, the weather conditions are not really ideal. If you are traveling further tonight, please use caution. We look forward to serving you again."

At the car rental counter, Amanda jokingly asked the agent if Fargo were always foggy.

"No, it's just been bad lately. You gonna be here long, Miss Wilson?"

"Actually, I'm on my way to Jefferson, Minnesota."

"Jefferson, huh? You be careful. They've had this stuff even longer than we have. I guess it's really thick over there. I'd wait until the mornin' if I was you."

"Thanks. I'll be fine."

"I dunno. Some people are callin' it the killer fog. Heard a fella up there killed himself by runnin' headfirst into the side of a house. People thinkin' it was somethin' like cabin fever, ya know?"

"I'll be careful."

"Well, not that you're nuts or anythin'. Just watch the roads. Ya never know when some crazy'll do something stupid. Drive defensive. Y'll be fine."

Amanda agreed to be wary of any "crazies" on the road. After she and the rental agent plotted her route on the Minnesota map, she directed the white Mercury Topaz eastward across the Red River and deeper into the fog.

## 3

Amanda's headlights cut through the darkness and parted the fog like Moses's staff at the Red Sea. Led through the night up the valley and across the White Earth Indian Reservation into Jefferson, Amanda was unaware of what the fog had done to the town, to the people. She did not understand what had led her there or even that she had been led.

She took a room at Dale's Motel, showered to relax her tense shoulders, then lay on her bed, planning the next day's research to find her birth mother. Her efforts did not last long as sleep and visions crowded in upon her.

The Word showed her the world which she had entered, and though the faces were indistinct and unfamiliar, she felt at home, a part of the whole.

Amanda's mind relaxed into the dreams. She observed detached, yet integrated, into the design of the fabric. She saw a black Mercedes roadster parked in front of the Plains Cafe, a place she had never seen. A group of men rushed through the streets. A young woman lay in bed too frightened to sleep. An anger-scarred man leered from a window. She watched the erotic dream of a lust-filled woman too ashamed to sleep next to her husband.

And she saw Beecher writing words in the sands of her California beach, words that would soon disappear.

4

Outside, a thin vine of fog climbed the wall and surrounded Amanda' s window. The leaves of mist became fairy-like creatures crawling over the glass, watching Amanda in bed turn to the wall. The creatures smiled at each other silently a moment, then melted into a single face, that of the laughing woman. The vine grew into a body with arms and legs clinging to the corners of the window. The woman then kicked herself from the window, turning a somersault before landing.

The darkness and the fog disguised the woman's features, but they could not erase the familiarity of her immovable smile.

Amanda's presence confused the woman, yet her face remained unchanged, as if the smile were carved into stone. She squatted next to Amanda's car, thought, and pointed back up at Amanda's window trying to find an answer. Then she threw back her head and laughed. Her merriment stopped abruptly. She turned her head from side to side, listening, holding her breath. A voice called her. She scrambled back to the motel window. Inside, Amanda slept calmly, peacefully. The voice the woman had heard wasn't Amanda's.

The call pierced the night again. The laughing woman turned toward the highway, recognizing the voice. She looked back into the room, watched Amanda breathing deeply, then touched the window softly. Again, she heard the call. She pushed herself off the window and danced away into the night toward Grave Swamp.

# VII ART BENSON

## 1

The Word spoke to the Sufis, the mystics of Islam, teaching them that life's work is a twin task: first, to recognize and remember the Truth; second, to help others do the same. For centuries Art held the Truth inside himself and saw. He heard the wind of verity and caught it in his mouth. He recalled the face of life, created and sustained by honesty and hope. He understood. But others would not listen or see.

His appearance, his locked jaw frightened everybody but the Frank Thorstads of the world. The image of his contorted body and the sound of his deep, clipped grunts caused both children and adults to squirm and move away. Even though they needed to hear, he could not teach what he felt or what he knew. His stiff jaw and his crumpled posture prevented him from talking clearly or anybody from listening to him. Yet the Word chose Art to instruct Beecher. Then It had confused him by adding Amanda Wilson to the lessons, someone he never knew.

Amanda Wilson arrived in a cauldron of bubbling egos and emotions that emitted the fog of the Matchi-auwishuk, the fog of delusion and self-deception. When Art first saw her, he ignored the Truth, ran from its fire, and, like Jesus' disciple Peter, denied that he had ever known it. Now, however, was the time to confront it and to help Beecher and Amanda do the same. That was why, even though Amanda was at Dale's Motel, he had to follow the laughing woman's flight back to the beginning, back to Grave Swamp.

## 2

Art hid on the ridge, looking down at the island with its wounded cedar towering silently over the bog. At the tree's base, he saw the Earth Man, lying in a drunken stupor with his entourage scattered about the ground around him. Some had joined their master in inebriated slumber. Others cavorted over the bog, weaving their way through the brush, then darting up through the bare branches to skim low like sparrows back to the island where they tumbled playfully at the foot of the cedar. The Matchi-auwishuk had adopted pastoral personae – dryads, naiads, and fauns. The nymphs pulled the fauns to their feet, lining up the "goat-men" around the shore of the island, and, like children on a playground playing leapfrog, proceeded to play "leapfaun." The fauns playfully stomped in indignation, shook their gruesome torsos, and grabbed at the laughing female spirits that flew overhead.

Most lit harmlessly on the shore or bounced off the knitted vegetation that covered the bog. One unfortunate nymph, however, landed on the Earth Man's sleeping head. The man coughed and sputtered, flailing his arms wildly. Frightened spirits scurried in disarray across the surface of the island and into the brush. The man opened his eyes and gazed angrily over what remained of his apprehensive throng. His sweeping glare paralyzed every being in sight. Behind the sentinel cedar to his right, the nymph who had landed on his head ventured a giggle, but froze instantly when the giant turned on her and bared his teeth.

His form bent and shifted, slowly metamorphosing into that of a snarling wolf. Step by slow, stalking step, he advanced hungrily on the trembling nymph. Saliva dripped from his mouth and light burned from his vile, yellow eyes. Shakily, the nymph held her ground, staring directly at the wolf-god until he was within inches of her face.

Just as he opened his mouth to devour her, she reached behind her back for a grape, plopped it onto his tongue, and clamped his jaws shut with her hands. His eyes widened with surprise and struggled briefly to free his mouth. Then he swallowed.

He changed instantly. As if the grape were a goblet of intoxicating wine, his anger relaxed, his form shifted again to human. When he was fully himself, the nymph grabbed his hands, and they danced about the island, leaping, gliding, twirling. Finally exhausted, they fell embracing at the foot of the tree. The man kissed the nymph lustily. At first the nymph felt relief, but when she opened her eyes, she saw his yellow eyes sneering down at her. Before she could breathe, he rose, picked her up and flung her roughly over his shoulder. Turning to his followers, he pointed one finger to the sky, then brought his finger to his mouth to bind them to secrecy. The crowd smiled and nodded. The nymph fought hard, kicking and pounding the man's back as he carried her through the hole at the base of the tree and disappeared into the earth.

En masse, the followers rose with the fog and rested in the top branches of the brush, eyes fixed upward and deliberately ignoring the rustling below. The centaurs, nymphs and fauns eased away from the tree, taking care that their games would not disturb their master again.

Art's back reminded him of his own battle with the Earth Man years earlier, the one that had left him deformed and nearly mute. He rubbed the pain, then slipped off back to Thorstad's Perfect Plumbing, his earthly job. As he slipped through the brush he contemplated his next move, preparing to accomplish his life's twofold task: to recognize the Truth; second, to help Beecher do the same.

# VIII BEECHER JONES

## 1

In Jefferson the fog hung above the town like a leaden umbrella. Below it, the community awoke sluggish and aimless, mourning the death of Karl Jurgens, unsure and apprehensive of the new day. Beecher stood at the kitchen window. No apparitions danced across the lawn. During the night there had been no more nightmares. As he looked across the back yard, he could see houses and trees into the next block. Signs of recovery, he thought. Despite Karl's death, there would be school. One small step toward normality, Beecher thought.

Even Sarah was more upbeat. At breakfast she suggested installing a new shower stall in the upstairs bathroom. She told Beecher if she had time she would run over to Thorstad's and see what was in stock and get an estimate from Frank.

Beecher could not explain why, but he didn't want her to go to Thorstad's. Frank's history, the rumored physical altercations with his wife Sammi, his facial scar, and his incessant scowl induced chills and crawling skin. He frightened Beecher just by existing.

The legend of Frank Thorstad was more than anyone in town wanted to deal with. It began when he was a teenager.

One brightly moonlit night in Mid-July, Frank and two of his friends, Lennie Evenson and Andy Krosting, had spent the evening drinking and shining deer near Grave Swamp. Chasing a wounded buck, they ventured out onto the muskeg. Andy, the only one not carrying a gun, became fascinated by the wavelike motion of the floating earth. He jumped repeatedly, giggling wildly as the ripples tossed Frank into the bushes. As Frank pulled himself to his feet, he and Lennie saw Andy jump one last time. The earth, the two said, rose around him like the jaws of a hungry bear and swallowed him whole. What they had actually seen was Andy breaking through the surface and vanishing into the muck below. Nobody ever found his body.

Just days later, Lennie hanged himself from his girlfriend's clothesline pole. Within a week of Lennie's funeral, a highway crew found Frank in a gravel pit, lying in a fetal position next to his rusted-out Dodge, blood streaming from self-inflicted knife wounds on his face, arms and chest as he mumbled, "Kill me, too. Kill me, too." He survived physically, but one violent incident after another wracked his emotional recovery, culminating with him breaking his teacher's jaw. The three years at the mental hospital in Fergus Falls did little to improve his effect on the Jeffersonian impression of him.

Whether it was Frank's connection to the Grave Swamp legend, his constant rage, his disdain for a world that had made his life hell, or simply his whole demeanor that reeked of vengeance yet to be inflicted, Beecher feared being in the same room with him.

Beecher wanted to tell Sarah they could probably find cheaper fixtures in Bemidji, but then again he didn't want to dampen her enthusiasm. Besides, the unwritten rule of commerce in Jefferson prohibited him. Anybody else in town could shop elsewhere for the best bargains on appliances, cars, services, whatever; however, city and school employees, because they were, in effect, paid by the town, had to do their business locally. So reluctantly Beecher told Sarah to go ahead, check out Frank's. After all, he thought, maybe the price would be too high, maybe she'd be as afraid of Frank as he was, or maybe Frank would be run over by a truck. Then they could shop out of town. Beecher laughed at his paranoia. Sarah seemed happy. He should be, too.

Later that morning at school, teachers, still dazed by the news of Karl's death, struggled with their grief and their sense of duty to their jobs. When the students flooded through the doors, the noise and activity proved a welcome diversion.

By 8:30, calm settled over the building. Students relaxed into the class routine. Even though the halls were empty, the building vibrated with life. In his office, Beecher leaned back in his chair and closed his eyes. The Word spoke.

At first, Beecher heard the air sliding in and out of his lungs. Then school faded far off into the distance, and he was alone on a cool spring night, resting against a tree next to a lake. The quiet water mirrored even the smallest stars twinkling above him. Across the lake two moons rose over the forest; one full to overflowing, its light dripping down from the sky and spilling across the water to where Beecher lay; the other a crescent that hung like a giant handle by which one could grasp the heavens.

"Well, that's basically impossible," Beecher thought. He smiled. He knew he was dreaming, but he accepted the incongruity as benevolent and inviting. Within that dream he stood, took off his clothes and moved to the water's edge. He dipped his toe into the water, surprised by its warmth. He bent down, cupped his hands, scooped water from the light, and poured it over his head. Again he stood. He closed his eyes and raised his hands above his head, breathing in the night air that caressed his moist face. The peace of the night drifted over him, through him, below him. The night air flowed through him, about to lift him toward the moons when he heard a rustle in the brush behind him.

He turned. There next to the tree was the laughing woman. At her side crouched a growling wolf, its fangs bared. Draped about her neck was a hissing, red-eyed snake, its tongue flicking the air. Beecher stood before them naked, defenseless.

The three advanced slowly, menacingly toward him. There was nowhere to run. Then Beecher felt the warm water at his feet. He looked down and saw the full moon's beam, solid as a plank below him. He turned and saw the full moon smiling at him, inviting him to walk across the water to safety. Next to him the crescent lowered itself and dipped its corner down for him to hold so he could steady himself on his race across the lake.

At first, Beecher resolved to remain steadfast and defiant, but his strength faltered. For all his previous bravado, he could not face down the woman, the wolf, and the snake; and as beneficent as the moons promised, he could not force himself to trust their offering. Instead of racing across the plank of light holding tightly to the crescent moon, he plunged headlong into the water on his own. Before he had swum twenty yards, he was out of breath and out of strength. When he looked up, the moons rose into the sky and disappeared behind a cloud.

Desperation gripped him; he knew he could not swim across the lake, and he could not return to the shore with the laughing woman, the wolf and the snake. He kicked. He flailed....

He started. The intercom on his desk buzzed harshly. Beecher sat up, caught his breath and answered.

"Yes, Peggy?"

"Mr. Swenson and Tony Thorstad to see you, sir."

"Okay. I'll be right there," Beecher said. He stood up and tried to shake the remains of his daydream from his head. He took a long breath and slowly exhaled before opening his door.

In the outer office, Arnie Swenson, an English teacher, probably the school's most patient, paced furiously in front of Peggy's desk. In the corner sat Tony Thorstad, fuming and sucking on a skinned knuckle.

Resolving conflict between students and teachers was part of his job, but this was an unlikely pair of combatants. In six years, Swenson had sent but three students to the office for chronic tardiness. No one – students, fellow teachers, even his own mother – remembered Swenson in a bad mood. Tony was much the same. Unlike his father Frank, Tony was small, known more for his amiable smile and enthusiasm for life than his inclination for conflict. Yet here Tony and Swenson both were, their hands separated from each other's throats only by Beecher and Peggy's presence.

"What's this about?" Beecher asked Swenson.

Swenson glared at Tony, seething. "In the middle of class discussion, Tony started beating the crap out of David Thompson. If some students and I hadn't pulled him off, I think he would have killed him."

Tony slumped in his chair, crossed his arms, and looked down at the door sill. Beecher looked at Swenson quizzically. "David Thompson? He's twice as big as Tony."

"I know!"

Beecher silently examined them both a few moments. "Tony?"

Tony kept his eyes set on the door sill and mumbled, "Yeah. What he said."

Beecher waited for more, but when Tony's fixed eyes and set jaw promised no further explanation. Beecher turned to Swenson. "Where's David now?" he asked.

"Down in the nurse's office. He's got a few cuts, but I thinks he's going to be all right."

Beecher looked at Tony who rubbed his sweaty palms against his thighs.

"Let's go inside," Beecher said, opening the door and letting the two into his office. Tony slid sulkily into a chair in the corner; Swenson sat opposite Beecher.

"Mr. Swenson, let's hear your side first."

Swenson took a deep breath. "We're studying literature. We were talking about how the setting affects a story, the author's choice of subject matter, his theme, even his own reputation. I gave the example of Mark Twain and the Mississippi, Charles Dickens and Nineteenth Century London, and Edgar Allan Poe and his gothic settings of dark, lonely castles, dungeons, and tombs. Then we started talking about our recent weather and what kind of story it would inspire. David said something – I didn't hear what – and before I could ask, Tony jumped him. He knocked David out of his desk, threw him down on the floor and just started swinging his fists at David's head. I had to have three boys pull him off and get him out of the room."

Beecher turned to Tony. "What did David say?"

Tony glared back at Beecher. "He said he'd write a story about screwing some whore in the fog."

Beecher pursed his lips, then said, "Okay. Rather crude, but why did that make you so angry?"

"Because I..." He stopped and clasped the arms of his chair. His breathing became labored and his shoulders tensed as he forced back his original thought. When he regained control, he continued, "Because his attitude makes me sick. All he talks about is sex, who he's had it with, where he's had it. It's all a bunch of shit. He'd be lucky to make it with a drunken goat. I just got fed up. I snapped. I'm sorry." He lowered his head and gazed at his outstretched feet.

Beecher looked at his desktop and stroked his cheeks. There was more to the story, he knew, but it would have to wait. He took a deep breath, then looked up at Swenson. "What would you like me to do?" he asked.

Swenson shared Beecher's thoughts. He glanced at Tony. The boy gazed at the floor and pulled at the seam of his pants. He was angry, to be sure, but he also looked pitiful. After a moment, Swenson turned to Beecher and said, "Whatever you think is appropriate."

Beecher nodded. "You probably better get back to class. I'll talk to you later."

Swenson nodded and let himself out, closing the door behind him. Beecher went to his file cabinet and pulled out Tony's file. He sat down, opened it, and looked over the contents. Tony did not look up from his feet. Finally, Beecher threw the folder onto his desk and examined the silent boy in front of him.

"I don't get it, Tony."

Tony's front teeth chewed at imaginary gum. There was no response.

"You've never been in trouble. What's this really about?"

Tony shrugged.

"Something at home?"

Tony shook his head. Beecher tried to see his eyes, but the boy kept them hidden. "Kind of like Art Benson," Beecher thought.

He took a deep breath. "Well," he said, "I don't have a lot of choice here. I can't have fights in my school. I'm going to have to suspend you."

Tony nodded again.

"Five days."

Tony sucked in his lower lip, bit it, and wrung his hands in his lap. Finally, he looked up. "You gonna tell my dad?"

"I don't have any choice."

Beecher saw fear in Tony's expression, fear tinged with anger. He hadn't even asked about David. "Are you going to be all right?" Beecher asked.

Tony bit at his lip a moment, then whispered, "Yeah, I'll be fine."

Hesitantly, Beecher dialed the plumbing shop, all the while watching for Tony's reaction. When Frank Thorstad answered the phone, his voice was harsh and demanding. However, when Beecher identified himself, the response was silence. Beecher listened, and just when he assumed he'd been cut off, Frank grunted, "Yeah?"

"I have Tony here in my office. He's been in a fight. I have to suspend him."

Beecher kept watching Tony, whose eyes had become stony and cold. Again there was silence. Then Frank's gruff voice responded, "Hmm. How long?"

"Five days."

"Yeah, okay, fine. I'll tell his mom."

Beecher could tell Frank was about to hang up. Hurriedly, he asked, "Say, Frank, on a totally different subject, have you talked to my wife today?"

This time Beecher thought the silence had an edge. "No, why?" Frank asked.

"Well, we're thinking about installing a new shower stall upstairs, and she was going to get an estimate."

"No, ain't seen her." Frank grunted and hung up.

Beecher looked at the silent receiver a moment before placing it back on its cradle. "That is one strange man," he thought.

Tony kept looking at his hands. "What did he say?" he asked Beecher.

Beecher tried to reassure the boy. "Remarkably little," he replied.

Tony shifted uneasily in his chair. "Can I go home now, Mr. Jones?"

Beecher looked at Tony empathetically. "I'll give you a ride."

"I can walk."

"I know you can, but humor me. Okay? Go get your jacket and books and meet me back here, all right?"

Tony nodded silently and rose. Beecher opened the door for him and followed him into the outer office. As Tony walked down the hall to get his things, Peggy stopped Beecher.

"Mr. Jones, Joe Engstrom just called. He's over at Karl's house and wants you to call him."

"Now what?" Beecher said. He returned to his office, found Karl's home number, and called, assuming Joe would answer.

"Engstrom."

"This is Beecher. You wanted me to call?"

"Yeah. Can you come over here? To Karl's house? I've got some stuff I need to show you."

Beecher looked at his watch. "Well, I guess so. I have to take a student home, then I'll be right over."

As Beecher hung up the phone, Peggy came to the door. "Anything wrong?" she asked.

Beecher looked at her and managed a smile. "Based on the way the rest of the morning has gone? Probably." They both forced a laugh. "May I borrow your van? I have to drive Tony home."

Peggy tossed him her keys. Beecher found Tony at his locker, and the two walked in silence to the parking lot.

The drive across town was also silent. When they pulled up in front of the Thorstad house, Beecher turned and looked at Tony. His lower jaw worked his lips between his teeth; the thumbnail of one hand clicked against the thumbnail of the other. He made no effort to open the door and leave.

"Is there anything you want to tell me," Beecher asked, "about..." He hesitated. "About anything?"

Tony took a deep breath, then looked at Beecher. Beecher could see the words starting to form in the boy's mind, but then Tony turned away and shook his head. He opened the door, and just before he was about to leave, he muttered, "Thanks for the ride, Mr. Jones. I'll see you later."

Tony walked up the sidewalk, a lonely defeated figure burdened by a secret that separated him from the rest of the world. Beecher shook his head to remove his mind from writer's mode and back into principal mode. He pulled away from the curb, frustrated by his own inability to help.

As Beecher drove, the van, like the air, felt heavy. He looked up into the trees that lined the street. The fog perched in the trees, gazing down at him, smiling maliciously, knowingly. He knew the laughing woman was hiding high among the branches, "like a malevolent Puck relishing the pageant of my mortal trials and follies." Beecher forced his eyes earthward, pounded both hands on the wheel, and muttered, "Gah! Sanity control, Beecher. Sanity control."

Just before Beecher turned the last corner, the black Mercedes he had seen outside Joe's office sped through the intersection ahead of him.

Beecher watched as the foreign car roared down the street, then took a sharp left toward the highway. "Who the hell is that?" Beecher wondered. He'd have to stop by the Plains later. Somebody there would certainly know. He drove on to Karl Jurgens' house, wondering what Joe Engstrom had to show him.

Beecher pulled up behind Joe's squad car outside Karl's house, then let himself in the back door. The kitchen was small, barely large enough to hold a table and a couple of chairs. On the counter next to a coffee cup encrusted with two-day-old grounds lay a spiral notebook. The name *Laura* was written diagonally across the cover in multicolored block letters. The attempt to make them three-dimensional instead made them comically awkward and unbalanced. Beecher grinned at the innocence of Karl's undeclared love for Laura Grapnic and opened the cover. Nothing was written on the sheets inside, but a small wriggling strip of paper clung to the wire spiral. "Must not have liked what he wrote," Beecher concluded. He closed the notebook and called, "Joe, you here?"

"Upstairs," Joe answered. Beecher found him inside Karl's cramped bedroom. He was sitting on the bed, reading another spiral notebook. The cover had been torn and repaired with long strips of masking tape, each strip bearing a female name.

"What's that?" Beecher asked.

Joe shook his head, closed the notebook and tossed it toward Beecher. "I don't know. I think it's like a diary or a journal or something like that."

Beecher picked up the notebook and began to ruffle through the pages. "Karl trying to be a writer? That's a surprise."

"Not as surprising as what he wrote. Read a few pages."

Beecher looked apprehensively at Joe, then opened the notebook and read. His eyes widened. Amid the scratching and scrawling, nearly obscured by the barely legible handwriting and numerous spelling errors, was a vivid description of Karl's sex life. Whether the scenes were real or imagined was unclear, but as Beecher paged through the book, the activity became more lewd and violent, more pornographic. The image of a licentious and depraved Karl instead of the lovable janitor/Father Confessor Karl sickened Beecher. He closed the book and threw it back on the bed.

"Well..." Beecher sighed. "He certainly was... imaginative."

Joe looked up at him. "It's not all imagination."

"You can't think all this is true?"

"The acts? No. They're probably a bunch of harmless fantasies. But I noticed something. Look at the cover."

Beecher picked up the notebook and examined the cover front and back. "What?"

"They're real girls."

"What?"

"The names. Look at them. 'Nancy B.' 'Julie K.' 'Penny N.' They're all girls from school. Nancy Brandt. Julie Karsten. Penny Nichols. For every girl's name on the cover and in the story, there's a girl at school."

Beecher touched the cover. "All of them…"

Joe nodded. "Hot. Yeah… Sorry. I probably shouldn't say that."

Beecher sat down on the bed, eyeing the offensive notebook. "Probably not, but still…"

He looked at the names on the cover and paged through the filth of Karl's imagination. Joe was right. All the names were those of students. Again, Beecher felt his stomach turn. He swallowed hard and whispered, "God, Karl. They're just girls."

Joe took a deep breath and nodded. "It's gets worse."

Beecher looked at him, afraid of what could be worse.

"There was something about the physical description of the girls that seemed too detailed, too realistic. I mean, these descriptions are more than just girls he saw in the hall. I got curious and did a little looking around in here. I found this under the bed."

He pulled a shoe box from under the bed. "It's pictures," he explained. "Photographs taken in the shower room at school probably by a hidden camera.

He's got naked shots of every girl in that book. Go ahead. Look."

Beecher eased the cover off the box. There were two stacks of black-and-white photos, just as Joe had described. Beecher lifted a few to see if the subject matter were the same throughout the box. It was. He replaced the cover and set the box next to the notebook. He leaned forward, wishing he could curl up under the bed and make the room disappear. "I didn't need to see those," he said.

"Yeah, you did. And you need to know there are more," Joe said.

Beecher looked at him hopelessly. "More?"

Joe got up from the bed and opened the closet door. He pushed Karl's clothes aside and revealed three stacks of shoeboxes, each labeled chronologically dating back five years. "I'm afraid he's been at it awhile," Joe said.

Beecher was stunned. He gazed at the closet. "How did you...?"

"Think to look? I found this in the kitchen when I first came in this morning." Joe pulled a piece of paper from his jacket "It's what made me curious to start looking around."

Beecher took the paper and read:

> *Deer dairy – I cant do it no more. I got to turn over a new leef. I cant think them bad things. I don't want them grils no more. I want Mis Grapnick, but the only way I can git her is if I giv up those grils. An there jus grils.*
>
> *No.*
>
> *Less then grils, jus pitchers of grils i cant never touch.*

> *But Mis Grapnick – Laura – now shes a womin. I cood have her. If i give up my bad thots, mabe she'll no i'm not so bad, that i'm not jus Karl the janitor. Mabe she'll see Karl is her good word.*
>
> *But then i'd have to give up them pitchers – but i can do it. A guy said he'd buy em. I woont jus haveta throw em away. I kin do it. I'd give up anthing for Laura.*
>
> *I love her.*
>
> *I shoold tell her. After that thing with coche, i think she likes me.*
>
> *Yah, i'll go tell her. wish me luck.*

Beecher lowered the paper.

Joe said, "He was starting a new notebook. It was on the kitchen table. I figure he wrote that just before he went over to Miss Grapnic's house."

Beecher nodded. He rose and walked shakily to the door. He stared at length at the boxes. He thought for a moment, then turned back toward the room confidently. He walked back to the bed, picked up the notebook and shook it at Joe. "This is the snake," he said.

"What?"

"The pictures, the fantasies, the journal. This is the evil, the snake, he was offering up to Laura as a sacrifice for her."

"What? The snake in her dream?"

"Yes."

"That's crazy. How could Miss Grapnic dream what Karl was going to do? That doesn't make sense."

"Nothing makes sense, Joe. Does this fog make sense? Do all those sparrows running into Benny's wall make sense? Of course not. Neither does Karl having a closet full of pictures of naked school girls, running into a wall, and killing himself. But it's real. It happened." He shook the notebook at Joe again. "Karl's love offering being Laura's dream snake? So far this week, it's the only thing that does make sense."

"And the guy wanting to buy the pictures. What's that?"

"I… I don't know." Beecher's voice quavered and he sat on the bed. "Who would he sell them to?"

Joe put a hand on Beecher's shoulder. "Beecher, I think he was just writing. Look. I know Karl's death is a shock, and then all this on top of it… but be logical. This is not a metaphor. It's just a sick man writing. There's no way for Miss Grapnic to dream what *Karl* was thinking. Life doesn't work like that."

Beecher looked at Joe. "Of course, it does," he thought. "He just doesn't understand. We're not in control anymore. Not of our thoughts, our actions, our lives. The world is falling apart."

But he kept his thoughts to himself. He simply nodded and muttered, "What are we supposed to do now? What do you want to do with all this stuff?"

"Well," Joe said, "I don't see any need for this to get out, do you? It will only embarrass and hurt those girls. As far as Miss Grapnic's concerned, she's been through enough. Karl… Karl's dead. I would rather he be remembered for 'What's the good word?' and being a nice guy than for this." He hesitated, then added, "I'm thinking it's best to destroy it all."

Beecher looked curiously at Joe. "Is that legal?"

Joe shrugged. "Does it matter if it's what's right?"

Beecher nodded his agreement, then looked at his watch. "I should be getting back."

"If that camera is still in the locker room, we need to find it and get rid of it."

"God, I forgot about that." Beecher tried to organize his thoughts. "Okay. Meet me at the loading dock about nine. I'll let you into the locker room. You'll take care of this other stuff?"

Joe nodded. "Sure. You gonna be okay?"

"Yes," Beecher mumbled absently.

He left the house, got into Peggy's van and slammed the door. He sat silently, trying to comprehend what the Word had said, trying to make sense of all that had happened. This morning he had been so hopeful, so sure things were getting better. Now he doubted they ever would. He knew the Evil One. He felt the Matchi-auwishuk. Anger rose within him, and he pounded the steering wheel with both fists and cursed. As he leaned forward, his head on the wheel, sorrow erased his anger. Sobs burst from his lungs, and he leaned over onto the seat, weeping. After several minutes, he turned and looked up through the windshield. He saw the fog poised just above the trees like a gray leopard about to pounce on its prey. He sat up and shouted at it. "What? Are you going to kill me, too? Running out of the easy and the weak? Birds? Karl?"

The air was silent. The fog was motionless.

He sat up, started the van, slammed it into gear, and drove back to school. When he got back to his office,

Peggy was surprised to see him. "Mr. Jones. I didn't think you'd be back until this afternoon." She paused, trying to be tactful, but finding no other way, she asked, "Everything all right? You don't look so good."

"Thanks, Peggy. I love you, too. I'll be fine. How are things around here?"

"Fine. No more fights."

Beecher sighed. "That's good. I'm going to go downtown for lunch. I'll be at the Plains if you need me."

Peggy could barely reply with a muffled "Bye" before Beecher was gone.

## 2

The Plains Cafe was much the same as the citizens of Jefferson; appearance was far different than reality. Outside, false brick made of cracked and weathered plastic covered the front wall of rotting wood as high as the base of the wide, aluminum-framed windows. The tinted windows were great artless rectangles gouged out of the once masterful 1920s façade. The first owner had emblazoned the glass with "The Plains: Good Food and Company" in barely legible red-and-white script that no one had bothered to refurbish. Above the windows a slightly matching red-and-white awning sagged under its own weight, and a shrouded, clunky air conditioner protruded from the warped wooden siding like a giant carbuncle. Hanging over the entrance was a rusty Coca-Cola sign which creaked every time the heavy door opened and closed.

Inside, the family dining room was clean, warm and friendly. Surrounded by wood-paneling and an astounding display of softball and bowling trophies, the local widows, clergymen, salesmen and farmers feasted on the good food and company advertised on the window. Here nurses from the clinic, grocery store clerks, and bank employees escaped their humdrum workplace for an hour and mingled with travelers, clinic patients, shoppers, and other commoners, but not, if it could be helped, "those people," which referred to any racial minorities, refugees from the assisted living home down the street, and Swedes. In the kitchen a radio playing an eclectic mix of country-western music, local news, and rebroadcasts of Paul Harvey's *The Rest of the Story* diverted the stream of banter between cook/ proprietor Hattie Long, the dishwashers, and the waitresses.

Beecher knew the Junta had sequestered themselves in the back room, safely away from the rabble, probably deciding his future. Right now he didn't care. As a school administrator, Beecher was a de facto member of the group, but today he had no desire to listen to their directives nor listen to their theories on the fog and Karl's death. Neither did he have anything he wanted to tell them. He thought a second about the black Mercedes, but today, he just wanted to eat by himself in silence.

He took a seat in the corner booth by the window. Clarice, his usual waitress, brought him a glass of water and a menu, but before she could ask Beecher why he was sitting up front, Hattie called her back to the kitchen to pick up an order. Beecher only gave the menu a cursory glance before laying it on the table. His stomach had already had enough upheaval for one day; he was not going to mess with his diet. He'd just have his usual chicken basket.

Across the hazy street, squatting between the buildings, Art Benson muttered to himself and squinted through the fog at the Plains' front window. "Who's he talking to?" Beecher thought, searching up and down the street.

Then a disturbing idea struck him.

"Is he talking to me?" he wondered.

He shook his head to clear his mind, closed his eyes, took a deep breath, and rolled his head around his shoulders.

Out front a car pulled into the vacant spot usually reserved for Joe Engstrom. "Now what?" Beecher thought. He opened his eyes, half expecting to see the Mercedes, but instead he saw a white Topaz. A woman pulled a hood over her head and bent over to pick up something from the passenger side of the front seat. As she opened the door, Beecher tried to see who would so impudently break local tradition by parking in the policeman's space. However, as the woman arose, the hood hid her features. She emerged from her car, clutching a book bag with a broken handle to her chest like a mother nursing her child,

Beecher sat upright. This woman, her hood, her walk, the way she carried the bag close to her chest – he had seen her before.

"Not that it matters," he thought. He closed his eyes and continued his deep breathing to relax his mind. The bell above the front door rang as the door opened and closed. Beecher opened his eyes. The woman entered the restaurant and laid her bag on the table two booths in front of him. Beecher pretended to stare out the window as she pulled back her hood, revealing her blonde hair and freckled face. He looked down into his water as she laid her cloak on the back of her booth and sat facing him.

When Beecher looked up, Clarice was bringing the woman water and a menu.

"Hello dere, ma'am. I'm Clarice, and I'll be your waitress. The specials are on da board up dere: salmon loaf dinner vit' mashed potatoes and creamed peas; meat loaf dinner vit' mashed potatoes and gravy, and steamed carrots; and turkey melt sandwich basket. Any a dose sound good to ya, or wouldja like ta check da menu?"

The woman looked up and smiled at Clarice. "I think I'll look at the menu for a little bit."

"Okay. I'll be back in just a jiffy den."

Even though the woman had only said a few words, Beecher recognized the voice, the dark tones resonating again inside his belly, at once exciting and terrifying him.

"You wancher usual den, Beecher?" Clarice's voice startled him, and he jumped. She put her hand on his shoulder. "I'm sorry, honey. Did I scare ya?"

Beecher tried to hide his embarrassment. "No, that's all right. I was just... Yeah. The usual. That will be fine."

When he handed Clarice his menu, she was looking across the street.

"What's wrong?" he asked her.

She looked a bit longer, then asked, "Is that Art Benson hidin' between the buildings over dere?"

Beecher followed her gaze. Art still sat, mumbling. "Yeah. I think so."

"That guy's really nuts. You know that?"

Beecher nodded. "Yeah, I kinda agree with you."

"Did you know he's a half-breed?" her eyes fixed on the hunched body squeezed between to bulging walls.

"I heard that. Yes."

"That's probably why he's crazy. Too much Chippewa. ' Course any is enough to make ya bat-shit bonkers."

Beecher shuddered inside. He always detested the anti-Ojibwe remarks he heard everyday in Jefferson. But even more, he detested his inability to say anything to stop them. His job dictated that he keep peace, and part of that, at least so he thought, was ignoring comments like Clarice's.

"Better to pretend she never said it," he thought.

Beecher touched her arm. "Clarice?"

She looked down at him."Yeah?"

"My food?"

She laid her hand on his shoulder and laughed. "Oh, yeah. Sorry 'bout dat. I'll have it right out to ya," she said, turning toward the kitchen.

Beecher could not force himself to look at the woman sitting in front of him. Instead, he took the water glass in both hands, and again stared into it.

"It can't be her. She was just a dream in the fog," he thought, but when he glanced up, it was the dream woman. The downcast eyes, the blonde hair, the freckles, the quiet innocence, the hooded cloak, the voice – it was Amanda Wilson.

His glance transformed into a stare, despite his best efforts to resist the change. As she lowered the menu, took a notebook from her book bag, and began writing, Beecher knew. She was no apparition. She sat not twenty feet away, placid and stately, oblivious to his presence. If he could touch her...

As if she heard his wish, she slowly raised her eyes. Her smile spoke of a centuries-old acquaintance.

Beecher squeezed his eyes shut, covered them with both hands, pretending to rub his forehead. He turned to the window. When he finally dared, he opened his eyes and looked across the street. Art had disappeared, but high atop the drug store across the street stood the laughing woman. She gave Beecher a mock scolding, shaking her finger at him. Then she laughed, whirled, and vanished into the air. Beecher bit his lip in anger, grabbed his glass with both hands, and glared down into the water, his anger mounting.

He did not know yet what Amanda represented or whose side she was on.

# IX AMANDA WILSON

## 1

She was on Beecher's side, the side of the Word. She, Beecher and Art would confront the Earth Man, the laughing woman…

Art hesitated. "There must be a third," he thought as he shuffled down the street through the fog. Although he knew much of the workings of the Word and the Earth Man, he did not know who the Earth Man's third was. He wasn't even sure if the laughing woman was the second. True, his vision had increased the past few days, but there was so much more to see. His mind turned to Amanda Wilson.

For Amanda the moment of Beecher's awkwardness was comical. She laughed to herself. She hadn't meant to embarrass this stranger, but he could have been a little more discreet in his examination of her.

When she first saw him, his face looked familiar. She couldn't help herself. She smiled. For some reason that innocent smile had so disarmed him, he nearly spilled his water glass all over himself, trying to look inconspicuous and turning to the window.

When the waitress came for her order, Amanda handed her the menu, asked for the salmon loaf special, and then reached into her bag for her journal. Outside, she saw the fog had slunk down onto the street. She furtively glanced at the man in the booth in front of her and saw him steadfastly gazing out the window, avoiding her eyes. Amanda grinned and began to write.

A moment later she heard the crack and spray of shattered glass, looked up and saw the man hurrying for the door. The cafe door slammed behind him and she watched out the window as he stalked away angrily into the fog, holding both of his hands in front of him in pain. His walk, his face reminded her of somebody she knew. In the instant they had looked at each other, she recognized him and he her.

An image stirred in her memory, but before it was completely formed, it disappeared into mist as the man had just done. She attempted to recapture the image by reflecting on the fog-enshrouded street before her, but its surrealism and dreaminess only distracted her more. She returned her attention to her journal and began writing.

Two booths away, a shattered glass stood on the table. Drops of blood mixed with the glass shards and spilled water.

Beecher was gone.

# X ART BENSON

## 1

In his role of herald, time and space slipped through Art's fingers like water. As seer, he stood among the clouds of vision and reality, the fog which confounds and corrupts the world. He felt the rain of the Word drench him with its truth. After centuries of spells and otherworldly experiences, he no longer searched for rational explanation. He simply accepted and experienced all. How it is possible to transcend place, thought and time, he did not know nor care; he was simply aware that everything is, was, and will be – now, then and forever; here, there and wherever. He knew the Word sees all, knows all, and reveals what it will, when it will, to whomever it will.

Even while he observed Beecher's struggle against the Matchi-auwishuk, Art awoke to the scene when the man in the black leather jacket slid noiselessly into the plumbing store. At the sales counter that had once housed hundreds of bowling shoes in the dilapidated building's former life, Frank pawed through a pile of sales slips under the cash register, increasingly incensed with his nonexistent filing system.

The man slapped the counter and roared, "Hey there, partner. Interesting place you got here."

"What the…?" Frank started, and the sales slips scattered across the counter and floor like confetti. "Shit!" Frank glowered at the man. "Who the fuck are you?"

"Sorry. I didn't mean to scare you. Here, let me help you pick up this stuff."

"Just leave it! Whattaya want?"

"Name's Wayne Diego. Just checkin' out the place here. Heard a lot about it downtown. Thought I'd see for myself. Used to be a bowlin' alley, they say,"

"Yeah. And a pool hall. And a Legion Club. So?"

"Nothin'. Kinda cool how you kept some of the decor. The gutters, the ball returns, that giant scoresheet on the wall. A perfect 300 game. 'Thorstad's Perfect Plumbing.' Pretty clever and original for a plumbin' shop. Interestin'."

"Yeah. Thanks. You here to buy something?"

"Nope. Actually, since I can see you're so imaginative, I have a business proposition might intrigue you."

"Business proposition?" Frank huffed. "Ain't interested. Got enough problems with this one." He knelt and began picking up the slips off the floor behind the counter.

Diego leaned over the counter and smiled. "Oh, I know, but I think this will be right up your alley…Hah! Alley. Get it?"

Frank scowled. "Yeah, I got it. Whattaya want?"

Diego leaned over the counter and looked up at Frank's face. Frank fingered his scar protectively. "Let's just say you can make a lot more with me than you can selling plumbing fixtures and cleaning up other people's shit."

Frank looked up. "Yeah? How do you know?"

"Been watching you," Diego said. "You're just the man for the job I have in mind. Sellin' somethin' people want, to people who wanna buy. Lots of 'em eager to buy. For tons of cash. No records to keep. No taxes to pay. In just a few days, you'll make a helluva lot more money than you could in a year in this place."

Slowly, Frank stood, captivated by the sound of Diego's voice and the promise of riches.

"Shall we go talk in your office?" Diego asked. He pointed to the door. "That the 'pool hall'?

Frank nodded, then called, "Art? I need you to watch the front."

The crumpled man in the warehouse scrunched behind large packing crates and did not answer.

"Art! Damn it, where are you?"

The Word held Art silent and still behind his shield.

"Fuckin', lazy-ass Indian. Just like the rest of 'em." Frank went to the front door and looked out on the empty street. "Well, shit. Ain't nobody around anyway. Damn fog."

"Shall we?" Diego said, gesturing toward Frank's office.

Frank nodded and led the way inside. Closing the door behind them, Diego let the sweet syrup of flattery drip from his voice, softening Frank's rage.

Hidden in his makeshift cubicle, Art heard Diego's words for what they were, but had no way to stop Frank's ears against their seduction. The promise of riches and Diego's charm relaxed Frank's inherent volatility into good-natured humor and affability. The two joked and laughed. Their laughter turned to talk of business, first, as quiet banter, which soon led to conspiratorial whispers. In hushed tones, their words droned through the shop, monotone and unintelligible. Art didn't need to hear them articulated. He had heard them before.

Art rose from the boxes  and wandered into the showroom just as Beecher's wife Sarah pulled up outside and parked next to Diego's black Mercedes. She wore her black cloak with the hood up and sat in her car, listening to the radio.

At the same time Frank and Wayne Diego in the next room worked on the details of their impending business deal, the Word spoke to Art. He heard Sarah inside her car. He could feel what she felt. He thought what she thought.

The heater blasted warm air into her face and onto her feet. Still she shivered. A lightness filled her chest, and her hands trembled in her lap. Fear had brought her here, but fear also kept her from getting out and entering the shop.

Her thoughts spoke of the two sleepless nights she had spent reliving the jumbled, flashing images of sex on a frosty lawn. Long ago, she reminded herself, she had abandoned the base urges she felt that night. Over the years she had built up her defenses and cultivated respectability in place of hedonism. However, since her surrender Monday night, Sarah alternately craved the excitement and the sheer perversion of the moment, and loathed herself for her weakness. She agonized over her betrayal of what she had become – wife, mother, businesswoman – but feared she would never again experience the total submission to sensuality she felt in that foggy darkness. She yearned for both the tranquility of the dutiful wife and the electricity of the decadent slut. Her thirst for momentary pleasure terrified her. That she had come to Thorstad's Perfect Plumbing to pursue it paralyzed her.

Boredom could not justify, erase, nor explain her actions of Monday night. Nor could it account for why she was here "to buy a new shower stall." Instead of making choices, she thought, choices were making her.

Just as a night of heavy drinking could lead to a torturous hangover, Sarah's night of passion had its price. She had gone to The Man clean, but empty. Now she was neither. Whenever she closed her eyes, she choked on the smoky smell of his hair; grew dizzy from the whirling, dancing fog; and feared the identity of that other voice. She remembered the shame of feeling the cold ground on her naked body. Worse, she felt the filth still oozing from her pores, sometimes staggering her with its stench.

For once, she longed to return to innocence; again, she realized the futility of her wish. Something was growing inside her. She could feel its cells dividing and multiplying, forming an entity she struggled to define: an infection, a disease, a growth, an indefinable deformity conceived in a moment of depravity long ago that lay dormant for years and now fed off her body, mind, and soul. She hated it; she loved it.

Behind Art, the door to Frank's office opened and the two men stepped out. Frank smiled and shook Diego's hand.

"I'll see ya in a bit down at the Plains. I got a couple things I gotta take care of," Frank said. He saw Art and bellowed, "Damn it, Art! Where the hell have you been?"

Before Art could answer, Diego smiled and said, "It doesn't matter now, does it? He's here. Now, don't go standing me up, Frank. If we're going to get this by the city fathers, I'm going to need a local guy to show 'em what we can do. I can't think of anybody I'd rather have."

Frank laughed. "Yeah, well, someday let me tell ya what people think of me around here."

"Ah, it's all a matter of perception. I got 'em all set up one by one. Now all we have to do is bring 'em together. That's where you come in."

"I'll do what I can."

The phone rang. "See you in a bit," Frank said, waving and returning to his desk. Diego closed the office door, and turned to Art.

Though the two had never met in their present incarnations, Art knew Diego's face and Diego knew his. Art heard different names in his head, yet he could not find the right one. The nuns at the reservation school would have called Diego "The Shining One" or Lucifer. The Hebrews would call him Satan or "The Adversary." The Muslims knew him as Iblis. He was none of these. Milton most accurately referred to him as Beelzebub, the prince of demons, who commanded legions of the Matchi-auwishuk, the Evil Ones, on their destructive mission. Disguised as human, he had yet to reveal himself to man, but the time was near. Like an immature schoolboy, his pride prevented anonymity.

He belonged to the Earth Man. He was the Second. He was the adversary Beecher must overcome. Art wanted to scream Diego's identity to the heavens, but he could do nothing.

As Diego stood at the door, sneering at him, Art realized Diego knew Art's role in the coming struggle better than Art did himself. The nature of the battle to come was clear to Art, but he could not fight. He could only warn, speak as the Word directed. In himself Art was nothing. Diego felt the Word within and around Art, but defied Its authority. He smiled insolently and unmasked himself.

The smooth, handsome face bubbled, then withered as his body stretched to the ceiling, tautening skin against skull and bones. The flesh turned ashen and his eyes sunk deep into their sockets. He opened his mouth and his jagged teeth dripped blood of freshly killed meat. His breath reeked with the stench of death and decay, filling Art's nostrils and nauseating him. The air in the room crackled and bristled with cold.

Then Art knew. Western religion did not know this creature. This was not Milton's Beelzebub nor the demons of the nuns and priests. This was not a Matchi-auwish Art's Anishinabe mother spoke of, yet it did reside in the same cosmos of the manitous. Wayne Diego was Weendigo. He would not be alone.

Art remembered that the Weendigoes eat of human excess and lust, always craving more. They seek out the self-indulgent, the greedy, the licentious, the narcissistic. Just what the Great Masking exposed. And each new passion and desire destroys judgment, leading man ever closer to destruction, for the Weendigoes have no goal but to devour men and women enthralled with their own desires.

In Anishinabe tradition, the Weendigoes were everywhere — in the forests and swamps, in the reservation towns, even in the winter winds that chilled Ojibwe houses.

When Art grew up, his mother regaled him and his friends with tales of the terrors of the Weendigo. The nuns and priests, eager to replace Anishinabe superstition with their own, blunted his mother's horror stories with the words of King David. Of all the words given Art by Buddha, Lao Tzu, Jesus, and Mohammed, as well as the promised protection of a host of manitous, it was those Davidian verses the Word spoke at that moment in Thorstad's Perfect Plumbing to and through Art as he gazed into the sepulchral eyes of the Weendigo:

*Though I walk through the Valley of Death*
*I shall fear no evil…*

Art looked to the heavens beyond the ceiling and cried,

*For You are with me.*
*Your rod and your staff, they comfort me.*

Both Diego and Art blinked in surprise at the clarity of the verses, but they also both knew it was the voice of the Word that had spoken, not Art. Momentarily stunned, the Weendigo shrank before the broken Indian. Gone were the bloody teeth, the sunken eyes, the skull-like face. Again, he was Wayne Diego, the man in the black leather jacket, now staring straight ahead, almost catatonic. Then gradually, his skin glowed with life and he regained his sight.

He looked at Art and grinned, speaking in the voice of his master. "Once again, huh?" he asked.

Though the voice was that of the Earth Man, Art knew Diego was powerless before the Word. Art nodded. "Once 'gain."

"This time it will be different. No Teachers, no Buddhas, no Messiahs."

"Never different. New names, new places, but always same. Word constant. Word strong."

"Of course, it is," Diego snickered, "but how's your back?"

Unseen arms grabbed Art's shoulders and twisted him, wrenching his back and forcing him to the floor. Pain pounded up Art's spine and into his forehead. He gasped for breath and clutched for the Weendigo's leg, but he deftly danced away, bent down, gave Art the Jefferson two-fingered salute, and left.

As the door shut, the metal, porcelain, and plastic of plumbing fixtures and material warmed the air, and Art's pain subsided. Although the Weendigo was gone, the essence of his being hung from the walls like poisoned mucous. Art pulled himself to his feet and shuffled to the front door. Outside, Diego stood next to his Mercedes and leaned against Sarah's car, motioning for her to open her window.

She lowered the glass, and through the door Art felt Diego salivate at the smell of her blood.

"Waiting for me, Princess?" he asked her.

Sarah shook her head. "No, I'm just...just..." She didn't know what to say. The stranger should have frightened her, but her memories distracted her from the moment.

"Just what?" Diego asked. When Sarah couldn't reply, he reached his hand through the window and said, "Name's Wayne Diego. What's yours?"

Hesitantly, Sarah held Diego's bony hand weakly in her own. His grip was cold, almost fleshless. She couldn't answer.

"My god, you're a beautiful woman," Diego told her. "How'd you like to come with me to California? I can make you famous."

"I bet you can," Sarah whispered. Unaware of who or what he was, she forced a weak smile.

"You'd like that, wouldn't you? To be famous?" His voice oozed and dripped from his mouth like sap.

Sarah finally looked at him. He reminded her of a television evangelist, who beneath the promise of hope and salvation is always selling something. Still she could not sense his evil. Her own depravity blinded her to the foulness seeping into her car. She turned away and watched the shop door. She said nothing. Diego followed her gaze, thought a moment, then nodded.

"Another time then," he said.

Sarah mumbled, "Another time."

Diego slid behind the wheel of his car and started the engine. He sat for a moment, revving the engine, and when Sarah wouldn't look, he honked his horn until she did. She finally turned to him, annoyed by the noise. He smiled and gave her the same two-fingered salute he had given Art. Feebly, she waved back.

The Mercedes backed into the street. Diego again revved his engine, then burned rubber to the intersection. Turning left onto the highway, he headed downtown. Sarah stared at the empty lane where the car had disappeared. "Small penis," she thought. "Arrested maturity and a small penis."

# XI SARAH JONES

1

Sarah turned back to the plumbing store. "There's no sense just sitting here," she said. She put her keys into her purse and entered the shop to pick out her new shower.

Through the hodgepodge of sinks, toilets, faucets, and other supplies scattered in any open space on the floor, Sarah threaded her way toward the service counter. Unlike the precise, displays set up on the old bowling lanes, the lobby was a cluttered maze" that belied the name "business place." Sarah rubbed her finger across the edge of a random sink near the counter, checking for dust.

Something was wrong in this room, she knew, but she did not know what. Only Art knew what she sensed

– the Weendigo's presence that still hung in the air, fouling the light and crusting over the ancient wood paneling.

Art, unsure what to say, waited at the counter, his lips forming unvoiced words.

Sarah saw Art but quickly turned away. Apprehension danced about her, and Art's appearance did not ease her mind. His very posture questioned the veracity of the persona before him, just as Sarah did herself.

She took a half-step back as if to escape, then reconsidered and rested her hands on the counter that separated the two of them.

Art smelled Sarah's panic and knew its source. She feared the Weendigo, Art, Frank, Beecher, herself.

For a moment, she twisted her wedding ring and avoided Art's eyes. Wiping crumbs from Frank's ham sandwich from the counter's edge, she pasted on a smile and said, "Hi, Art. I need an estimate. Beecher and I want to put in a new shower in our upstairs bathroom."

"Mm," Art grunted. He wanted to alert Sarah to the danger of Wayne Diego, but words would not form in his mouth. His grunt inadvertently challenged her credibility, and she shifted her weight nervously from foot to foot. Art would have reassured her, but he could talk of nothing more than plumbing business. "Not good… with numbers," he told her. "Frank's on… phone."

Behind the office door, the phone crashed to the floor. "Shit!" Frank yelled.

"Off now," Art said. Sarah smiled at him.

Frank flung open the door and burst from his office. "Art, I have to..." When he saw Sarah, he halted abruptly. He struggled to put on his business face. "Mrs. Jones. I was just talking to your husband."

"Yes, I have that reaction to him myself sometimes." She smiled shyly.

Art watched their faces, then turned to the door. The Weendigo had driven away in his Mercedes, but his laugh still echoed in Art's ear.

Frank forced a grin. "It was about my son. Got suspended. Damn kid," Frank explained. "Anyhow, I hear you wanna buy a new shower."

"Well, we're just thinking at this point, trying to figure out prices, and so on."

Art cringed as Sarah examined his back. Its doubt-filled curvature made her uncomfortable. In the window, Art watched her reflection as she rubbed her neck.

"So you want an estimate. Come into my office an' we'll see what we can figure out."

"Okay." Sarah replied. As she walked into Frank's office, Art turned and watched her. She felt his stare follow her, Art knew, but she would not turn. Frank shut the door behind them.

Slipping into the warehouse, Art again hid among the crates. He invited the spell by closing his eyes. Instantly, the Weendigo's bony face stared down at him, snickering. Despite that Diego's laugh annoyed more than terrified, Art turned his face to the ceiling, searching for the Word. Instead, he heard the Weendigo's laughter stop as the grinding of its teeth drowned out the rumbling of its stomach.

"So, what kinda shower d'ja want?" Frank asked inside the office. "A simple stall? Combination tub and shower? Steam?..."

Sarah sat in a rickety and scarred wooden chair facing Frank's desk. "Well, I don't know. I thought I'd just see what you have, and..."

"How big is your bathroom?"

"I don't have measurements. It's pretty good sized, I guess."

"Well, it would be a hell of a lot easier to know what to show ya if I knew how much space we were talkin' about," he laughed. "God! Women! Don't know shit about nothin', not even what they want, and then they get pissed 'cause we men can't figure 'em out." He leaned back in his chair, both hands behind his head and his feet crossed on top of the stack of plumbing catalogues on his desk.

His arrogance rankled her. She hated him, but she wanted him. Why, she could not explain. He was everything she detested in men and in herself. And yet here she was. She sat up in her chair and began picking at the stuffing peeking out of a hole in the arm cushion. After she had regained her composure, she looked at him.

"Frank," she began, "do you really think I'm here to talk about a stupid shower?"

His sneer oozed across the desk. "Like I just said, how the hell should I know?"

"I want to talk about what happened Monday night and what we're going to do now."

Frank snorted. "Monday night? What happened Monday night?"

"You know what happened Monday night."

He raised his eyebrows and shrugged. Sarah sighed, exasperated. "Monday night, when you and I… you know," she said.

"What the hell're you talkin' about?"

"On your lawn? When you and I… had sex?"

"What?" Frank howled as he sat up, his feet hitting the floor with a crash.

"Shh. I don't want Art to hear."

Frank strode to the door, opened it and, seeing Art was not in the showroom, locked the door. He turned to Sarah. He lowered his voice to a hoarse whisper, but retained his disbelief. "You're sayin' you and I fucked on my lawn Monday night? Where the hell was I?"

"You were there. First, you were inside watching TV, but then you came outside to smoke. I watched you from behind the tree. At first I was scared you would see me, but then I realized you already knew I was there. I stepped out so you could see me."

Sarah paused as tears formed in her eyes. Had she just imagined it? "You came to me, undressed me, and took me. Right on the lawn. You took me."

"Lady, it may be warm for March, but it's still fuckin' cold. Why would I want to do that? I'm not as crazy as people say."

She looked up at him, her voice quavering. "I don't know why it happened, but it did. And even as we lay there in the snow, I didn't want to love it, but I couldn't help myself. I wanted more, and then..."

Her voice broke and she looked down at her hands. "And then, just as I came, I heard a voice – I don't know who it was – but you were gone."

She raised her eyes to him again. "You left me, naked, on the lawn."

Frank stared at her, then finally went back to his chair and leaned forward, his arms on his desk. "And they say I'm nuts. Look," he said, "I know I spent all that time in Fergus, but you'd think if I fucked you, I'd remember."

Sarah wiped her face, then continued picking at the chair's stuffing. "You must remember. I do… every sound, every breath, every... I can still feel you on me, in me." She looked up at him and sniffed. "What happens if I'm pregnant?"

"Lady, if you're pregnant, it ain't me. Hell, I wouldn't touch your tight ass with a crowbar."

She stared at him. His sardonic smile increased her frustration, her anger, her shame. Sniffling and biting her lower lip, she stood to leave, but looked at him one more time. His grin sickened her. She turned and walked to the door, defeated. Just as she was about to open it, she paused, thought, and checked the lock, making certain it was secure. She turned back to him, lifted her head, and stood erect.

"You don't remember?" she asked, haughtily. She unhooked her cloak, dropped it to the floor, then she slowly began to unbutton her blouse.

The smile disappeared from Frank's lips. "What are you doing?" he asked.

She smiled at him and said nothing, slipping out of her blouse and letting it slide to the floor. Stepping forward, she unhooked her bra, held it out, and dropped it on his desk. She stood before him, her bare breasts mocking his denials. "You don't remember these?"

Frank looked at her, pursed his lips and shook his head. He rose slowly from his chair, picked up her bra, and handed it toward her. "Put this back on," he commanded.

Sarah ignored him, pulling off her slacks and panties. Then she stepped back and lay naked on the pool table in the middle of the room.

Frank stepped around his desk. He threw her bra on her nude body and growled, "I said put this on."

She smiled up seductively. With one hand she rubbed her pubic hair. "Or this?"

Frank sighed and turned. As he bent for her clothes, Sarah grabbed one of his hands and pulled him to her. He fell back onto the table next to her, and before he could react, she thrust his hand between her legs. "Tell me you don't remember this," she whispered, biting his earlobe.

He jerked away from her, rolled off the table and scrambled up. "Put your clothes back on," he ordered.

Sarah sat up, fuming, matching rage with rage. "Tell me you remember!" she demanded, slapping his face.

Frank grabbed her shoulders and pushed her back down on the soft felt. He lay on top of her and hissed in her ear, "Stop it, you bitch!"

"Fuck me!"

Frank began to push himself away, but Sarah grabbed his hair, pulling him back to her. "I said 'Fuck me!' I'll scream if you don't."

She smelled his hair and felt his breath on her skin. As he struggled against her, she saw his eyes. This was not the Frank on the lawn. This was someone, something else. That Frank would not, could not have stopped. That Frank was more animal, more predator.

She stopped struggling. Maybe the stories were true and this was the Frank that was lost in Grave Swamp years ago.

Frank stood and thought a moment, straightening his shirt and debating what to do. Two forces struggled within him, the animal that wanted to devour her, the animal Sarah craved, and the man who wanted to save her from herself. His tears fell on her face and he collapsed on the table next to her.

Sarah's toes and fingers throbbed with anticipation and confusion. Like the tree limbs Monday night, the ceiling tiles seemed to swirl above her. Both Frank's lust and fear fought inside the silent body next to her. Sarah did not know which side of him she wanted to win.

Finally, Frank rolled off the table, stood, composed himself, and turned to her. He surveyed her nakedness until she could not bear his eyes any longer. Her jaw began to tremble and she covered her eyes with her hands. Frank leaned down, took her hands in his and and raised her to a sitting position. Sarah struggled to stifle her sobs, as Frank lifted her chin and wiped the tears first from her cheeks, then from her naked breasts.

She caught her breath and clamped her eyes shut as his fingers wiped her skin dry, then lingered on her nipples.

She wanted more, but nothing happened. In his fingertips, no lechery, no craving, no ardor led him on. Instead, his touch was gentle, calming.

"You don't want to do this," he said. "You have a good husband, a kid, a nice house. Ya don't wanna screw that up. Now put on your clothes and go home."

Hesitantly, she took her bra from him, then stood and bent to pick up her clothes from the floor.

"There's a bathroom over there if you need to wash your face or… whatever," he said.

Sarah nodded. Silently, she went inside, dressed, and reapplied her mascara. When she came out, Frank sat on his desk, his arms crossed holding her cloak, his eyes focused on the floor.

"I better go," she whispered, taking the cloak from him. Then she added, "I'm sorry."

"Me, too," he said.

They looked at each other in silence. Then Sarah turned to leave. He stopped her.

"I…uh…really don't remember," he said, earnestly. Then he tried to laugh. "But then again, I'm crazy. I don't remember much."

Sarah smiled a moment. Maybe she *had* imagined it all. "Sorry," she said guiltily turning to go. Frank returned to the chair behind his desk.

"Oh, one more thing," he said.

She turned. Frank leaned back in his chair and lit a cigarette. He took a long drag and blew the smoke high into the air. He nodded at her and growled, "Nice tits."

His eyes turned a vile yellow and the old sneer slithered across his face. The attack animal was back. He laughed wildly and bared his teeth. His eyes sunk into his head and the flesh of his cheeks pulled tight against his jaw. He rocked his chair forward and stood up. He rose high above his desk as Sarah fled the shop.

Inside her car, she momentarily fumbled with her keys, and strained to breathe. She glanced inside and saw the creature's shadow advancing toward the office door. The engine turned over, and she pulled out, narrowly missing Betty Nordhaus's Buick. As Sarah sped off toward downtown, she did not hear the sound of Betty's horn.

"Art! Art! Where the fuck'd you go?" Frank yelled from the show room. His face was normal, but Art still huddled against the shop wall behind the crates, his forehead straining against his eyes as he willed Frank away. In Frank's office Sarah had seen an animal; Art had seen an infant weendigo. Unlike Wayne Diego, Frank had yet to become manitou. Spirit had yet to swallow the man. He could not yet see through walls or hear the hearts of others. But as a fledgling Weendigo, he sought to satisfy his hunger, and he clomped to the door. Art heard his keys in the lock as he bolted the door behind him. Art's vision did not follow him, but instead found Sarah again.

## 2

Sarah parked in back of her dress shop "Sarah Jo's." What she had seen was impossible, she knew. A hallucination caused by stress. But why had she gone to the plumbing shop in the first place? Why could she not suppress what she had grown to hate? What had she become?

She leaned her head back on the headrest. She needed to relax, to sort things out. Home was impossible. Too many reminders of Beecher and Jeannie, of life chosen over life desired. The store was no better… Then she realized. The store was perfect. It was a world of her own making, a world which she controlled. She got out of the car and let herself in through the service entrance. Throwing her cloak onto her desk, she walked briskly into the showroom. There were no customers, nor had she expected any. Since the fog arrived, business ceased to exist. Her two salespeople stood at the window, watching the nearly empty street. "No customers?" she said a little too loudly, startling the two workers.

"I have an idea, ladies. Why don't we all just go home?"

They looked at her as if she had fallen off a truck. "I'm serious," she reassured them. "There's nobody here. I'll even pay you for the rest of the day. How's that for a deal?"

"Really?" they asked.

"Yes. Go home. Watch soaps. Clean the bathroom. Take a nap. That's what I'm going to do. Go on. I'll see you later."

So they left, bewildered, but happy for the time off. Sarah locked the door and closed the blinds behind them. Leaning back against the door, she let the silence sink in. She tried to erase the hallucination of Frank's face, to feel numb, to feel nothing. She stood alone, locked inside the store and herself, and breathed deeply.

As Sarah's heart slowed and she again felt a part of reality, she looked about the store. A brief smile of self-satisfaction crossed her lips.

Despite the dire predictions and exasperating barriers erected by the Norske Junta, her dress shop had become one of Jefferson's most successful businesses through Sarah's sheer determination and strength of will. Now, in the quiet she inspected her merchandise, walking around the racks, touching the clothes, trying on the jewelry, and smelling the perfume. She emptied the cash register into the bank bag, turned off the showroom lights, took the money back to the office, and stuffed it into her purse.

As she was about to leave, she noticed a light still burning in the dressing area. She pulled back the curtain of one of the rooms, revealing her reflection in the full-length mirror. She froze. For the first time, she saw herself the way Beecher saw her, the way Frank saw her, the way the intimidated voiceless men and huddled jealous housewives of Jefferson saw her. The woman in the mirror emanated beauty – her raven black hair; her piercing gray eyes; the perfectly seductive lips; the captivating curve of her neck that dragged one's eyes down to her stunningly powerful chest, narrow waist and trim hips...

She stood transfixed before the mirror as the room around her disappeared. The face before her, the face she had examined so many mornings , the face she knew better than her own soul, was not just the play of light across a glass surface; the reflection was a Sarah she never knew, at once more ethereal and more tactile.

She cocked her head. The image in front of her had a depth, a resilience found only in humanity, yet Sarah knew if she wanted, she could reach through the mirror and touch the woman – touch herself – feel her warmth, her breath, the response to her own caress.

A single hair fell across her left eye. When she reached toward the mirror to wipe it away, she watched her hand pass through the glass. She felt her fingers gently close her eyelids and trail tenderly to her mouth. The fingers that gently pressed against the mirror pressed against her own lips, and she kissed them. When the back of her hand stroked the cheek in the mirror, she leaned her head toward the loving affection delicately brushing her own face.

The serenity of the moment exhilarated her. The terror of Frank's face evaporated. The self-torture of the past few days vanished. At this moment, she loved herself completely. She opened her eyes and saw herself smiling back.

Loving hands fondled her shoulders and she kissed each one. She leaned back her head and sighed. Leaving the temporal world far behind, she closed her eyes.

She felt her own hands upon herself. The sound of her breath escaped from the depths of her lungs, filling the air about her. She felt her body writhe in desire from her own touch. Her moans emanated from the walls, the ceiling, the floor. As she yielded to the moment, her body convulsed in ecstasy until it lay spent and motionless on the dressing room floor while the walls reverberated with her cries.

When the room was silent again, Sarah rested on her side, powerless and exhausted. She smiled in self-satisfaction.

She had surrendered completely to the woman in the mirror. This was not lustful desire for flesh. This was the ecstasy of love, love of life, love of self. The world of reality disappeared and a new truth opened to her.

Sarah opened her eyes, rose, and stood naked before the radiant reflection. She smiled and shivered under the woman's gaze.

Sarah tilted her head back and closed her eyes again, bathed in the mirror woman's glow. Putting the backs of her hands together, Sarah touched her chin with her fingertips. Slowly, almost imperceptibly, she brought them down along her throat, across her collarbone, and down to the soft flesh of her abdomen. She spread her fingers, interlaced them, and placed her palms flat against her belly. Prayerfully, she lowered her head, breathing in the wonder of existence.

Silence and peace filled her again so she could no longer hear the sound of her own breathing. She felt pure, complete, strangely virginal, lost in the beauty of a world she had not believed in since childhood.

Sarah took a deep breath and felt her fingers separate. The movement distracted her from her reverie, but she kept her eyes closed and tried to refocus. Again, when she inhaled, she felt her hands move slightly farther apart. Against her will, she opened her eyes and looked at her reflection.

It had changed. She didn't recognize this figure at all. It was at once angry and terrified. Its eyes were swollen. And its belly grew as if some creature inside were pushing its way through the taut skin. She looked down and saw her own stomach, struggling against her, repelling her hands. Desperately, she fought to force it back, to make it flat again, but it continued to bulge, distend and distort. Panic gripped Sarah's throat, cutting off her air. She fell to the floor and fought for breath. In the mirror, she saw a face, the face of evil pushing against the skin of her abdomen

The same sneer on Frank's lawn, the same sneer in his plumbing office struggled to escape her abdomen.

"No!" she gasped. "No!"

Then, the face was no longer Frank's. It twisted and contorted, tormenting her with excruciating pain.

In agony Sarah fell to her knees, her eyes intent on her tortuous abdomen.

The face inside her bubbled and turned and then she saw. The leer of Wayne Diego, the man she had seen in the leather jacket driving a black Mercedes. He had invaded her body and now pressed against her belly, his teeth bared, trying to eat his way out of her.

Sarah doubled over and fell to her side in pain. In the mirror, the woman's tearstained grimace accused Sarah of inflicting agony on them both. Sarah wept, shook her head. "No, please," she gasped, reaching forward to feel mirror woman's healing touch again, but the image retreated behind the glass and fled.

This agony would be Sarah's alone. All the lust she had ever felt made her responsible, and even self-love could not purge it. Instead it increased her pain. The violence inside her, the cold glass staring back at her, and her unrelenting remorse seized her body, twisting, pushing, wringing life from her. She fought frantically, clutching the air. A frenzied hand brushed something hard on the floor behind her. Desperately, she struggled to grab whatever it was. Once. Twice. Three times. At last her fingers clasped the toe of her shoe, and in one last hopeless effort to free herself, she heaved the heel at the mirror, bringing the room crashing down around her.

## 3

The spell had been broken. Sarah's reflection lay around her in shards of broken glass, and again, she was left alone. She looked down at her body. Her stomach was smooth. There was no evidence of the vicious faces she had seen, but she still felt their embryonic presence growing within her. She stood and gingerly stepped around the shattered glass. Afraid shards were embedded in her clothes on the floor, she slipped through the darkened store, selected a new outfit from the racks, and dressed. As she picked up the larger pieces of the shattered mirror, she saw her appearance was the same as she had seen in Frank's office bathroom, but she knew she was not the same person. She would never be the same again.

While Sarah vacuumed the remaining slivers of glass from the carpet, the meaning of the past became clear. She must consider her options. There didn't appear many, but for once she must do what was right. However, what was right was no longer clear to her. Propriety was pretense. The choices that convention, society, and her invented self viewed as appropriate were no longer valid. Truth and reality had changed. So had she. By the time Sarah discarded the glass and her old clothes in the dumpster, she had made her decision. She had to go home.

She was about to leave the store, but she couldn't remember if she had put the "Closed" sign on the front door. Walking back to the front, she let her hands trail across the top of the racks of dresses and blouses. At the perfume counter she sprayed her left wrist, rubbed it against the right one, paused and smelled their sweetness.

"You're stalling, Sarah," she said to herself. "Check the door."

She pulled back the blinds to check the sign. It still read "Open." Sarah sighed and turned it to "Closed." Outside, the dense fog had thickened and drooped menacingly to street level. It would be difficult to drive, she thought, but she had work to do at home. She was about to turn away from the window when she saw a man come out of the Plains Cafe, holding his hands and hurrying toward the clinic.

Her anticipation did not allow her to recognize her own husband. There was so much to do, so much to rectify. "Never the same," she mumbled, rushing out the back door to her car.

Moments later, a car door slammed. Wayne Diego stood waiting at the front door of the Plains. Frank Thorstad tossed his cigarette into the gutter and greeted him. Diego shook Frank's hand and patted him on the shoulder. The two grinned, entered the café, and walked through the dining room and kitchen. Diego slung his leather jacket over his shoulder and knocked on the back room door. Einar Nordhaus opened it and smiled, welcoming them both into the inner room.

Outdoors, Joe Engstrom inched his patrol car past Frank and Diego's parked cars. He stopped momentarily outside the Plains, strained to see through the tinted window. He could make out nothing.

"What are they up to?" he wondered. He considered the possibilities, then drove on. He would find out soon enough, he thought.

The fog already knew.

At the plumbing shop, Art's vision faded and he crawled from behind the crates. He slipped out the door and then hurried through the alleys to find Beecher.

The laughing woman. Matchi-auwishuk. Weendigoes. Sarah. The Earth Man. Amanda Wilson. Beecher. The Word. The forces were all present, he knew. It was time to begin.

# XII BEECHER JONES

1

Art sat on the school steps, watching Beecher's hazy form make its way down the sidewalk. Occasionally, he'd stop, glance behind him, look down at his bandaged hands, then continue on his way. Art heard his thoughts.

It had taken six stitches in each palm to halt the bleeding, but the only permanent damage, Doc Benham said, would be a scar interrupting Beecher's lifelines.

"Interrupting, but not ending. Right, Doc?" Beecher joked nervously.

"No, not ending," Doc said, as he finished dressing the wounds. "That does bring me to another subject, though. Nancy says your blood pressure's pretty high. She tell you?"

"No."

"Yeah. I'm thinkin' maybe we should give you a complete physical soon."

"Well... Things are a bit hectic right now. It's probably just stress."

"Yeah. Probably. The thing with Karl. The fog. And I'm sure Einar and the boys have been on you about closing school. Right? But we want to make sure. Don't want a heart attack or a stroke. Have the physical. Maybe think about a spring vacation."

"Can't. There's no such thing as a substitute principal. That's why I get the big bucks."

"Well, we'll keep an eye on it and check it again when you get the stitches out. Try to take it easy, though. Okay? Eliminate the stress and you'll live at least a couple more days."

They laughed, but Beecher wondered what Doc knew. Could he even conceive of what Beecher had seen and heard? Of monsters and spirits empowered by the fog ripping apart the security of his life. Of unseen evil hidden everywhere in everything and everybody, maybe even himself.

"What was it Art called it?" Beecher thought. "Matchi-who-what?"

He turned and crossed the street, and as the questions in Doc's office replayed in his ears, he stopped in the intersection and examined his hands again.

He thought, "First, Amanda Wilson. Then, the laughing woman. The dream and then the nightmare. What next?"

His thoughts turned back to the scene at the Plains. When he turned away from Amanda and saw the laughing woman, the fog specter, outside the window mocking him, his water glass became his tormentor's throat. At least he wished it had. He interlocked his fingers, pressed his thumbs against the middle of the glass, and squeezed it until it snapped. Gory shards penetrated deep into his palms, spilling water and blood over the table. It was foolish, Beecher knew, to let his emotions take control. Then again, he thought, when had he ever had control? Plus, it didn't help. When he glanced out the window, the woman still laughed at him.

A car horn blared next to him and Beecher jumped back. The driver, an elderly woman whose face Beecher knew from church but whose name he could never remember, raised her palsied hands from the wheel as if to ask, "Well?"

"Sorry," Beecher mouthed, then waved as he hurried to the curb. The woman shook her head, muttered ancient Norwegian curses under her breath, and sped away.

Beecher's heart raced, not from the near accident, but from reliving the scene at the Plains. "Of course, my blood pressure is high," he thought. All he believed of the people around him, of the world's natural order, of his own sanity, all was askew. Thousands of suicidal birds slamming into concrete walls? The almost saintly Karl Jurgens a voyeur? Now dead? And how could he have seen Amanda Wilson, an acclaimed Hollywood screenwriter, sitting at the Plains Cafe in Jefferson,

Minnesota, ordering lunch? It had to be that damnable laughing woman, torturing him everywhere he turned. Still, he knew, more troubles lurked in the shadows, crouching in the crevices of his brain, waiting to attack with more brutality than before.

At times Beecher swore the fog had bored its way into his head and now directed his thoughts and actions. When he saw Karl's hoard of pictures, he wanted to surrender, to demean himself before whatever power had invaded the town, and cry, "What do you want? I'll give you whatever it is. Just stop this shit and go away!" In more noble moments, he wanted to rebel against the invader, to destroy it and eradicate all evidence of its existence. To do so, however, the element of surprise was vital, and Beecher was under constant surveillance. He had no way of catching this entity off guard. Its agent, the laughing woman, haunted him, stalked his every move, mocked Beecher's meager efforts to defy her, and goaded him into new, ever-increasing idiocy – like smashing water glasses with his bare hands.

Although it was barely two o'clock in the afternoon, the streetlights flickered on along the darkened street. Beecher glanced up and stopped short. Through the fog, he recognized the white Topaz parked outside the main door of the school. He stopped. The vision of Amanda Wilson had anticipated his movements. Again his imagination poisoned his sanity.

He needed to escape, so he closed his eyes and shook his head, striving to hang on to every scrap of lucidity he had left. When he opened his eyes, he discerned Art sitting on the school steps.

He approached apprehensively. When he was within speaking distance, Art nodded and told him, "Real."

He stopped. "What?"

"She's not dream. Real. She's here."

Beecher blinked and shook his head. "Who... What are you talking about?"

"Amanda… Wilson. Real. No 'lusion."

Stunned, Beecher stared first at the car, then back at Art. He couldn't be right, yet he had to be. Beecher turned his head skeptically and examined Art's eyes. No deception clouded them.

Beecher knew Art was no longer the "drunken blue-eyed Indian." The veracity of the crumpled man's words validated his presence and the knowledge he would impart. Though he didn't know what It was, he knew something bigger than his memory, the Word, spoke to him. Slowly, he sat beside Art and looked toward the Topaz. Unlike before, Beecher was willing to hear.

"What is it you know, Art?"

Art raised his head and looked up toward the streetlight across the street. "Word. His chosen… angels. Know Earth Man and manitous, demons."

"Demons."

Art nodded. "Matchi-auwishuk, weendigoes..."

"Weendigoes. What are they? Are they like the Matchi-... Matchi-...?"

"Auwishuk." Art shook his head and whispered, "Worse."

"Worse." Beecher weighed the word.

Again Art nodded. The two sat quietly, Beecher gazing at the bandaged hands in his lap, Art watching the sky. Art rubbed the corners of his jaw, hoping he could form more words. "Beecher needs to know," he thought.

He pointed at his own chest. "See dreams," he said.

"Like what?" Beecher asked.

Art shook his head. "Not what. Whose. Mine. Yours. Laura Grapnic's. Sarah's. Amanda Wilson's."

Beecher turned to Art. He wanted to ask what the seer had seen, but decided he wasn't ready. "How do you see?" he asked.

Art shrugged. "Just do. Word shows what am to know."

"And what is the Word showing you about this woman? This Amanda Wilson."

"Here for you."

Beecher smiled and shook his head. "Not unless your Word condones bigamy. I'm married. Remember?"

"Married. Not married. Not matter. Not yours… in way world… understands. Exists for you, within you, without you. You for her. Will understand."

"When?"

"Soon. Very soon."

"Will you tell me or will she? Or is this another thing that must come from the Word?"

Art brought his face back to earth and examined Beecher's face, searching for signs of ridicule. There were none. Art placed his hand on Beecher's chest. "Will know," he said.

Beecher brushed Art's hand away and looked at the car, then the school door. He hesitated, then said to Art, "I have to go in."

Art watched Beecher eyes. They shone clear. There was no deception. Beecher did not speak simply to dismiss Art and his incomprehensible rambling. He was not simply going back to his principal's job. He believed. He knew he was not crazy nor was Art. By some twisted perversion of nature, all he had seen and felt was real. The Word had spoken and he had heard.

Art nodded at him. Beecher stood, patted Art's shoulder, took a deep breath and entered the school. Art raised his eyes back to the sky and in his vision watched as Beecher walked down the hall and entered the office.

## 2

Peggy squinted at her computer screen, updating the attendance files.

"You're going to go blind if you get any closer to the screen," Beecher joked.

"I'm not used to these bifocals yet," she said. She glanced up at him and saw his hands. "Good Lord! What happened to you?"

"Got in a fight with a water glass at the Plains. Glass won," he said. "Sorry I didn't get back till now. Everything okay?"

"Yep. No more fights. No more phone calls. Oh, Mr. Jones, this lady's here to see you."

Beecher turned and saw Amanda Wilson in the chair outside his office, waiting patiently. She stood and moved toward him.

He had expected her. As she drew nearer, he knew that this woman, this Amanda Wilson, was not his fog-induced delusion, a television image, nor the Plains hallucination. This Amanda was real, not five feet away. He heard her breath, smelled her perfume. If he reached out, he could touch her. Beecher stood silently as words collided in his brain, unable to find their way out of his mouth.

Neither spoke while the undefinable energy vibrating through the air said more than their words ever could. It told of lives long ago entwined in ways Beecher and Amanda could not know, but somehow did.

"Amanda Wilson," Amanda said, automatically moving to shake Beecher's hand. He responded, but the sight of his bandages stopped them both. Amanda looked at the hands as if her gaze could heal the wounds. "I'm sorry. I... I didn't mean to embarrass you today." Pointing to his hands, she asked, "That must hurt. Is that why you ran out of the cafe?"

Beecher's face flushed as he struggled to gain composure. "Yes," he said. "Kind of stupid, huh? You get many drinking glass murderers in L.A.?"

Amanda smiled shyly. That he knew she lived in Los Angeles should have surprised her, but it didn't. Because of the one glimpse he had of her on the Oscar telecast, he knew who she was, where she was from, how she walked, how she lived. And strangely, she knew him.

Peggy felt like a spectator at the climax of a magical ballet. She leaned across her desk and asked, "Have you two met?"

Beecher, still struck by Amanda's presence, replied as if she had spoken instead of Peggy. "Uh… no. I… um… I recognize you from television."

Feeling herself fading from the dance, Peggy interrupted. "Television?"

"Yes." Beecher shook himself. "I'm sorry, Peggy. This is Amanda Wilson. She won this year's Academy Award for best original screenplay for *Bright and Shining Star*."

"Really?" Peggy rose, pushed in front of Beecher, and grasped Amanda's hand. "Well, congratulations and welcome to Jefferson. I'm Peggy Nordahl." This was as close to stardom as Peggy had ever been or was ever likely to be. However, as she held Amanda's hand, Peggy quickly understood this was not her place.

"Nice to meet you," Amanda said. Then she turned politely but deliberately to Beecher. "I'm sorry. What was your name?"

"Oh, sorry. Beecher Jones." Forgetting his wounds, Beecher raised his hand to shake. When Amanda hesitated and pulled back her hand, Beecher looked down at his bandages, then laughed at himself. "Oh, yeah. How about we just wave?"

Amanda laughed. In unison they raised their hands, turned them like parade princesses, smiled, and said, "Hello." The tension vanished. Peggy giggled.

"I'm sorry," Beecher said. "Did you want to talk to me?"

"Yes. If you have a few minutes."

"Sure. Come on in."

Beecher opened his door to let her into his office. As she passed him, Beecher saw Peggy's quizzical look. All Beecher could do was shrug and sigh. He closed the door and directed Amanda to a chair.

"Beecher," Amanda said. "Interesting name."

He laughed, sitting behind his desk. "I know. My foster parents were closet Presbyterians. Spent their lives emulating the Beecher family."

"Beecher family?"

Beecher nodded. "From the 1800s? The patriarch was Lyman Beecher, who preached temperance – a great Presbyterian virtue, or so I was constantly told. His son was Henry Ward Beecher, a writer and preacher who tried to reconcile the Bible with evolution. Strange concept, I know, but my dad admired him. That's where he got the idea for my name. Then, of course, there were the girls. The eldest daughter Catharine Esther was a great supporter of women's education. And, of course, daughter Harriet... Harriet Beecher Stowe of *Uncle Tom's Cabin* fame?"

"Quite a family. Shows you how sheltered my life has been. I thought they named you after the tree."

"Tree?"

"Beech tree. Hardwood. Strong. Hearty."

Beecher laughed, held up his arms, flexed his biceps. "Oh, yes. I've always been the manly man you see sitting here before you. At birth I had sixteen inch biceps from doing push-ups in the womb."

Amanda's laugh relaxed him, as he continued. "We don't have many beech trees in Minnesota that I know of, but I like the image. My wife keeps telling me I need to be more assertive."

"You're married?"

Beecher nodded. "Yes." He relaxed even more after he had said it. He wanted Amanda to know about Sarah, how much he loved her, how important she was to him. Surprisingly, Amanda seemed more comfortable too after he had said it.

"Any children?"

"One. Jeannie. This is her." Beecher reached over and handed Amanda the framed picture from his desk.

"She's pretty."

Beecher smiled proudly. "You should see her mom."

Amanda lowered his eyes, then asked "You said something about your foster parents? Are you adopted?"

"Mm-hm."

Amanda looked at his eyes and felt their paths converging again. "Did you ever meet your birth parents?"

"No. I guess my mother was from Wisconsin." He hesitated. "You sure you want to hear this?"

"Please."

"Nothing special. Same old story. Mother was a small-town girl. Young. Unmarried. Gave me up when I was born. Folks raised me just east of here. In Bemidji. Good people. Both teachers at the college." Why he was telling her this, Beecher did not understand. He hadn't talked about his parents for years, but Amanda's smile and quiet bearing put him at ease.

"They still live there?"

Beecher shook his head. "They both died a few years ago. My wife's family died in a car-train accident when she was in high school, so Jeannie has no grandparents. I feel bad for her. Christmases feel a bit empty."

Amanda handed Beecher the picture of Jeannie. "Anyway," he said, "enough about me. What is a big-time Hollywood writer doing in Jefferson, Minnesota, in the middle of the foggiest spring ever?"

"Well, believe it or not, I'm here to find *my* birth parents."

Beecher sat back in his chair. "Really. You're adopted, too?"

Amanda nodded.

"And?"

"All I know about my history is that I was born here in Jefferson and raised in Sand Creek, Michigan. Like you, I had great foster parents, although we were more on the Methodist order. Anyway... I always wondered how I got from here to there and why. So after the Oscars the other night, I decided to take some time off, come here and find out."

"Sounds… adventurous."

"Well, I tried to do it once a long time ago right out of high school, but… it didn't work out. Family emergency. You never wanted to?"

"What? Find my real parents?"

Amanda nodded.

Beecher tilted his head to one side. "I guess, but one thing I learned a long time ago. I don't handle guilt well."

Amanda smiled. "Me neither. But for some reason, I have to know... I don't know what I have to know, just that I do. Ever since I moved to Hollywood, I think I've grown further from what I am. Maybe I'm seeking redemption for what the movie business has made of me."

"Redemption. Isn't that what *Bright and Shining Star* was about?"

Amanda looked up and smiled at him. "You read all that press release crap, too, huh? Yes, it was about redemption and salvation, but despite what *Entertainment Weekly* would have you believe, Geri is not me. She's a fictional character I grew to admire as I created her, but I could never be her," she said. "She's too solid, solid but ethereal, grounded but free. You know? Me, I'm just floundering my way through life."

Beecher laughed. "At least you're floundering. Floundering is life. Besides, maybe it's better to be ethereal yet solid, free yet grounded," Beecher said.

"You think I'm ethereal?"

Beecher caught himself, then stammered, "Well, I… uh... yeah, I guess. At least by Jefferson standards. Wait. That didn't sound right, did it?"

Amanda shook her head and smiled.

"Sorry. Sometimes the mouth doesn't work the way it should. Anyhow, back to your parents. What have you found so far?"

"Nice recovery," she said, remembering his look of embarrassment at the Plains before crushing the glass. "Not much. I went to city hall and the hospital this afternoon to examine the records..."

"And they wouldn't let you see them."

"The lady at city hall said birth records were kept at the county courthouse in Adams. The woman at the hospital said their records had been transferred to someplace in Grand Forks, North Dakota. Then they both gave me this owl-like stare that said, 'If you know what's good for you, you'll just leave this alone.'"

Beecher nodded. "That's the way we are. We expect outsiders to respect our privacy and to keep their own lives private as well."

"You mean people here don't like to talk about others? That's different from where I grew up."

"I didn't say that. Sure, we'll dig up and spread all the dirt we can find on people we know, but outsiders we just ignore, and it would be better if they just ignored us. But then, maybe what these women did was innocent. Maybe your reaction to their attitude was just your conscience making you feel guilty for asking the wrong questions."

Amanda nodded. "Maybe."

There was an awkward silence until Beecher asked, "So… what did you want from me?"

"Well, I realize this is a long shot, but I was wondering if the school library had yearbooks from thirty, thirty-five years ago. Something like that. I'd like to look through them and maybe… maybe see someone familiar, someone who looked like me… something. It was so frustrating talking to those women. I just need to do something. Even if I don't find anything, if I could just spend a couple hours getting an idea of what this place was like when my parents were here."

"How do you know they were in school?"

"I don't," she admitted. "But it's worth a look. Tomorrow I can go to the courthouse, maybe Grand Forks. But for now, I can do this."

Beecher examined her face. He had not noticed the freckles during the few seconds she was on television. Probably the work of a makeup artist and a soft-focus lens, he thought. So her face was not the dreamlike ideal he had pictured in his porch dream just two nights ago. It was, in fact, profoundly human, vulnerable and inquisitive. Although it was girl-like, still there was a strength of conviction in the way she set her jaw after she spoke. "The woman is a paradox of innocence and wisdom, faith and doubt," he thought.

He looked at her a second and smiled. His "writer's imagination" was getting away from him. He leaned forward and picked up the phone. "Well, let me see what we have."

The school did indeed have a collection of yearbooks that dated all the way back to the Great Depression. According to librarian Brooke Langford, the yearbooks were kept on reserve "to prevent the little creeps from cutting out pictures of their parents or writing crude comments on the autograph page."

When Beecher told Brooke he was sending her a visitor, she adamantly reminded him school was over in an hour and she had to get home before the fog got worse. Beecher looked at Amanda's calm, expectant face and decided to risk incurring Babbling Brooke's wrath. He was, after all, her boss. The visitor, Beecher told her, was a famous writer researching the history of Jefferson. He assured Brook that her invaluable documents would be safe in this person's hands. Reluctantly, the "guardian of the books" assented, and Amanda had access to the "special collection" room. Beecher would lock up everything when he left.

"I can't stay too late. I have to be home about 5:30," he told Amanda. "Is that going to be enough time?"

"I might have to come back tomorrow," she answered, "but yes, that will be great. Thanks."

Instinctively, they both stood and moved toward the door. There was more that Beecher wanted to ask her, but couldn't remember what. Again, Beecher raised his hands and the sight of his bandages re-injected the room with the initial energy both had felt in the outer office. They paused, looked at their own hands, then at each other. Shyly, Amanda glanced up into Beecher's face, reached forward, took Beecher's thumb between her fingers and shook it. Rather than pull it back, Beecher laughed.

"I think the wave worked better," he said.

Amanda smiled. "Yeah, probably." She raised her hand and waved while Beecher did the same.

Beecher opened the door and led her into the outer office. "Peggy, will you find someone to show Miss Wilson to the library, please? She needs to do some research."

"Wait!" Art Benson said, limping into the office.

Amanda, Beecher, and Peggy turned to toward the interruption. Beecher cleared his throat and shifted his weight nervously. "Art," he said, "I'm sorry. If you can wait just a minute, I'll be right with you."

Misunderstanding Beecher's body language, Peggy said, "Mr. Jones, do you want me to call Joe?"

"No," Art said as he looked from Beecher to Amanda. Beecher knew Art belonged. "Time to speak. You must speak." Art pointed first at Beecher, then at Amanda. "Both of you."

Amanda's face questioned both Beecher and the deformed man.

"Art, not now," Peggy said, standing and moving to escort Art from the room.

"No. Now. You know," Art said to Beecher. Then, pointing at Amanda, he added, "She knows. Ask her."

"Knows what?" Beecher asked. "She's never been here before."

Amanda examined Art's face curiously. She showed no fear or apprehension. "What is it you think I know?"

Art flinched as the pain in his jaw grew excruciating. He immediately recognized the pain. "The Earth Man," he thought.

"Remember dreams," he said to Amanda. "Drowning man."

She blinked. "The drowning man? How do you know about that?" she asked.

Invisibly, the Earth Man grappled Art's voice to stem the Word. Art grimaced, took a deep breath and gasped, "Altar... altar and flame."

Beecher's mouth clamped shut. He had not told anyone his vision.

"Art, Mr. Jones is really busy," Peggy interrupted. "And Miss Wilson has..."

"No, that's okay, Peggy," Beecher said. "I'll talk to him. Come on in, Art." He turned to Amanda. "Can you... Is it all right for you... I mean do you have time?"

Looking at Art, Amanda thought for a moment. She saw herself on the beach, watching a naked man splashing playfully in the sea. "Sure. Sure, that will be fine," she said.

Amanda went first, and Art followed. Peggy stopped Beecher. "You sure you don't want me to call Joe?"

"We'll be fine," Beecher said, but just as he was about to close the door, he peeked out and said, "But *you're* not going anywhere, right?"

"Right," she said, nodding and patting the phone. "Speed dial is a good thing."

Beecher smiled and closed the door. "Please, sit down," he told Amanda as he sat at his desk. "Amanda Wilson, this is Art Benson. Please, Art, sit."

"No. Like stand."

"Okay. Miss Wilson, Art is... I'm not sure what he is."

"Anishinabe," Art told him.

"Right. That's the local Native American tribe here. Sometimes called the Ojibwe or Chippewa..."

"I know," she told him. Then she asked Art, "Are you a shaman?"

"Shaman. Seer. Keeper of Word," Art told her.

"What is it you see? What is it you know?"

"He sees dreams," Beecher said. "The altar and the flame is a dream I had a few nights ago. I haven't mentioned it to anybody, yet he knows. I'm guessing you had a dream about a drowning man. Am I right?"

Amanda nodded and watched Art's face for reaction.

Beecher continued, "Art and I have been having some discussions about the fog and some other events which have been happening around here lately. People acting a little crazy. One of my employees appears to have killed himself..."

"The one who ran into a wall?"

Beecher looked at her. "You heard about it?"

Amanda nodded. "At the airport in Fargo."

"There have been other things, too, but it would take too long to explain. Anyway, Art has a theory it's all the work of evil spirits called... I can never get it right."

"Matchi-auwishuk," Art told him.

"Right. He says he knows this from the Word. Now, I'm not sure what that is, but evidently I have some mission from this Word I am supposed to accomplish. Somehow you, who I've never met before, are supposed to help me with this quest or whatever it is."

Beecher tried to sound skeptical, but he could not. He leaned back in his chair, looked up at Art and asked, "Did I get it right?"

Amanda watched both men and waited quietly. Art shrugged.

"Am I close?"

Art nodded.

"So what is going on, Art?" Beecher asked.

Art nodded at Beecher. "Started, but must do more."

"I've started? Started what?"

"Tell Story."

He tilted his confused head. "What story?" he asked. "I don't know what you're..."

"What have seen."

"When?"

"Since Friday."

Beecher reached for a paper clip and began untwisting it as he thought. "You mean the birds?"

"And...?" Art urged.

"What? You want me to talk about now?"

Art nodded toward Amanda. "Must hear."

"She's going to think we're crazier than she already does. I'm sorry, Miss Wilson. Maybe I shouldn't have asked you..."

"No, that's fine. I'm curious now. What else have you seen?"

He shrugged, nervously.

Art urged him. "Miss Grapnic, your wife, Karl. Dreams." Art tilted his head toward Amanda. "Her, flame at altar. Tell."

He leaned forward on the desk. "All right, Art. Enough. I want to know. How do you know my dream? No more of this magical Word stuff. What's going on?"

Ignoring him, Art turned to Amanda and asked, "Drowning man?"

She looked at Beecher. She began slowly, "Yes. It was you. Art's right. I dreamed of you night before last. After that dream, I wanted to come here. I don't know why, but maybe Art..." Then she turned back to Art. "How do you...?"

"Word speaks to me. The Word in you."

"Which means what?" Beecher challenged. "Damn it! What is this Word you keep talking about?"

"All." The pain in Art's jaw subsided. His face almost felt normal, as if words could speak themselves through him.

"All? All what?" he asked

"All Spirit. All Light. All Life. All Truth. That is what I know. I know the truth. As do you. Both of you."

"The truth about?"

Art walked around the desk and stared quietly out the deepening fog. The words came. They would be heard. "Lao Tzu said:

*Names and concepts only block your perception of the*
*Great Oneness...*
*Those who live inside their egos are continually*
*bewildered: they struggle*
*frantically to know*
*whether things are large or small,*
*whether or not there is a purpose,*
*whether the universe is blind and mechanical or the*
*divine creation of a conscious being.*
*Look behind your beliefs, and you will discern the*
*deep, silent, complete truth of the Word.*
*Embrace it, and your bewilderment vanishes.*

Beecher tossed the straightened paper clip on the desk and stood next to Art, trying to see what he saw. "Is the Word in the fog?" he asked.

Art shook his head. "The fog is Great Mask, tool of Earth Man, tool to take what he craves."

"Who is the Earth Man?" Amanda asked.

Art turned from the window. "Evil One."

"Is he Matchi-auwishuk?"

Art shook his head. The tightness came back to his cheek. "Matchi-auwishuk plural. Are his servants. But more. Men. Women. Weendigoes."

"Weendigo? Is that a man or woman or...?"

"Not man. Manitou."

"Manitou. I've heard that word. What does it mean again?" Amanda looked at Art quizzically.

"Spirit," he told her.

The pain in Art's face drove him to a chair. He gasped and grimaced. Amanda grabbed his shoulders.

"Are you all right?"

Art took a deep breath and nodded. The two forces, the Word and the Earth Man, fought for his tongue. He had to let the Word speak the truth. He waved his hand toward Beecher and said, "You will see Earth Man. He is here, stronger than Matchi-auwishuk, birds, Karl, laughing woman..."

"You see the laughing woman?" Beecher asked, reaching forward and touching Art's arm.

He nodded.

"Is she Matchi-auwishuk?"

Art shook his head. "What she is, even she… does not know. All will know… one day. Soon. Not now. Word reveals only to those who will see."

"But I don't want to see her. I'm sick of her."

The pain in Art's jaw throbbed. He marshaled his strength, raised his hand and pointed at Beecher's chest. "Chosen. To see. Tell. Save."

"I've seen enough."

"Tell what have seen. Only then will it stop."

Beecher struggled to keep his voice calm. "What will stop? I don't understand what you're telling me."

"The Earth Man," Amanda said.

"Yes," Art replied, "and fog… and death… but only if… he tells Story."

Reluctant to accept his responsibility, caught between the role of savior and deserter, Beecher said, "I can't tell stories. I can't even say the right thing. Ask Miss Wilson. She knows. Why can't she tell the story? She's the writer!"

"Not her story. She brings…and holds Flame."

At the name, the pain eased. Art sat straighter and stretched his mouth.

"What is the Flame?" Amanda asked.

"For him to tell."

"What is the Flame?" she asked Beecher.

"Hell, I don't know," he shrugged.

"Yes," Art told him. "In dream. Fire that cleanses… and burns…and brings Story to light. Until you accept it…from her hands, Story goes untold. There must be Three. Herald." He touched his own chest.

He then pointed at Amanda, "Flame."

Then nodding toward Beecher, he said, "Storyteller. Storyteller… you. As long as Story untold,… the stronger Matchi-auwishuk become – and Weendigo and… ultimately Earth Man. Longer you keep silent,… longer fog creates illusions; The more you deny Word, more Earth Man controls thoughts and actions."

"My thoughts and actions? So it's all an illusion?"

"Not illusion."

"Okay, bottom line, Art. What's the worst all this could lead to?"

"What you have seen."

"You keep saying that. What is it I have seen? Will you give me a straight answer for once instead of all this mystical bull shit?" he shouted, crossing the room.

"Death," Art answered. Beecher stopped short, looked quizzically at Art, and slowly moved back to his desk.

"Confusion. Lust. Sin. But ultimately, death," Art continued.

Beecher sat, picked up his paper clip and began bending it back into its original shape. "I've seen it. Yes," he said quietly. "You mean Karl."

Liberated, the message of the Word flowed from Art's mouth.

"The Karl you knew was body. Body dies physical death. Is natural. Dust to dust. But spirit lives in body after body. To lose one body is only new beginning for spirit. Lives through cycle after cycle…of life, death, and rebirth, gaining insight, refining self, becoming pure, constant, and unwavering, seeking immortality. Earth Man cares nothing about killing body. Seeks to kill spirit…by using it as he wishes, destroying beauty and good…through hate and evil, arrogance and pride, drunkenness and lust. Tosses remains into abyss where no new body, no new life. Spirit dead forever.

"Here in Jefferson spirits fight for life. Some already lost. Still more will lose. Until you…speak, struggle continues. Until you speak, spirits die."

"So if I don't tell whatever story the Word wants me to say, spirits will be lost forever? The eternal salvation of this town is my responsibility? How did I get this job?"

Art shook his head. "Responsibility with each person. At birth, each knows truth…of good and evil. Word lives within us…and we spend lives deciding… whether to follow it. When life difficult, what we do not want to face, we ignore. We cover our own reality behind masks. Right?" he asked Amanda.

Her face transformed from confusion to certainty. She nodded.

"And now comes fog, Earth Man's tool, to unmask us, to reveal his manitous…by allowing us to be…who we want to be. But even Earth Man blind. Does not know Word's manitous. Does not know you,…either of you. That is why only you can tell Story."

"Why not you?" Amanda asked.

"People not listen. Even now, both you doubt. Hear my voice falter, yes? How hard words stick. Jaw locked. You see back is weak. Not for me to speak. Can only awaken the Story…within you."

Beecher's mind jumbled. Thoughts tripped over questions which tripped over answers. "And who do I tell it to? I'm sorry. I still don't understand."

The door burst open, and Einar Nordhaus barged into the room.

"There you are," he bellowed.

Peggy pushed in behind him. "I'm sorry, Mr. Jones. I told him you had people..."

"It's all right, Peggy," Beecher told her.

"Ah, hell, it's only Art," Einar said, dismissing Art with the back of his hand, but then he saw Amanda. "Who's this?"

"Einar, this is Amanda Wilson. Miss Wilson, this is our mayor Einar Nordhaus."

Amanda extended her hand, and said, "Hello, I'm glad..."

"Yeah, me too," Einar grumbled. "Beecher Jones, I want you to meet Wayne Diego. Wayne, get in here."

Diego entered the room, smiling broadly, and reaching out his hand. Beecher hesitated, then showed his bandaged hands and said, "Sorry."

Pointing an imaginary gun at Beecher, Diego laughed. "Gotcha, guy." He turned and saw Amanda. "And who's this?"

Amanda's stomach shuddered and turned. She crossed her arms and said, "Amanda Wilson."

"Wayne Diego," Beecher thought. "Wayne... Ween... What was the word Art said?"

"Weendigo," Art whispered, stepping toward the incognito monster.

There was a moment of imbalance. The air shuddered. Finally, Einar asked, "He know you?"

The Weendigo bit his smiling lip and nodded. "Yes, we've met. Good to see you again. Let's talk sometime," he said and patted Art's twisted back. Art's muscles tensed and turned, but he fought back the pain.

"Can I steal Beecher from you folks for a few minutes? Wayne an' me got some important business to discuss with him. If you don't mind."

Beecher looked down at his bandaged hands. His fingers trembled and his palms pulsed with pain. He sensed the enemy. The Story had to wait. "Peggy," he said, "did you find someone to take Miss Wilson down to the library?"

"Sure. Right this way," Peggy said. Amanda walked to the door. She hesitated and looked back at Beecher.

"Mrs. Langford will take care of you," he told her. "I'll be down to lock up about a quarter after five. Okay?"

Amanda nodded warily and then followed Peggy's blonde, acne-faced freshman student aide to the library.

"Hey, Art! You don't mind, do ya? There's a bottle a whiskey in it for ya if ya leave now. Okay?"

"Don't want whiskey."

Einar and Wayne both laughed derisively. "Woh!" Einar said. "So-o-or-ry. But get out of here. Okay? 'fore I haveta call Joe ta haul your half-breed drunken ass outta this public building."

Beecher stepped between Einar and Art. Putting his arm over Art's shoulder, he led him to the door. "Art, maybe you better leave. I'll talk to you later. All right?"

Art nodded and glanced back into the room. "Weendigo," he whispered to Beecher. Beecher glanced back at Diego, then nodded and patted Art's back.

"Okay." He closed the door behind Art. Art watched the door until Peggy's stare reminded him it was time to leave. He walked out of the building, crossed the highway, leaned on the hardware store wall, and listened while Einar and the Weendigo unfolded their plan.

## 3

"That was rude, Einar," Beecher admonished.

"What? Art? Shit. He won't remember in the morning."

"And Miss Wilson?"

"Yeah. Hey! Who is she? If I weren't an old married man, by God, I'd liketa... Hell, I'd liketa anyway. Right, Wayne?" He elbowed Diego in the side. "Well, never mind. Beecher, ya gotta hear about this."

"What now?"

"Well, let me tell ya. This is big, Beecher. Really big. Wayne here's a talent scout from Hollywood, lookin' for some high school kids for a movie they're filming in Fargo."

"Really?" Beecher said sitting at his desk and motioning to the two men to sit down. "So why are you in Jefferson?"

Before Diego could answer, Einar broke in. "He's looking for something different, you know, more wholesome, more rural,"

"What? Fargo's not different, wholesome, or rural enough?" Beecher smiled.

Diego bared his teeth in an unsettling smile. "I didn't see what I was looking for there, so I've been scouring the countryside. Something happened to me when I came to Jefferson. Everything felt right. So I've been looking around last few days, and I like what I see," Diego said.

"How could you see anything in the fog?" Beecher asked. His hands itched, as if allergic to the bandages.

Diego and Einar laughed. "Yeah, it's been tough," Diego said, "but..."

"His hair's too perfect," Beecher thought. "So how can I help?" he asked aloud.

"Like I said, he wants to talk to some of the kids," Einar said, beaming.

"When?" Beecher kept watching Diego's eyes. They were an odd color, lighter than hazel, almost yellow.

Diego looked at Einar, smiled, and said, "How about now?"

Both men laughed and shot two thumbs up at each other.

Beecher shook his head. "Can't do that. There's little more than an hour left of the day. I can't take students out of class. Teachers have to have some warning. Besides, there's the liability. I'm going to need parental permission slips. That'll take..."

Again Einar interrupted. "Oh, come on, Beecher. Who wouldn't jump at the chance to have their little girl in a movie?"

"Girl?" Spiders of apprehension crawling out of Beecher's palms and up his arms.

Diego scowled briefly at Einar, then smiled again. "Nothing like a young, pretty, northern Minnesota girl to make a movie."

"I'm sorry. I don't mean to... But I'm going to need some credentials, a couple days to set things up with the faculty..."

"Damn it, Beecher!" Einar broke in. "Why do you have to be so difficult? Me and the boys already said it was okay. Just let us call the girls down to the gym and..."

"But, Einar, why only the girls? Doesn't that worry you? Listen, I don't care what you and the Junta decided, I..."

Einar stood and slammed his hands on Beecher's desk. "Damn it, Beecher! Will you stop usin' that word? It makes us sound like a bunch of Mexican commies."

"Sorry. Anyway, I can't do it, Einar."

"Like hell you can't. You're the principal, for God's sake!"

Diego held up his hand. "No," he interrupted. "Mr. Jones is right. He doesn't know me. He's only looking out for the girls' safety."

Despite the fact Diego had taken Beecher's side, his smile made Beecher's teeth itch.

"Besides, he's had a tough week," Diego continued. He moved around the desk and leaned close to Beecher, whispering in his ear. "Einar told me earlier. About your custodian? What was his name? Karl? I'm sure that had to be quite a shock."

Beecher felt the spiders crawling down his back. "Yes... Yes, it was."

Diego nodded, his yellow eyes streaming malevolence that pressed into Beecher's wounds. He said, "We can wait, Einar. We want to do things right."

Einar glowered at Beecher, harrumphed and nodded reluctantly.

"Two days enough? I'll get you my resume and references, the parental releases... Anything else you need?"

Although Beecher's nerves tingled and his fingers trembled, he shook his head. "No, no, that will be fine."

"Great!" Diego said, reaching out and playfully punching Beecher's shoulder. "It was good to meet you."

Beecher tried to rub his shoulder with his forearm instead of his bandaged hand. He felt the lie. His meeting Wayne Diego was not good, he thought, just inevitable.

## 4

After the Weendigo and Einar left the office, Beecher returned to his desk, and Peggy returned to her attendance report.

Down the hall in the library "special collections" room, Amanda stopped her study and replayed her meeting with Beecher and Art. The words she had heard at once confused and enlightened. Their truth excited and frightened, but the Story was incomplete, she thought. The writer in her wanted to hear it, to finish it and relate it. And despite the fact she knew Art had the answers, she acknowledged that only Beecher could fill in the blanks. In Wayne Diego and Einar Nordhaus, she recognized Beecher and the Word's antagonists, though she felt she had yet to see them all.

Beecher leaned back in his chair, looked up at the ceiling tile and counted the sound holes until the room faded away. All that he had seen, felt, and dreamed raced in blurs and fits and starts through his mind — LauraWallybirds. Sarahwoman. AmandaKarlLaura. SnakeWoman. Amandawoman. ArtAmanda. ArtWayneDiego.

Words and ideas searched for coherence — WordFlameStoryteller. EarthManWeendigolaughing-woman. Evildeathlife. Realitydreamspirit.

He thought of the sanctity of the number three. He recalled the nuns teaching… the Holy Trinity: Father, Son, Holy Ghost. Three crosses. "On the third day…." the "Sacred Trio" he always looked for in literature, composed of whatever the writer chose to save the protagonist. Three. Holiness. Sanctity. Purity.

Then Beecher felt the darkness slipping away. Whatever was arranging and shaping his life was also leading him somewhere he hadn't known existed. The school dismissal bell startled him and the commotion outside his door distracted him before his thoughts could stray to Amanda working in the library.

Art turned to walk back toward the plumbing shop. For the moment he was finished with Beecher and Amanda. It was time to let the heavenly shape the earthly. Beecher and Amanda would need him again, he knew, but later. Humans treading between heaven and earth are easily sidetracked from the path, he knew. If the Earth Man knew who the two were, he would not let

Diego and Einar leave the room so easily, but it did not matter. The Word and the Flame spoke in Beecher and Amanda's dreams; unbeknownst to either, they had each other, even though they did not know why. Once they knew and Beecher told the Story, the Word had won.

But Art knew the Earth Man would fight to the end, using all the weapons at his disposal, including the irrepressible arrogance of the Weendigo.

Art stepped out to walk across the highway when Diego's Mercedes Roadster roared toward him. Before he could step back onto the curb, the headlights popped out of the fog, and the car squealed to a stop in front of him. The engine behind the grill growled like a snarling hound from hell, while inside the car, Diego smiled, flashed the lights, and saluted. In an act of defiance, Art raised his head toward Diego and sniffed. Surprised, Diego gaped and considered the man in front of him. Then he threw his head back, laughed, swerved around Art, and drove on.

Art looked into the dark, fog above him, listening. The sound was unmistakeable to him. The Earth Man's forces gathering in the mist. Many were in town. Still more gathered around their leader out at Grave Swamp. Along the highway, the fog was thick and hung low to the ground, drifting like curtains in the breeze. Art closed his eyes and heard the laughing woman tiptoeing across the schoolhouse roof.

"I must not drive her away," he thought. "This is where she belongs."

Art sat down on the sidewalk and leaned against the flower shop. In his spell, he saw the school he had just left.

Sliding down the schoolhouse wall, the laughing woman hastily checked the street that ran past the building. She peeked in the top of Beecher's window and scratched her head a moment. As she turned to look eastward toward Grave Swamp, her brow furrowed. Tapping her teeth with her fingernails, she searched for the answer that eluded her. Then she turned back and looked downtown.

Art heard her thoughts.

Somewhere in the fog, she knew, the cold, dark Weendigo waited, while inside the building was light and warmth. She stroked her jaw, unable to loosen her smile. She hesitated a moment then scrambled up the wall. Sitting on the roof, she tried to remember why she had come to the school and why she couldn't leave.

Art's vision turned to Beecher.

Beecher instinctively knew of three. He thought he could identify both the Holy and Unholy Trios: First, the Word, the Flame, and the Storyteller; and secondly, the Earth Man, the Weendigo, and the laughing woman.

Art knew Beecher was close to knowing the truth, but something was not correct. The laughing woman was important, he knew, but not on the same level as the Earth Man. Or the Weendigo. Her uncertainty outside the school just now, indicated she was lower. "Still," Art thought, "the solidity of the Unholy is shaking."

## 5

The insight of Art's vision of what was inside the school revealed what the laughing woman could not perceive. True, she could see on Beecher's desk lay a small pile of mutilated paper clips. He had moved from the small size clips to the larger, thicker gauged, less easily manipulated ones.

But she could not hear Beecher's thoughts. Art could.

*The Story.*
*The Word.*
*The Earth Man.*
*Eternal salvation.*

The words reverberated from the walls. How had the burden of the future been placed in his broken hands? His devout parents would tell him to pray, pray for knowledge, for guidance, for strength, but he had forgotten how to pray. Even if he remembered how, he realized, he was now unsure to whom he should pray.

There was a knock. Beecher looked up as Wally Forseth peeked around the door. "Oh, good. You *are* here. Can I talk to you a minute, boss?"

"Sure, Coach. Come on in."

Wally walked in and sat down in front of Beecher's desk. "Holy shit! What the hell'd ya do to your hands?"

Beecher sighed and smiled sheepishly. Again Beecher related the story of the water glass. It was already getting old.

"Ya get stitches?" Wally asked.

Beecher nodded. "Six each. No muscle damage, Doc says. Just have to be careful around water until he can take the stitches out. What's up, Wally?"

Wally bent forward, his legs spread, his elbows on his thighs. "Well..." he began, "I been thinkin' an' I got me an idea."

"About what?"

"About Laura's play."

With Karl's death, the laughing woman, and images of Weendigoes infesting Beecher's brain, Laura Grapnic's production of *Our Town* had fallen off his table of concerns. Something so important just days ago now felt insignificant. "Wally, we're not going to get into that until she comes back. She has enough to worry about without arguing with you about practice time..."

"No, that's what I was thinkin'. Ya know she's so damned stubborn about getting that thing done an' her kids doin' all that work an'..." He took a deep breath. "Anyhow, I got curious 'bout why this play was so damned important to her. I mean, I understand the work thing an' all, but it's just a play, right?"

Beecher shrugged. "Where is this going?" he wondered.

"Anyway," Wally continued, "I went to the library an' checked out a copy of *Our Town* – an' I read the thing. You read it?"

Beecher nodded.

"Well, you know that whole idea of appreciatin' the world when you're alive, 'every every minute'? I thought that was pretty deep stuff to pull off, especially for teenagers. But then I thought about Karl dyin' an' I thought, maybe that's why it's important, for kids to think about things that're important to 'em. So anyhow, what I thought was, how 'bout lettin' me finish off the play for Laura? I mean the kids already know their lines an' stuff. They just need someone around to supervise while they practice a couple times, doncha think? That'd let 'em perform and let Laura get over this other thing."

Beecher sat back in his chair and examined the coach's face. He wasn't joking. There was no sign of sarcasm or facetiousness on Wally's face, only sincerity and concern for the students and Laura, the woman who had nearly performed rhinoplasty on his nose with a letter opener. Beecher considered a moment, then said, "That's pretty generous, Wally, but what about track? You'd have to..."

"No, I know. But the track kids can practice on their own for a week. They're just conditionin' right now, or I can get them to help with the play an' stuff, or..."

Beecher held up his hand to interrupt. "Wally, that's okay. I think we'll just wait and see what Laura wants to do."

The coach sat back and began to pick nervously at the dirt under his fingernails.

Beecher watched him a moment, then asked, "Wally, why do you want to do this? Just a week ago, everybody in the play was a loser. Is this a peace offering because of what happened in here?"

Wally shook his head adamantly. "No!"

Beecher cocked his head. "Really?"

"Seriously. No."

He paused, then slumped a little. "Okay, maybe a little. But the major thing is Karl, ya know?"

"Karl?"

"Yeah. I mean I can't believe he did that. Running head first into a house, for God's sake? I mean that's no accident or anything, right? It had to be on purpose. I mean..." His hands searched the air for the right words. "I mean... isn't life short enough already? An' then last night I figured it all out."

"You did?"

"Yeah. Karl understood what's been takin' me years to realize. It's all bullshit."

"What is?"

"Life."

"Life is bullshit?"

"Yeah. There's not one thing that's real. Not even us." He shifted in his seat. "Hell, did you know I never wanted to be a coach or a teacher?"

Beecher raised his eyebrows.

"No, I wanted to be a minister."

Laughter burst from Beecher's mouth before he could stop it.

"What?" he sputtered.

"I know. I know," Wally said. "I swear too much, I drink too much, an' I'm hornier than an Irish setter humpin' a teddy bear."

Beecher leaned back and laughed even louder.

"Seriously, Boss. Ya ever seen that?"

Beecher wiped a tear from his eye. "Unfortunately, yes," he said, still chuckling.

"Well, that's me. I'm the setter. But it's kinda natural, ya know? In high school I was this great football player and that's what football players did – swear, drink, get laid. I couldn't break the habit. Besides, who's got time to read all them books?"

"But a minister?" Beecher asked.

"I don't know. I always liked sittin' in church, lookin' up at the cross, prayin' and listenin' to the choir sing 'Amazin' Grace.' But there was my image. So I just bought into it, played college ball, got the only degree that made sense to everybody but me. Now I ain't got nothin'. I don't do nothin'. I just spend all day teachin' these kids to play games. Games! What the hell? I mean, there are people like Karl, bashin' their heads against the walls, and I'm teachin' kids to play fuckin' games?"

Wally sat back in his chair and took a big breath to relax.

"Sorry. Didn't mean to use that word," he said.

"I understand," Beecher replied.

"An' then I read this play… an' I get it. I screwed up! I mean, I shoulda done what was right all along. I don't wanna be like all those dead people in the play, waitin' to find that part of myself that's eternal. I wanna find it *before* I die. I wanna be what I'm s'posed to be, not just stand around playin' games and watchin' everything go past."

Tears formed in the big man's eyes.

"I gotta do something, ya know? An' if finishing this play will help those kids and help Laura, it'll help me, ya know?"

Beecher inconspicuously pushed a box of tissues toward the coach. He understood Wally's feeling. Beecher too had to do something, a charge to fulfill, an obligation bigger than himself. His conversation with Amanda and Art, as well as the arrival of Wayne Diego and the torture of the laughing woman, had convinced him. However, his challenge was more daunting. Wally's self-loathing was but a low hurdle; Beecher's terror was insurmountable. He had lived in fear his whole life – fear of abandonment, of death, of the uncertainty of life.

He looked down at his injured hands. "Everything is upside down," he thought. "Kind and gentle Karl Jurgens turns out to be a sexual deviant, while boorish and belligerent Wally Forseth becomes introspective and wise. Things are definitely out of order."

He considered the earnestness in Wally's face. Quietly, calmly, he said, "You're like the Greeks, Wally, looking for balance, an equilibrium between the physical, intellectual, emotional, and spiritual."

"That's my point! My life is unbalanced. It's *all* games. I don't mean just sports. I mean everything. I play games with the people I know, with my job, with what I do for fun, with my whole life. Equilibrium? Hell,

I gave up the spiritual. I deny the emotional, and I haven't had an intellectual thought since..." He hesitated. "I've never had an intellectual thought." He laughed and reached for a tissue to blow his nose. "Like I said, I don't wanna do this jus' for me. It's for Laura and her kids. I jus' wanna help, ya know?"

Beecher nodded, then began rearranging his pile of paper clips. "Well, I'll tell you what. I'll call Laura, see what she thinks. I'll probably have to call the paramedics to revive her after I tell her what you want to do, but it's very nice. I'll get back to you. Okay?"

Wally nodded.

"You going to be all right?" Beecher asked.

The coach nodded, and murmured, "Thanks, boss." He stood and turned to the door. He hesitated at the door, and said, "Um, you won't say anything about the minister thing, will ya?"

Beecher smiled. "Not until you enroll in the seminary."

"Thanks," Wally said, extending his hand. Beecher showed him the bandages and they both laughed. Wally patted Beecher on the shoulder and turned to leave.

"Uh… Wally?"

"Yeah?"

Beecher thought of what he had learned the last few days, what he had seen, the words he had heard. He considered their importance, how they were all related. He considered the Sacred Trio. The Unholy Three.

"Would Wally understand?" Beecher wondered. He examined the coach's face. All he saw was innocence.

"I really appreciate the thought. You're a good man."

Wally clapped his hand on Beecher's shoulder again. "Thanks," he said and closed the door behind himself.

Beecher had almost spoken. The Word stirred within him. The time was near.

Beecher looked down at his watch. Five o'clock. Time to face Amanda again. This time he would be close to who he was, he knew. Still, his lower jaw trembled.

# XIII AMANDA WILSON

## 1

In the tiny cubicle dubbed "Special Collection," Amanda pored over picture after picture, searching for someone with her own nose, chin, or eyes. For nearly two hours she examined each obscure, minuscule face in photos of the student council, the ushers club, the band, the football team, the cheerleaders. Finally, in the last book she had pulled from the shelf, she saw something, somebody that made her stop.

It was a smile. Among eighty other smiles in a concert choir obviously coached to grin on cue, this one was genuine, inviting. Amanda was certain she had seen this girl before. The old black and white picture revealed little detail, but Amanda assumed the girl was blonde from the hair that was two shades of gray lighter than that of either girl standing next to her. From the left of the picture, Amanda counted heads in the girl's row, then counted the same number of names beneath the picture: G. Dahlgren. The girl's name was G. Dahlgren. No first name, just the initial *G*. "What does *G* stand for?" Amanda wondered.

Amanda marked the page with a slip of paper and paged back to the class pictures, first checking the seniors. Nothing. No *G. Dahlgren.* No Dahlgrens at all. She found no more answers with the juniors and sophomores. She examined each class all the way back to the seventh graders. No one with that name.

Beecher opened the door and stepped in. "Sorry to interrupt, but I have to go home. Find anything?"

"I don't know," Amanda said. "Do you know this girl?" She turned the book around so he could see clearly.

Beecher leaned over the table, then picked up the yearbook to have a closer look. The girl did look familiar, especially the smile, but the book had been printed long before he arrived in Jefferson. Beecher turned the book over and checked the cover date. The picture had been taken close to the year he was born. He shook his head and smiled. "Mmm. No. I don't think so. You think this is your mother?"

Amanda took the book and looked at the picture again. "I don't know. Maybe. Maybe not. I just think I've seen her before somewhere. I know that face."

Beecher brought the book closer to his face. "You know what? Me, too. An older version maybe. What's the name?"

"G. Dahlgren."

"G?"

"That's all it says."

"Hm. No. That's not helping me. Sorry."

"Well, at least I have something to look for tomorrow." She stood and picked up her cloak from the back of her chair. Beecher watched her as she put it on, and he narrowed his eyes. His stare made her pull the collar tighter about her neck. "What?" she asked.

"I didn't notice before, but my wife has a cloak just like that, only black."

Amanda smiled. "I guess we won't be going to any parties together," she said smiling and walking past him.

Beecher locked the library door. As the two walked down the hall, Beecher crossed his arms tightly across his chest and said, "Um, Miss Wilson..."

"Amanda."

"Amanda, about what happened in my office. I mean Art and..."

"Yes. I wanted to talk to you about that, but..." She looked at her watch, then patted his arm. "You have to go home. Do you need a ride?"

"Yeah. Sure." Then he stopped. "Um... No. I can't. It's a small town. People will talk."

"Okay. Tomorrow? Your office again?"

"Yeah. Maybe. Wait. No. Karl's funeral is tomorrow. Give me a call here at school in the morning. Okay?"

"Sure."

The two walked to the door, both thinking the questions that could never be answered in the few remaining steps to Amanda's car. Amanda unlocked the

Topaz and thanked Beecher for the use of the library. Beecher smiled and said, "I hope you find... you know... whatever it is..."

"Thanks."

Beecher turned and headed home.

"Mr. Jones!"

Beecher looked back. Amanda gave him her best parade princess wave and grinned. Beecher laughed and waved back.

Art huddled in his hideaway in the plumbing warehouse. He relived the day, especially the conversation with Beecher and Amanda Wilson.

All seemed calm, yet he knew. The aching he felt in his back reminded him of earlier conflicts.

This time, the Earth Man did not see yet the connection the Word had made with the Storyteller, with Beecher, nor did he see the influence the Flame held over Amanda, but he would. He had defeated hundreds of others over the centuries. He would not stop. He hated to lose.

Art's jaw throbbed as he rose and walked toward Beecher's home.

# XIV SARAH JONES

## 1

In the misty gray, as Art walked the streets of Jefferson, he watched flickering orange flames rise from the sidewalk, thick red blood trickle from streetlights and buildings, a shimmer of gold around the edges of his vision. From the deserts of the past, he heard the words of Muhammad: "One who can control himself when in anger, in passion, in fear, and in attraction is safe from the hands of the devil and the fires of hell." That was the purpose of the fog in Jefferson, to dissolve restraint. As each person surrendered to his personal obsession, the earthly domination of the Matchi-auwishuk, the Weendigoes, and the Earth Man increased. No one was safe from himself.

Blocks away, Sarah sat on the porch couch, waiting for Beecher to come home. The truth of her past, her reality, had returned. For years she had hidden it, ignored it, suppressed it. Now there was no longer escape. The night with Frank, today at the plumbing shop, her reflection in the store mirror, Wayne Diego – they all scraped away the layers of the past and laid her soul bare before her. It was now time either to reject it or embrace it. She had made her choice.

After leaving the store, she stopped at the bank, then drove home to make the necessary phone calls. She worked frantically, cleaning the kitchen, making beds, balancing the family checkbook, and writing a daily menu for the next week. The house was neat, orderly, spotless.

In the hallway near the front door stood two suitcases crammed with all the essentials – the entire contents of her underwear drawer, a romance novel, a picture of Jeannie, and enough clothes for two weeks. Between the suitcases sat a shopping bag stuffed with five pairs of shoes. Her hooded cloak and a spring jacket hung over the banister.

The fog thickened again. The streetlight glowed like a yellow torch in the mist, and the trees and houses across the street were mere shadows. Images of a long repressed memory flickered and grew in Sarah's mind.

*Upon the beach*
*Three white altars*
*Three glasses*
*Three bottles of red wine*

*Springtime mist*
*Blackness of night*
*Torches*
*Shadows*
*Three women*
*Six men*
*Sacrificial calf*

The calf made Sarah wince. She leaned forward, her chin in her hands, closed her eyes and allowed the long-smothered memory to play.

2

The idea had been born in Sarah's comparative religion class at Bemidji State, a thoroughly boring course until the syllabus reached the rituals of the Bacchus/Dionysus cults. The Maenads, the Bacchantes, and their abandon to vicious pleasure and violence dominated the after-class discussion at Hobson Union. A particularly obnoxious frat boy named Ryan…or Brian…or Wade…Sarah couldn't remember…suggested the class hold their own Dionysian ceremony at Diamond Point Park. At first everybody at the table laughed.

"Seriously. A class orgy. Think of it as primary-source research."

Again the table laughed.

"Hey! What's better – reading about it in the library or living it?" the boy asked.

The laughter was not quite as genuine and an uncomfortable quiet followed as the proposition sank in. It was Sarah who finally asked, "Why not?"

A girl…for some reason, Sarah thought her name was Prudence…responded, "Because it's illegal!"

"So's smokin' dope, but you do that, doncha?" Ryan/Brian/Wade challenged.

"Yeah, but…"

Prudence went on to list all the legal, moral and scholastic ramifications such an act would have if they were caught. After ten minutes of Prudence's whining, Sarah had enough. "If you don't want to join us, don't. Just stay up in your tidy little room and knit doilies or something. Who cares? The least you can do is shut up. God Almighty!"

Prudence stared at Sarah and the uncomfortable, yet determined faces of her classmates. She stood. "Fine," she said in a quiet voice. "If the cops find out, don't say I didn't warn you." She walked away shaking her head.

Sarah remembered the smile on Brian/Ryan/Wade's face… Why was such a simple name so hard to remember?... His leering grin approved as she laid out her vision of how the ceremony should be conducted, and his nodding endorsement as the ritual unfolded on paper. Each step was choreographed, from the opening procession, to the wine, to the sex, and to the final sacrifice. However, as the plans solidified, becoming increasingly risky and explicit, the number of willing participants dwindled to Sarah, two other women, Wade/Ryan/Brian, and a horny sophomore boy from Newfolden. Ryan/Wade/Brian assured the rest he could get more men from his frat if they were really serious. Sarah looked at the rest and asked, "Well?"

The girls looked at each other, shrugged, then nodded. "Yeah! Let's do it," Horny Boy responded. "I even know where I can steal us a calf."

As word spread through the class, there were more than enough men in class willing to take part and to carry out the ritual with the seriousness Sarah demanded. This was not to be simply rampant sex, but it was to be a religious experience. Under Sarah's stern eye even Horny Boy tempered his lasciviousness. Concern over police interference was relieved when Brian/Ryan/Wade said he had connections with the city police and knew which officers could be bought off for a couple cases of Grain Belt beer.

Wade/Brian/Ryan… What the hell was his name?! … always seemed to have an answer for any problem which arose. He was like a teaching assistant watching the plans unfold, suggesting refinements here and there, grooming his charges for something greater. At first Sarah resented his proposals. True, the ceremony had been his idea, but it was the women, particularly Sarah herself, who had perfected the concept. As time went on, however, she realized his knowledge of Bacchanalia and his depravity excited her. His recommendations, his leering glances encouraged her own perversion, so rather than clashing, their two personalities complemented each other and promised to drive the ceremony to new levels of debauchery.

## 3

The night from the past unfolded in Sarah's mind. In his own brain, Art watched and recognized what she could not, what had eluded him throughout the Great Maskings old and new. The Missing Third.

For centuries, for millennia actually, the Earth Man had searched for the Wondrous One, the woman or soul capable of satisfying his desires, the female third of the Unholy Trio, and nowhere among the spiritual and temporal worlds, nowhere amidst his millions of seductions, had he found anyone to fulfill his insatiable hunger and at the same time worthy of sharing his eternally evil existence. Year after year he had sent his minions to scour the earth, selecting and grooming potential mates, only to have them fall short of his demands.

Wade/Ryan/Brian was one of those minions. Sarah had no way of discerning that or anything else from the spiritual world. Since her family's death, she had resented the spiritual, rebelled against it, denied its existence, all the while maintaining an air of innocence and modesty. To achieve her freedom from restraint, she now looked to Wade/Ryan/Brian and his ceremony. The Dionysian ritual would be her vehicle for achieving pure decadence, of giving herself over to depravity. Blind to Wade/Ryan/Brian's deception, she embraced the ceremony, careless of its outcome or consequences, unaware of who actually orchestrated the event.

Over the ages Art had seen the ceremony many times – the women in gray, the men in blue, the altars, the wine, the burning torches stuck in sand, the frightened calf. He had watched as rituals degenerated into wantonness, wantonness into violence, and violence into death. He heard the moans of human pleasure. He watched blood run from the side of the sacrificial calf torn with tooth and nail. He felt the calf's heart beating frantically as it was ripped from its protective rib cage. He smelled death as frenzied worshippers gnawed at heart, flesh and bone, leaving few scraps for flies and crows.

In the ancient rituals, the calf represented Dionysus feeding his followers' hedonistic lust, dying that they might live in the pleasures of wine and flesh. But that night in Bemidji, Sarah saw the calf as something else. It was the remnants of purity that had lived in her beyond her family's death, the innocence that haunted and constrained her.

As she lay in the sand, excited by wine and sex, she could no longer bear the destructive confinement of morality. She had to destroy it. It was she who first attacked the calf. It was she who goaded the men to tear the animal apart, stretching and pulling its legs until the bones snapped. It was she who cheered as Ryan/Wade/Brian waded through the calf's blood and dug the heart from the chest. She smiled as he knelt before her and handed the heart to her. She held the heart aloft, teasing the sky with the life the bloody mass represented, and then the first bite, relishing the death of innocence.

The other revelers scrambled over themselves to eat of flesh and muscle, life and death. Only Wade/Ryan/

Brian ignored the remains of the calf. Instead he rose, sneered viciously at Sarah. Wrapping her in his arms, he kissed her neck and licked the calf's blood from her mouth. His thin hands stroked her sides, her back, her breasts. Sarah groaned angrily, then pushed him away and stepped back.

"What?" he asked, confused by her rejection.

Sarah looked at him and his bloodstained face. She looked past him and saw. She saw the table/altars overturned, the broken bottles and glasses. She saw the broken remains of the calf. The air was as still as the mist which hung over the quiet lake. Truth dripped from the trees, and Sarah knew. She shrugged and smiled at Wade/Ryan/Brian. "It's not enough," she said.

"What?" he asked. "Me?"

She shook her head. "You. This. Any of it. It's not enough. That's why nobody follows Bacchus. The human body can't contain or withstand enough pleasure to ever be satisfied. If you can't be satisfied, what's the point? If you can't have it all, why have any of it? Fuck it. I'm done."

Sarah waded into the cold water and dove under to wash off the calf's blood. After scrubbing herself, she slowly walked back to the beach. The others lay sleeping on the beach, dead to the spirits moving about them. Chills reminded Sarah how alive she was. She took a deep breath of the night air, picked up one of the robes and covered herself. Wade/Ryan/Brian stood naked in the fog, watching her. She could feel his eyes. As thrilling as the night had been, this man was nothing to her. She turned and walked past him, then stopped.

"Thanks," she said.

"For what?"

She turned to him. "Now I know."

Wade/Ryan/Brian smiled and nodded. When Sarah turned and headed back to the football stadium at the edge of the park where she had left her clothes in a neatly folded pile, she did not see the boy's face stretch tight against his skull as his body stretched upward. Nor his eyes sink into their sockets. While she dressed behind the arched entryway, she did not see him open his mouth nor the blood that ran from his teeth. She could not smell his rotten breath or hear him when he whispered her name and memorized her face.

## 4

To be one with the god, to have him inside, to be inside him – that was what the early Dionysus worshippers had sought. To achieve perfect ecstasy. To reach the orgasm of the soul. It was what Sarah had sought and found impossible to achieve. So rather than suffer from the overwhelming power of imperfect excitement, she ran from her desire. She ran to the mundane. She ran back to Jefferson. She ran to Beecher.

For years she hid behind her mask of motherhood, her mask of dutiful wife, her mask of businesswoman. Then came the fog and the night with Frank. The fog had revealed her for what she was, what she wanted to be.

She realized now Frank was only prelude. She would have more, so much more. It was near, somewhere in the fog.

A car horn in the distance distracted Sarah's thoughts. She looked up and through the lace curtains saw two headlights racing up the street. "Too fast," she thought. "He's driving too fast." She hurried to the window as if her attention could slow the vehicle. The horn blared again as the fog swirled ahead of the car. Growling, the car emerged from the haze and squealed to a stop behind Sarah's Buick, which was parked on the street at the end of her sidewalk. Sarah recognized both the car and driver. Wayne Diego. He sat in his black Mercedes Roadster, peering through the mist, waiting for her. "Why would he look for me? How did he find me?" she wondered.

Sarah stepped onto the porch and leaned her head against the storm door window to watch him. Diego revved the engine again, the male mating call she remembered from her youth. "Definitely a small penis," she thought.

Diego leaned across the seat, smiled out at her and beckoned her to join him. Sarah scowled and stepped outside.

"C'mon, Princess. Let's go for a ride," he yelled. Again the engine raced.

Sarah laughed sarcastically and shook her head. "I'm not your princess," she called back.

"Hey, c'mon. I can show you somethin' you've never seen before."

"Yeah, but nothing I want."

Diego raised his hand and shrugged. "Oh, yeah? Ya never know."

Sarah regarded him for a moment. She had seen him before today, but couldn't remember where. He smiled his sinister smile and said, "C'mon, Princess. Whattaya say?"

And then she recognized him. The hair, the voice, the mannerisms, the leer.

"I know you," she said.

Diego smiled.

"Wade?" she asked.

"Wade or Wayne. What difference does it make?"

"Or is it Brian?"

"Brian's okay, too."

"Ryan."

Diego shrugged. "I'll be whoever you want me to be."

Then Sarah knew. Diego was not human. He was an invention, a manifestation created to be her lover. Like Wade/Ryan/Brian, Wayne Diego was a cheap replica of something she craved, but would never have.

She looked at the clothes, the car, the hair, then shook her head.

"Who do you work for?" she asked him.

"What?"

"Who do you work for? I mean, fancy car, fancy clothes. You obviously don't work around here."

"Well, I…"

"You know what I think you are? Nothing. There is no Wayne Diego or whatever you say you name is. You drive around in your fancy car, harassing women, looking for some sign you really exist. Whatever you're supposed to be, you're not very good at it. Fact is, I bet this isn't even your car. I bet it's your boss's car."

Diego blinked.

"Probably stole the boss's car to steal the boss's woman, right?"

Diego's face was blank.

"And when that didn't work out, you just kept on driving to Jefferson."

"No, I… You don't understand. I just…"

"Forget it. I know who you are. We both remember. You weren't what I wanted back in Bemidji. You're not what I want now. Send your boss next time. Him, I might want to meet."

Her words flustered the Weendigo. He was confused, but scrambled to reestablish his charm. "All right, Princess –"

"I told you –"

"Ah, yes. Princess isn't enough. You want to be queen. Well, your majesty, remember that kings come and go, but it's only a matter of time before everybody wants Wayne Diego."

His words masked his bewilderment, but his actions betrayed him. He slammed the car into reverse, backed up without looking, and stopped. Leaning forward over the steering wheel, he gave her his two-fingered salute and hit the gas, only to rocket backward another fifteen feet. Embarrassed, he braked, shifted into first and drove forward, his downcast face avoiding Sarah's eyes. His disorientation nearly took him into the back of Sarah's car, but he managed to swerve at the last moment and drive away. Sarah laughed.

She did not see the pompous manitou's fingers shrink on the steering wheel. She did not see his jaw tremble from starvation. She did not know she had defeated a weendigo. Rather than defeating him with moderation, she had defeated him with an all-consuming lust that outdid his. She would not be satisfied with an underling; she wanted the king. Although she had won, she did not know the prize.

## 5

As Sarah waited for Beecher, she rehearsed her lines, anticipating his reaction, reasoning out her responses. He'd never understand the truth, and there was no good lie. However, she had to tell him something.

The fog continued to grow thicker. Sarah sat on the porch couch again and leaned forward, her elbows on her knees. Nervously, she rubbed her forehead, trying to erase all her memory, but sitting only made her remember more. She had to move. She stood, pushed her hair back from her face, and paced in front of the couch. Dreams and images attacked mercilessly. Beecher. Jeannie. Her parents. Her brother. The train. The car. Frank.

Sarah reached up and squeezed her head between her palms, hoping to crush the contrasting images flashing through her brain. The pain forced her to the couch again. Visions flickered rhythmically, insistently, swelling in intensity. Frank and the trees. The unknown voice. Sarah the victim. Frank and the fog. Sarah the slut. Frank the beast. Over and over. Diamond Point Park. The calf. The heart. The blood. Wade/Ryan/Brian. Brighter. Faster. Then new faces. Diego. Beecher. Her reflection in the shop mirror. Her standing on an altar, devouring the calf's heart, grinning maniacally. An unknown man. An unknown woman. Faces flashing swiftly, harshly, pressing closer, growing larger until Sarah's head felt as if it would burst.

"No!" She screamed, flinging her arms down and springing to her feet. Struggling for breath, she leaned her hands against the window frame and rested her head against the pane.

Through the mist, Sarah saw Beecher walking briskly, his hands stuffed into his coat pockets. When he reached their sidewalk and turned toward the house, he stopped and picked up *The Shopper*, which a careless delivery boy had left on the lawn instead of the porch. It was then Sarah saw the bandages. Instinctively, she rushed to the door and called, "What did you do to your hands?"

Beecher looked up sheepishly. "Long story."

"What happened?" she demanded, hopping down the steps and hurrying toward him.

"I broke a glass down at the Plains."

"With your hands?"

Beecher nodded. She grabbed the paper from him and cast it aside, then took his hands and examined the bandages. "How bad?" she asked.

"I'll tell you inside."

The pain of Beecher's wounds coursed through his bandages into Sarah's hands and up to her brain. New images swarmed about her. His broken glass. His pierced hands. Blood. Wine. The horrible face struggling to push through her womb. Teeth sinking into flesh. Animal flesh. Her flesh. The shattered mirror lying in pieces around her. Great shards rising from the carpet. She let go of Beecher's hands, grabbed her head and raced into the house, leaving Beecher alone on the sidewalk.

"I didn't do it on purpose," he called after her, mistaking her grimace for anger. "Sarah, wait. I want to tell you who I met today at school."

Beecher retrieved the paper and followed her into the front hall. Sarah struggled to put on her black cloak. The suitcases and the bag of shoes formed a phalanx in front of her as she grappled desperately to fasten the clasp. Beecher stood in the open doorway, confused, as Sarah battled ineffectually against cloth and metal. Her hands wouldn't do what she wanted them to.

"What's this?" he asked.

She took a deep breath, steeled her jaw, and said, "I'm leaving."

"You're going on a trip?"

"No, Beecher. I'm leaving. I'm leaving you."

He blinked. The words did not register immediately. They hung in the air a moment until Beecher finally understood. He lowered his head, took a deep breath, then asked, "Why? What did I do?"

"You didn't do anything." She paused, picking the predetermined sentences carefully. "Beecher, I know you don't understand, but I have to go. I wish I had a better explanation, but I don't."

He placed *The Shopper* on the hall table and let his bandaged hands fall to his side. He looked at the floor a moment, then back at her. He turned his wrists and raised his wounded hands to her as an offering, as if he had been wounded for her. When she stepped away and leaned back against the closet door, Beecher's hands flopped back to his side in futility.

Sarah knew he needed more. She pulled the cloak around her and held it tightly, as she searched for the right phrase.

"I know you don't need more stress, but… I have to go. Once I'm gone, things will be better."

Beecher stood quietly, biting his lower lip.

"I have already done so much to hurt you," Sarah continued. "Not just my bitchiness, but things… things I don't want you to know."

Beecher snorted. "Things you don't want me to know. That's ironic."

"Why?"

"I already know too much."

Sarah turned to him sharply.

"I know the secrets of the universe," he said, only half believing the hyperbole. "Everything I've learned in the past few days hurts like hell. I'd just as soon live in ignorance, but no. According to Art Benson, I have a 'mission to save the world.' I must tell what I have seen and somehow everything will be all right."

"What are you talking about? Art Benson? Since when do you listen to crazy, old Indians like Art Benson?"

Beecher winced. "Since the world began to fall apart and he seems to know why." He leaned on the banister. "Sarah, I don't want you to go. I... God, I love you."

"I know," she replied, scratching her head, "but it doesn't change things."

Quietly, Beecher asked, "What did you do?"

Sarah's shoulders tightened. It shouldn't hurt, but she couldn't face him. He was as innocent as the calf. She turned her face to the closet door. The bile of guilt rose in her throat, and she brought her fist to her mouth to keep it down.

"Sarah, please look at me." Beecher said.

She couldn't. She closed her eyes, wrapped both arms about her stomach, and refused to move.

She heard the rustle of the shopping bag as Beecher breached her hastily erected defense. She cried as he gently took her shoulders and turned her to him. With the back of his bandaged hand, he wiped a tear from her cheek.

Sarah flinched. His touch burned, the revenge of the guiltless. She would not move. Masochistically, she ground her teeth and endured his scorching fingers.

"You don't want to do this," Beecher told her. "Stay and we'll figure it all out. Okay?" He leaned forward and kissed her forehead. The flame spread through her body as if her blood were gasoline. "Okay?" He put his arms around her and held her close. The pain was so intense she grasped his coat and whimpered into his chest. "Shh. It will be all right," he told her

"But it won't be all right," Sarah thought. "Staying will destroy him and Jeannie. It will destroy me." She had to resist. Mustering all her strength, she tightened her grip on Beecher's coat. Building deep within her chest, her whimper became a growl and burst into a scream as she thrust him away. Beecher fell backward and crashed into the doorjamb. His head bounced off the frame and he fell sideways onto the stairs.

"Damn it, Beecher! Why are you so fucking nice?" she yelled. She pulled on the back of her neck with one hand, vainly searching for the words she had rehearsed. No matter how deeply she rummaged for them, she could not find them. Her breath was short and erratic. She had to stop this.

Viciously, she leaned toward him and vomited the words into his face. "All right. You want to know what I did? I cheated on you. All right? I had sex with another man, out on his front lawn in the middle this damned fog. We fucked like animals, and you know what? I loved it. I loved everything about it. I loved having him inside me. I loved having his hands and tongue all over me. I loved it when I came and nearly fainted. And I loved it even more when he came inside me and I could feel him dripping out between my legs."

She leaned back. "You wanted to know what I did? That's what I did."

Beecher did not react. She wanted him to. She needed him to. Bending closer until her face was inches from his, she spat, "You want to know something else? I'd do it again."

Nothing more would come. Her face contorted, and she retched at the acrid taste in her mouth. "I'd do it again," she choked. She could not bear Beecher's lost expression. Averting her eyes, she left him alone on the stairs as she escaped to the living room sofa.

Beecher lay stunned. He couldn't fight. He couldn't move. "The Word chose the wrong man," Beecher thought, but he didn't care anymore. He didn't care about matchi-auwishuk or weendigoes or laughing women or Karl or Wally or anything. He wanted his family. But he had no illusions. His world was gone. Right now his greatest desire was to curl up under the stairs and sleep through the approaching Apocalypse.

After several minutes, Beecher groaned and picked himself up from the stairs. He crossed the living room and sat silently in the easy chair. Sarah huddled on the sofa, her cloak pulled tightly around her shoulders.

Beecher leaned forward and rested his arms on his thighs. "Why?" he asked quietly.

She huffed and shook her head. "Shit, Beecher. I don't know."

"Who was it?"

"It doesn't matter. If it hadn't been him, it would have been someone else."

Her head ached. She looked down and began examining the clasp on her cloak. "There's something inside me, Beecher, that just... I saw it at the store today in the mirror. There was this... this gruesome... absolutely hideous creature growing inside me struggling to rip me apart. I don't know. Maybe I'm just going crazy."

"We can all go away," Beecher suggested, but she shook her head no. "Why not?"

She paused. "I think I'm pregnant. When I looked into that mirror, I could tell."

Beecher looked up at her incredulously.

"I know that sounds stupid," she said, "but I could. That's why I can't stay here. That's why you and Jeannie can't go with me. If we were together, every time I'd look at you, I'd see what I'd done. So would you." Sarah paused to consider her words. They were only partially a lie.

"Where is Jeannie?" Beecher asked.

"Over at Ralph and Bonnie's. I asked them to take care of her until you got home."

"Do they know you're leaving?"

Sarah shook her head. "I just told Bonnie I had some things to do at the store."

"The store. What are you going to do about the store?"

"Franny can run it until I can find a buyer."

She watched as reality finally began to settle in Beecher's mind.

"Where are you going?" he asked her.

"I won't know until I get there. I'll phone."

"You're leaving tonight?"

She nodded.

In a final desperate grasp, he asked, "What am I supposed to do for a car? Karl wasn't finished with the Chevy and I haven't had time..."

"I took care of it," she interrupted. "Jeff Arnold is going to try to finish it tomorrow or the next day. Until it's done, though, he's going to loan you one off his lot. His brother Jerry is bringing it over tonight."

Beecher sat back, exasperated. "You've thought of everything."

His bitterness strengthened her. It was easier to tolerate his anger than his grief. She felt the turmoil inside him, yet she marveled how he remained in control. "But of course he would," she thought. "That's what makes him Beecher." She nodded and finally clasped her cloak about her neck. "I'm ruined," she told him. "I'm no good to anyone anymore. Especially not you, Beecher. I was never any good. Just let me go, okay?"

"Are you going to him?"

"No." She paused. "No. I can't. I'm just... I'm..."

"Running away?"

"If it makes you feel better to think that, yes."

"From me? From Jeannie?"

Sarah shook her head. "I'm no good for Jeannie. Hell, I feed her Spam, for Christ's sake. Motherhood is a sham for me. You know that. I just go through the motions. I have no flair for it."

She watched as Beecher sucked his lips between his teeth. "I don't get it, Sarah. This... This isn't like you."

She sighed and felt the anger returning. "No, this is exactly like me. Beecher, you know I wasn't a virgin when I married you."

"Well, yes, but..."

"I had lots of sex. I should have been ashamed, but I wasn't. It's what I did. It felt good and I liked it. But promiscuous sex is not a good business practice in Jefferson, so I became what I wasn't. Respectable. I married you and had Jeannie. I accepted everybody else's morals – the church's, the town's, my parents', yours. I had to in order to survive. But it isn't me. I love decadence – the freedom, the thrill, the complete abandon to the inner animal..."

"So your morality is immorality."

"Oh, God! Beecher, don't preach to me. That's what I'm trying to tell you. This is what I am. A slut. A whore. Whatever you want to call me. I'm worthless and irredeemable. Art says you're supposed to save the world? Fine. Maybe he's right. Do it. But you can never save me."

Sarah caught her breath and knelt in front of Beecher, looking up into his tear-filled eyes. "Look. You can tell everybody I have to visit a friend who's dying. After a while, when you're more settled and sure of yourself, you can tell Peggy, then maybe Ralph and Bonnie. Pretty soon everybody will know or will have guessed. You won't have any trouble. Everybody here likes you better than me anyway."

"What am I supposed to do about Jeannie? What do I tell her?"

"I don't know. Just love her and hug her a lot." She patted his knee. "Jerry will be here in a little bit with the car, then you have to go get her. I have to leave before it's too difficult to see."

Beecher didn't move, not when she rubbed his leg, stood, and kissed the bump on his head; not when she struggled carrying her suitcases to the car; not when she came back for the bag of shoes. He sat slouched in the chair, his bandaged hands hanging limply over the arms of the chair, his legs splayed carelessly in front of him. Sarah knew she was leaving him silent and empty, but the Great Something awaited her. She stood in the doorway and whispered, "I'm sorry." When he glanced up at her, she was gone.

Inside the car, Sarah sat motionless, staring back at the house. Through the fog, she saw the faint glow in the living room windows. She laughed. The living room? The dead room. There was no more life. The corpse of her marriage lay in the casket of that room, and she was the one who killed it, a sin for which she could never atone.

"And the wages of sin is death," she remembered.

"Sin." The word reverberated in her mind.

Sarah gazed at the house a moment longer. "Hmph. Sin?" she said, laughing and shaking her head. "Wrong god." With new resolve she started the engine and turned on the headlights. The fog danced and swirled madly about the car, but defiantly she inched the car into the street and drove away, intent on accomplishing her own mission.

## 6

The night was full. Sarah. Beecher. Amanda. Weendigoes. The laughing woman. The Earth Man. Art could not tell where he should be. So many lives to follow. So many spirits. He closed his eyes and let the Word lead his sight. When the vision cleared, his sight was still with Sarah. Her final destination was clear to him, though not to her. The Earth Man and Grave Swamp. How she was to get there neither she nor Art knew. The darkness tingled about the car as she drove.

It would have been faster to leave town just by taking Carlson Avenue to Highway 2. Instead she wove through the streets and alleys until she reached the T-intersection of 5th and Manning. Across the street in front of her stood Frank Thorstad's house. The fog had stopped its frustrated dance and hung like a veil in front of her. Sarah could see lighted windows, but little else. She pulled into the intersection, turned slowly, staring intently toward the house. "I need to see Frank one last time. I need to tell him," she thought.

When he did not come out, she circled the block and stopped at the T again, one house back from the intersection. She turned off the headlights and the engine. The air inside the car was stifling. She rolled down the window and waited. The air hung still and silent as she watched the front door of Frank's house. She knew he would eventually come out for a smoke.

As she waited, she saw the tree behind which she hid that night, praying for a glimpse of Frank's hard and violent sneer. Even without the legend of Grave Swamp and its aftermath, the man exuded danger, a danger that thrilled and aroused her whenever she thought of him. Sarah shifted in her seat. She saw the porch step where he had sat that night, arrogantly blowing smoke rings while she trembled in fear, anticipation, and lust behind the tree. She saw that spot on the lawn where she had eagerly shed her clothes and given herself up in one more sacrificial rite of gratification. All the sounds, smells, sights of that night rushed over her and she leaned her head back against the car seat, knowing that a far greater experience awaited her, one her body could not contain, the one she had sought that night on the beach long ago, the ultimate pleasure that far exceeds physical constraints, the orgasm of the spirit.

She unbuckled her seat belt, leaned her head back against the seat, and closed her eyes, as about the car, fog spirits frolicked and danced in anticipation. She thought of all the men she had ever had, especially those at the Dionysian ritual. She relived Frank pushing back her hood. She unzipped her pants and her right hand slid under the waistband of her panties as she remembered his lips, his tongue, his hands...

And then she saw another face, heard another voice. The man at the plumbing shop. The one in the Mercedes Roadster. Her hand stopped.

"Everybody wants Wayne Diego," he had said. The words amused her and she giggled. The creature did not understand his limitations, she smiled. He had made the mistake of taking human form and no human could supply what she was after. Not Diego. Not Frank. Nobody. Her thoughts drifted to an as-yet-unknown face, their meeting, the moment of consummation, of fulfillment. Her fingers reached down, pushing, probing. After several minutes, she groaned, sighed and sat up. Absently, she brought her hand to her nose and sniffed her fingers. Lost in her vision was the mission that was now upon her.

A storm door slammed across the street. Sarah glanced quickly at the house and saw Frank standing on the steps. The fog hung as thickly as that previous night, but as she watched, a small window in the mist opened before her. Sarah could just make him out, sitting on the porch, lighting his cigarette in the same arrogant fashion, blowing the smoke high into the air and looking out over the street.

Four laughing and inebriated fog spirits rose out of the street and hovered nearby, awaiting her next move. As soon as she saw them, she knew. First Diego. Then Frank. Now these spirits. Her return to this spot had a purpose. Sarah sank low in the seat, her eyes barely above the dash simply watching, awaiting her moment. Her nerves buzzed with anticipation.

To her left, Sarah heard footsteps on the sidewalk. As the window of fog opened wider, Sarah saw a woman approaching, dressed in a hooded cloak much like hers, only forest green. In the dim light of the fog the woman's cloak looked almost black, but Sarah's fashion sense appreciated the difference from her own. The hood was up so Sarah could not see the woman's face.

"Where did she get a cloak like mine?" Sarah wondered. Sarah had asked Beecher to special-order hers from a store in Los Angeles for her birthday. In Jefferson it was one of a kind, yet here was somebody else with the same design.

Sarah heard a cough and looked back at the house. Through the cold night air, she saw Frank's face brighten. He stuck the cigarette in his mouth and stood, cramming his hands into his jeans pockets and sauntering down the sidewalk to meet the woman.

Amanda ignored him as she walked past, until he called, "Hey!"

She stopped and turned toward him. "I thought you might be back for more," Frank said in a voice that carried easily through the fog.

"Excuse me?"

"That's not me," Sarah whispered. The fog spirits looked back at her, nodded, and returned their attention to the scene before them.

Frank looked confused. The woman's voice wasn't whose he expected. He stepped toward her and tried to see under the hood, but couldn't. "I'm sorry," he said. "I thought you were somebody else."

Amanda turned and began to walk away.

"But, hey, you'll do."

The fog spirits turned to Sarah.

When Amanda did not stop walking, Frank said, "Wait a minute. Who are you? You live around here?"

Her steps strengthened in stride and purpose, determined to leave this irritation behind.

"Who are you?" Frank called louder.

With even more resolve, Amanda continued her escape.

"Hey, I'm talkin' to you, bitch!"

"That's not me," Sarah muttered aloud. Again the spirits nodded. They smiled, shrank to the size of hummingbirds, and flew back to the open car window, lighting on Sarah's shoulders.

Amanda stopped, turned back to him and pulled off her hood. Sarah did not recognize the face or the blonde hair.

"Bitch?" Amanda asked. She was soft spoken, but her low, deliberate, calm, and forceful voice carried strongly through the night and made Frank take a step back.

He regarded her a moment and said, "I just wanted to know who you are."

"And calling me a bitch was your way of saying hello. You need a better opening line."

Frank smiled.

Sarah was furious. She no more wanted Frank now than she wanted Diego, but watching him with Amanda brought the taste of bile to her mouth again. This time it was not the taste of guilt or remorse; this time it was jealousy. The drunken fog spirits felt Sarah's rage and grinned.

Frank sat on a stump that jutted out from the tree and leaned back against the trunk. He took a long drag on his cigarette. "Shit. Yer all bitches to me. Ya only got one thing I want or need," he said.

"And what would that be?" Amanda asked.

Frank smirked, looked directly at her crotch and grabbed his own.

"Charming," she huffed as she turned away.

"Hey, I bet this can thaw out that frigid cunt of yours," Frank persisted. "It gets kinda hot and hard to control at times, but I ain't never had any complaints."

By now Sarah heard nothing. Her fury roared in her ears, drowning out all other sound. The fog spirits laughed and flew out of the car, whirling about it, encouraging her to take action, leaping and dancing in joyful anticipation. Sarah rolled up the window and started the car.

As Amanda stalked away, Frank stood before the tree and in one final drastic fit of bluster, rubbed his crotch, and said, "Ya got enough room for all this, baby?"

"That's not me," Sarah snapped loudly, turning on the dome light. "This is me." She glanced at the four corners of the car where the spirits had gathered, gleefully nodding. She threw the car into drive and slammed the gas pedal to the floor.

As the car roared across the intersection, Frank was unaware of anything other than the mysterious woman fleeing his taunts. A loud bang of something bouncing off the curb jolted his attention. He spun and saw the Buick borne by four drunken spirits flying out of the mist toward him. Inside the car, Sarah's gray eyes flashed maniacally under the dome light as she screamed, "This is me!"

Frank had no time to react. The bumper caught him in the midsection, drove him into the tree, and wrapped its metal arms around the trunk. For a split second, Sarah saw the recognition in Frank's face just before his blood exploded over the front of the car and the force of the crash slammed her head through the windshield. In a long, torturous moment, Sarah felt the glass gouge into her forehead and peel the skin back from her skull.

Sarah sprawled across the hood and through her own blood saw Frank pinned between the car and the tree, his head hanging limply next to hers. The strange woman dashed to Sarah's side and cried frantically, "Oh, God! Oh, God! Are you all right?"

Sarah turned her head and felt the large flap of skin and hair hanging loosely above her own eyes. She looked through a stream of red into the stranger's face, a face framed by long blonde hair. Sarah whispered, "You're not me." She turned her eyes back to Frank. His face was blank. The yellow snakelike eyes, the sneer, the lust had vanished. Sarah looked back at the woman. The fog spirits floating behind the woman's head nodded and smiled. Sarah smiled back, closed her eyes, and in a last moment of semiconsciousness, watched the Dionysian calf's face dissolve into the face of an unknown man.

From blocks away, Art had seen it all. He huddled in the doorway of the hardware store across from the school. The din of screams, splintering bones, cascading blood, and death filled the night. The Earth Man had turned on Frank, an infant weendigo, one of his own. Art did not understand why. He raised his face to the darkness, seeking through sorrow and pain for answers. He found none until the Word spoke.

*Their egos,*
*Their emotion,*
*Their lust seduces them.*
*Physical demands,*
*Extravagance,*
*Hunger for power enslaves them.*
*The reign of calamity and confusion begins.*

Art listened for hope, for promise, and heard.

*In times of chaos*
*Superior people arise*
*And lead others out of the swamp,*
*Away from the grave.*

Art opened his eyes and stood.

He knew.

Beecher's time had arrived.

# XV BEECHER JONES

## 1

Art scrambled across the highway, past the school, through the fog and dark to Thorstads' house. He heard the screams as Frank's wife Sammi found her husband's crushed body bending over Sarah Jones' car hood. As the night crackled, and blue, white, amber, and red flashes split the darkness, Art watched Sammi's son Tony frantically tugging her away as she tried to tear the car from the tree and Frank's corpse with her bare hands. He felt Sammi's convulsive sobs against her son's chest as he repeatedly murmured, "It's too late, Mom. It's too late."

Unseen Matchi-auwishuk sped past Art through the night, laughing and dancing their way back to Grave Swamp and their master. Exulting in their victory over normality and the Word, they ignored everything around them. Art was invisible to them, nothing more than shadow and dust. He was not surprised. Matchi-auwishuk exist in an unseeing, unhearing universe, leading the mortal world to blindness and deafness. In their ears the sound of Art's footsteps was but a whisper of wind amidst their celebration. He easily slid through their dance and found the destruction at Thorstads'.

Amanda had pulled Sarah several yards from the wreck in case the car caught fire. She and several neighbor women sat on the ground next to Sarah, guarding her unconscious body until the ambulance arrived. Tony held his mother in his arms in the soft glow on the porch steps, while a heavy woman in a flannel nightgown, hair rollers, and sneakers patted her hand and whispered banally, "It will be all right, Sammi. It will be all right." A clump of five men stood back from the car, looking for a method to release the tree and Frank's lifeless body from the bumper's embrace.

No one noticed Art, and there was nothing for him to do. He looked to the sky and listened. The Word directed him to Beecher to ease the news, to focus his task, to engage his will. Art nodded, then scuttled along the sidewalk, avoiding overhanging branches and bounding fog fairies.

Five blocks later at Beecher's house, Art watched Beecher through the window of revelation that came with his spells.

## 2

The knot on the back of Beecher's head throbbed and his shoulder ached from trying to break his fall. He stood and wobbled a second before gaining his balance. Banging his head, along with Sarah's verbal onslaught, had left him dazed and unsteady. He stabilized himself by leaning against the wall, then eased his way to the front door to look at the fog-inundated street.

The car was gone.

It was true. Sarah had left.

Thickening haze floated down in front of the street lamp, dimming its harsh illumination. Beecher waited patiently, expecting the laughing woman to rise from the sidewalk or for Amanda Wilson to appear before her altar or some such delusion.

There was nothing – no visions, no sounds, nothing but a muffled siren somewhere in the distance.

His equilibrium slowly returned, but he still held the railing as he climbed the stairs to their bedroom. The empty, sterile room chilled him. Sarah had taken both her latest romance novel and her picture of Jeannie from the nightstand. In the closet, she had left most of her summer outfits; nevertheless, her essence had abandoned them. The closet stood occupied but totally deserted. She had also cleared the bathroom, her personal sanctuary, of her make-up, her shampoo, her robe. Beecher wandered into the spare room where Sarah had slept for the last week. Here she had left no trace of her existence.

Beecher crossed into Jeannie's room. He breathed deeply, searching for Sarah's scent somewhere amidst the stuffed animals and dolls. On the nightstand he found the picture of Jeannie clinging to her mother's neck after a Disney World Goofy had inadvertently startled and horrified her. In the photograph Sarah smiled as she tried to calm the frightened little girl. Beecher stroked the frame of the picture, then sat on the bed and examined the image. Jeannie was right: That was a better time.

Who would calm Jeannie's fears now that her mother was gone? Certainly not Beecher. He could not calm his own. His own fears were legion – the fog, Karl, Amanda Wilson, the laughing woman, Matchi-auwishuk, Weendigoes, the Earth Man, the Word...

Outside, another siren wailed in the night.

"What the...? That's the second one I've heard. Must be something big," Beecher wondered.

In college, he could discern the difference between ambulances, police cars, and fire engines by their different sirens, but he had since lost his ear. Besides, what difference did it make now? What difference did anything make?

"Where the hell is Jerry with that car?" he wondered. He walked down the stairs and looked again onto the street. Still nothing. Distracted by anger and frustration, Beecher did not notice the thickest fog had sunk lower. Instead he meandered into the living room and sat on the couch, leaning his head gingerly against the cushion. He didn't even have the energy to find the television remote control.

He covered his face with his bandaged hands and cried. His tears shook loose scrambled images of Sarah,

Jeannie, the laughing woman, Karl, Laura, Wally, Amanda Wilson, Art Benson...

His world was collapsing, yet something else was pulling together. Life? The world of spirits? What? Beecher groaned in frustration. It didn't make sense. It didn't make any sense.

Great sobs wracked his body and he pushed his hands harder against his eyes. In his anguish, the colors behind his clenched eyelids shifted from black… Sarah… to gray… the fog… to green… Amanda… to yellow… flame… to red… what? Red? Blood. Blood red. Beecher lowered his hands. His palms had bled through the bandages. Clutching his hands to his chest and rolling onto his side, he tried to escape into sleep.

3

On this night, sleep provided no refuge. Beecher recognized part of the dream when he saw the red eyes moving through the trees above him. It was the snake again, the one he had seen at Laura Grapnic's house after Karl died. Abandoned on the cold ground at the foot of a twin oak lay Sarah's lifeless body. The snake had descended through branches and the fog and crushed the life out of her. On the other side of the tree, Jeannie clutched her stuffed Tigger and cried, "Mommy, where are you? Mommy!"

The tree hid Sarah from Jeannie. Beecher had to get her away. Just as he moved toward her, he saw the snake crawling out on the limb immediately above her. "Jeannie, run!" he yelled.

"Daddy, where's Mommy?"

"Jeannie, please just run, sweetheart! Just run!"

Jeannie refused to budge, and Beecher watched helplessly as the snake drew closer. He tried to run to her, but he felt like he was running through water. The snake dropped down from the tree and coiled itself around Jeannie's feet. The frightened girl closed her eyes and wailed even louder, "Mommy!"

The snake encircled her legs, slithering and climbing to her waist. Beecher's lungs and muscles ached as he inched closer. Jeannie felt nothing as the snake wound its way up her body. She embraced her Tigger tighter and cried yet again for her mother. Beecher reached her just as the snake wrapped itself around her arms. Beecher grabbed the snake's head and began to peel it from her body.

"No, Daddy," she shrieked. "Mommy. I want Mommy!"

Dream or not, Beecher knew he had to stop the snake. No more death. Not Jeannie. Sarah was gone. He could not lose his daughter. Madly, he pulled at the snake as Jeannie continued to scream, "I want Mommy."

Despite her cries, Beecher pushed and pulled, plied and peeled, struggling to free her from the snake's clutches. Suddenly, the snake's attack veered away from Jeannie to Beecher. It slithered around his arms and constricted them firmly to his sides, rendering Beecher helpless as it slid once around his neck. With its new adversary now powerless, the snake turned its head to Beecher's face, gazed at him with its glowing red eyes, flicked its tongue at him, and began to squeeze itself around his throat. Beecher fought to free his bound arms, but couldn't. He fell to the ground gasping for breath, and battling to retain consciousness. He cried for Jeannie, but only dry, gagging sounds escaped his lips, immediately lost in the night air. Jeannie could not hear him as she wandered into the fog weeping for her mother.

## 4

The phone rang in the kitchen. Beecher jolted awake, finding himself on the living room floor. His mind still half lost in the dream, he clambered across the living room floor to escape the snake and pulled himself up on a dining room chair. He weaved through the kitchen door, stumbled into the wall, grabbed the jangling receiver, and grunted.

"H'lo?"

"Beecher? Joe Engstrom."

"Now what?" Beecher thought. Joe's voice sounded higher, excited.

"Beecher, are you there?"

"Yes, Joe. What's wrong?" Beecher's words sounded groggy and slurred in his own ears.

"It's your wife."

"Sarah? What about her?"

"She's had an accident. The EMTs are working on her right now."

Beecher's mind suddenly cleared. All trace of his snake-filled nightmare vanished.

"Where?' he demanded. "What happened?"

"She ran into a tree over here at Thorstads'..."

Beecher dropped the phone and ran into the fog. Art met him at the end of the block, stepping into his path.

"Wait!"

Anxious and angry, Beecher stopped for a moment, then tried to push by Art, who would not be moved.

"Damn it, Art! Get out of my way."

"Can't …save her. She's… lost."

"What? You mean she's dead."

"Not dead. Lost. To Matchi-auwishuk. To Earth Man."

"Art, I don't need this shit now," he said, attempting to shove past the annoying obstacle.

Art would not be ignored. Stepping in front of Beecher, he said, "Is time. The Word…"

"Art, I don't care about your Word, your matchi-bull-shit. If you don't get out of my way… I'm not a violent man, but..."

"Word in you now," Art said, poking Beecher's chest. "Must tell story. Now. Karl… lost. Frank… lost. Cannot save Sarah. But can save…Jeannie, Amanda Wilson, Jefferson."

"I told you I don't care!" Beecher growled, shoving Art's shoulders and thrusting him to the sidewalk.

As he strode past, Art scrambled to his feet to stop him.

"Do care. Must stop evil, snake," Art blurted as he grabbed Beecher's shoulder.

Beecher turned and threw off the offending hand. "Damn it! I've told you before. Don't touch me, Art. I'm warning you."

His hands clenched into tight fists.

He glared at Art, considered, then asked, "What snake?"

Art took a step toward him. "Snake Karl saw. Laura saw. You saw."

"I never saw..." he protested.

"Just now," Art said. "In dream." He touched Beecher's temple to reinforce the words.

Beecher stood staring at Art. His cheekbones tensed as he ground his teeth. Before Art's could say another word, Beecher's right fist crashed into his face and sent him sprawling to the ground.

"I told you not to touch me. I don't care about any snake. I don't care about your Indian spirits. I don't care what your Word needs. I have to see my wife. Now, leave me alone."

Art raised himself to his knees as Beecher sprinted away. If Beecher would not hear, Art thought, if he would not see, the Earth Man had won all. "No! Wait!"

Even though Art's knees rooted to the spot, he was still with Beecher, in him as he ran the five blocks to Thorstads'. Each time Beecher's feet struck the sidewalk, Art felt his head throb. At the same time, Art lived within himself, struggling to his feet to follow. Sharp pangs shot through his back as it straightened, but he could move faster. His jaw swelled painfully, yet flexed easier than before. Beecher's pain doubled Art's own so his head pulsated with Beecher's; like Beecher's hands, Art's palms ached. And still his body carried him faster than ever, carried by need, strength, inspiration.

When Beecher turned the last corner, he saw Thorstads' house ablaze with flashing yellow, blue, and red lights of emergency vehicles. On the front lawn, Joe Engstrom, firemen, sheriff's deputies, and Jeff Arnold struggled to remove Sarah's car from the tree. Sammi and Tony watched the operation from the porch. A female EMT climbed into the back of a city ambulance parked on the sidewalk. Her partner, a man half her size, slammed the doors behind her, hopped into the cab and drove away.

"Wait! Damn it! Wait!" Beecher called, staggering down the street after the speeding ambulance.

"Beecher! Stop!" Beecher heard Joe Engstrom chasing him, but he couldn't stop. He had to catch up with Sarah.

Before he had run ten feet, though, Beecher's body rebelled against his mission. His feet tangled beneath him, and he stumbled to the pavement. Struggling to rise, his legs and arms gave way, and he fell flat. He lay still for a moment, resting his cheek against the cold asphalt.

"Holy shit, Beecher!" Joe exclaimed, rushing to Beecher's side. "What happened to you?"

"What?" Beecher asked, sitting up.

"You're covered with blood."

Beecher looked down at himself and in the flashing lights saw his shirt covered with the dried blood from his hands. He could only imagine what his face looked like. "Nothing. I'll be fine. What happened, Joe? What did she do?"

"She ran into that tree back there. Went right through the windshield and ripped her face up pretty bad."

"Through the windshield? That can't be right. What happened to her seatbelt?" Beecher asked, his hands beginning to shake.

"She wasn't wearing her seatbelt."

"That's wrong. She always wears her seatbelt."

Joe shrugged. "Not this time."

"Is she going to be all right?"

"They don't know yet. Right now she's alive. That's the important thing. Now what about..."

"How could she run into a tree?"

"I don't know. We're still trying to sort all that out. There are… indications..."

"Indications of what?"

"Well, it's just speculation, but she may have done it on purpose."

"On purpose? What? You mean like Karl? There's no way she..."

"Beecher, calm down."

"Calm down? You tell me that my wife tried to kill herself, and I'm supposed to calm down?"

"I never said she tried to commit suicide, just that she may have crashed the car on purpose."

"That's ridiculous." Beecher turned to follow after the ambulance. His feet did not want to follow where his brain led them.

"Beecher!" Joe caught him by the arm. "Jeez, are you all right? Have you been drinking?"

"No. I just bumped my head at home and I'm not feeling real steady. I'll be fine."

"Where'd that blood all over your face and hands come from?"

Beecher looked weakly at his hands. "I cut my hands on some glass today. I probably broke my stitches."

Joe looked at him skeptically. "Okay. For right now, sit down. I'll get the patrol car and take you to the hospital."

"I'm fine, Joe! Just tell me what's going on."

Joe examined Beecher's face a moment, then nodded. "Come on," he said. "Let's sit down."

Beecher sat on the curb, and Joe sat next him. "We don't know the whole story, but... How has Sarah been feeling lately? Things okay at home?"

Beecher was slow to respond. "What do you mean?"

Joe noted the hesitation. "Well, you know. Has anything been bothering her? Has she been… you know… stable?"

Caught between the truth and Sarah's honor, Beecher rubbed his forehead before answering. "Sarah's always been stable." He turned to Joe. "What kind of question is that?"

"Beecher, she killed Frank Thorstad."

"Weendigo," Art whispered, watching and listening to the scene safely far down the street.

Beecher blinked. "Wee… Killed...?"

"Pinned him against the tree." Joe pointed to where the team of rescuers were prying the bumper away from the tree. Frank's dead body hung above the car's hood like a broken limb. "Bastard never had a chance. Probably died on impact."

Beecher pulled up his legs and dropped his head to his knees. He thought for a long time. "Is that what you think she did on purpose? Kill Frank Thorstad?"

Joe shrugged his shoulders. "Don't know. The woman who found them said before Sarah passed out, she kept telling her, 'You're not me.' You have any idea what that means?"

"No. Do you?"

Joe shook his head.

"Who's this woman who found her?" Beecher asked.

"An out-of-towner. Name's Amanda Wilson."

"Flame," Art whispered.

Beecher remembered the music, the altar, the cloak, Amanda offering him a ball of fire. He remembered the paradoxical face of innocence and wisdom he had seen just today in his office. Beecher swallowed and held his head.

"You okay?" Joe asked.

Beecher nodded. "It's just been a horrible day."

"You know this Miss Wilson?"

"No. I mean not really. I just met her this afternoon at school. She's a writer doing research here at the school library."

"Did Sarah know her?"

"I don't think so. I don't know how she could. Did this Miss Wilson see it happen?"

Joe nodded. "She says she was just out for a walk, looking over the town. She walks by here, and Frank starts talking all this shit to her, almost like he knows her. Well, you know what a prick he is. His wife and kid just inside and he's out here trying to pick up stray pussy. In Jefferson? Anyway, Miss Wilson confronts him, an' he says something like, 'I'm sorry. I thought you were somebody else.' So she walks away. But Frank keeps after her, asks her name, and she keeps on walking... until he calls her a bitch. She comes back to tell him off, and he tries to act real smart, leaning up against the tree, dragging on his cigarette, asking her if she wants to go at it right here on the lawn. Then, all of a sudden, she hears a car engine. There's Sarah's car, hopping the curb, coming right at Frank. Squashes him like a bug. There were no headlights, the lady says. We checked the car. She never turned 'em on. Why would Sarah be driving in this fog at night with no headlights?"

"Matchi-auwishuk," Art mouthed.

Beecher heard. He looked up and watched the workers struggling to remove the car from the tree.

"Beecher?" Joe nudged him. Beecher shrugged helplessly.

"Anyway," Joe continued, "there's nothing Miss Wilson can do to help Frank, so she decides to get Sarah away from the car before it blows up or somethin'. Sarah's layin' on the hood, and before ..."

Beecher was lost in the words echoing in his brain:

*"...He said he'd write a story about sex in the fog..."*

*"...Right out on his front lawn in the middle of the fog, fucking like animals..."*

*"...if she wants to go at it right here on the lawn..."*

Joe touched his arm to bring him back to reality. "Beecher, you sure you're okay?"

"Huh? Yeah. Where's this Miss Wilson?"

"Had a deputy take her down to the station to get her statement."

"I want to talk to her."

Joe shook his head. "You better go see your wife. Besides, Doc's gonna want to take a look at those hands."

Beecher nodded. "Yeah, you're right." Then he remembered and gave a pathetic laugh. "I don't have a car." He pointed toward Jeff Arnold and the group gathered around his tow truck working to remove Sarah's car from the tree and move it from Frank's corpse. "Jeff's brother was supposed to bring me one tonight, so I could go get Jeannie... Oh, my god. Jeannie."

"Where is she?"

"Over at Ralph and Bonnie Bjerkland's."

"Okay. I'm going to take you to the hospital. I'll get a hold of Bjerklands and see if they can take care of her at least until morning. Do you have any family you can leave her with?"

Beecher shook his head. "The closest thing I have to family is Peggy."

"Your secretary?"

Beecher nodded.

"We'll see what we can do. Come on."

When Beecher stood, he was still unsteady. "Better have Doc look at that head of yours, too," Joe said. He put his arm around Beecher to support him, walked him back to the patrol car, and sat him inside.

"The Word needs you," Art whispered through his loosened jaw. "Tell the Story."

Beecher looked at the street ahead, waiting for the laughing woman.

"Tell the story."

Beecher leaned forward and raised his eyes to the blackened sky.

"The Story is yours."

Sitting back, Beecher bit his lip, breathed deeply, and nodded. He then stared forward, barely blinking. A car approached slowly through the fog, and as it neared, Beecher recognized it. It was the black Mercedes Roadster. The car stopped in front of the patrol car and blinked its headlights at Joe. Einar Nordhaus opened the passenger door, stood, leaned on the roof, and bellowed, "What's goin' on, Joe?"

Joe walked over to Einar. Beecher sat quietly, watching as Joe explained and pointed, pointed and explained. In the Mercedes' dome light, Beecher saw Wayne Diego lean over to hear the details and examine the scene. Joe said something and Einar looked into the patrol car. Beecher turned away and looked out the side window. After a moment he heard Einar's door slam. Joe entered the patrol car and closed the door. The Mercedes inched forward and Diego gave the horn a quick beep. Joe and Beecher looked over as Diego gave a two-fingered salute and drove forward.

Art heard Beecher's thought. "Weendigo."

Art nodded as Joe started the engine and drove toward the hospital. Behind them, Jeff Arnold's tow truck pulled the wreckage of Sarah's car away from the tree. Frank's nearly bisected body folded over like a ransom note and crumpled to the ground.

# XVI AMANDA WILSON

1

Beecher grieved. Sarah hung between earth and eternity. The laughing woman wondered. The Matchi-auwishuk frolicked. The Earth Man waited. Above all was the Word.

Beecher heard, though he wanted not to. He saw, though he closed his eyes. The Word called, and he would not move, hidden behind the mask of denial.

Art knew his words were not enough. Though Beecher wanted to believe, the blue-eyed Indian was crazy. To trust him was insanity. In the midst of chaos, sanity was to be cherished.

Death and confusion surrounded the town, Beecher knew. He now believed in Matchi-auwish. He had seen the Weendigo. He knew the Earth Man reigned. The Word, he didn't understand.

Locked in darkness, he flailed against the light. Rather than embrace perception, he renounced it. Art realized that this was time for Beecher to take the Flame, but it was not Art's to give. And time was a hindrance.

Art decided he could not convince Beecher on his own. He must start with the Flame itself. He must start with Amanda Wilson. He must follow his visions to her.

Still wrapped in her forest green cloak, Amanda lay on her bed at Dale's Motel, tossing from side to side in the garishly lit room. Her life shaken, she could not rid herself of the images. The man. The fog. The car. The woman – her words. Screams –sirens – shouts. The police – flashing lights – blaring radios.

Amanda pulled the pillow from under her head and put it over her face, trying to forget. It was no use. She needed to talk to somebody, but Herb and Maggie were still in London. She tried to call Sherman, but he was not home, evidently molding somebody's manuscript into something salable. The only one left was her mother, but how would Amanda explain where she was and why? Instead, she lay searching for answers from a day and night that had only raised questions.

The touch of Beecher's fingers. His voice. Revealed dreams. Shared paths. Unseen, unknown forces – The Word, Matchi-auwishuk, Weendigoes, Manitous. She knew the names, though she had never heard. She felt their power, though she had never seen. They were as much a part of life as air.

She turned and faced the curtained window.

At the police station, the deputy sheriff doubted every answer she gave: "I was just passing by… I'm a writer… From California…No, I don't know either of them. I'm only in town for a few days… I'm looking for my birth parents… I only went for a walk." The answers were the same she gave at the scene to the Jefferson policeman. After the third time through, she evidently satisfied officers' curiosity, and they let her go.

Now alone in her cramped motel room, Amanda turned to her side and watched the clock radio minutes change. 08...11...13...

She reached for the television remote and turned on the television. She flipped from one channel to the next. The Jefferson cable system consisted of four channels from Fargo, the PBS station from Bemidji, three superstations, Country Music Television, and the local weather. Four times through the stations, she realized there was not going to be anything to distract her from the day's events. She turned off the television and watched the clock again. 17...18...19...

Behind the clock, the phone sat, deaf and voiceless. She turned onto her back, her hands behind her head. The flat beige ceiling stared back at her blankly, as vexing as an empty page.

A train whistle blared across the highway, momentarily deflecting Amanda's gaze, but when her eyes returned firmly to the blank ceiling, she saw the face from the yearbook. *G. Dahlgren.* She remembered the face, particularly the smile, the eyes, and…something else. Amanda decided she would have to go back to the school the next day and examine the yearbooks from the years before and after the one in which she found the picture. She could also check hospital records, if she could get past the woman at the front desk.

Her next day's itinerary set, Amanda rose, hung up her cloak, and lay down again, still in her jeans and USC sweatshirt. She first gazed at the ceiling, then at the wall to her left, and finally to her other shoulder to watch the clock on the bedside table. The numbers on the clock changed even slower...22...22…23…23...24… The phone still sat accusingly behind it.

"This is 'The Night That Will Not End'," she thought.

She turned to her other side and saw her suitcase standing against the wall. Her cloak hung near the door. It needed dry cleaning. Though the woman's dried blood was barely visible against the dark fabric, Amanda couldn't stand knowing it was there.

She turned back to the bedside table. The clock hadn't moved. 24...24...24… She checked her watch. 9:24. She tapped the face to make sure it was right. "If time is going to go this slow," she laughed, "I'm never going to get to sleep."

"In L.A. it would only be 7:24. In Sand Creek..." She hesitated. In Sand Creek, it would be 10:24. Too late to call her mother. Her mom usually went to bed at 9:00 "Maybe tomorrow," she thought.

But now the phone began to stare back at her.

"All right. Enough of this," she said. She rose and walked to the window.

Dale's was a single level motel where travelers parked their cars outside their door. The parking lot was only wide enough for one car per room and a single lane of traffic around the building. Beyond the lot were a ditch, the four lanes of Highway 2, the railroad tracks that ran parallel to it, and the vast prairie of the Red River Valley.

When Amanda looked out, there was nothing but a slow-moving grain truck crawling past on its way to Duluth. The fog was dense, and in seconds the truck's lights were barely visible. In a few hours, Amanda thought, the truck would be in Duluth. A few more, it could be in Sand Creek. She could be in Sand Creek. She could drive to Sand Creek. Her mother would love to see her. She looked briefly at the still-staring phone, then turned back to the window.

Outside, Art stood beside her car, waiting. At first, Amanda wasn't sure she saw someone. Even when she knew, she didn't recognize Art. She opened the door, and called, "Who is it?"

Art held onto the car and stepped forward into the light from the door and sat back against the Topaz's hood. "It's me."

She stepped forward. "Art, is it?"

He nodded.

She came out of the room, looked at Art's beaten face and disheveled hair, and stopped. "What happened to you?" she asked, coming forward and touching his jaw.

Art couldn't think of what to tell her. He felt the Flame within her, but, even though Beecher had loosened his jaw, the words would not come. "I… I'll be all right. I just..."

"Do you want something?"

Art nodded.

She tilted her head quizzically. She reached forward and touched Art's jaw. The Flame radiated from her fingers as he held her palm against his face and felt its warmth. Her eyes saw and her fingers heard what happened.

"Beecher," Art said.

"He did this to you?"

Art nodded. "For me. It's all right. A gift from the Word. Now the Flame. Words come easier. He freed me. Now he needs you."

She dropped her hand to her side, looked down at the ground, then at Art's bruised face.

"Why?" she asked.

"His time is here," Art said. "He needs the Flame you bring. You must save him."

She stared into Art's eyes and knew. She nodded. "Where is he?" she asked. Not "What's wrong?" "What can I do?" or "Why me?" Just "Where is he?"

"You drive. I'll show you," Art said.

She stepped back into the room, changed into a hooded sweatshirt, and grabbed her keys. As they pulled up to the highway, Art saw the laughing woman crouching on the other side of the road, watching, waiting. "Turn left, but be careful," Art told Amanda.

Assuming he meant the fog, she tentatively crossed the westbound lanes and turned left into the nearest eastbound.

Just as the car began to accelerate, the laughing woman dashed in front of them. Amanda slammed on the brakes, and the tires screamed. The woman, stood illuminated in the headlights, smiled, pointed directly at them and motioned for them to follow.

"Holy…! Is she nuts?" Amanda asked.

Art shook his head. "No, it is the laughing woman."

Amanda turned to him. "Beecher's laughing woman?"

"Beecher's, mine, yours. She belongs to no one, not even the Earth Man. Although he does not know this yet. She will be with us, for us."

The laughing woman nodded and stood patiently, waiting for Amanda to continue.

"What should I do?" Amanda asked.

Art watched and listened as the woman cocked her head teasingly and began to tiptoe down the road.

Art glanced at Amanda, then said, " You know her."

Amanda peered into the fog after the woman, then began to nod. "Yes, I think I do. I'm not sure how, but yes. I know her."

Art smiled. The Word had spoken. "Follow," he said.

Amanda inched the car forward and the laughing woman led them. She walked, ran, skipped, encouraging Amanda to drive faster, always staying in front of them, provoking them on. When they reached the hospital service road, the laughing woman ran to the parking lot entrance and directed Amanda to pull in.

"The hospital?" Amanda asked.

Art nodded. "He is here."

Amanda turned in and parked as the woman sprinted to the hospital door and leaned against it jauntily, waiting for them.

The parking lot was virtually empty. There was only one other car in the visitors' lot and three cars in the staff lot. The laughing woman clambered up the wall and remained outdoors as Amanda and Art walked into the lobby. There was nobody at the desk.

"Hello?" Amanda called. Nobody answered. Tentatively, she walked through a double door and saw a nurses' station down the hall. The blue glow of a television lit the small waiting room. A disheveled man in a bloody shirt sat alone in the flickering light, dozing in his chair with his head resting on one of his freshly bandaged hands.

"Is that…?"

Art nodded.

"What am I supposed to say?"

"Listen to the Flame within you. You will know what to say."

"Why is he here?"

"Ask him." Art motioned for her to go on.

"And you?"

"I will wait."

Amanda nodded and walked away. Art returned to the lobby, sat down, and watched the ceiling.

## 2

As Amanda approached the desk, she sensed another presence. She quickly scanned the room and saw nobody except Beecher. Quietly, she advanced and touched him on the shoulder. "Beecher?"

"Hm?" He looked at her groggily. "Miss Wilson?"

"Amanda," she nodded. "Are you all right?"

Beecher rubbed his eyes and sat up. "Yeah, I'm fine."

"What are you doing here?"

He wiped his cheeks with both bandages as if he had just walked into cobwebs that kept clinging to his face. "My wife," he mumbled.

"What's wrong with your wife?" Amanda said, sitting in the chair next to him.

Beecher looked up at her. "You were there."

It took Amanda a moment to understand. "That woman in the car was your wife? My god. I'm sorry. I didn't know."

There didn't seem to be any more to say. The two of them both stared straight ahead, looking for words on the opposite wall. Finally, Amanda broke the silence. "How is she?"

Beecher pursed his lips. "Don't know. Doc's still inside trying to assess all the damage. He's not sure whether to airlift her to Fargo or what. Especially with the fog."

"How about you?"

He weighed his response, before saying, "I'm fine."

Amanda pointed to the blood on his shirt.

Beecher looked down at himself and scowled. "Oh. My stitches broke. Got blood all over my hands and face. Only took a second for them to fix. I'll be all right."

She reached to touch his head. "You look a little pale," she said.

He raised a hand defensively, and turned his face away. He whispered, "I'm fine," then paused. "I'm sorry. I'm just upset."

Amanda nodded and examined her own hands. She had seen his wife lying on the hood of the car. She had dragged her from the wreck. She had heard her words.

"She said, 'You're not me.'"

Beecher turned to look at Amanda. She smoothed the nonexistent wrinkles from her pants leg.

"When I found her, she said, 'You're not me.'"

Beecher leaned forward and looked down at the floor between his knees. "That's what the police told me."

Amanda leaned her head back against the wall. "I've been trying to figure out all night what that meant."

"Did Frank think you were Sarah?"

"Frank?"

"The man who was killed."

"I don't know. Maybe. She was wearing a cloak like mine. Different color, but the same style. I guess he could have mistaken us for each other in the dark. But..."

"But?" he asked.

"It didn't sound like she was talking to me about this Frank person. It was more like..."

Beecher looked at her, willing her to finish. "Like what?"

"Almost like she was talking about… well… about you. But I couldn't have known that then. I didn't know she was your wife. How could I know that?"

Beecher's face twisted. He shook his head and turned away from her.

"I'm sorry. Did I say something wrong?" she asked.

"No," he said, as he absently leaned his head against the wall. He recoiled in pain as the lump on his head met the hard concrete. "Shit!" He rubbed the sore. "I'm sorry, but, God, that hurt."

He stood and walked away from her. Amanda examined him from behind. Even though she could not see his face, she knew. She considered her words carefully. "She… uh… She hurt you, didn't she?"

Beecher grabbed a tissue from the desk and wiped his nose. "What?" he whispered.

"Your wife. With this man. She hurt you. Didn't she?"

Beecher turned to her. His mouth moved, but nothing came out. His hands flopped in circles at his waist.

"She told me she was leaving, that she…"

His neck muscles tensed. His mouth twitched. Finally, the words found their way out. "I think so. Yeah."

He sat next to Amanda again, leaned his head against his fists, and let the tears come. Amanda felt all the hurt, all the unspoken emotion. She closed her eyes, and the Word revealed images of Sarah, of Frank, of Beecher, of his daughter. The truth of Art's words and the enormity of Beecher's task unveiled themselves to her. In the darkened room, with Beecher suffering under the combined weight of betrayal and duty, Amanda heard and awaited her time to speak.

When the sobbing subsided, Amanda touched his bandaged hand and said, "Mr. Jones… Beecher… I didn't mean to pry."

"It's okay," he sniffed.

She got up and brought him another tissue. When she sat next to him again, he asked, "Why are you here?"

Equivocation no longer existed. All she knew was truth. "I'm here to save you," she said.

He looked at her quizzically, then laughed halfheartedly. "I think you're a little late."

She shrugged.

He looked at her and knew. "You've been talking to Art again."

She nodded. "Talking and listening. He can speak better now that you hit him."

"He told you that?"

Amanda thought a moment, remembering the Flame as she touched Art's face. "I knew."

Beecher hesitated. "I hit him. I was trying to get to Sarah. He was in the way, wanting to talk about the Word and his manitous. I…I just hit him."

Amanda smiled and nodded. "That's probably why he sent me instead of coming in himself."

Beecher smiled, too, and looked down at his hands resting on his knees. "What else did he say?"

"Just that you needed saving."

"So you're supposed to save me so I can save the world."

"I am to give you Wisdom and Passion."

Amanda's words sounded foreign to Beecher. He turned to her. "What?"

Again, she smiled. "Yes, I am supposed to save you so you can save the world."

"Hmph. I'm not sure the world's worth saving."

"What is it you believe, Beecher?"

Beecher thought for a moment. "I believe everything's falling apart, that the world is disintegrating faster than anyone can comprehend, that no matter what I say or do, nothing will stop it."

"Why do you believe the world is falling apart?"

His temper rising, Beecher said, "My quiet, small-town wife screws a crazy man in the fog and then kills him with her car. The school janitor, one of the kindest, gentlest men ever, secretly takes pictures of naked high school girls in the shower room, then kills himself by running his head into a wall. I walk to school one morning, get lost in the fog, and find my way only because I hear the screams of hundreds of birds crashing into a concrete wall. I keep seeing this imaginary woman who won't stop laughing at me. And finally, there is this fog that will not go away. It just keeps closing in and strangling us. I guess that's why I think the world is falling apart.

"But somehow," he continued, "I'm supposed to have the answers to stop it all. Art keeps babbling about his Matchi-auwishuk and Weendigoes, his Earth Man and the Word. He's wrapped up in this whole cosmology I've never heard of, yet I'm supposed to understand. My lord! I'm a Lutheran, not a Chippewa."

Amanda leaned forward and began arranging the aging magazines on the glass-topped table.

"What do you believe in?"

"Huh?"

"You say you're a Lutheran. What does that mean?"

Beecher thought. "I'm not sure."

"Do you believe in God?"

"I don't..."

"Or do you believe in coincidence, chance?"

"I'm not sure what you mean?"

"Do you believe things just happen or do you believe they happen for a reason?"

"I don't know. What possible reason could there be in everything that's happened?"

"It doesn't matter what. Just that there is. You want it all to stop."

"Yes."

"Therefore, you believe it can be stopped, that it's not just occurring randomly. You believe there is something behind it all, some force or forces leading to all this chaos."

"I...guess."

"Isn't that what Art refers to as the Earth Man and the Matchi-auwishuk?""

"Maybe," Beecher conceded.

"And isn't it conceivable that if there is a power that creates havoc, there is another, one that can stabilize the universe? What Art calls the Word?"

"I guess so, but why haven't I heard of this Word?"

"You have. Just by different names. Every culture hears it differently. Art hears it in the names of his manitous. You and I heard it in the name of Christ. Others hear it in the name of Buddha or Vishnu or the Tao or Allah or Yahweh or whatever."

"You're saying all religions are the same?"

"Religions? No. Religions are not the same. Man creates religion. Because man is different, religions are different. The Word, however, is the same no matter what. It is the Creator, the Eternal Unity. It exists with or without religion, with or without man."

Beecher stood and walked to the nurses' station for another tissue. He blew his nose and found a wastebasket. Finally, he asked, "And Art taught you all this?"

Amanda shook her head. "I just heard it now."

"Heard it? You mean *thought*."

"*Heard*. That's what Art taught me. To hear, to listen, to see."

"Yeah, well, I guess I'm not as quick to catch on."

"That's okay," Amanda said, grinning. "It's a woman thing."

Beecher sat beside her again. "What else do you hear?"

"I hear the Flame."

"The Flame is a person?"

Amanda nodded. "It is Wisdom. Understanding. A Right Mind. Passion to learn, to seek the way of the Word."

"What does this Flame say?"

Amanda listened, then spoke the words:

*I was the first of his works,*
*Before life,*
*Before death;*
*I emerged from eternity,*
*Before the beginning,*
*After the end.*
*Before there were oceans,*
*I was given birth;*
*After the heavens die,*
*I will live on.*
*Created before man,*
*For man,*
*I burn in the soul of a child,*
*Throughout time,*
*Leading him to the Word.*

There was no trance, no otherworldly aura, no possession by another spirit. Just a simple declaration of the Flame's relationship with the Word. Amanda listened, trusted the voice, and told what she had heard. Beecher sat quietly.

"I know it's hard to believe there is good, that the Word can set things right," Amanda told him, "especially after tonight. But why else am I here? Although we had never met, you dreamed of me and I dreamed of you.

And for some reason, here I am. Something brought me here. Something inside each of us."

Beecher started to shake his head, but Amanda interrupted. "What you're feeling is not insanity. What you're seeing are not hallucinations. I'm not imaginary. Nor is the laughing woman. Art and I saw her on our way here tonight."

"Art's here?"

"He's waiting for your revelation. He felt it would be easier if I talked to you first."

"He's not mad about his jaw?"

Amanda smiled and shook her head. "He said it was a gift."

Art stepped around the corner and sat opposite them under the television. There was an uncomfortable silence in the room as Beecher looked from Amanda to Art and then to the floor.

"So…are we the next Trinity?" he asked, half-smiling.

"No," Art said. "What is next is yours. You must listen. You must speak."

"And my dying wife? My daughter? I'm just supposed to forget them?"

"Where is your daughter now?" Amanda asked.

"She's staying with some friends."

"So she has a place to stay."

Beecher stood and walked to the darkened window. "At least for the night. I don't know what I'm going to do in the morning. Both of the people who are taking care of her work tomorrow."

Amanda glanced down at her hands, then at Art and the soundless television. She suspected Art could hear her thoughts, so she stood and looked down the empty hallway. "This town isn't safe," she thought, recalling Frank, Sarah, and the crash.

Amanda turned and watched Beecher at the window. "So fragile and alone," she thought. She walked over to him, studying her fingers on the way. Haltingly, she began, "Beecher… Mr. Jones, I know you don't know me. You have every reason to believe I am Matchi-auwish or a Weendigo, but like Art, I speak truth. I'd like to help with more than speech. If you want..." She paused. "While you do whatever the Word would have you do – take care of your wife, confront the Earth Man, whatever – I can watch your daughter for you. It's been a long time since I've entertained a six-year-old, but..."

Beecher spoke to the darkness. "She won't know you. I don't know if…"

"Do you need a ride or anything?"

"No, the local car dealer dropped off a vehicle for me. Sarah had arranged it before…before she…"

"Okay," Amanda said. "As long as you're all right.

Beecher nodded. "I'm fine. I have to wait and find out what the doctor says, and I… I have to think."

"All right," she said. There was no more to say. "I'm staying at Dale's Motel, room 14."

"Thanks," he said, returning to his chair and staring up at the flickering, but silent television.

Amanda thought a moment, but she had no profound words. "Art, are you…?"

"I'll walk," he told her, rising and joining her by the desk. They both looked at Beecher, then at each other.

"Good night," she said, patting Art's hand.

As she turned away, Beecher stopped her. "Miss Wilson?"

"Yes?"

Beecher looked exhausted. "I'm… I'll see… Room 14?"

Amanda smiled and nodded.

"I'll call you in the morning and let you know. Okay?"

"Sure. Or anytime. Seriously."

Beecher nodded and turned back to the television.

Amanda leaned toward Art and asked, "Will he…?"

Art shrugged. "Some things the Word does not reveal to me. You have given him the Flame. What else needs to be done comes from Beecher."

"And you? What will you do?"

"Like you and Beecher, I will wait."

She raised her hood over her head, pulled on her gloves. "You sure you don't want a ride?"

Art shook his head. "Thanks."

The two walked together to the front door. As Amanda walked to her car, Art stood at in the cool, wet air, watching, listening to her thoughts.

Inside the Topaz, Amanda thought for a minute before starting the engine. Finally, she nodded to herself, turned the ignition and drove to the motel. It didn't matter how late it was. She had to call her mother.

Art watched her drive away, then looked behind him toward the hospital roof. The laughing woman sat on the edge smiling at him. She stood, pirouetted, and flew off to her swamp. Art sat on a bench and let his vision follow.

3

Miles away, Grave Swamp was a mess. Six nights of reveling, not to mention what had happened this night, had taken its toll on the brush, the island, and the entire party of carousers. This night's intensity exhausted them.

At the height of the festivities, with his attendant fairies stroking his great beard, nibbling on his ears, and kissing his bare chest, the Earth Man suddenly leaned back his head and bellowed in ecstasy to the blackened sky. Casting off the fairies, he burst from them and ran headlong through the brush, breaking off twigs and handing them to his followers. When each had been armed, he sprang up and stood atop the nearest centaur. In a great sweeping gesture, he ignited their branches to serve as torches burning blue, red and yellow.

Then calling down music from the wind, he led them all in a dance, darting, spinning, bounding above, under, and through branches and brush. The light and shadows flickered and played off the fog above them in haunting, fantastic images. At each turn, each leap, every beast and spirit punctuated its move with a draft from the master's wineskin, a vessel that replenished itself instantly at his command. He held the skin above them and the wine flowed and spilled over each eager mouth which clamored for more. The air shuddered with the energy of light and frolic. The muskeg swelled in large waves and tossed the delighted partiers through the air and into the branches. Even the solid ground under the tree shook with merriment.

Above them all, the laughing woman sat on a limb of the wounded cedar, observing, contemplating. She watched as one by one, the participants dropped to the ground in drunken weariness – first, the nymphs, then the satyrs, the centaurs, and finally the master himself.

In the silent air, a giant hangover weighed over the marsh. Nymphs, those that could move, crawled to resting places far away from the noise of leaves decaying in the melting snow and whispering branches. Centaurs and satyrs occasionally attempted to rise to their knees, but found their rebellious limbs would not cooperate. To speak truth, the beasts did not much care if they ever rose again. They fell back to the party floor and lay motionless, praying for an end to the aching in their heads or to life, whichever was quicker.

The lightning-wounded tree propped up the Earth Man, their peerless leader, as he leaned against the trunk, his drowsing head periodically bobbing against his chest. Now, hours later, their misery was just as poignant as their pleasure had been during the night. The revelers lay scattered throughout the swamp – hanging from branches, huddled in groups beneath the tree, faces tilted up like baby robins, their tongues seeking more wine.

The charred debris of broken twigs that had ignited the sky during their festivities now littered the swamp floor. Bushes were bent, broken, uprooted. Trampled and torn by hoof and foot, the ground of the island had been worn bare. For all the life and joy manifested during the celebration, the aftermath revealed destruction and pain.

The laughing woman dropped from the tree, landed lightly, and surveyed the scene from ground level. She ventured out into the bog, pulling hanging nymphs from their branches and tenderly laying them on the gently rolling soil. As she floated from one creature to the next, her permanent smile ached. Back on the island, she passed a satyr which raised its head, stirred by her activity. When it opened its eyes, the beast's head swayed, dizzied by the woman's movement. It closed its eyes again and burrowed its nose into the soil. The woman dragged herself to the lightning-scarred cedar and sat down next to her master, her arms wrapped around her legs, her eyes studying the scene.

The master rolled away from her, and his body slid to the ground. He sighed, pillowed his head with his arm, and returned to sleep. A trickle of drool trailed from his open mouth into his matted beard. The woman regarded him a moment, turned back to swamp and rested her chin on her knees.

She knew morning was just hours away over Angler Hill behind her. It was not yet time, but she had seen the Weendigoes. She had heard Amanda and Beecher. The hour was soon. The woman pulled herself up and considered the master a moment. Finally, she shook herself free of her reverie, awoke the fairies, and glided off to Jefferson, the fog stumbling after her.

# XVII SARAH JONES

## 1

The lights above the hospital parking lot shimmered in the fog. Inside Beecher wept at his wife's bedside. At Dale's Motel, for the first time since she had left L.A., Amanda phoned her mother Lois. Through the night, the laughing woman flew from Grave Swamp toward Jefferson. Art smelled the Matchi-auwishuk and the Weendigoes already gathering.

He needed to do something. He needed to move, to strike against Earth Man. He needed to assemble the forces of the Word against the attack, but the Word did not need him. It spoke to him on a bench in the darkness outside the hospital:

*Life is in you,*
*but not about you.*
*The battle will be won through you,*

*but not by you.*
*Have you not learned?*
*Have you not been told,*
*"The ego is a monkey*
*swinging from one desire to the next,*
*one conflict to the next*
*one self-centered idea to the next"?*
*Let go of the self.*
*Let go of the monkey,*
*Let the senses go.*
*Let selfish desires go.*
*Let conflicts go.*
*Let the fiction of life and death go.*
*Offer up the battle into My hands.*
*Just remain in the center, watching.*

*Then forget that you are there.*

Art lowered his body to the ground and rested his head against the bench. Watching seemed worthless, but the Word had spoken. The words given the ancients through the voice of Lao Tzu still echoed. Art must "remain in the center, watching." He closed his eyes and ears and plunged into Sarah's world.

Time was out of focus. Reality merged with hallucination and fantasy. Inside her broken, bleeding body, the temporal and spiritual fused in a world of agony and fear.

Excruciating pain pierced Sarah's eyelids, dug into her skull and lifted her into the space. She hung suspended above the world, her body swinging in a great arc, oscillating between the agony of sensation and the emptiness of oblivion. Not the swinging of the ego, but the pendulum swing between the temporal and the spiritual. Slowly the pendulum arm climbed toward consciousness, hesitated, then fell backward until it began its ascent on the other end toward death. Back and forth she swung blindly, helplessly. As she rose toward consciousness, the physical agony obliterated thought; as she swung back toward oblivion, the insentient void terrified her. The bottom of the arc was the most bearable.

Finally, she could bear the swinging no longer. She twisted and struggled against the forces of gravity and motion. How long she fought she did not know. Time became a feather of reality that floated just beyond her grip. Each minute seemed endless. Each hour seemed momentary. Despite her efforts, she continued her pendular journey.

As Sarah spun and swung, space became a blur. Occasionally, she glimpsed a house, a car, a bed, but she could never tell exactly where she was. Everything moved too fast. She wanted to scream out against the forces controlling her, but she could not speak. Finally, as momentum brought her toward consciousness again, she thought she saw or felt or heard shadows reaching for her. Desperately, she turned to them, grasping at the air and mouthing empty syllables, but again gravity snatched her away and they were gone. She had to get back to them. She reached up and jerked at her tether. The swinging became erratic as Sarah tugged and twisted and jumped and fought. Finally, the rope broke and she fell, through the darkness past planets and stars, through the sunlight past clouds and trees. Sarah clenched her eyes against the impending crash.

There was no crash. Instead, something slowed her fall, and she simply reached down with her feet and found herself walking on the soft ground. But it didn't feel like ground. Sarah opened her eyes.

The world before her did not exist in her memory or anywhere she knew. Colors shifted. Shapes melted, grew, collapsed, ran, and transformed into thought. Things became words. The line between fantasy and reality wavered, faded, and disappeared.

The universe had stopped whirling and swaying, and she stood on a pond of green and black. She did not sink. The water and land had become one. A cool purple sun rose above a great hill behind a tall yellow tree.

From behind the tree floated hazy images of two creatures she had only seen in picture books. Half goat, half human. What were they called? She couldn't remember. Tentatively at first, they inched forward until Sarah smiled at them. Then they burst into the opening with a host of other creatures. One grabbed her by the waist and began to dance with her seductively, nuzzling her neck, one of his animal hands cupping her breast, the other pulling her forward so she straddled his hairy thigh while he rubbed himself against her.

Inexplicably, Sarah laughed. She leaned back her head and howled. Freed from all constraints of pain, she relished pleasure. She wrapped her arms around the creature and held him tightly. This was no shadow; this was real. Around her and the creature, nymphs played and frolicked joyously.

Suddenly, a loud trumpeting arose from the base of the tree. Immediately, all the creatures dropped to the ground. Sarah's beast released her and stumbled across the pond into the brush. Only Sarah remained standing as a large manlike creature emerged from the ground, followed by Frank Thorstad and Wayne Diego.

As Art watched, he recognized the creature. It was the Earth Man. His hair was long and unkempt, yet there was an air of royalty about him. All the spirits around Sarah lay prostrate as he strode forward to where she stood. He stopped in front of her and looked back questioningly to Diego and Frank. Both nodded. The Earth Man examined Sarah a moment, slowly circled her once, and nodded his agreement. He held his hand out to her. Without hesitation or thought, she took the hand and let the Earth Man lead her toward his home beneath the tree.

At a lightning-created fissure that was the entrance to his den, the Earth Man turned and held Sarah's face in his hands. The sky brightened into a vivid crimson, and Sarah leaned her head back, inviting his lips to hers. He kissed her, and she felt holy and sacred. Nature had healed her, blessed her, exalted her, and gloried in her perfection. The blood-red sun rose over the hill above the tree and warmed Sarah's face. Manitoussiwuk, little manitous or sprites, lit on her bare shoulders and fanned her eyelids. Sarah smiled, turned her head into her protector's chest and stroked it in gratitude.

Just as she was about to kiss her protector's bare nipple, a shadow fell across them and all was dark.

"It's all right, Sarah. I'm here," a voice said.

Sarah felt rough cloth gently rub across her arm, trying to calm her, as she emerged into a world of shadow. She struggled to open her eyes, but all was gray and formless. She stopped and listened for the voice.

"I'm here," it whispered. Sarah lay motionless, unsure if the voice were real or part of another dream. Again the cloth, a bandaged hand, stroked her forearm. It held her fingers and raised her hand. Lips kissed her palm. "I'm here," the voice said.

"Beecher?" she thought. "Where am I?"

"Beecher," another voice said, "I'm going to have to ask you to leave. She's going to need her rest."

Whose voice was that? The bandaged hand gently laid her fingers on the bed.

"What happens next?" Beecher's voice asked.

"As I told you, when she's stabilized, we'll move her to Fargo. They can handle something like this better than we can. They can deal with the plastic surgery, the psychotherapy…whatever she needs. We're just not equipped. All we can do is try to put the pieces back together and hope she wakes up."

"Will she wake up?" Beecher asked.

There was a pause.

"We're hopeful. She's breathing on her own, but... We don't know. I won't lie. The damage to the skull and eye sockets is severe. So many fractures. I can't predict. It was a... a bad accident."

Sarah hovered on the edge of consciousness. The voices were real, she thought, but she couldn't respond. She could not move, she could not speak, she could not see.

"Accident?" she thought. She remembered the face of the woman outside Frank's house, the blonde woman with the hooded cloak. The crash had been no accident.

"If she survives," Beecher asked, "how bad...?"

"Her face? Well... again, I won't lie to you. There will be a lot of scarring, but..."

"But?"

"She'll be alive," the voice said. "That's the important thing."

"Alive?" Sarah thought. Beecher did not respond. "What does that mean?" she wanted to scream. "Alive? Being alive is nothing."

The voices in the room faded, but the words of the doctor echoed – "Plastic surgery... Fractures... Scarring..." and then the voices were quiet.

Again the pendulum swung, but the arc was softer, calming, peaceful. Sarah rested. When the swinging stopped, she sighed. She heard her own breath. How long had it been? She wondered. Had she slept?

Beecher kissed her hand again and held it to his cheek. She opened her eyes and saw him bending over her. The room was bathed in a green light filtering through the walls.

"I love you, Sarah," he said, kissing her forehead. There was no pain in his touch.

"Beecher, what happened?" She thought. Her lips could not move. Her voice made no sound.

"You're going to be fine," he said. "You just hang on and everything's going to be all right."

"My face..."

"You are so beautiful."

*He's lying,* a new voice told her. The voice was masculine, more inviting than reproachful. *You're only beautiful to me. He just wants you back,* it said. She looked behind Beecher and saw the Earth Man waiting for her.

Haltingly, she began to Beecher, "About tonight..."

"It's all over. All that... When you get out of the hospital, we'll work everything..."

*You don't want to go back. You were made for me, not him. He's given you nothing. I can give you everything. Stay with me. You don't want to go back.* The voice was soft, inviting.

Sarah shook her head at Beecher. "No, Beecher. I can't work on anything. I'm done. I'm not good for you or Jeannie or even myself, especially after what I did."

The Earth Man smiled.

"There is no past..." Beecher said.

"Not what I did before. What I did with the car. I killed Frank, Beecher. I saw him standing there and I killed him. He was talking to that woman and I decided he had to die."

"Frank was an evil man. It's not your fault what he did to you."

Sarah stopped. "You knew it was him?"

Beecher squeezed her fingers. "I knew. I'm your husband. I knew almost before you did."

She had always thought he could read her mind. She could never hide her feelings from him. "Maybe that's what love is," she thought. "Living within another person, hearing thoughts as they formulate, tasting desire as it arises deep inside."

*If you love him, leave him. It's what he needs. You knew that when you saw the other woman. You weren't taking Frank away from her. You were giving her to Beecher.*

"I don't know what you mean," she said.

"We are one, always meant to be, now and forever," Beecher said.

Sarah felt the pendulum start to swing again.

*Don't listen. Don't think,* the Earth Man said. *You don't live there anymore. You live with me now.*

Beecher quietly stroked Sarah's arm with his bandaged hand.

"He's hiding something," Sarah thought. "What's he not saying?"

"Sarah, I don't know what to do with Jeannie until you come home..."

*You can't go back!* The Earth Man's voice hissed at Sarah.

"Beecher?" Sarah thought, reaching for him. He knelt beside the bed, took her hand, and held it to his cheek.

"I am going to stop all this," Beecher said. "No more hurting, no more killing, no more fog. The words inside me demand a voice. I don't know how this all works, but I'm going to speak Truth, Life, Love. When I'm finished, all this will be gone."

The Earth Man's face shriveled in anger. *Ignore him!* He said. *The only truth is with me. Your life is here. You love me. You love my life, my world.*

"Sarah, it's hard to explain," Beecher said, "but none of this is real. I know it's going to sound like I've become a religious fanatic, but the only thing that exists is the Word. We are all a part of It and It lives inside us. To love the Word is to love ourselves and each other. The past is nothing. The future doesn't exist. The present is false."

*No! Now is all we have. Accept it. Live it.*

"Everything we see and think is false. It's all illusion. Ironically, I think, the fog that makes it so hard to see the buildings and cars and the prairie…that fog has stripped away the lie and shown us the truth about ourselves, who we are, what we are. With the truth of the Word, we can now find out why we are."

The Earth Man fumed.

Beecher kissed Sarah's palm. "I don't know whether any of this makes sense to you. I'm not sure it makes sense to me. I just know it's right. And that's what I want, Sarah. I want everything to be right. I want you to come home."

Sarah felt the darkness gathering in her brain. She was tired. She realized she had said nothing, that only

Beecher had spoken, that he had posed her questions for her in his own mind. She was barely in the room herself. Sarah looked beyond Beecher and saw the Earth Man's scowl. She tried to digest Beecher's words, but thinking made her face hurt.

Sarah sighed. "Beecher, I'm tired. You must be, too. Go home for a while. Get some sleep."

"Doc told me I can't stay very long." He stroked her hair with one hand while his other pressed her fingers to his cheek. "Please, Sarah. Wake up. It's all over. I love you," Beecher said as his tears ran down her hand.

The Earth Man snorted. *"Over." Right.*

Sarah lay still, feeling Beecher, listening to him. "Beecher, go home," her mind whispered. "I'll be fine."

Beecher rose and wiped his cheek with the back of his hand. Then he leaned over and kissed her forehead. "I better go and let you rest," he told her. "You sleep well."

Sarah smiled. "Thank you," she thought as Beecher left the room. After the door closed, the Earth Man leaned against it, smiled at her, and held out his hand to her.

*You know he didn't hear you*, he said, almost as a question.

She put her hand in his.

*You're in my world now*, he said as he kissed her forehead.

Sarah closed her eyes and sighed.

Art paid no more attention to Sarah and the Earth Man. Instead he rejoiced.

Beecher saw! He heard! He spoke! The Word was alive in him. There was no pretense, no distortion. He had spoken honestly, simply. He spoke the Truth. He was becoming the Whole, something Art could never be. The Story could be told.

Art rose from the ground and headed downtown. At the end of the hospital driveway, he heard the building's glass door open. He turned and saw Beecher walk toward his loaner car on his way to pick up Jeannie. He walked with purpose, with strength. Inside, his thoughts took form, although to the remnants of his human intellect, they seemed jumbled and amorphous. He had trusted the Word, but had yet not learned to trust himself and what was happening to him.

He must learn for himself, Art knew. The Word told him to watch, so he stood behind the Emergency Room sign as Beecher entered his car and drove across town to the Bjerklands.

Art touched his jaw. It was loose and the pain was gone. He couldn't remember it being pain-free. For the first time in centuries, he felt the music in his mouth. He raised his hands to sing the song of praise to the Word, the Kitchi-Manitou, the Creator.

Instead he heard the words of the ancient psalmist Asaph:

*O God, do not keep silent;*
*be not quiet, O God, be not still.*
*See how your enemies are astir,*

*how your foes rear their heads.*
*With cunning they conspire*
*against your people;*
*they plot against those you cherish.*
*"Come," they say, "let us destroy them."*
*With one mind they plot together;*
*they form an alliance against you –*
*Cover their faces with shame*
*so that men will seek your name,*
*O Lord.*
*Let them know that you, whose*
*name is the Lord –*
*that you alone are the Most High*
*over all the earth.*

The words had spoken themselves. They remained in Art's ears and on his tongue. He knew. The night was full. The end was near.

# XVIII ART BENSON

## 1

Art hurried down the street to the highway and toward town. The light in Amanda's room at Dale's Motel was still on, but he passed by. He could not stop. Through the gloom of dark and fog, he heard voices rise in anger. He felt the movement of spirits – Matchi-auwish and Weendigo. Past the school and Benny's Amoco, he hurried, following the current of rushing sound and the pull of the Imperative. Rounding the corner at the stoplight, he saw the cars gathered outside the Plains, all of them familiar, all of them dominated by the presence of Wayne Diego's black Mercedes Roadster. Under the cover of night, the Norske Junta met, their task too hideous for the day.

Art scurried across the street and peeked through the greasy-fogged window of the front door. The dining room was dark except for a dim glow behind the kitchen doorway. Art closed his eyes and saw. Hattie's, the Junta's chamber, was full. They were all there. The city council. The school board. Einar Nordhaus stood at the end of the table. To his right sat Wayne Diego, smiling insidiously. Art turned his back to the wall and slid down to the sidewalk to listen.

"I'm tellin' ya. Now's the time," Einar said. "If we're gonna do it, we gotta do it now."

"But, Einar…"

"Ain't no *but*'s, Pete. This here's the perfect opportunity. Beecher's mind ain't gonna be on work. Hell, his wife just killed Frank Thorstad and just about killed herself. If she dies, he's gonna be in mourning. If she lives, she'll be on trial for murder. Ya think he's gonna care about goin' to school? Anyway, a man who can drive his wife to murder will be a bad influence on the students. We can't have our kids around that kinda thing, can we?"

"But, Einar, what you want the girls to do is no…"

"My god, Pete. I know. It was a joke, ya little twerp." The room echoed with laughter.

Pete Carlson, the diminutive electrician, was tenacious. "What about Sam?"

"Haake? We hired him. He ain't gonna say nothin'. 'sides, he's still out of town. Him and a couple other superintendents is havin' a big powwow wit' da governor tomorrow."

"I don' know."

"Ah, fer Christ's sake, Pete. You were all for this a couple hours ago."

"I know, but it just doesn't seem right."

"You gettin' religion on us? Listen. Think a the money. You an' Belle always wanted to go to Maui; now's your chance."

"But Beecher …"

"That's what I'm tellin' ya. After tonight, ya don't haveta worry about Beecher. He's… He's going on an extended leave of absence." Einar looked down at Diego. The two grinned at each other. "Yeah, that's it. 'An extended leave of absence'."

The men at the table laughed again.

"I don't know. It seems kinda cruel. What are people gonna think?"

"Whatever we tell 'em to think! Dammit! Beecher's been in the way the whole time. Now we've got the perfect chance to get him out of the way, an' you're worried about being too cruel? What are you? A pussy? Beecher's history. He's gotta go, an' he's goin'."

"But even without Beecher, what are we going to do about Joe?"

Einar smiled again at Diego. It was Diego who replied. "Joe Engstrom? Jefferson's finest? We don't have to worry about him. In fact, I don't think it will take much at all to bring him over to our side."

There was a hush. "You mean money?" someone asked.

Diego shrugged. There was a murmur about the table.

"Hell, there's more'n enough to go around," Einar said, raising his voice. "Like Wayne just said, it ain't gonna take much."

"I don't know," Pete said. "We've done a lot over the years, but we've never done anything like this. Are you sure it's legal?"

The whole table laughed at the question. "Legal?" Einar bellowed. "Who gives a shit about legal? Hell, we're the law. Of course, it's legal."

Einar looked around the room, then raised his eyebrows. "An' if it's not, we can just make it so it is. So are we agreed?"

There was a general nodding of heads around the table.

"Pete?"

There was a pause. All eyes in the room bore down on the reluctant member. "Yeah. I guess so. When are we gonna do it?"

"Hell, tonight. Can't waste time."

"But it's so late."

"All the better. It'll be over an' we can start with the girls tomorrow. Pete, you call Joe an' get him over here. Beecher's prob'ly still at the hospital. Who wants to go get 'im?"

"I will," someone said.

"I'll go with you." Two men stood and moved toward the door. Art rose, hunched over, hurried between the buildings and hid in the darkness as the two came out of the café, hopped into a Ford pickup, and drove toward the hospital. Beecher was on his way to the Bjerklands, but the Junta would find him soon.

Art searched his mind for a plan to stop them, and saw the swirling images of Beecher, Sarah, Jeannie, Amanda, and the laughing woman. Among them swam the forms of the Earth Man, Wayne Diego, Frank Thorstad, and the members of the Junta.

Again, Art sang the song of Asaph. The Word answered:

*The world is one within Me.*
*Good and bad,*
*Self and others,*
*Life and death:*
*Why affirm these concepts?*
*Why deny them?*
*Seek instead to keep your mind undivided.*
*Dissolve all ideas into the Word.*
*Be one with Me.*

Art realized that assembling the thought-pieces of his brain into a mind undivided would take longer than the Junta's search for Beecher. Art wanted to be one with the Word. More so tonight, he wanted the Word to be one with Beecher.

However, what the Word wanted was unclear. Art slid from his hiding place and rushed to find Amanda.

# XIX AMANDA WILSON AND BEECHER JONES

## 1

As Art shuffled through the fog, he knew Amanda lay on her bed, staring at the blank television screen and reliving the conversation she had held hours ago with her mother. Amanda had told her mother everything, all that had happened to her and around her. She explained why she had come to Jefferson and about the face in the yearbook; she told her mother about Beecher and about Sarah's car crash; she attempted to explain the Word and the Flame; she recounted her dream of saving the drowning man and Beecher's vision of her; and she struggled to make sense of her own actions.

Through the telephone lines, the Word spoke to both Amanda and her mother. It opened Amanda's heart and mouth. Over Amanda's feeble objections, It led her mother to insist on coming to Jefferson. Depending on the weather off Lake Superior and how far east the Jefferson fog extended, the trip would take nine to ten hours, her mother explained as she began her packing.

Amanda heard the air speaking. The Flame burned brilliantly inside her and she was glad. On the human level, she knew that even if G. Dahlgren, the woman in the picture, still existed and was her birth mother, Amanda still needed Lois Wilson, the mother she had always known. She needed the sense of home and security she left years ago and had been avoiding since. In the spiritual world she had lived since her dream on the beach, she recognized the forces pulling all the necessities into place.

Art's knock on her door startled her.

"Who is it?"

"Art. We must go."

She opened the door. "Go? Go where?"

"To find Beecher. They want him."

Amanda stepped aside to let Art in. "Who wants him?"

Art stayed in the doorway. "The Matchi-auwishuk. The Weendigoes. The Earth Man."

Amanda's eyes searched Art's face until she understood. She grabbed her keys from the top of the dresser and asked, "Where is he?"

Art turned from the door and faced the night sky. "With Jeannie."

"His daughter."

Art nodded. "We must hurry." Behind the motel a dog barked. Several houses away another dog answered. Then another and another. Birds screeched in the trees. The sky resounded with animal warnings. Even they knew the time was now.

Amanda grabbed her car keys off the night stand and stood next to Art in the doorway. She stood a moment listening. She heard the voice behind the barking. She smelled the fetid breath of the Weendigoes. The moisture in the air reached toward her face and clung to it like a cobweb. Brushing the stickiness away, she closed the door behind her.

"You know where?" she asked Art.

He nodded. Then she unlocked the car and they drove into the blackness to find Beecher.

## 2

Beecher parked Jeff Arnold's massive, dark brown 1972 Mercury Marquis outside the Bjerklands' house across town. The engine chugged almost a full minute after he switched off the ignition.

When the engine puffed its last, Beecher patted the steering wheel. "Not much," he thought, "but it gets me where I'm going,"

In the fog, Ralph and Bonnie Bjerkland's darkened two-story relic from the 1930's loomed over the neighborhood houses, a behemoth among pygmies. It had always intimidated Beecher, but tonight he welcomed its size as a protection for his daughter.

Peering through the murkiness, Beecher debated with himself. Bonnie had told Joe that both she and Ralph had to work in the morning. Beecher could wait until they woke up at 6:30 or so. Or he could wake them and take Jeannie home now. He glanced at his watch. 2:30 a.m.

Beecher looked down at his injured hands. The bandages were clean, white. He tentatively stepped from the Marquis / tank, and looked down the tree-lined street. In this part of town, the fog had diminished, now only a light mist, barely visible in the glow of the streetlights, harmless, innocuous. However, Beecher's hair bristled. He knew the Matchi-auwishuk were close by, waiting for him.

As Beecher slowly walked up the sidewalk, he surveyed the trees in the yard and the bushes next to the house, half-expecting another guerrilla attack by the laughing woman.

Nothing.

In the distance he heard the barking dogs, but nothing moved around him. He heard the screeching birds and remembered their suicidal destruction at Benny's just days ago. Here at Ralph and Bonnie's, the turmoil seemed far away. The night air was still, almost stagnant.

As he surveyed the yard, Beecher heard the Word's truth. The laughing woman was not the real enemy, not even a member of the Unholy Trio. She was merely a pawn of some higher intensity, an influence far too immense and powerful for a wraith like her to resist. He gave an understanding nod, stepped onto the Bjerklands' porch, and knocked on the front door.

At first there was no answer, but after Beecher's constant pounding, somebody upstairs finally turned on a light. Ralph's heavy footsteps pounded down the steps. Beecher heard a stumble, a muttered curse, and a forgotten toy slammed into the wall at the bottom of the stairs. The porch light startled Beecher, making him squint at the peephole in the middle of the door. "Ralph, it's me. Beecher. Let me in."

Ralph opened the door, baseball bat in his hand, and, in a voice hushed to avoid waking Jeannie and his daughter, said, "Shit, Beecher! Ya scared the hell out of us. Is everything all right?"

Beecher heard Bonnie's loud whisper at the top of the stairs. "Ralph, who is it?"

"It's Beecher."

"Just a minute," she said. "I'll be right down."

"Is Jeannie okay?" Beecher asked Ralph.

"Yeah, she's fine," Ralph said, leaning the bat against the wall, rubbing his ample stomach and scratching his head. "How 'bout Sarah? She gonna be all right?"

"I don't –"

"God, Beecher. What's goin' on?" Bonnie asked, pulling her robe around her and padding down the stairs in her overstuffed moose-head slippers.

"Nice feet," Beecher joked.

She looked down, yawning and speaking at the same time. "Like 'em? Ralph and Chelsea bought 'em for me for Christmas. Sarah gonna be okay?" With her free hand, she pushed several strands of electric hair from her eyes.

"I don't know. Maybe. Yeah, I think so. Doc says he just wants to make sure she's stable, then they'll move her to Fargo."

"How long's that gonna take?" Bonnie asked.

"Maybe as soon as tomorrow morning... or this morning. God, I don't even know what day it is."

"Are you goin' down there with her?" Ralph asked. Bonnie put her finger to her mouth to quiet him.

"Well, yeah." Beecher replied. "I guess so. I don't..."

Bonnie and Ralph looked at each other. Ralph hesitated. "The reason I ask is... Well, as far as Jeannie goes... I mean we'd love to keep 'er here, like ta help, ya know? But I don't think either of us can get off work that long... I don't think she's gonna wanna go ta school. Ya know?"

Beecher interrupted him. "No. No. That's okay. I know. That's why I'm here. I came to take her home."

"What are you gonna do? They won't let her into the hospital while..." Bonnie said.

"I know. It's okay. I'll work out something. Don't worry."

"Are you sure?"

Beecher nodded, waving off her question.

"Holy shit, man. What the hell'dja do to yer hands?" Ralph asked.

Beecher looked down at his bandages and again weakly explained what had happened at the Plains. The story seemed so old and practiced now, simply worn-out words – a sermon delivered once too often. Ralph and Bonnie watched Beecher's hands as he spoke, and he felt the stitches pull against his palms. He hid his hands under his arms.

Bonnie asked, "You think you can carry Jeannie? She's gonna be too tired to walk."

"I'll be fine."

"You sure?"

Beecher nodded.

"Okay. I'll get her," Bonnie said. "Be right back,"

When the two men were left alone, Ralph stood, shifting his weight from one foot to the other. Finally, he asked, "Beecher, what the hell happened tonight?"

Beecher shook his head and bit his lower lip. "I'm not sure. Joe's still trying to sort everything out."

"Joe Engstrom? RoboCop? Shit. He can barely find his dick with a tweezers, let alone solve crime. He's as useless as tits on a boar. What's he toldja so far?"

"Not much. Just that Sarah ran into Frank with the car. He's dead... And Sarah's... she's... Her face is all..." His hands swarming about his face, Beecher struggled to hold back his tears. Ralph dropped his cynicism, reached out and grabbed Beecher's arm.

"Hey, it's okay. I'm sorry. I didn't mean to... Here. Sit down on the steps."

Beecher sat and lowered his head in his hands. Ralph looked up the stairs to make sure Bonnie was out of earshot.

"Beecher, I promised Bonnie I wouldn't say nothin', but I thought you should know. I heard the Junta was havin' a meetin' tonight."

"About what?"

"You."

"Me? What about me?"

"I dunno, but with that bunch, ya can bet they ain't plannin' no Parcheesi tournament."

The stairs creaked and Bonnie came around the corner with the sleeping Jeannie hanging over her shoulder. "Here's Daddy," Bonnie said as Beecher reached to take Jeannie from her. "Careful of your hands," she told him.

When Jeannie was safely in Beecher's arms, Bonnie handed him Jeannie's stuffed animal. "Here," she said. "Gotta have Tigger."

Before Beecher could try to find a way to squeeze the wide-eyed, grinning doll between him and Jeannie, she grabbed it from Bonnie's hand and clutched it to her, as if it were the only piece of security she had left in life.

Beecher patted her back and said. "Listen, guys. Thanks a lot. I'm sorry to wake you up like this. I just... you know."

Bonnie nodded. Ralph led them to the front door and opened it. The night air had turned colder. "Here. Let me getchya a blanket," Bonnie said. She reached into the closet under the stairs, took out a green and white striped comforter, draped it over Jeannie's shoulders and tucked it between the sleeping girl and Beecher.

"I wish we could..." Bonnie said.

"It's fine. I'll talk to you tomorrow."

"I'll open the car door for ya," Ralph said. The two men walked in silence. Jeannie instantly fell asleep heavily against her father's shoulder. When they reached the car, Ralph opened the back seat. Kicking at the rust on the bottom of the door, he smiled and asked, "New car?"

Beecher smiled. "Loaner from Jeff Arnold."

"Figures. Couldn't get anything bigger, huh?""

Beecher set Jeannie on the back seat and buckled her in. She simply slumped over onto the seat hugging her Tigger. Beecher wrapped the blanket around her and shut the door quietly.

Ralph looked back at the house, then said to Beecher, "Beecher, you haveta be careful. Somethin's up. I can smell it. You ain't made too many friends wit' Einar and da boys. An' now they got this here Wayne Diego character. He's no good. I can tell. An' he's got somethin' against you."

"The Junta and Diego. Matchi-auwishuk and Weendigo," Beecher thought. "And the Earth Man is near."

"Thanks for the warning, Ralph. I'll watch myself," he said aloud.

"If you need any help with them, you call me, ya hear? I ain't gonna let those pricks do nothin' to you and Jeannie."

"Thanks, Ralph."

"An' Sarah…?"

"As soon as I find out anything, I'll let you know. Thanks." He turned the key, gave Ralph a quick wave, and drove away.

# XX ART BENSON

1

Fog swirled around Amanda's car and Art knew why. The night was alive. The Word had enlivened it with dreams. Again, It revealed all and Art was forced to watch.

Laura Grapnic once more saw the love-struck Karl Jurgens standing outside her window offering her the snake. This time, however, she saw Beecher across the street beckoning to Karl. Karl paid no attention, his eyes fixed on Laura's window. He raised the snake higher so Laura could see its face. The head seemed human, hungry. It flicked its cleft tongue between skeletal jaws and hissed viciously. When Laura refused the gift, the snake slithered out of Karl's arms, gave Laura a reptilian sneer, devoured Karl in one swallow, and headed for Beecher. Beecher stood still, defying the serpent to approach. Laura ran to the door, opened it, and yelled for Beecher to run, but he refused.

Just as the snake stretched its jaws to engulf Beecher, Laura awoke. Breathing in short gasps she lay, trembling in her bed. She remembered the dream she had the night Karl died, how she had found him dead the next morning beneath her window.

Whether dreams come true or not, Laura knew Beecher was in danger. She dressed, not knowing where she was going or why.

"Daddy?"

Chelsea Bjerkland stood at the side of her parents' bed, shaking her father's shoulder. Ralph blinked and grunted. He had barely turned out the light again.

"Daddy, wake up."

"Shit!" Ralph whispered. Bonnie heard him and jabbed him in the back with her elbow. Ralph switched on the light. "What is it, Chelsea?"

"Daddy, where's Jeannie? She's not in her bed."

"It's okay, Chelsea. Her daddy came and took her home."

Chelsea shook her father's shoulder. "No, Daddy! He can't. You have to stop him."

Ralph propped himself on one elbow. "Why? What's wrong?"

"Somebody's trying to hurt Jeannie's daddy."

"What do you mean?"

"Bad men. I saw them. There were lots of them in cars and there was one really bad man and they all wanted to hurt Jeannie's daddy."

Ralph reached out and stroked his daughter's hair. "Where did you see them?"

Chelsea thought for a moment and began to cry. "I don't know," she sobbed.

The normally rough Ralph melted at his daughter's tears. He sat up, lifted Chelsea and hugged her tightly. Bonnie turned over. "What's wrong?" she asked.

"She had a bad dream," Ralph told her.

"No, Daddy. It wasn't a dream," Chelsea insisted. "I saw them. They were bad and they wanted to hurt Jeannie's daddy." She pushed back sharply and looked into her father's face. "What if they hurt Jeannie? Daddy, you gotta stop them. I don't want them to hurt Jeannie." She clung to her father's neck.

Again, Ralph hugged her hard. "Me either, Chelsea. Me either."

Bonnie came around the bed and rubbed her daughter's back. "Maybe... It wouldn't hurt to go over there an' check it out," she told Ralph.

He looked at her. "You think they'd do somethin' tonight?"

"I don't know, but... It would make Chelsea feel better."

Ralph nodded. "Okay, Chelsea. I'm gonna go over to Jeannie's house. I'll be right back. Mommy'll take care of you. Okay?"

Chelsea nodded, sniffed, and rubbed her nose on her father's tee shirt. "'kay."

Ralph grabbed his pants from the chair and began to dress.

"Ralph," Bonnie said, as Ralph pulled a flannel shirt from the clothes hamper, "you may want to get someone to go with you… just in case."

Ralph looked down at her as she tucked Chelsea into his side of the bed. He nodded and buttoned the shirt.

"No!"

Wally Forseth tossed back the covers and sat up. His voice still reverberated from the walls of his apartment. Outside, the streetlight glowed a ghastly yellow. Wally rubbed his hand over his disheveled hair, got his bearings, and then leaned back against the headboard. The dream that had been so clear a second ago was now as foggy as the town had been for days.

He reached for the lamp on the bedside table and knocked his Bible to the floor. Turning on the light, Wally leaned over to pick up the book. He laid it on his lap and let the pages fall open. Slowly, a word at a time, he read aloud, and as he read, the words stripped away the fog from his brain. He remembered the dream.

Again, he saw the bloody face and hands, heard the screams, and smelled the stench of death seeping from the ground. Again, he wanted to push through the crowds to save the man, but he was afraid – afraid of the soldiers, afraid of the officials, afraid of the disciples.

Again paralyzed by indecision, he watched silently. When the man cried out, Wally looked up and saw not the face of the crucified Jesus but of Beecher Jones.

Wally stood at the window, looking down at the street. He had heard about Sarah's accident and knew it would mean trouble for Beecher, especially with that group of men Beecher called the Norske Junta who met down at the Plains everyday. The whole faculty knew the school board didn't like Beecher for some reason, but he had plenty of support in the community and among the teachers and kids. Why would anyone want to hurt him?

Besides Wally did not believe in prescient dreams, if that was the term. They may have happened in the days of Joseph and Daniel, but not today. Then again he wasn't sure he believed in modern psychological interpretations either.

Still, as Wally looked out at the fog, he could not shake the idea that something was wrong, very wrong. He could not force himself to go back to bed and lie down. He picked up the Bible and stared at the words floating about the pages in front of him. He could not decipher the meaning. His eyes no longer focused – until the telephone rang.

Amanda stopped at a stop sign just as a large older car drove past. It was too dark to see inside the car, but as Art watched the taillights, he knew.

"It's Beecher. He's going home. Follow him," Art said.

Through the fog, Amanda trailed him as closely as she could.

Beecher wondered who was following and why. Several times he checked his rearview mirror, but the glare of the headlights masked the whole car. It could have been the Junta, but with Jeannie in the back seat, he wasn't going to run.

When Beecher parked the car in front of his house, Amanda pulled her white Topaz close behind him. The headlights now hidden beneath the trunk of his car, he recognized both Amanda and Art in his mirror. He knew the time had come. He stepped from his car. Amanda and Art walked to him and stood next to him in the glow of the Topaz's lights.

"What's happening?" he asked Amanda.

"They want you," Art told him.

"The Junta?"

Art nodded.

"But it's more than the Junta, isn't it?" he asked.

Again Art nodded. Beecher looked through the window at his daughter sleeping on the back seat. "What do I do with Jeannie?" he asked.

Art looked at Amanda. She took a deep breath and said, "I'll take care of her."

Beecher turned back to Art. "It is time," Art told him.

He knew. "I'll show you where she sleeps," Beecher told Amanda. He opened the car door, carefully picked up Jeannie, and led Amanda to the house.

Art walked back to the Topaz and turned off the lights, then waited at the curb, frustrated with his role.

He fumed silently. He wanted to do something! Attack the Earth Man and rip the fog from the sky. Scream a warning to the world like the dogs and birds. Something.

His thoughts flashed back to the present when Beecher turned on the porch light and came back through the door. As he walked down the steps, Art saw Amanda's face pressed against Jeannie's darkened upstairs window. When Beecher was halfway down the sidewalk, he stopped and gazed down the street to his left. Two headlights crawled through the fog. Beecher inched slowly to Art's side, and they watched the lights approach.

The car stopped behind Amanda's. Beecher and Art looked at each other as the engine and lights died. The door opened.

"Beecher, you have to come with me," Joe Engstrom said, standing and leaning against the inside of the door.

Beecher looked steadily at Joe, as the friend became the policeman, shoving a nightstick through his belt and closing the door of the patrol car behind him.

"I hoped you would be on my side," Beecher said.

Joe rubbed his nose between thumb and forefinger. He sniffed, then grimaced. "Me, too."

"What do they want?"

Before Joe could answer, two more sets of headlights emerged from the fog in the opposite direction. Wayne Diego's Roasdster led the original Junta search party of Tim Arneson and "Stinky" Fish. The two cars stopped on the other side of the street. Diego and Einar Nordhaus got out first. While Diego strutted and Einar waddled across the street, Tim and Stinky stayed by Stinky's car, each lighting a cigarette, and leaning against the front fender.

"You're a hard man to find," Einar said.

"I've had some things on my mind," Beecher replied. "A little thing with my wife."

"I bet." Einar turned to Diego, who stood grinning at Beecher and Art. "Say, uh, me and the boys would like ya to come down to Hattie's. We'd like to talk to ya 'bout somethin'."

Beecher looked at his watch. "Tonight? It couldn't wait till morning?"

"C'mon," Diego taunted. "What would be the fun in that?" His sneer transformed Art's hand into a fist. When he stepped forward, Beecher's bandaged hand on his shoulder held him back. Art turned to him. Beecher's face was peaceful. He shook his head.

"What do you want with me?" Beecher asked Einar and Diego.

"Just ta talk," Einar said.

"It takes four men and a policeman to get me for a talk?"

Einar and Diego moved toward him. Across the street, Tim and Stinky threw their cigarettes to the pavement, pulled themselves erect and began to swagger toward Art and Beecher. Behind him, Art heard Amanda open the door and sit on the porch steps. No one saw her. They were too intent on Beecher.

Like the friend he had once been, Joe put his arm around Beecher's shoulder. "Beecher, come here." He led Beecher up the sidewalk a few steps, put his hands behind Beecher's neck and leaned his head forward until it met Beecher's. The conversation was quiet, not meant to be heard. It didn't matter to Art. He had heard it before.

Diego came and stood next to Art. "So, Simon…still living in denial?" he asked.

Art looked at him. Diego smiled, then leaned his head back and laughed.

"What's so funny?" Einar asked.

"Nothing. Just an old joke between me and ol' Art here." He wrapped his arm around Art's neck. The stench of his breath slapped Art's face, but he stood motionless.

Joe looked at Beecher and asked, "Okay?"

Beecher stood motionless. "Do what you have to do," he said.

"He's comin' with me," Joe told Einar. "If you want, you guys can follow us,"

"I don't think that's a good idea," Diego said.

"Why not?" Joe asked.

"No offense, Joe, but I don't trust you. You two just might drive off into the night and we'd never see you again," Diego said with a snarling grin.

"He's not going to leave his kid."

Diego looked at Beecher. “I dunno. Looks pretty desperate to me.”

Beecher, his hands hanging at his sides, stood facing Diego. “You don’t want him to hear, do you?” he said.

Diego looked quizzically a moment, then sneered. “Hear what?”

“Who you are. Where you’re from. What you really want.”

“And you know.”

Beecher nodded. “I know.”

“Well, good for you,” Einar said. “Now get in the car.”

“Does Einar know?” Beecher asked Diego.

“Of course, I know. I told you. He’s Wayne Diego. He’s from Hollywood. He wants to make movie stars out of our kids.”

Without turning, Beecher raised his voice and called behind him. “Miss Wilson, have you ever heard of Wayne Diego?”

Amanda rose from the steps and joined the group.

“Who’s this?” Einar asked.

“I told you in my office. Remember, Einar? This is Amanda Wilson. She’s a Hollywood writer who won an Academy Award this year.”

“You didn’t tell me that. You just told me her name.”

“I wanted to, but you were in a hurry. Anyway, she’s in the business. She knows a little more about Hollywood than you or I. Miss Wilson, have you ever heard of a talent scout named Wayne Diego?”

Her eyes fixed on Diego's face, she replied, "No. No Wayne Diego."

"Well, L.A's a big city..."

"Einar, there is no Wayne Diego. There is no talent scout. What you see standing here is not even human."

Einar, Tim, and Stinky looked at Beecher, then at Diego, who smiled, shrugged, and twirled his index finger next to his temple to indicate Beecher was crazy. The four burst out laughing.

Beecher stood motionless, barely blinking. His stare quieted the laughter. "You came here to fire me, but he wants more than that. He wants you to kill me," Beecher said.

Einar turned quickly to Beecher. "Nobody said anything about firing. How did you know...?"

The wisdom of the ancients, the expression of the Word spilled from Beecher's mouth.

*"I am old,*
*Older than the story.*
*I am new,*
*Newer than your next breath.*
*I am every life.*
*I am the innocent and the guilty,*
*The virtuous and the profane."*

Einar gaped at Beecher while Wayne Diego shifted his weight nervously from foot to foot. "What is that supposed to mean?" Einar asked.

"It is the Word," Art said. "It is speaking to Beecher, through him. Diego knows what it means."

"What?" Diego asked

"It means I know," Beecher said. "I have known you forever. I knew you before you were made. I knew you before you came to Jefferson. I knew you before you bought Karl's pictures from Joe."

Diego and Einar turned on Joe quickly. Joe raised his hand and stepped back. "I didn't tell him. Honest, Einar, I…"

"Then what the hell were you two talkin' about a second ago? Engstrom, you dip shit! If you screwed this up…"

Beecher held up his hand. "He didn't have to tell me. I know it all. There's more:

*I live in every man and every woman,*
*In every people,*
*In every generation,*
*In every country.*
*I live in every rock and every tree,*
*Every lake and every stream,*
*Every deer and every bear.*
*All –*
*All live in me,*
*Unknown, unknowing.*"

"There you go with all that crazy shit again. What the hell are you talking about?"

"All Joe said was that I couldn't stay in Jefferson, that I should just leave my resignation on my desk, leave town, and everything would be fine. But he doesn't know the Word any more than I did last week, any more than you do now. Diego doesn't want you to know."

"What's to know?" Diego challenged.

Beecher replied:

*"The shimmering Word that excites the eye,*
*The honeyed Word that lies sweet and savory on the tongue,*
*The healing Word that nurtures and caresses,*
*The ambrosial Word whose perfume intoxicates the gods,*
*The melodious Word waiting to be sung.*
*The Word that Man ignores."*

Diego howled. "You're as loony as old Art here."

*"I am old, but never tired..."* Art said.

Beecher finished the Word's invocation.

*"Young, but never blind.*
*The Story lives in me.*
*It must be told.*

You don't know what Diego really wants," Beecher said to Einar.

"And what is that?" Diego challenged.

"Einar's soul. The town's. The world's."

Again, Diego bellowed. The other men laughed. Beecher, Amanda, and Art stood quietly. "Who the hell do you think I am? Satan?" Diego demanded.

"You want to be, but you're not that smart," Beecher said. "You want to be part of him. That's your goal, your inspiration. You would be him if you could because you want the same thing. And he supports you because the more destruction you can wreak on the world, the happier he is."

"Satan?"

"Satan, Lucifer, Beelzebub.... Whatever you choose to call him," Beecher said.

"The Earth Man," Art added.

Beecher looked at Art and nodded. "The Earth Man," he repeated.

Diego wiped his upper lip with the back of his skinny hand.

Einar glanced at Diego. "You okay?"

Diego bit his lower lip, breathed deeply, and nodded his head.

Einar looked at him again and turned back to Art, Amanda, and Beecher.

"You on some kind of God thing with these two, Beecher? Really? A broken-down half-breed, a woman, and a frickin' high school principal? Shit."

"Not God as you know, Einar. The Word is God as It is."

"What does that mean?"

"All things and nothing."

Einar started to speak, but he coughed in confusion, the words lost in his straining mind. "All and noth–... What the hell?"

"In us you see race, gender, occupation. The Word that resides in humans is all races, both genders. The Word is found in all occupations. Yet in Himself, It has no race, no gender, no job. It simply is."

Ignoring the sweating Wayne Diego next to him, Einar huffed, "Simply is WHAT?"

"All and nothing. Light and darkness. Color and space. Flesh and spirit. It is in all things, all people."

"Ha!" Einar exploded. "Even the likes of you three?"

"The likes of all. Ojibwe-Norwegian. Female-male. Teacher-mayor."

Einar shook his head in disgust. "All right. Enough of this shit. Beecher, come on. We're going to Hattie's," he ordered.

Diego turned his head from the two groups and shuffled a few steps off, wiping his forehead, imperceptible growls forming in his throat.

The sound of a car engine and another set of headlights distracted him as he reached for Beecher's arm. The car pulled in behind Joe's patrol car. Wally Forseth opened the driver's door and stood up.

"You okay, Mr. Jones?"

Ralph Bjerkland got out the passenger side, followed by Laura Grapnic from the back seat. Laura stood with Beecher, Amanda and Art, while Ralph and Wally confronted Einar and Diego. "Einar, what are you guys up to?" Ralph asked.

Two carloads of Junta members pulled up and parked behind Stinky's. They emptied out and formed a threatening phalanx behind Einar. All except Pete Carlson. He stayed at the curb by Joe's patrol car.

"Einar, I thought we were going to do this quietly," Pete whimpered.

"Well, that was the plan," Einar grumbled, "but Joe had to go open his frickin' mouth."

"I didn't," Joe protested.

Diego withdrew furtively behind the group of Junta members when Beecher raised a bandaged hand and shouted, "Stop!"

The group turned to Diego. Even in the fog-filtered dimness of the headlights, they could see his face had paled. His hair, usually slicked perfectly, now hung ragged and limp about his face. His cheeks sank and his eyes receded into his skull.

"They need to know," Beecher said.

"Are you okay?" Einar reached for Diego, but the con man shook him away. His shirt hung loosely from his shoulders.

"Tell them yourself, O Great Reluctant Messiah. Or don't you have the guts?" Diego growled. "Of course not. You're all pussies! All of you who've ever been. You're all pacifists, 'seeking enlightenment,' pretending to be men, speaking of *love* and *honor*. Shit!"

His back hunched, and he advanced. The smell of his breath scattered those around Beecher. Diego leaned his face close to Beecher's and spat. Beecher did not flinch. "You're worthless. When the battle's on, you just stand there, silent, keeping this big secret, expecting them to learn it on their own. Come on. Speak. Tell them who I am. Tell them who the Earth Man is. Tell them who you are."

"You are Weendigo. The Earth Man is ultimate evil. You have faced the Word before and lost wherever and whenever you have. The Truth always finds and destroys you."

"And you're the Truth?"

Beecher shrugged.

"Yeah. Right," Diego sneered. "Who made you this century's Messiah?"

"Messiah. That's what you call me," Beecher said.

Diego waved his hand in a sarcastic gesture, then brought it down across Beecher's face, his nails leaving wide scratches across Beecher's cheek. "That line's been used. Can't you even be original?" he snarled.

Wally immediately started for Diego, but Beecher held up his hand. "I do not speak for you," Beecher told Diego.

"Speak for me," Einar said.

"I will speak only for those who will hear the Truth."

"What's truth?" Einar challenged.

"The Truth is what we were always intended to be – one with ourselves, whole, courageous, indestructible, one with the Word."

Diego interrupted. "But Truth is a Lie. And so is the Word. What's real is what we can see and hear and touch…"

"And grasp? No. There is truth, but to see THE Truth, you must recognize the Lie. And to do that, you must look beyond the surface. There is more to see than what is before our eyes. There is more to hear than the roar in our ears. Yes, True and False exist as one, but Truth is the way things are, ever have been and ever shall be. The Lie is the way man would have them be to his own destruction. The Lie is the deception of the world, the temptation of the Earth Man – the lust of the eye, the lust of the flesh, the desire for that which can never last."

Beecher turned to Joe. "That is why you sold him Karl's pictures. You wanted to destroy them, but you believed the Lie. You believed the promise of riches. You relished the image of naked flesh. The promise of pleasure consumed you. He offered it to you and you believed. You took his money and you believed and believed even stronger."

Facing Einar and the Junta, Beecher continued. "You all did. The lives of your daughters, the future of Jefferson – none of it meant anything as long as you got yours.

"And that's what makes him stronger," he said, pointing at Diego. "That's what he feeds on – excess, lust, and greed. No, he's not Satan, but he's not even Wayne Diego. He is a Weendigo."

Diego's legs seemed to grow as he hunched over farther.

"You said that twice. What's a Weendigo?" Pete asked.

Art stepped forward and answered. "A manitou, a spirit of my people. He comes from the Earth Man. He would be part of the Earth Man, but he fakes loyalty even to his master. The Weendigo lives only for himself. When man believes the Lie, when we live to satisfy desire, when we replace our sacredness with gluttony, we feed his hunger. Without our weakness and indulgence, he starves. Look at him."

The Weendigo rose to his full height. Towering thirty feet above the gathered, his skin stretched tightly against his bones. His clothes split and fell in rags at his feet. In the glow of the Junta's headlights, his skin turned ashen. Blood dripped from his lips torn by his jagged teeth.

Amanda rushed back into the house to protect Jeannie, while the Junta fell back and scrambled across the road to their cars. Einar crawled into Diego's Roadster and frantically tried to start the engine. The Weendigo's bony hand sliced through the roof and plucked the old man from the seat. Einar kicked and screamed as the Weendigo lifted him into the air. Its teeth grinding as it grew taller still, the Weendigo held Einar to its sunken nostrils and sniffed him.

"My god, no!" Einar wailed.

The Weendigo smiled. "Your god," it sniffed, tossing Einar into its mouth and clamping its razor-like teeth upon his legs. Einar screamed, but the Weendigo's teeth crashed into his skull, smashing his cries. The night crackled as the monster ground on Einar's face and carcass. Laura screamed, doubled over and hid her face in her arms. Ralph, Joe, and Wally grabbed her and pulled her behind the double oak. The Junta's cars sped away with poor Pete Carlson clopping down the street after them.

Only Beecher and Art remained facing the Weendigo.

"There's your Truth," its raspy voice said.

Art stood facing him silently, watching, waiting.

"Do you remember, Indian boy?" the Weendigo asked. "The night in Grave Swamp? Did he tell you that, Messiah? I could have done this to him, but the Earth Man stopped me. That's how your 'blue-eyed Indian' got his hunchback. That's how his jaw became so tight. But, of course, you healed that. Ever the savior."

"It's over," Beecher said, stepping forward. "The Truth is known. You've revealed yourself. They may have run, but they know. They see."

The Weendigo's hand wrapped around Beecher's body and lifted him high into the air. "It's never over. I could swallow you whole, Messiah," it hissed.

"Eat me and you will starve. Nothing in me exists for you."

The Weendigo hesitated. "Nothing? So this world means nothing to you? Is that what you mean, Messiah?"

A look of defiance on what was left of its face, the Weendigo placed Beecher in a fork of high branches from the double oak. In one step it was at the house, reaching toward Jeannie's window.

"Jeannie! No!" Art cried. Beecher sat paralyzed and speechless in the tree.

Art could no longer watch. No longer the hapless herald, he ran toward the house, but before he could reach the steps, the Weendigo shrieked in agony as a window crashed outward into its face. Art looked up and watched the Weendigo stumble backward holding the shredded skin of his cheeks. A flaming, whirling light burst from the house and spun around its head. In a blinding flash, the Weendigo's eyes exploded in a flood of steaming yellow slime that ran from the beast's now-fleshless fingers. Groping wildly, the Weendigo stumbled and fell against the tree, but the spring-like branches pushed his weakened form forward toward the street. The elongated, emaciated body twisted, staggered, and crashed to the pavement.

Its remaining skin snapped and ripped, revealing nothing beneath but bone. The Weendigo's teeth clattered and clacked as the monster lay dying. With a gigantic thunk, its joints shattered, and the skeleton collapsed into a mound of rubble.

The night became still, save the sound of Laura's weeping. Beecher climbed down from his tree and stood with Art next to the pile of bone on the street.

He looked at Art and asked, "What happened?"

"I don't know. I heard the window break, saw a flash and…"

"It was her."

They turned and saw Amanda walk out the door, pointing toward the house. Floating in the air next to Jeannie's window was the laughing woman holding a ball of fire.

The laughing woman landed at the bottom of the steps and waited for them all to approach. Beecher rushed forward. "Where's Jeannie?" he asked.

Amanda and Art walked immediately behind him. Amanda touched Beecher on the back and said, "She's safe."

Beecher looked back at Amanda, who nodded, repeated, "She's safe," and nodded once again. Beecher stopped for a second, smiled at Amanda and approached the laughing woman.

Bewildered and frightened, Ralph, Joe, Laura, and Wally followed cautiously. They did not know the names the *Word* or the *Earth Man*. They did not know of the Flame. They only knew what they had just seen with the Weendigo. It was beyond what they had been taught. It was beyond anything they could conceive.

The time for explanation to the unknowing would come, but there was more to do. Beecher had seen the fire in his dream. This time, Art heard the voice within him say, he would not reject it. He reached out his hand for the ball of fire, but the laughing woman pulled it back and shook her head. Beecher did not understand her refusal. He stepped back and looked to Art for answers, but Art's thoughts focused on the woman's smile.

There was much she wanted to say, but could not. Her eyes expressed many emotions – fear, anxiety, sadness, determination – but her lips could not move. The Earth Man had petrified her mouth into stone-like hilarity. As she struggled to speak and no words could be formed, Art's loosened jaw ached in sympathy.

Though frustrated by her condition, she walked past Beecher and offered the ball to Amanda. It was then Beecher knew. The Flame had been a gift from Amanda to the laughing woman to protect Jeannie. He could not claim it for himself. His baptism of fire had to come from

Amanda, the Flame's chosen priestess. Through Art, his ears and his eyes had opened. Through Amanda, his heart would open, also. He stood quietly, waiting. Art waited next to him.

The flame burned brighter in the laughing woman's hands, as if it had seen and recognized Amanda's hands as home. Amanda reached out her hands, and the laughing woman gently placed the ball into them. Cradling the fire before her, Amanda's face beamed. The fire nestled into her fragile grip and she was not burned. She gazed into the flame, occasionally glancing up at the laughing woman. The laughing woman's smile no longer hurt. The flame rose from her hands, and Amanda squinted through it to see behind the laughing woman's smile to the spirit beneath it.

In the darkness far to the East, thunder rumbled. Grave Swamp beckoned the Matchi-auwishuk, the living Weendigoes, and the slaves of the Evil One. The laughing woman looked to the sky, then at the circle of humans now surrounding her and Amanda.

The ground beneath the assembled trembled, and the flame in Amanda's hands billowed. Awareness fell from the sky like rain. The reality of what they had seen, what they had heard, and what must still come rose about them like floodwaters, immersing them in the inconceivable.

Joe knew the woman's name first. "Oh, my god!" he gasped.

"What?" Laura asked.

"It's Geri Dahlgren!"

Amanda blinked, but the softness of the laughing woman's eyes calmed her. "Geri Dahlgren? *G.* Dahlgren?" she asked. "The woman in the picture?"

The laughing woman nodded and cocked her head. Amanda thought for a moment, then remembered. "You are the woman I met at the truck stop when my dad died..."

Again the laughing woman nodded.

"You've been in Jefferson before," Beecher said. It was not a question; still Amanda nodded.

"It's where I first thought of *Bright and Shining Star.* This is the real Geri," she said.

Beecher examined the woman's face. With the clarity of goodness streaming from her eyes, he understood and nodded. She was not the enemy he had feared. She was here to lead, and though the destination was dangerous, the peril was not from her.

The light of the Flame bathed them all in its glow. Joe no longer lived outside the Word; he stood with the knowing. As yet, Ralph, Wally and Laura had not heard the air speak. Instead, they stood, fascinated by the cleansing fire and unsure how to engage the spirit. Wally turned to Joe and asked, "Geri Dahlgren. Isn't she one of the ones who…?"

"Disappeared in Grave Swamp? Yeah, that's the story," Joe said.

"What happened to her?" Laura asked.

"Vanished many years ago in a snowstorm out by Angler Hill," Joe explained. "We found her car the next day in a ditch out on Highway 2. It was full of her stuff, almost like she was movin' away somewhere. We looked all over for her, but she was gone. We figured she started to walk, got lost, and ended up in the woods. We searched as far as the ridge above Grave Swamp, but found nothin'." Then he addressed the laughing woman, still standing there. "That *is* where you ended up, isn't it?"

The laughing woman nodded.

"What are you now?" Laura asked, standing next to Beecher. "Are you a spirit? A ghost?"

The woman strained to form words, but her mouth would not change shape or expression. Helplessly, she waved her hands as incoherent squeaks and grunts came from her throat. It was Wally's turn to understand.

"She's the Rebellious Saint," Wally said, as if he'd been told.

The laughing woman nodded.

Art did not remember the name, but Wally had heard a voice from the trees speaking to and through him. Art knew the name was true. In the laughing woman's face he saw her rebellion against the world, the Earth Man's traitor, the saint of the Word. Wally's face brightened as the Word spoke through him.

"The Earth Man lured her into the swamp, destroyed her body, and imprisoned her spirit to become his servant underground. She belonged to him and she served him well. But she is no longer his."

Now Art had questions. "No longer his?"

The laughing woman shook her head.

Wally continued, "All through her life, she always knew the Word, followed it, loved it. But at Grave Swamp, she lost more than her way. She lost what she was. The Earth Man imprisoned her, wanting her to be his queen.

"Until he brought her back here. He didn't know she could return to the Word. But as he, the weendigoes, the matchi-auwishuk came back to Jefferson, she heard the Word speaking to Art, to Beecher, to Miss Wilson. She knew what she always knew and she deserted the Earth Man to serve whom she always intended to serve. She listened and the Word sent her here, along with Miss Wilson and the Flame, although they didn't know it, to undo all the Evil One's treachery."

It was Ralph's turn to hear, his turn to speak. "It's the Flame that killed Wayne Diego. The Flame saved Jeannie, Beecher… all of us."

The laughing woman smiled and nodded.

"And it's what brought us here, isn't it? That's what woke up Chelsea. That's what made us dream…" Ralph said.

Amanda stepped forward. "I didn't know until just now…"

Again the laughing woman nodded.

Wally looked to the rest of the group and said, "If we in this circle accept the Flame as Geri did, her rebellion against evil will be complete. She will finally be the completed saint the Word intended her to be."

"How do you know this?" Laura asked, her ears still stopped.

Wally looked at Beecher, Ralph, Joe, and Art, and smiled. "I hear."

"We all hear," Ralph added.

The words were true, Art knew. He survived ancient trials because of the Flame. With it he stood in Grave Swamp and battled the Earth Man and the Weendigoes once before. He saw it around the face of Jesus, Mohammed, and Buddha. He heard it in the voices of King David, Lao Tzu, and Vishnu. He held it in his hands as one of the countless saints of the countless faiths east and west, north and south. He tasted it now on the tongues of prophets and seers in distant worlds as the Word springs from their mouths to unnamed, unknowing peoples.

Amanda's smile affirmed Wally's words as well. She had received and shared the Flame. She knew.

Wally, Ralph, Joe, Laura, and Beecher knelt around the circle, and Amanda invited Art inside to fan the flame higher. He stood before her and waved his hand above hers. The fire crackled and rumbled upward, nearly overflowing her cupped hands. Amanda turned first to Laura. The tiny teacher lifted her head and closed her eyes. Amanda opened her fingers and let flame drip through them onto Laura's angelic face. The fire ran over her like water. Next, Amanda baptized Wally, Ralph, Joe, then Art.

She had saved Beecher for last, but she hesitated. She was unsure. Through her mind, Art heard the same doubts John the Baptist had when he baptized Jesus. He understood, and so did Beecher. His face reminded her that what must be done, must be done. This was the instruction of her dream on the California beach. This was how she would save the "drowning man." She looked down and smiled. The Flame fell onto Beecher's head. The fire was no longer thin like water, but thick and golden like honey. It flowed over him, through him.

As the Flame burned within each of them, the trees sang and the ground resonated the sound to the sky. All raised their heads to the darkness and watched their light burn straight upward through the fog until their glow reflected in the stars.

The Word spoke again. Beecher heard it first and lowered his gaze to the laughing woman. As the Flame had cleansed them and carved a hole through the fog, the laughing woman huddled at the center of the circle. Beecher rose and plucked a spark from Amanda's ball. He held it in his right hand and fanned the spark into a flame with his left. As the fire grew, he rolled it into a ball between his hands. The fire burned away the bandages and stitches on his hands, healing his wounds. The light of the Flame filled his body and shined through his skin and bones. He walked to the laughing woman and lovingly took her face in his right hand. He stroked her jaw with his thumb. Her smile, once mocking and grotesque, a frozen charade of hilarity, melted into joy under Beecher's touch.

Then, again Beecher fanned the flame in his hand. The fire grew until Beecher had to hold it in both hands. Then like Amanda had done with us, he raised his hands above the laughing woman's head and let the flame drip through his fingers, through her hair, and over her body until she stood purified by the fire, her life with the Earth Man eliminated.

Beecher smiled. "You can speak," he told her.

She looked at him and tested the newfound movement in her mouth. Her laugh was genuine as she nodded and answered, "Yes."

Amanda, who still held the flame in her hands, asked the laughing woman, "Are you really Geri, my Geri?" Even though she knew the answer, she needed to hear.

"Yes, I am," the laughing woman said.

"And are you… are you my mother?"

Geri smiled and said, "I was your mother."

"Are you dead?"

"My original body is gone, but you can see me, hear me, touch me." She held out her hands to Amanda. Amanda held them with her own, caressed them, and raised them to her lips to kiss them. She felt the flesh, tasted its purity, and smelled the perfume of the Word. She ignored her own tears and looked into her mother's eyes.

"How is this possible?" Amanda asked.

"You see me because you want to. You hear my voice and touch my skin because you want to. The Flame is within you."

The phone rang inside the house. The sound broke Laura's attention from the scene. "I'll get it," she said, rushing up the steps and through the door.

"There is more to be done," Geri said. She stood behind Wally and Joe, resting her hands on their shoulders. She turned to Beecher, and said, "There is more to be told. You must lead them." Turning back to Amanda, she said, "You must go with him. The Flame in your hands will lead him to his destiny and burn away the fog."

"And I?" Art asked.

She looked at him and placed a finger on her lips. "Shh! Listen."

He stood quietly and closed his eyes. Beyond the choirs, like a rush of wind, he heard the Matchi-auwishuk hurrying back to Grave Swamp. He saw the spirits of the Earth Man scurrying about the wounded cedar. He saw the snake and heard the skin stretching against the skulls of Weendigoes. The laughing woman interrupted the vision.

"You have been there before," she told Art. "You know. This time the path is different. It is not yours to lead, but you will arrive at the same place."

"I can't just…"

"Remember what you've been told – *It isn't necessary to struggle to maintain unity with the Word. All you have to do is participate in it,*" she said.

In the hymns of the still-singing choir, Art heard the trees sing,

*I have sent the Truth.*
*You have seen His light.*
*I have sent the Flame.*
*You have seen Her strength.*

*The Once-Mighty will fall, for*
*Against the One,*
*None can stand.*
*You have seen The Victory*
*Once.*
*Twice.*
*Now.*
*Forever.*
*Watch and rejoice!*

Art opened his eyes and knew. What was once would be again.

"Mr. Jones!" Laura cried, bursting through the door. "The hospital! Your wife… They just had to put her on a ventilator. You need to go."

"She's not there," Geri said.

"What are you talking about?" Laura demanded. "Where do you think she is?"

She was still too much in the world. Grave Swamp would devour her. She could not go.

"As I am here, though my body is dust, Sarah is in Grave Swamp," Geri explained. "That is where Beecher needs to go." Thunder rumbled in the East again. Geri cocked her head and listened. "The Earth Man's waiting," she told Beecher.

Amanda dropped her fire into Beecher's, took his hands, and wrapped them around the flame. She pressed the hands tightly together, and the gathered felt the warmth spread within him as the flame infused him with courage and passion. When she let go, Beecher lifted his head and closed his eyes.

His voice was distant. “Laura, will you please go inside and take care of Jeannie?”

Laura cleared her throat and whispered, “Yes.”

Still speaking to the sky, Beecher said, “Ralph, you, Joe and Coach find whoever you can, whoever will come, and meet us at the swamp.”

“After what we just saw, who would go? Who would we find?” Joe asked.

“Any and all. Those who saw, those who ran, those who want to know.”

“Know what?” Wally asked, innocently.

“What you have seen,” Geri, the laughing woman, told him. “Not just with your eyes, but here,” she said, laying her palm flat against his chest.

Wally nodded, but Joe still stalled.

“Einar…”

“Einar is gone,” Art said. “Go. You’ll find Miss Wilson’s car on Highway 2 at the bottom of Angler Hill. Enter the woods there. The Word will lead you to us on the ridge above Grave Swamp. Hurry.”

Wally understood. “Come on, Joe,” he said.

“It’s what we have to do,” Ralph said, taking Joe’s arm. Joe nodded and the three hurried to Joe’s squad car. With lights flashing, they drove toward downtown to recruit whoever would come.

Art walked to Laura. “You must go inside now. She needs you. We will be back.”

“Mr. Jones?” Laura looked to Beecher for approval.

Beecher quietly listened to the thunder growling in the distance. Art did not know what to say to Laura.

Amanda broke the silence. Taking Laura's face in her hands and looking deeply into her eyes, Amanda said, "Jeannie needs you now."

Laura swallowed. "Okay." She walked awkwardly up the sidewalk, turning back to watch Beecher, Amanda, Geri, and Art before she went inside.

As Art opened the car door, Amanda called back to Geri. "Aren't you coming with us?"

"I'll meet you there," she answered. She whirled round and vanished up through the hole in the fog into the sky.

Amanda looked at Art and asked, "Will I ever get used to this?"

Art smiled and shook his head.

Beecher began walking toward Amanda's rented Topaz. It was time.

# XXI BEECHER JONES

## 1

Beecher, Amanda, and Art found Geri standing on the top of the ridge above the western edge of Grave Swamp. The fog thickened over the bog so the woods were barely visible. Still, the Flame burned within them so they saw without light, they heard without sound. Geri, her face glowing, looked to the dark sky, listening intently. She nodded and smiled at the Sacred Trio. Then they heard it, too – the choir of the Word, singing in the voice of the trees, the birds, the air. Geri leapt into the air, clapped once, spun three times, and disappeared into the mist.

The three were alone.

"Where is she going?" Amanda asked.

"Sh!" Beecher said. "Listen. Behind the choir." Amanda and Art stood without speaking. Then they heard it, too. A more primitive sound, not a choir, but a collection of crude wooden flutes and drums playing somewhere beyond the ridge, somewhere out in the swamp, playing as in celebration of an ancient rite.

"Out there," Amanda said, pointing ahead. Far ahead, down among the scrub brush, the fog lightened and they saw a yellow glow flickering in the darkness. Above the light, the silhouette of the cedar rose from the brush and disappeared into the dark.

"Should we wait for the others?" Amanda asked.

Beecher shook his head, looked at Art and told her, "Art will wait for them here. You and I must go on. They will find us when it is time."

He expected Art's protest, but he had none. He had resigned himself. It was his duty to wait. To wait and watch. The Word and the Flame had spoken.

Beecher took Amanda's hand, and cautiously the two eased their way down the embankment. The hillside was moist and slippery from days of fog, and twice Amanda's feet slid out from under her. She stifled her scream, and Beecher managed to catch her both times before she could fall to the ground and slide noisily to the swamp floor. Without words, Beecher showed her how to dig her heels into the soft soil to keep her balance.

At the bottom of the hill, they could barely see the light through the brush ahead, but the music was louder, more rhythmic and enticing. They had no choice but to move forward, pushed on by the choir of the Word, lured by the flutes of the Earth Man. Having gained assurance walking down the hill on her heels, Amanda confidently stepped forward onto the flat surface of the bog. Without warning, the ground sank under her weight. She grabbed for Beecher's arm and nearly toppled them both. Waves of muskeg rose around them as they struggled to regain their balance on the floating floor of the swamp.

Once the two restored their equilibrium, they inched across the swamp toward the light, feeling the ground sink and swell with each footstep. As they grew nearer the light, they saw that it came from an island. Soon the glow grew bright enough to illuminate Beecher and Amanda's path around bushes and branches, leading them toward the island.

Amanda suddenly clutched Beecher's arm. Her grip twisted him around toward her, and again he nearly fell. He looked up to her for explanation. She raised a hand and pointed at the bushes ahead. Through the branches ahead slid a multitude of large snakes. Their red eyes illuminated their heads as their tongues tasted the air. Like a vast moat of slithering reptilian flesh, they surrounded the island and protected it from invaders.

Beecher took Amanda's hand. The Word spoke the Truth to them. The Earth Man had set the snakes there as a distraction, not as a weapon. They could not harm Beecher and Amanda. The Flame burning within them was stronger than the snakes. The two pressed forward with their eyes set steadily on the island. Still, the snakes did their best to intimidate, dangling from the branches close to Beecher and Amanda's heads. Long, slippery tongues flicked at Amanda's ears and hot breath from steaming nostrils raised the hair on Beecher's neck. The two moved past the snakes, untouched, undeterred.

The island was now within reach. Beecher and Amanda saw that the light radiated from a fissure at the base of the tree they had seen from the top of the ridge. The rustic music swept across the swamp and shook the air. Beecher and Amanda crouched behind a bush to watch the flurry of excitement before them.

It was a festival of spirits. Centaurs, fauns, and nymphs danced and cavorted about the tree, drinking, laughing, grasping at each other. Manitoussiwuk, the childlike fairies of the Ojibwe, cannonballed out of the tree, landing roughly on the hard ground and rolling into the brush. When the last one had wheeled into the bushes, the manitoussiwuk all laughed and flew up to the highest branches of the cedar, only to dive again.

Just feet in front of the tree, two of the centaurs, one whose face resembled Karl Jurgens, busily fashioned two logs into sparkling thrones. The music, still unsophisticated and wooden, piped and pounded faster and faster, as if signaling that all tasks and frivolity must quickly end.

A clatter of bones shook the ground, and a giggling nymph sprinted from behind the tree chased by a weendigo. Salivating and growing taller as he ran, the weendigo was not in a playful mood. He was starving, and, deprived of human food, would settle for an annoying nymph. He caught her up in his bony grasp, lifted her high above the earth, and licked at her ears, tasting and torturing her.

Amanda was the first to recognize the lecherous sneer. She nudged Beecher. He followed her gaze and quickly distinguished the eyes, the scarred face, and the curled lip. Frank Thorstad. They both watched speechlessly as the creature lifted the nymph above his mouth.

The music stopped unexpectedly, distracting the weendigo. For an instant, he loosened his grip and the nymph flew from his hand landing in a bush yards away. The weendigo had no time to react. All the creatures – the snakes, nymphs, manitoussiwuk, centaurs, and other weendigoes – scrambled past him to the island's shore. Caught up in their wake, the Frank-like weendigo followed, and everyone fell to their knees, facing the tree.

The thrones were ready. Before them, the creatures were still and reverent. In two long lines, the Matchi-auwishuk, the Evil Ones, paraded from around the tree. The leader of each line held a crown of golden grape leaves in its hands. The lines moved past the supplicants, around the island, and back to the thrones. Each leader stood, head bowed, on either side of the two thrones. Patiently, the congregation and the Matchi-auwishuk waited for the ceremony to begin.

Amanda and Beecher felt the music of the Word vibrating within them. From his spot above the swamp, Art felt it, too. However, the inhabitants of the island heard nothing. The voice of the Word had eluded them. They knelt anticipating the arrival of someone else.

Art heard a branch break behind him. The others from town had arrived.

## 2

On the island, a single note, different in tone from the song just ended, a high trumpet, soft and clear, sounded from somewhere in the darkness beneath the earth. At the sound all the creatures, even the snakes, hid their faces.

"What's goin' on?" Pete Carlson whispered in Art's ear.

Art jumped. Pete's presence surprised him. The member of the ruling council most skeptical of Wayne Diego and his ideas, the last man to join in the Junta's scheme to sell the girls of Jefferson into pornography, but the one who ran fastest from the Weendigo, Pete was the only one to join the force against the Earth Man. The other members of the Junta had run further, scattering and hiding throughout the countryside. Nobody else in town believed Ralph, Wally, and Joe's story of Diego and Einar's disappearance. But Pete knew. He had seen, and he believed what he saw. He believed Wayne Diego had been sent. He also believed whoever or whatever had sent Diego could and must be stopped.

"Close your eyes and watch," Art told him.

"What?" he exclaimed.

"It's all right," Ralph told him. "Close your eyes."

Ralph and Wally's sight had already been opened. Each one put a hand on Pete's shoulder. The timid little man closed his eyes so he could observe what was happening on the island.

Those on the ridge, as well as Beecher and Amanda in the swamp, watched the light from the base of the tree intensify into a harsh glare. Another trumpet note, lower in pitch, harmonized with the first. Then there was a third and a fourth. The notes wove around each other, gently at first, then furiously, swarming like bees until the night air throbbed. The light and the trumpets drove Pete to his knees. He buried his eyes and ears in his arms and pulled his head to his thighs. He quivered in fear. He had not received the Flame. The rest of the observers held their positions.

The light dimmed and each trumpet held its harmonious note. A large man with flowing hair and dressed in purple robes rose from the fissure at the base of the cedar, silhouetted by the light. The man stood momentarily before the light, then strode a bit unsteadily to the throne on the left. Facing the crowd of disciples at his feet, he smiled arrogantly.

It was the Earth Man. Though they had never seen him, the observers knew him at once. His was a presence that demanded recognition, even from those who had never known of him. Unlike Diego who relied on disguise for power, the Earth Man renounced it. Instead, he relied on his very being to intimidate and coerce, to flatter and confound, to astonish and deceive.

With a flourish of his outstretched arm, the Earth Man turned back to the tree. An elegant woman, dressed in a black cloak with purple, vertical stripes, ascended from the hole and walked regally to the throne on the right. She and the man bowed to each other, took hands, and faced the crowd before them.

It was Sarah. Whole. Uninjured. Alive.

She took the crown from the matchi-auwish next to her, kissed the golden leaves, and turned to the Earth Man. He bent down and smiled broadly as she placed the crown on his head.

The man then took the other crown and, leering at Sarah, kissed it with an added salacious lick along the brim. He then lifted the crown to place on her head.

"Sarah! No!" Beecher commanded, standing and stepping from the brush.

Manitoussiwuk and nymphs scattered into nearby bushes. In a clatter of hoofs and bones, the centaur and fauns raced to the bog, tearing up the ground of the island. Even the weendigoes scattered into the swamp, their bony feet breaking through the muskeg and sending dark brown muck into the air. Frantically, they grasped for the brush and pulled themselves from the thick dark water and clutching roots of the brush, crawling away from the island like the snakes. The Earth Man, his long hair falling about his face, staggered backward in surprise.

Beecher strode forward, Amanda just behind him. Sarah saw who it was and stood erect and defiant, waiting for them.

When they stepped onto the island, Sarah said, "Beecher, why are you here? Go home."

"Come with me," he replied, approaching her.

Sarah halted him with a quick gesture. "I can't!" she snapped. "Look at me."

"I am. You're beautiful."

Sarah sighed, exasperated, as if there were no way to make Beecher understand what was perfectly clear. She looked down, examining her fingernails as if reading a script. "Beecher, in this swamp, in this form, yes, I am beautiful. I *am* beauty. I am queen. However, at home in my earthly body, my face would be gone, hidden by a mass of scars; my body would be bent and shriveled like Art Benson's. My spirit would drown in anger and hatred for what I've been and what I am."

Beecher reached for her, and she stepped back. "Sarah, there is healing," he told her. "There is forgiveness. You'll be as beautiful as ever. Even more so."

Sarah shook her head. "I know the truth of what I am."

As Beecher watched, Sarah's face shriveled into a lump of scar tissue, her left eye hidden within folds of flesh. Her right cheek stretched upward over her skull so her long dark hair grew only from the left side of her scalp. In a bucktoothed mockery of a Halloween pumpkin, her teeth separated, half of them falling to the ground like pebbles. Hunching toward her head, her left shoulder seemed to grow out of her left ear. Her clothing mutated from the black and purple royal cloak into blood red rags hanging over her shoulders in shreds across her chest and back.

Sarah wheezed, "Is this what you want to wake up to the rest of your life? Is this the mother you want

Jeannie to see across the breakfast table? Tell me you can look at me and not remember what I did with Frank, what I did with all the other men before I met you."

Beecher stood calmly, gently smiled, and repeated, "There is healing. There is forgiveness. You don't have to stay. You can come home."

She held up her hands and stepped to the side. "Home to what?" she challenged."

"To Jeannie. To me. To the Word."

"Ha!" the Earth Man, bellowed. He leaned back in his throne, smirking, his crown slightly askew. He knew what Sarah's answer would be.

"I am already home," Sarah said. "Beecher, this is beyond anything you know."

"But I do know," he told her. "The Word showed me."

Then turning to the Earth Man, he said, "And He sent me to tell you it's over. Let her go."

The Earth Man smiled and taunted Beecher. "The Word sent you. Wonderful. The Great Confrontation once again. 'Oh, please, Mister. Let her go. The Word sent me.'" Then he shrugged. "I'm not making her stay. It's..." again he smirked. "It's what *you* call free will. Isn't that what you saviors preach? Humans have free will? Well, it's her will to be with me instead of you. Sorry. It's out of my hands."

"But you lie to her."

"There's that word again. 'You *lie* to her. All you do is *lie*.' Why do you people think you have a monopoly on truth? I told her the truth. I showed her the truth. This *is* what she'll be if she goes back to her body. If she stays with me..." The Earth Man waved his arms restored Sarah's beauty and her royal robes. "See? If she stays with me, her past is fulfilled. She will become what she always wanted to be. She will be a queen."

"Your queen."

Again the Earth Man shrugged. "All right. So it's not much. It's still royalty."

"You're looking for another sacrifice."

"As if you'd offer one. You and I both know you didn't come here to bargain with the devil. You came hear to defeat me. You got rid of Diego and you believe you can do the same to me. It doesn't work that way, Sonny. You may be one with the Word, but you are not the Word. Her choices are me or the real Word. And since I already have her and since you have nothing else I want, she's mine. As she said, go home."

For a moment, Beecher stood silently, listening to the choir of the Word. Finally, he said, "She needs to know everything."

Sarah's face contorted with anger, as she spat, "Damn it, Beecher. Don't you ever listen? This is where I belong – for me, for you, for Jeannie, and –" She paused, then pointed to Amanda. "– and her."

Amanda moved forward and stood next to Beecher.

The Earth Man howled in laughter. "Oh, yes. There she is. Another virgin. There always has to be a virgin," he bellowed. "What is it about you 'purveyors of light' that there is always a virgin in your story? It's as annoying as that damned flood story. 'Sex is evil.' Bull shit! Do you think *I* invented sex? That was your guy, not me. I just make it fun."

He awaited Beecher's response, but then a new idea struck him. "Oh, wait! It's a pagan thing. The whole Lord and Lady idea," circling Amanda and Beecher. "Hah! This is novel. The Word has become pagan. What a concept! But for something really outrageous, I have a better idea. You two, me and Sarah – a foursome. Think of the possibilities. Sacrificing the virgin princess... Oh, yes. That should excite everybody. A sacrifice *and* a virgin. That'll make your big guy very happy."

"You were right before," Beecher said. "Nobody's here to sacrifice. We're here to rescue, to save."

"Shit. No sacrifice. Damn. How 'bout the sex, though?" the Earth Man said. Then he leaned his head close to Amanda's ear. "You'd like it. I can be a lot of fun. That's what Sarah's here for. Fun." He draped his heavy arm around Sarah's shoulder. "Isn't it, honey? She tried it. She liked it. She stays."

Beecher shook his head. "She doesn't know."

"I don't know what?" Sarah challenged. "I don't know who he is? Who I am? Of course, I know. It's you who doesn't know."

"But I do. I know the Word is universal, unconstrained by space and time; all powerful, unhampered by nature and death. The Earth Man is limited by all the Word has made, all that the Earth Man is himself. You don't know what you are worth..."

Before Beecher could finish, Sarah walked deliberately to him and roughly grabbed his head with both hands, pulling his lips to hers. Beecher closed his eyes and felt her mouth open, inviting him in. He did not move, even when her tongue shoved inside his mouth and met his as it had thousands of times before.

Something was different. Her mouth tasted dry, like dust and soot. Beecher's body stiffened, but still he did not pull away or encourage her. His resistance only caused Sarah to hold him tighter. She swept the inside of his mouth with her tongue until he gagged. His stomach knotted. He couldn't breathe. He tasted death. Still her tongue, prompted by his resistance, pushed deep into his mouth, reaching back to his throat.

Beecher's body rebelled against death's attack. Vomit erupted from his stomach into Sarah's mouth, and she pushed him to the ground. Triumphantly, she laughed and wiped her mouth as Beecher knelt at her feet retching. "I told you. I know. He is death, and I am his queen," she said, pointing at the smiling Earth Man. "And yes, I know death is forever."

"That's not true. That's what he wants you to believe." Beecher coughed, wiping the vomit from his face. "Look." Sarah and the Earth Man turned and looked up into the branches of the cedar where Geri sat, watching and listening.

"He killed her, but still she lives. He took her body, but we still see her," Beecher said.

"Another satisfied customer," the Earth Man sneered.

"So satisfied she killed your Weendigo. So satisfied she's been forgiven and sanctified with the Flame. So satisfied, she's no longer dead."

"What?!" the Earth Man exclaimed, jumping up from his throne.

Geri leapt from the tree and floated to Amanda and Beecher's side. The Earth Man growled, and Sarah stepped away from him, terrified of his pent-up anger.

"You bitch!" he screamed at Geri. "After all I've done for you? I made you happy, and you turn on me? Out of what? Jealousy? You're jealous? Is that it? Before you wanted nothing to do with me. *Now* you want to be my queen?"

"No," Geri said calmly, "I don't want to be your queen. I never wanted to be here at all."

She turned to Sarah. "In Jefferson, I was happy. I was innocent."

Again confronting the Earth Man, she said, "But then you sent that man. I listened to his lies, your lies, and believed. I gave in to my lust. I became pregnant. and then you sent the whispers. *'Slut... whore... abomination....'* they said.

"Through the whispers you convinced me to give up my child. Even after she was born and gone, the whispers continued: *'Disgrace to the town...slut...whore...'* They never stopped. They came from the truck stop walls. They came from the tables. For twenty years. No matter what I did. No matter what I said. The whispers tormented me. I couldn't live in Jefferson any more, so I packed my things and left.

"And when that deer ran in front of my car on Angler Hill in the middle of that snowstorm, that was your doing. You knew the storm was so bad, nobody would find me. I tried to get back, trudging through the snow.

"But your music led me here. Everything was the same as it is now: the island, the manitoussiwuk, the weendigoes, the throne. Except that man was here, too. Him, you rewarded. Him, you turned into spirit, a manitou. Him, you made into Wayne Diego, the weendigo, your partner.

"Me, you wanted to be your queen, your perfect third. I wouldn't. You had already destroyed me once. And when I refused, you grabbed my hair and pulled me to the ground. You straddled me, thrust your thumbs into my mouth and pulled up and out against my cheeks, forming that hideous smile I could never lose. You set it in stone by spitting in my face, and told me it would stay until I found you another queen."

Geri raised her head defiantly and said, "And as time went by, you thought I forgot, but I didn't. I remember it all."

The Earth Man gnashed his teeth as his eyebrows protruded, hiding the blood-red eyeballs beneath them. In a moment, however, he relaxed, smiled, and turned to Beecher. "So there's your villain, savior. She's the one who brought your wife to me. I was just sitting on my throne out here in the swamp, and she..."

"It doesn't matter what she did with you. She's been forgiven," Beecher said. "That is not the smile you gave her. It is her own, the one given her by the Word. The Flame restored it. And the Flame destroyed your weendigo. You have no third. You are no longer in control here. That's what I've been trying to tell Sarah. No matter what's happened, the past is not eternal. She can be restored. Everybody can be restored."

Beecher and Amanda held out their hands. A flame began to glow in each palm. Sarah hesitated, then took a step forward. She looked down into the fire, then up into Beecher's forgiving eyes. Then she turned to Amanda, who also offered Sarah her flame. Sarah heard Geri's voice – or was it another voice. Sarah couldn't tell. The voice said, "Take it. It's yours if you want it."

Sarah wavered, then turned to the Earth Man. He felt the uncertainty inside her. Quickly, he waved his arm over her, and again she was the scarred, misshapen wretch. "Remember, this is truth," he hissed.

"But this is truth and *life,*" Beecher countered, holding his flame out for her.

Sarah reached forward her trembling hand toward the flame. She began to hear the choir of the Word.

"Sarah," the Earth Man said.

She turned to him again.

"My queen," he said, leering at her.

She saw her distorted reflection in his eyes. She saw the scars, the humped-back, the sagging eyes, the torn scalp, the blood-red rags. And then she saw the vision transform into that of the erect beauty dressed in the cloak of royalty. The trumpet of the Earth Man clashed with the choir.

She glanced again at the fire in Amanda and Beecher's hands. Pursing her lips and shaking her head, she whispered, "I'm sorry, Beecher. I can't."

She looked up and tried to smile, but couldn't. The Earth Man held out her crown to her. Tentatively, she lowered her head and let the Earth Man place it on her head.

On the ridge above the swamp, Pete Carlson heard, but did not understand the Word. He became brave and foolish in one moment. He shook off Wally and Ralph's hands and cried, "Mrs. Jones! Don't! Don't do it!"

He sprinted down the hill, tripped over a dead log, and tumbled down the embankment.

Ralph, Wally, and Joe bolted after him, sliding through mud and branches, trying to grab Pete before he could reach the muskeg. Their shouts echoed across the swamp.

The Earth Man grabbed Sarah and sneered up at Beecher. "What's this? A posse? The Word needs reinforcements now? He's gettin' soft. I'll bet the blue-eyed Indian is hidin' around here someplace, too."

"I'm not hiding," Art said. "I am here, watching."

He had not moved. He had not shouted. Still the Earth Man heard and saw him. The Earth Man looked up the ridge. Above Art the air shimmered and sang. With the sound of a million voices and the light of a thousand suns, the Word and the Flame filled the sky.

"What? Again? Can't You leave me alone?" the Earth Man cried. At his side, Sarah stood enthralled by the sound. He saw her captivated face and shouted in defiance, "Not this one. She's mine." Then to his followers quivering in swamp, he bellowed, "Take them! Take them all!"

His disciples sprang from their hiding places to meet the men scrambling down the hill. Pete reached the bottom of the ridge and charged onto the muskeg. He had only advanced five yards when a centaur jumped high into the air, landing next to Pete and tearing through the surface. The ground disappeared beneath Pete's feet and he sunk into the muck. His hysterical hands clutched for a branch, a bush, anything to pull himself up. However, the centaur had hold of his foot and pulled him below the surface. As soon as Pete's head disappeared, a matchi-auwish flew over the gash in the muskeg, closing it, and trapping Pete and the centaur in the bowels of the swamp with the souls of the thousands who gave the swamp its name.

"Get the others!" the Earth Man screamed.

Pete's disappearance only detoured the others. Wally and Ralph circled to the right, still doggedly trudging toward the island. Joe drew his gun and circled to the left. Leading Ralph through the brush, Wally pushed aside a branch and a fattened snake fell from it, wrapped itself around Wally's head and dragged him to the ground. Ralph tugged at the snake's body, trying to loosen it so Wally could breathe, but a matchi-auwish tackled him from behind and pushed his head into the muskeg. Wally struggled for air, but the snake coiled tighter until its victim fell to the ground breathless, silent. The matchi-auwish sneered at the sky as Ralph's body went limp in his hands.

Still the Earth Man had not won. The choir of the Word sang louder. The light reached into the shadows, exposing the lurking spirits. Joe crouched on the ground and fired his pistol at weendigoes, centaurs, and matchi-auwishuk. His bullets had no effect, but the music and the light were too intense for the spirits. They could no longer fight the force of the Word reaching deep inside them.

They rose from the swamp, leaving their opponents behind, and sped toward the island. Manitoussiwuk and nymphs swept past Beecher, Amanda, and Geri, and disappeared into the gash at the bottom of the cedar.

"No!" the Earth Man yelled. He could not stop the exodus. Snakes and centaurs streamed by him. His disciples mobbed the tree, pushing, crowding, brawling to get through the hole. Realizing his fight was over, the Earth Man hoisted Sarah onto his shoulder and shoved his way toward the hole. He stopped in the midst of the pandemonium and shouted back at Beecher, "I killed your men, Savior. And Sarah refused your forgiveness. I win. Admit it!"

"As always, you take lives to death," Beecher said. Then nodding his head toward Geri, he added, "The Word brings life *from* death. He will again. In Him there is no death, only passage. That is something you never understand. Again, you lose."

The Earth Man grimaced and bellowed above the choir and confusion, "Aaaahhhhh!" He stamped his foot and the ground shook violently. The impact rattled the rock deep beneath the swamp and built a giant wave that lifted the muskeg and threw the rescuers – Ralph, Joe, and Wally – back to the shore at the foot of the ridge. The wave also threw the Earth Man's remaining soldiers high into the trees above Art. The creatures clambered down the trunks, over the men's motionless bodies, and across the bog toward the safety of the island.

Above it all, the choir sang and the sky burned.

Geri urged Amanda and Beecher away from the cedar and toward the ridge. They didn't need her prodding. The Word called them in His song.

The Earth Man bellowed again like an enraged bull at the sky. He too heard the Word and knew the end had come. Then, in a swirl of purple, he and Sarah disappeared through the hole at the base of the great cedar.

Quickly, the remaining matchi-auwishuk gathered in formation around the tree and began circling it. In a moment they disappeared in a swirling gray blur of wind that blew back the brush in the bog. As the wind from the island pushed at their backs, Amanda and Beecher struggled over the waves and through the clutching branches. Geri flew ahead of them, fighting to create a path.

On the island the blur grew darker. The creatures flew faster and faster, spiraling upward in a large funnel cloud that sucked the island up out of the bog. The wind picked up Geri and dropped her at Art's feet.

Immense waves of muskeg billowed and threw Amanda and Beecher above the brush into the side of the ridge. They turned over and watched from the bank as the island rose higher into the air. The violent rush of the spirits uprooted bushes and lifted them into sky with the island. The waters of Grave Swamp opened and Pete's body rose from the depths. It landed face down in the brush next to Ralph, Wally, and Joe. Debris from the swamp flew over them like a protective blanket. Only Geri and Art at the top of the hill, and Beecher and Amanda halfway up were able to watch the ending.

The music and light crescendoed to its climax and abruptly stopped. The sky slammed shut, black and silent. Suddenly, lightning exploded all around the swamp. Flash after flash streaked across the sky, illuminating the shuddering woods. Thunder rattled the trees around the survivors. Still the island hung in the air, quaking and quivering, until a thunderbolt from high in the blackness crashed into the tree. The lightning crackled and burned the tree while shaking the island like a rag. A stream of electricity flowed through the tree, pulsed and swelled, then broke across the swamp in a blast of thunder and light. With a thud and a splash, the island fell back to earth. The muskeg billowed in wild undulations over the island, splashing and pounding against it until it sank into the muck. The swamp grew calm.

The air warmed and the fog began to disperse. Light began to filter through the clouds above and revealed all. The island, the tree had disintegrated. All signs of the Earth Man, Sarah, and the spirits of Grave Swamp vanished.

# XXII ART BENSON

1

At the Jefferson hospital, Doc Benham switched off Sarah's respirator and removed the tube from her mouth. In the middle of the night, lightning knocked out the power for the whole county. Doc and his nurse Nancy struggled frantically with flashlights and limited electrical knowledge to start the emergency generator. Their efforts were futile. In minutes only a lifeless body remained in the emergency room. Sarah was gone.

2

At Beecher's house Laura Grapnic stood on the enclosed porch, nervously checking her watch and watching the street. The power was still off. She sat on the couch and chewed her thumbnail as she watched the Weendigo's bones melt like Jell-O onto the pavement.

She heard a shuffling through the door behind her. When she turned, Jeannie stood holding Tigger at the end of the couch.

"Where's my mommy and daddy?" Jeannie asked.

Laura reached out to her and said, "Your daddy'll be home soon. Do you remember me? Miss Grapnic from Daddy's school?"

Jeannie nodded, but did not move.

"You want to come sit by me?" Laura asked.

The girl hugged her Tigger and looked at the floor, then inched her way down the front of the couch until she stood next to Laura's leg. Still watching for signs of Joe's squad car or Amanda's rental, Laura put her arm on Jeannie's shoulder, as much for her own comfort as for Jeannie's.

Jeannie crawled onto the couch and rested her head in Laura's lap. She lay quietly for a moment looking through the screened windows. Laura rested a hand on Jeannie's shoulder, leaned her head back, and closed her eyes. Suddenly, Jeannie turned, looked up at Laura, and said, "It'll be all right."

Laura looked down and saw both Jeannie and Tigger grinning at her. She stroked Jeannie's cheek and smiled back.

"Wanna know how come?" Jeannie asked.

Laura playfully poked Jeannie's nose. "How come?"

Jeannie turned and pointed out the window. "The sun's coming out."

Laura looked out. The fog had dissipated and sunlight now streamed through breaks in the clouds overhead. She smoothed Jeannie's hair, and the two of them marveled at the brightening day.

3

Beecher, Amanda, Geri and Art made their way down the hill to where Pete Carlson's body lay. At first an unwitting colleague of the Matchi-auwishuk, Pete had switched allegiances, had opposed the Earth Man and all his forces with nothing but will – no weapons, no Flame for protection, no knowledge. He had never read the Word spoken to the Buddha or Lao Tzu, Jesus or Muhammad; he had not heard it sung by the choir of the Word:

*Do what you should do*
*When you should do it.*
*Refuse to do*
*What you should not do;*
*And, when it is not clear,*
*Wait until you are sure.*

Though heroic in its intent, Pete's attack had been foolhardy.

Beecher crouched and placed his hand on Pete's back. After a moment, he looked up at Geri and Art and said, "He's gone."

Art nodded "From here," he said, "but not from everywhere and not forever."

Amanda bent down, took Beecher's hand, and raised him to his feet. Sunlight filtered through the branches overhead. The four of them looked up and watched the sun push away the clouds. They knew.

Art heard a rustle and groan in the bushes nearby. Wally awoke and pulled himself to his knees. Next to him, Ralph turned over and massaged his aching shoulders. A few feet away, Joe heard the sound of the wind and the birds, the voices of the Word, and rubbed the mud from his face.

Filled with the Flame, they had survived the Earth Man's attack. As all three rose to their feet, Art understood. They lived to tell what they saw and heard, how Beecher had told the Story to the Earth Man. It would not be easy, but they would repeat the words. They would recount the tale if any would listen. The Word was within them.

Geri turned to Art and said, "It's time to go."

He nodded and began to follow her up the ridge.

"Go? Go where? Aren't you going to help us?" Beecher asked. Confusion had again begun to seep into Beecher's brain.

"The time for my journey is now. Your own will come soon," Geri told him.

"Me? Where am I going?"

"You will go home," Art told him. "You will take your daughter and your mother. You will go with Amanda and you will be home."

Beecher glanced at Amanda. "My mother? Art, my mother is dead."

The losses of the battle – Einar, Pete, and Sarah – had distracted him. Art knew he still had one more lesson to teach. He walked to Beecher and laid his hand on his shoulder. Through Art's voice, the words of the ancients spoke.

"Listen to the Word:

*Whatever you have in your mind — forget it;*
*Whatever you have in your hand — give it;*
*Whatever is to be your fate — face it.*
*The Spirit of Truth has come*
*To guide you onto the Way,*
*Into all Truth,*
*Into all Light.*
*You have seen,*
*You have been*
*The light shining in the darkness.*
*Embrace it.*
*Believe it.*
*Accept that it is yours.*
*You need no longer seek,*
*For the seeker has found you."*

Beecher stared at Art blankly, then nodded as if he understood. However, words from Art's mouth did not speak to him. He still must hear them from inside.

Ralph, Wally, and Joe stumbled toward them.

"Take time to listen to what is said without words," Art told Beecher. "Obey what you hear within you, the law too subtle to be written."

First Wally, then Ralph, and finally Joe joined the others around Pete's body. "Close your eyes and hear," Art told Beecher.

He closed his eyes and lifted his face to the sun. He listened, smiled, then spoke deliberately. "I know what I always should have known, what has been taught to all the great teachers."

He opened his eyes and looked at Art.

"And what is that?" Art asked.

Beecher looked around him, then spoke to Art, to Geri and Amanda, to Ralph, Wally and Joe:

*"Love your life.*
*Trust the Word.*
*Seek love,*
*Perseverance,*
*And gentleness.*
*Return to the mere basics of life.*
*Become honest,*
*Simple,*
*True,*
*Virtuous,*
*And whole."*

Beecher paused.

"Yes," Art told him, "and what else do you know?"

*"Life is acceptance and denial.*
*Therefore, we must accept all,*
*Everybody and everything,*
*Given us by the Word.*
*Everything the earth throws in our way*
*Must be denied as falsehood and illusion.*
*By our own invitation,*
*The Flame has burned the Word within us,*
*And we must listen.*

*We no longer need seer nor sage,*
*Man nor manitou,*
*To know the truth —*
*The truth of healing and forgiveness*
*That not even death can stop."*

"And your mother?" Art asked him.

Beecher opened his eyes and smiled. "I hear nothing," he said, "but I will know that, too."

Geri took Art's hand and began to lead him up the ridge.

"Wait," Amanda said. "Mother, why are *you* leaving? Where are you going?"

Smiling at her daughter, Geri said, "Where you cannot follow."

"But I wanted…"

"You wanted what you always had. A mother. I gave you birth. I could do no more. Accept the Mother the Word has given. Love her. Cherish her. More now than ever."

"You mean Lois?"

Geri nodded.

"I do love her, but can't we, you and I…?"

Geri smiled and shook her head. Amanda was about to protest, but Beecher's hand on her shoulder stopped her. She looked at him and felt the Flame burning within her. She understood.

"Art? Please. Stay," Beecher said.

Art shook his head. "I must go find my own healing, my own absolution."

"And your death?"

Art smiled and looked at Geri. "I've been there before," Art told him.

4

The woods, long under the domination and at the mercy of the spirits of the Earth Man and the inhabitants of Grave Swamp, shook off the influence of death and fear. As the five carried Pete's body through the woods, birds flew overhead, chirping and singing amid the treetops. Farther on, a whitetail buck ran across their path, stopped, regarded them a moment, and walked slowly away. Squirrels rustled the wet leaf cover and chattered loudly as the party passed them.

At the highway, they laid Pete's body on the shoulder next to Joe's squad car. Joe called for an ambulance and turned on the squad's emergency lights. The five waited for the ambulance to arrive.

None of them wanted to leave. Wally sat in the ditch just below Pete's body. Ralph sat on the passenger side of the squad car, and on the driver's side, Joe sat inside the open door, his feet resting on the ground. Amanda and Beecher leaned against the Topaz.

The clouds had vanished and the sun warmed the concrete highway.

Amanda glanced toward the top Angler Hill and saw a single car descending toward the parked cars and flashing lights. The car slowed as it neared them and changed lanes. As the car passed, the driver looked to see what was happening. Just past the group, the car stopped suddenly and backed up to where Beecher and Amanda stood. The passenger window lowered.

"Amanda?"

Amanda looked inside. "Mom?"

Lois Wilson put the car in park, ran to her daughter and embraced her.

Beecher watched as the two hugged. The driver's tear-streaked face was familiar. The answer burned within him, but he did not listen. The lights of the ambulance appeared in the West.

## 5

The EMTs quickly examined Amanda and Beecher and found nothing wrong. While one checked out Ralph, Wally, and Joe, the other enlisted Beecher's help to prepare Pete's body for transfer back to Jefferson. Amanda sat in her mom's car and told Lois about Geri, Amanda's birth mother. Amanda explained how she and Geri met at the truck stop years ago, how Geri had given up Amanda to protect her from the voices of gossip. She did not tell about the Earth Man and why they were sitting at the side of the road. There would be time for that later.

Geri's story, Lois said, was similar to her own, the story Amanda had never known, the married man, her pregnancy, and the child's birth. She explained how she had given the baby to a Lutheran minister in Duluth, moved to Sand Creek and met Amanda's dad. Amanda smiled. Just a week ago, the story would have upset her.

Today, the Flame warmed her to the past and allowed her to accept her present.

6

Amanda rode back to Jefferson with her mom while Beecher drove the Topaz. When Beecher parked the Topaz in front of his house, Jeannie leapt to her feet, and still clutching Tigger, she ran out of the house to meet him. Laura followed close behind.

"What happened?" Laura asked. "Where are the others?"

"They'll be back in a bit," Beecher said. He lifted Jeannie, hugged her tightly and kissed her fine hair.

Lois pulled up behind the Topaz. Amanda got out and joined Beecher and Laura.

"What happens now?" Laura asked.

"We go on," Beecher said. "Jeannie, I want you to meet somebody. Can you look up?"

Jeannie raised her head from Beecher's shoulder and looked at Amanda.

"Jeannie, this is Amanda Wilson. Can you say 'hi'?"

"Hi," Jeannie whimpered.

Lois came and stood by Amanda's side.

"Hi, Jeannie. This is my mom, Lois," Amanda said.

"Hi, Jeannie. Is this a friend of yours?" Lois said, pointing at Tigger.

Jeannie nodded.

"What's his name?"

"Tigger," Jeannie said, barely audible.

"Trigger?"

"Tigger," Jeannie said a bit louder.

"Oh, Pigger."

"No, Tigger!" Jeannie scrunched her eyebrows in frustration.

Lois laughed. "I know. I'm just teasing him. Tigger and I have met before." She took one of Tigger's paws and said to him, "It's good to see you again. How have you been?" She looked Jeannie and asked, "Has he been behaving? He can be kind of nasty, you know."

Jeannie smiled and shook her head.

"He hasn't? Tigger! Shame on you! Jeannie, let's go somewhere and you can tell me everything he's done. Okay?"

Lois reached out for Jeannie and took her into her arms. As Lois balanced Jeannie on her hip, Beecher saw. What had been in Lois's face out at Angler Hill now reflected from his daughter's. He understood what the Word had spoken.

# EPILOGUE

Jefferson lives on. The Junta no longer meets. The legend of Grave Swamp now includes Karl Jurgens, Frank Thorstad, Einar Nordhaus, Pete Carlson, and Wayne Diego.

Tony Thorstad, Frank's son, had seen too much. It was his voice Sarah had heard that night in the fog with Frank, the voice that interrupted her pursuit of worldly ecstasy. Tony had seen his father for what he was. His mother Sammi already knew. It did not take much urging from Tony to persuade Sammi to move to Fargo and start over.

Wally Forseth gave up teaching and coaching to attend Luther Seminary in St. Paul. However, the truth he had seen at Beecher's and at Grave Swamp colored his perception of the school's teaching. His "education" did not last long. He already knew too much.

Joe Engstrom stayed in Jefferson, as did Ralph Bjerkland and Laura Grapnic. Joe and the remains of the Junta finally destroyed Karl's collection of photographs. They told no one what they had planned, done, or seen, and the pictures disappeared into smoke, as did the Junta.

Guilt drove Joe from his job as policeman. In penance, he chose to work as a cashier and shift manager at Ralph Bjerkland's grocery store. He often took breaks, sitting on the bench outside the front door, his eyes seeing what the world could not.

Ralph continued to run the store, but turned over most of his work to his employees. He spent much of his time sitting in the backyard listening to the night air, reading by flashlight, meditating. His wife Bonnie and his daughter Chelsea did not understand. His story of Grave Swamp confused and frightened them. The Flame had not touched them, and they could not hear. Bonnie moved in with her parents in Beltrami and took Chelsea with her.

Laura Grapnic continued to teach at Freedom High while earning her administration degree. The Word continued to speak to her in dreams, dreams that revealed the events of Grave Swamp, dreams that revealed the truth of existence. The Flame burned strongly within her and she loved life and the world perfectly, free of desire, free of greed, free of possessiveness. She never married.

Lois left Sand Creek to be near Amanda. The story Amanda told of Jefferson convinced Lois that Michigan was no longer home. Home was with family. Home was with Amanda. Lois's husband and the past were gone.

Amanda did not write *Bright and Shining Star II*. Instead she helped Beecher finish his screenplay while she wrote her first novel. Her agent Herb Strickland managed to sell both projects, even though their content defied his definition of commercial. Herb was skeptical when Amanda's college friend Sherman Lubovich said her book about a Norwegian-Ojibwe half-breed spiritualist would find an audience. He was incredulous when Sherman's prediction proved correct.

After Sarah's funeral, Beecher resigned and took Jeannie originally to Vancouver. He wanted to write, but California or New York seemed too big, too busy. The mountains of Canada were peaceful and far enough away from Minnesota. He could forget Jefferson and still hear the Word. He wanted to know Amanda and he wanted to know his mother. Yet he needed to learn to trust what spoke within him. He would listen. He would learn. He would love and teach Jeannie.

And he did write. While his film script *Defunct* did not win the Academy Award, nor any other award, it did, however, with Amanda's long distance advice, open the doors of producers willing to hear and tell the Story.

The Word spoke through Beecher and Amanda. They knew it. The Message lay within their work. The Truth lay within their lives. They loved each other beyond eros, above agape; neither like lovers nor siblings. Apart, they loved in spirit more than other human beings who love in heart and body; they loved like the Word loved the Flame. Though hundreds of miles apart, they lived lives that complemented each other and the universe. For five years, they seldom saw each other; yet the Word immersed them both in joy at the mention of the other's name. Many of their friends understood. Most did not.

Until their wedding high in the mountains near Vancouver. Those who were there, saw. Those who were not, felt. All heard the music of the Word, clear, uncluttered, the music that is always there, most often ignored. All knew. Beecher, Amanda, Jeannie, Lois – together. The Story was complete.

Art Benson lives on, in a new world and a new age. His role is different. His body is renewed. His back is strong. He speaks without pain.

He no longer waits and watches, for he is no longer bound to the partial religions of earth. He is no longer subject to their manipulations, their spiritual obstruction, their fanaticism. He is one with the Word, where the essence of life exists. He lives out of the shadows, following a road without detours, without barricades, without branches. Realizing the Truth of the Universe, he outlives time and space, with God and the Word, from creation beyond Armageddon, from birth beyond nirvana, across the blackness of the universe to the source of all light. He lives a unity of flesh and spirit, Word and Flame. What the Word intended, he has become.

Through Beecher's life, through his story, Art heard and understood. Through Beecher's revelation of forgiveness, healing, and love, through his strength, the Word destroyed the Earth Man's dominion over Grave Swamp and Jefferson. It liberated the unsuspecting world from itself.

Someday Beecher and Amanda, as well as all who lived the Story with them, will follow the path Art has taken. They are on the Way now, bringing the world with them.

When humanity understands, it will know the Word perfectly, and like the Word, it will reject the divisions of man. It will become One.

# ABOUT THE AUTHOR

Michael Frickstad has experienced much of the cultural and geographical vitality that is Minnesota, having been raised in the north woods, taught on the edge of the Red River Valley, and finished his working career in the Twin Cities metropolitan area. For over thirty years, he taught English and social studies, as well as coached speech and directed community and school plays. He and his wife Diane live in the northwestern exurbs of Minneapolis.